THE
GOOD
OR
EVIL SIDE

THE GOOD

OR

EVIL SIDE

MATAMOROS 1846

A SWIFT & DANCER ADVENTURE

DAN GOODER RICHARD

INKSPIRATION
MEDIA

THE GOOD OR EVIL SIDE: MATAMOROS 1846
Copyright © 2021 by Dan Gooder Richard

All rights reserved. Published in the United States
by Inkspiration Media, Arlington, Virginia.

Publisher's Cataloging-In-Publication Data
(Prepared by The Donohue Group, Inc.)

Names: Richard, Dan Gooder, 1947- author.
Title: The good or evil side : Matamoros, 1846 / Dan Gooder Richard.
Description: First edition. | Arlington, Virginia : Inkspiration Media, [2021] |
Series: A Swift & Dancer adventure ; [1] | Includes bibliographical references.
Identifiers: ISBN 9781939319326 (paperback) |
ISBN 9781939319333 (hardcover) | ISBN 9781939319296 (PDF) |
ISBN 9781939319302 (ePub) | ISBN 9781939319319 (MOBI)
Subjects: LCSH: Spies--United States--History--19th century--Fiction. |
Women war correspondents--United States--History--19th century--Fiction. |
United States--History--1815-1861--Fiction. | Mexican War, 1846-1848--Fiction. |
Manifest Destiny--Fiction. | Murder--Investigation--Fiction. |
LCGFT: Thrillers (Fiction) | Historical fiction.
Classification: LCC PS3618.I33374 G66 2021 (print) |
LCC PS3618.I33374 (ebook) | DDC 813/.6--dc23

Library of Congress Control Number: 2021909334

Produced in the United States of America
10 9 8 7 6 5 4 3 2 1

First Edition

Inkspiration Media supports the First Amendment and
celebrates the right to read.

For Synnöve

Once to every man and nation comes the moment to decide,
In the strife of Truth with Falsehood, for the good or evil side.

James Russell Lowell
"The Present Crisis" 1845

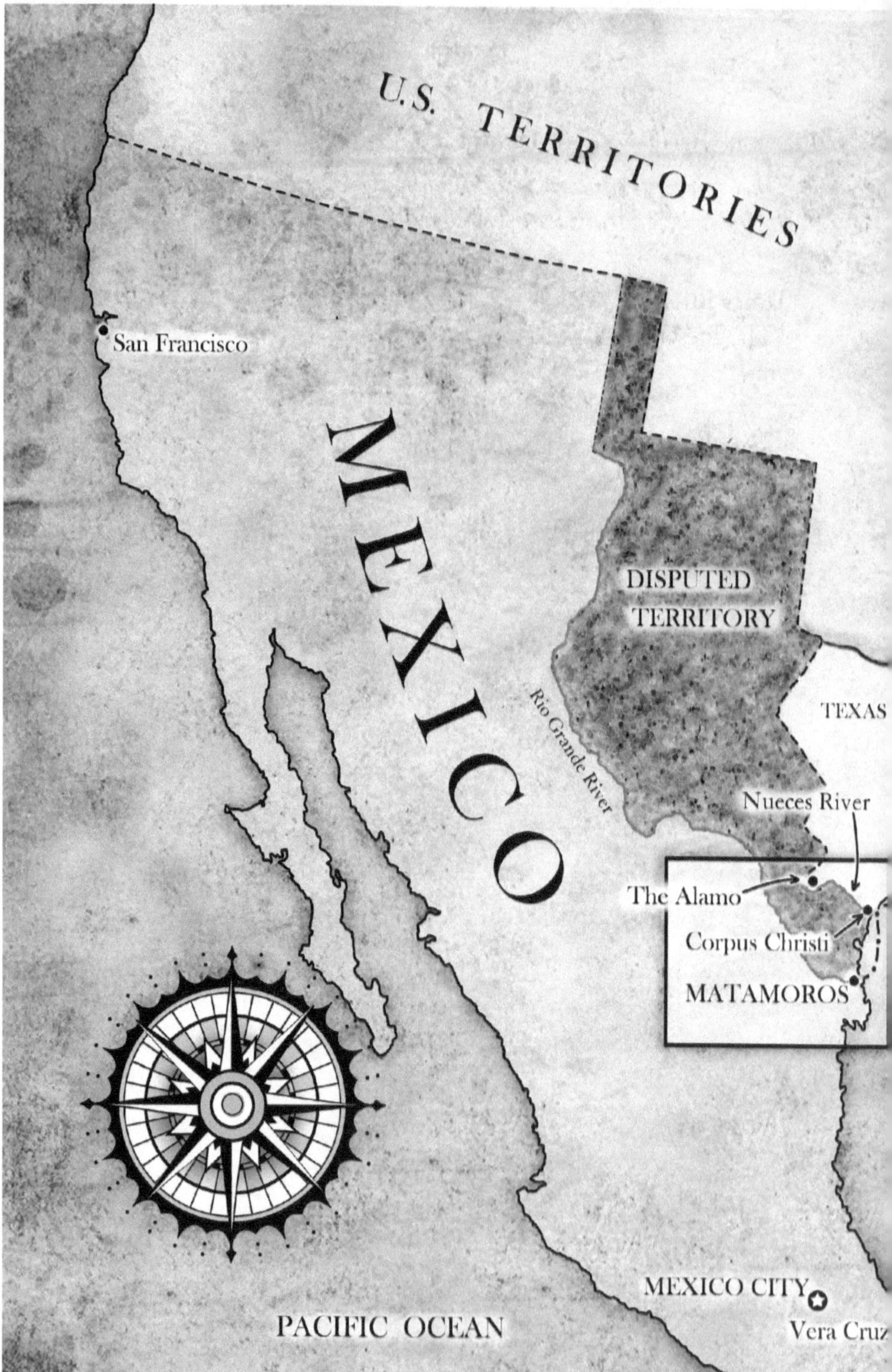

U.S. TERRITORIES
San Francisco
MEXICO
DISPUTED TERRITORY
Río Grande River
TEXAS
Nueces River
The Alamo
Corpus Christi
MATAMOROS
MEXICO CITY
Vera Cruz
PACIFIC OCEAN

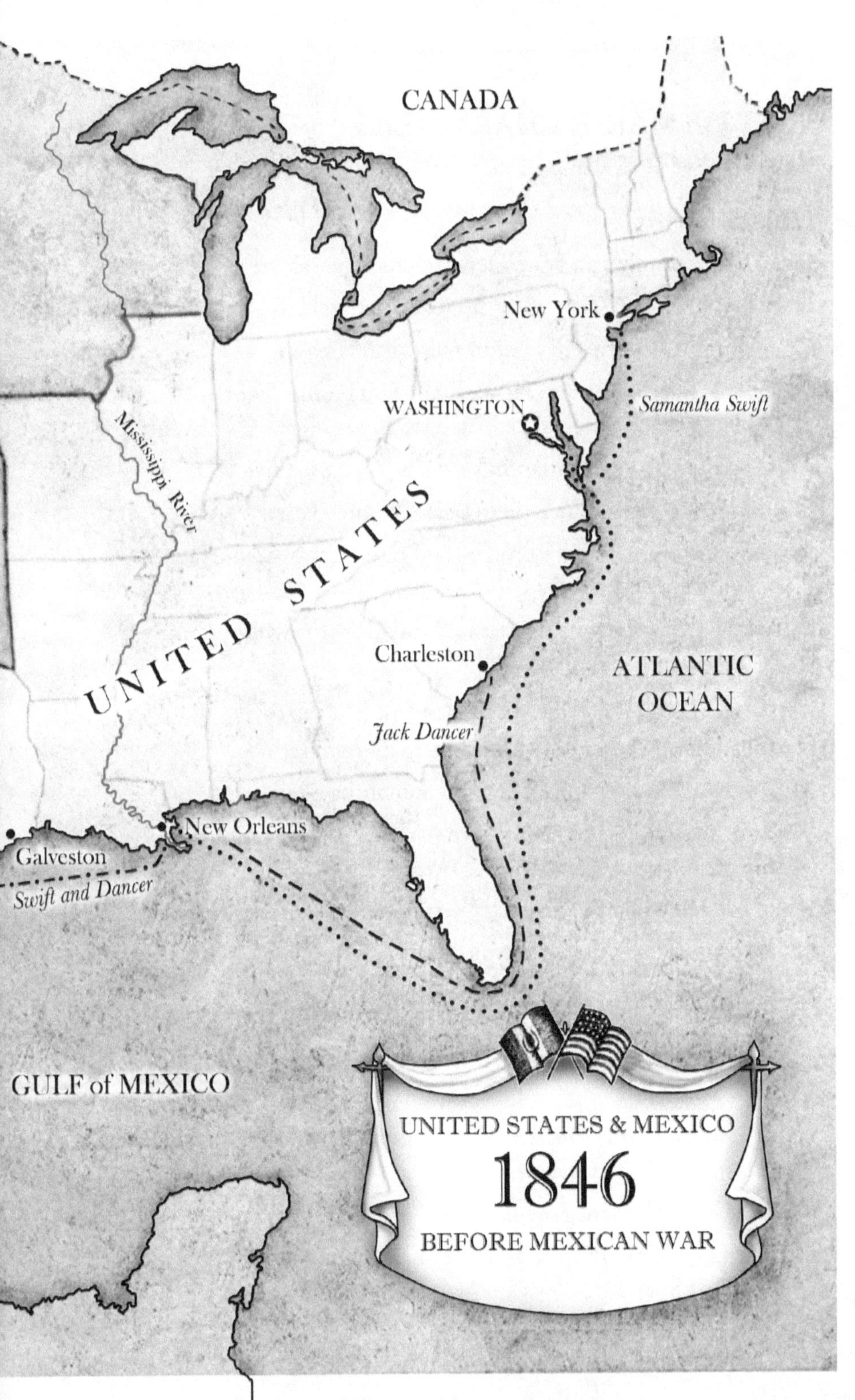

CANADA
New York
WASHINGTON
Samantha Swift
Mississippi River
UNITED STATES
Charleston
Jack Dancer
ATLANTIC OCEAN
New Orleans
Galveston
Swift and Dancer
GULF of MEXICO
UNITED STATES & MEXICO
1846
BEFORE MEXICAN WAR

CAST OF MAJOR CHARACTERS
(In order of appearance)

Fictional Characters

Jack Dancer: American State Department secret agent

Lady Belle Ashley: Mistress of the Ashley household

Colonel John Ashley: Charleston railroad magnate

Samantha Thomas Swift (Pseudonym: **S. Thomas Swift**):
War correspondent for the *Brooklyn Eagle*

Anne Thomas Swift: Samantha's mother (deceased five years)

Phillip Swift: Samantha's father (deceased three years)

Jacob Swift: Phillip Swift's brother and publisher of *New York
Examiner* newspaper

Patrick Harp: Irish-born American Army defector who formed
Saint Patrick's Battalion

Israel David: New Orleans lawyer

Natchez Jones: Captain of steamship SS *Decatur*

Mr. Penrhos: Banker and trustee for Samantha Swift's trust

William Beacon: Newspaper illustrator for *The Daily Picayune*
in New Orleans

Josephine Fitzwilliam: Madam of Josie's bordello in New Orleans

Scarface Flanagan: Patrick Harp's henchman

Henry Kaufman: Eldest of three Austrian brothers (Henry
immigrated to New Orleans in 1844) who became cotton and
dry goods traders as well as financiers with connections in
New York City

James Collingsworth Turner: War correspondent for *The Daily
Picayune* in New Orleans

Kelly the Weasel: Flanagan's sidekick

Michelena Anoche: Proprietress of Hotel Casamata (known as a
"Ladies Hotel")

Big Tim: Bouncer at Hotel Casamata

Don Carlo Juan Baptiste: Rancher and wealthiest man in
North Mexico

Luiz Juan Baptiste: Second son of Don Carlo Juan Baptiste

Father Daniel Thomas: Parish priest of oldest church in Matamoros

General Francisco Payaso: Commander of Mexican Department of
Tamaulipas and Matamoros garrison

John Stepptoe: U.S. Consul in Matamoros

Antonio Malvado: "Chapparal Fox"—a Mexican rebel and bandit
from Camargo Texas

Diego Juan Baptiste: Eldest son of Don Carlo Juan Baptiste

Historical Figures

(In order of appearance with military rank as of story dates.)

Don José "Pepe" Llulla (1815 – 1888): Master of Arms from Majorca Spain (renowned duelist and cemetery owner); owned fencing academy in Exchange Alley New Orleans

Major General Zachary Taylor (1784 – 1850): General of American "Army of Occupation" in Mexican War; became twelfth president of United States in 1849

Lieutenant George Meade (1815 – 1872): American officer in elite Corps of Topographical Engineers in Mexico; became American Civil War general and future victor at Gettysburg

Major Samuel Ringgold (1796 – 1846): American artillery officer credited with perfecting "flying artillery"

Lieutenant Braxton Bragg (1817 – 1876): Artillery officer for whom Fort Bragg is named

Lieutenant Ulysses S Grant (1822 – 1885): American infantry officer at battles of Palo Alto and Resaca de la Palma; became eighteenth president of United States in 1868

Captain Charles May (1818 – 1864): American officer of light-cavalry dragoon unit

Lieutenant Jacob E. Blake (1812 – 1846): American scout and officer of elite Topographical Engineers

Colonel William J. Worth (1794 – 1849): Second-in-command to Zachary Taylor; later celebrated as the namesake for Fort Worth Texas

Captain Samuel Walker (1817 – 1847): American captain of Texas Rangers company of volunteer irregulars

General Pedro de Ampudia (1805 – 1868): Major General of Mexican Army in Matamoros

Captain Seth Thornton (1815 – 1847): Commander of dragoon squad who was ambushed and captured 25 April 1846

Brigadier General Anastasio Torrejón (1802 – 1861):
Mexican cavalry officer to whom Thornton's dragoons
surrendered after clash at Rancho Carricitos

General Mariano Arista (1802 – 1855): General and commander in
chief of Mexican Army of North Department who superseded
General Ampudia

Major Jacob Brown (1789 – 1846): American commander of
Fort Texas that was renamed Fort Brown in his honor
(Brownsville Texas)

Captain Joseph K. F. Mansfield (1803 – 1862): Connecticut-born
officer in American Army Corps of Engineers who designed
Fort Texas

**Sarah Borginnis (c. 1813 – 1866; aka: Boginnis; Bourdette; Bourget;
Bourjette; Davis; Bowman; and possibly Foyle):** Camp follower;
"Heroine of Fort Brown" nicknamed "The Great Western"

Lieutenant Randolph Ridgely (1814 – 1846): American officer of
"flying artillery" first used in combat at Palo Alto

PART I

WILDFIRE

CHAPTER 1

JACK DANCER loved the smell of a woman. Especially in the afternoon. A southerly breeze off Charleston Harbor gave a slight riffle to the sheer curtains. Behind him the mistress of the house stirred.

"Darling…I thought I lost you there for a moment." She purred.

Dancer felt the sheet behind him billow free as he sat on the edge of the canopied bed. Belle Ashley rose on her knees and slipped behind him. He felt the sensuous sting of her sweat in the red claw marks she had left on his back. Now she slipped her hands under his strong arms then moved them down his sides. The breeze made her sharp nails on his ribs even more tantalizing as she pressed her damp breasts against his shoulder blades.

"Thought I'd lost you." She repeated the words in that low voice she used with men after love. "I say…I do believe we have time…if you're willing…Mr. Dancer." Her nails raked lightly down his belly. Then she probed his inner thighs. As his interest rose to her touch his hands slid back along her velvety legs as the idea of a third go began to appeal to him. He leaned back into her. His right hand reached behind and found her wetness with his fingers. He heard a gasp as she collapsed completely against him. The smell of powder on her flushed skin came to his nostrils as she cocked her chin against his neck. Then she slowly explored the space behind his ear with her tongue.

Just as Dancer stirred the front door slammed downstairs. The voice of Colonel John Ashley rose up the staircase from the central entry hall in the grand Old Charleston home.

"Hullo…Belle! I'm home!"

Belle Ashley separated from Dancer. "Oh…fiddlesticks. I believe our adventures must take a holiday…my love." She offered her sly apology as she slid backward and stepped out of bed. "Sounds like my other duties call. Since you are a guest of our house this will be your room. We'll be having supper with the Colonel and the girls at eight o'clock. Cocktails at seven. Be a gentleman and don't be late." She blew Dancer a kiss before backing out of the guest room while closing the door.

With that admonition Dancer moved into the adjoining anteroom of his third-floor suite. He filled the water basin from the ironstone pitcher to freshen himself and shaved for the second time that day. The image in the mirror (he knew) was of a man whom women found attractive. Especially the type of woman who enjoyed her pleasure with the thrill of trouble. Broad shoulders and strong hands made his six-foot frame look taller. With an easy stroke he combed his black hair straight back. Then checked the thin curl of his Lord Byron mustache. His dark eyes had the look of a gambler. *You're trouble.* The secret agent smiled into the mirror. *No telling where your orders from the Inner Circle will take you this time.*

✠   ✠   ✠

The Ashleys sent their butler to usher Dancer onto the breezy second-floor *piazza* porch for mint juleps before supper. Just as they had seen the custom performed in Charleston's old-money homes.

"Mr. Dancer." His host extended his hand. "I'm John Ashley. Friends call me Colonel." At age fifty-eight Ashley tended toward fleshiness. Yet the Colonel was more weathered from years spent outdoors than Dancer had expected. He knew this much: John Ashley was first an army officer under Zachary Taylor charged with moving the Seminoles out of the Florida Territory. And since 1840 he had been overseeing construction of his Louisville–Cincinnati–Charleston Railroad.

"I hope you find our humble home acceptable for your brief billet of invitation…sir."

"Most accommodating…Colonel. Most accommodating indeed."

"I see you've met my sister-in-law…Lucibelle Ashley."

"Pleasure to make your acquaintance…ma'am. Thank you for the kind welcome on such short notice." Dancer formally shook Belle Ashley's gloved hand as he bowed slightly.

"The pleasure is all mine." She returned Dancer's greeting with a mischievous nod.

The Colonel readied the iced juleps. "Good. Good. You may know…sir…the Ashley brothers married two sisters. When my brother and my wife both succumbed to influenza in the same season…rest their souls…Charleston society found it most natural for Belle to move in as mistress of my house. After all…she was already Lady Ashley and someone had to see to the education of my two daughters."

Dancer nodded toward Belle Ashley as they exchanged a meaningful glance.

The Colonel turned his gaze toward the *piazza* doors. "Here come my two lovelies now. Mr. Dancer…please make the acquaintance of my eighteen-year-old angels. May I present the Ashley Girls…Patience and Chastity."

As if on cue both colleens stepped forward. The identical twins wore matching peach-colored silk bell skirts as they fluttered into the space.

Chastity extended her hand. But Patience stepped in front to touch Dancer first.

Patience curtsied. "'The call of doves…sings the sweetness of spring…in a joyful ode.'" She whispered Tennyson with a smile not unlike her aunt's.

Not to be outdone Chastity pushed between them. She took Dancer's hand in hers. Led him as if he was her next dance at the Cotillion. "May I…my dear sir…serve you a julep? The finest ice has just arrived from Boston. I crushed the mint and mixed the sweet syrup myself."

"Ladies…there will be plenty of time to monopolize Mr. Dancer at evening supper. Please…girls…leave us for a while to talk business before we dine." Colonel Ashley ushered Chastity and Patience back toward the parlor.

"We never get to have any fun." Chastity pouted as the twins left the *piazza* porch.

"*Tout alors.*" Patience's eyes read "I shall be seeing you again shortly" as she tested her limited French gleaned from *Ladies' National Magazine* serials.

⊠   ⊠   ⊠

"Now…Mr. Dancer…let's get down to business." Dancer passed Ashley the forged letter from Congressman Jefferson Davis of Mississippi. Earlier he had taken care it was not the revealing second letter hidden in his room that outlined his true secret mission.

Dancer settled into a white wicker chair with flowered chintz cushions in a shaded corner of the *piazza*. Belle followed his lead. After a perfunctory glance at the letter the Colonel held forth at length.

"As you know…sir…I am a dedicated supporter of the South…as any Charleston native son like yourself can appreciate. We've just received word from Envoy John Slidell upon his return from his mission to Mexico. As expected his offers to the Mexicans to cede territory and repay Mexican debts have been refused. Slidell has returned empty-handed. But that is not the message we must take from this news." The Colonel gave juleps to Dancer and Lady Ashley. "It is no secret. I know in my heart that slavery is the natural order and we must do everything in our power to maintain and expand that glorious institution in the South. Northern abolitionists are the greatest curse of this nation!" Colonel Ashley turned red as the veins in his neck bulged. "I have made the proposal that California be divided into two states. The north half will be free. The southern state will allow slavery. With the labor of our African domestics we will build the greatest railroad — from San Antonio in Texas to the city of Los Angeles in California. Take my solemn oath…Mr. Dancer. If California is admitted as a free state then South Carolina will secede…and take the entire South with us."

Lady Ashley raised her kid-gloved hand. "John…remember your heart. You mentioned making good on Mexican debts. Is there an opportunity in that for us?"

"Yes…my dear. May I speak frankly…Mr. Dancer?"

"By all means…sir."

"Our vision is for the South to expand all its railroads. Then integrate them into a system that gives us independence and blocks the advantage of the radical abolitionists. As you know the main lifeblood of the South today flows by river and ocean. Shipping is our strength…and our Achilles' heel."

"There is much talk about a transcontinental railroad." Dancer said the words noncommittally.

"Exactly…sir. Once the railroad crosses the Mississippi in the north and extends to the Pacific Coast our crown jewel that is New Orleans will be reduced to a second-rate cottonseed. Not to say our bustling Charleston will suffer. This Holy City of churches is a seaport whose cotton exports to foreign lands are now third in America only to New Orleans and Mobile. Charleston will be smitten an unredeemable blow. The entire flow of trade will shift from its north-south routes on the Ohio and Mississippi through New Orleans to an east-west axis that will bypass our beloved South…and choke the life from us."

The Colonel paced. "As it stands today I am personally in debt three million dollars from pushing our railroad more than one hundred and thirty miles west from Charleston. Frankly…we face ruin unless we can join forces with other supporters in New Orleans and New York. We must turn the inevitable war with Mexico to our advantage. We must connect all southern railroads into our river system and connect that system to the Pacific Coast and the Orient by southern rail…or the South is lost."

"My instructions from Congressman Jefferson Davis are to assist in any way I can." Dancer lied. "The Congressman once did me a kindness. I am honor and duty bound to return the service to him through his friends. Please continue."

"Here is what we propose…sir." Colonel Ashley pulled two letters from his jacket pocket. He handed Dancer the smaller letter. "First… a group of us that use the code name 'Wildfire' for discretion has arranged for you to be supplied as a profiteer to provide material to General Zachary Taylor's Army of Occupation in Texas. All is explained in this note. Your commission is to leave immediately for New Orleans. Make contact with the Kaufman Brothers and Mr. Israel David in that city. They will provide you with details and all necessities to win the confidence of the Army."

"Being sure my persona has the smell of truth will be critical." Dancer played along.

"Yes…of course…no question. That is why we have arranged for you personally to benefit from any and all profits from your trading ventures. I understand the Army is actually bragging about paying premium prices. It will be like shooting fish in a barrel."

"There seems to be more to the mission than that hole-and-corner story. Am I right?"

With that question Ashley stopped pacing. He generously refilled his julep glass. Dancer waved off a second. Ashley took a seat across from Dancer and lowered his voice.

"Your real mission…and I personally consider this the most critical…is to get to the bottom of a mystery in Matamoros on the Rio Grande in Mexico."

Colonel Ashley handed Dancer the second letter.

Lady Ashley spoke up. "Through our contacts with Wildfire we've been informed of a…shall we say…business opportunity in Matamoros. Jefferson Davis informed us from Washington — and now Slidell has confirmed — that any debts owed by the Mexican government to Americans will be paid in full by the United States Treasury as war claims. We acted on that information…and Wildfire shipped one million dollars in gold half-eagle coins to Matamoros via our American Consul there to be delivered to the highest-ranking Mexican commander in the north." Dancer handed Slidell's letter back to the Colonel.

Ashley coughed quietly then sipped his julep before he continued. "We were led to believe that a loan to Mexico was a sure thing. A guaranteed investment that couldn't miss…or so we were told. If the Mexicans defaulted the American government would make good… plus add six percent interest. A tidy sum on one million."

Lady Ashley clutched her monogrammed handkerchief. "Greed and necessity led us down this path."

Ashley leaned closer to Dancer. "What we must have…to save the South…is to get from the Mexicans the signed certificates and notes and every official confirmation that the one million dollars in specie has been duly delivered to Mexico. The delivery of the gold shipment was an act of good faith. Now the Mexicans must come through with the documents."

"Let me get this straight." Dancer raised his index finger. "What Wildfire needs is finalized documents to prove the loan in the event it becomes necessary to make an official claim?"

"That is correct. We get the papers. The Mexicans keep the money." Ashley calculated. "But there is more."

Dancer listened.

"To qualify as a peacetime loan for our war claim the documents must be dated before hostilities begin. Perhaps more important we must obtain the documents from the Mexican authorities before they are in such disarray as to not know their bonds from their bums. Pardon my French. We must have those documents before the first shot is fired at Matamoros."

Lady Ashley made an impatient gesture. "The clock is ticking."

"Obtaining the loan documents should be straightforward." Dancer said. "After all...you have made your payment."

A cloud came over the Colonel's face. "True...but there is a problem."

"A problem?"

"That's the mystery of Matamoros." Lady Ashley's face clouded as if confiding a secret.

"Mystery?"

Belle Ashley glanced at the Colonel. "Yes. The million dollars in gold is...shall we say...missing. We know it reached Consul John Stepptoe in Matamoros and was given over to the Mexican authorities. But it has vanished."

"Where do you think the treasure could be?"

Belle Ashley's eyes narrowed. "Somewhere in Matamoros. Definitely. Only a small cadre knows of its existence...and it is too conspicuous to be carried away...or explained if caught red-handed."

The Colonel interjected after he emptied his fourth julep. "Due to the delicacy of Wildfire's position as purveyors of the payment...we are not at liberty to make any investigations ourselves. At this time. That is why we depend on you...Mr. Dancer. As a Southerner. As a Charleston native. And as a trusted associate of Jefferson Davis."

Dancer rubbed his chin. "The treasure of Matamoros..."

"Yes." The Ashleys had answered in unison. The next moment Colonel Ashley again took the lead. "We need you to find the documents. Secure the treasure of Matamoros. And deliver them both to New Orleans before they are lost forever."

⊠　⊠　⊠

Over supper Dancer's mind raced despite the interminable giddy chatter of the twin Ashley girls who seemed exhilarated by his presence.

Lost treasure...advancing slavery to new lands...a last-minute loan provided to the highest placed officials in Mexico...time running out... imminent war. This better be worth it.

"I will excuse myself...sir and ladies. Tomorrow is an early start." Lady Ashley held Dancer's hand a beat longer than a polite good night would require.

⊠　⊠　⊠

Jack Dancer removed his jacket and jackboots. From the settee he heard a soft noise come from the anteroom of his guest chamber. He looked up. There in the doorway stood one of the twins. Slowly she pulled the ribbon from her gathered tresses and they fell luxuriantly across one breast. Her white skin glowed in the guttering candlelight. She tossed her hair away from her shoulder. Then advanced toward Dancer wearing only her thin nightdress. Patience put both hands on Dancer's chest. Playfully she pushed him against the back of the settee. She moved closer to her intended. Raised her summer chemise. Pressed astride Dancer's legs. And artfully began to undo Dancer's string tie.

"Shush." She whispered the command. "Whatever is good for Belle is good for Patience. I watched you this afternoon from the anteroom." Patience lifted Dancer's hands and cupped them over her warm breasts.

Patience gripped Dancer behind his neck. Pulled his face toward her chest with both hands as she began to move her hips over his thighs.

At that moment something quite singular took place. Without warning the guest suite door flew open. All hell burst into the room. Chastity shrieked and pointed at the couple. "She's here! She's here...Daddy! They are fornicating! He has violated her!" Colonel

Ashley stomped into the room followed by two rough-looking roustabouts. Trailed by Lady Ashley.

The Colonel stopped. "What is this?" Ashley shouted the question. His face red. Sweat appeared at his temples. Veins popped on his neck like a steam engine about to blow.

"We caught you! We caught you!" Chastity trilled at Patience. "He's fornicating her! Look!"

"This…this…debauchery cannot be tolerated under my own roof!" Colonel Ashley blustered.

If you only knew. Dancer silenced his thought as he eyed an escape. Seeing none he pandered. "This is not what it seems." He pushed Patience to the side. "She hid in my room. Uninvited. I didn't do a thing. She's barely even a woman. She's just eighteen for God's sake!"

Patience's face twisted toward Dancer. "Not a woman? Why…you bastard." She feigned innocence. "He was seducing me…Daddy."

Patience straightened her nightdress and stepped toward Chastity. Without even looking Chastity gave Patience a sharp elbow in the ribs. Patience almost cried out but thought better of it as the twins sought protection behind their father.

"That will teach you!" Chastity hissed in a whisper to Patience. "You can't have anything I can't have. Daddy always says."

Patience gave a triumphant half smile. *Two for one. Got Dancer. Got my sister.*

Before Dancer could speak another word or even think about escape the railyard brutes pinned his arms behind him. Ashley fumed. "My own daughter! In my house! My darling Patience! How dare you…*sir!*" He slapped Dancer hard across the face with the back of his hand.

Stepping toward her smug sister Chastity angled to drive her heel onto Patience's bare foot. Only to be restrained by their Aunt Belle.

The Colonel motioned to his men. "We will show you what we do with fornicators in Charleston! Take this man to the wharf! We'll splay him from the dock!"

⌧　⌧　⌧

Hands tied and helpless Dancer was dragged across the wharf to the edge. To his left ankle one roughneck knotted a stout line and secured the end to a dock cleat. No escape. A second line was cinched around Dancer's right boot. With the second rigging in hand the other blackguard boarded the soon-to-depart SS *Decatur* steamer. Hidden by the great sidewheel paddle box he raced to the aft-railing post. And hitched the slack line to an iron stanchion. Then returned to the darkness of the steamer quay.

Belle stepped between Dancer and the Colonel. Then took her brother-in-law to the side.

"Dearest…let us think for a moment."

"That beast violated my little Patience!" Colonel Ashley fumed.

"Believe me…dearest. Dancer was not the initiator. After supper I overheard Patience and Chastity talking in their room. They flipped a coin to see who would take the dare to seduce Mr. Dancer. Chastity lost. There is no guilt on Dancer's part."

"What? Woman…I saw them with my own eyes!"

"What you saw was Patience pretending to be one of those magazine characters from *The Ladies' Companion* serial. She was playacting. Dancer is innocent."

"My honor is at stake! I must avenge this insult!"

"Dear brother…I have another idea."

"My darling…Patience was exposed.…"

"Yes. And Mr. Dancer was fully dressed. My dear…let's turn this to our advantage. He is worth more to us with both legs attached. We need Dancer to find the treasure in Matamoros and bring back the officially stamped loan papers. No one else can do it. That is what Wildfire wrote. Let me speak to Dancer. I will make him an offer he will understand."

"I won't hear of it! Alert the *Decatur* to cast off at once!" Ashley bellowed. The ship's steam whistle unleashed a deafening blast.

"Cast off bow line." The captain's call came sharply.

"Tear the scoundrel in half!" The Colonel shouted as he stomped across the wharf to his carriage.

"Then I will give him his final farewell." Lady Ashley moved toward Dancer.

Belle gave her orders: "Stand back boys. Take the Colonel back to his carriage. I'll give this randy scoundrel his last goodbye."

Lady Ashley smiled while moving closer to Dancer. Her cape-like mantelet and voluminous dome-shaped dress shielded any view of Dancer from the Colonel's carriage—now drawn two steamer-lengths distant from the wharf's dark edge. She whispered. "My love…I'm sure my daughters would be a disappointment after my attentions today. Hush…my darling. Don't protest. Just as you will be returning the consideration of Congressman Davis and Wildfire…I will do you this one last service."

Propped up exhausted against a wharf piling. Tied like a traitorous pig to be drawn and quartered. Dancer gaped at her in disbelief.

"If you live to see Matamoros then we shall say you owe me something in return. Is that clear? For my kindness now…your service in return is to find the treasure and secure the documents. Tittle for tattle…yes? I will help you. If you help me. Do you understand?"

Dancer blinked—dumbfounded at this bewildering turn.

"Don't think Wildfire is not watching your every move. Their men are everywhere. You'll probably never survive. But no threats…my love. Let me know when you return to Charleston so I can make myself presentable for you. *Adieu*…darling."

With that strange farewell the massive side wheels groaned and began to churn. The *Decatur* moved slowly away from the dock. The splaying rope tied to the aft rail splashed into the black water. Then in a blink the slack tightened. Jack Dancer was ripped off the dock and thrown into the oblivion of Charleston Harbor.

CHAPTER 2

SAMANTHA SWIFT felt like she was drowning. Vignettes of her life ricocheted about her brain. *How could this be? This was my home. I grew up in this library. This house. The Christmas tree there. Hattie and Jim. They always watched out for us. Peddlers calling in the street. Deliveries. Father's sweater and pipe. Smiling at Mother. How you glowed beside Father. Extending a quiet touch. Books. Always books. By the fire. In the garden behind the gazebo. My secret place.*

Samantha's gaze traced back and forth over the detailed craftsmanship of the elegant brownstone. In her mind there was no more perfect home. *Until the accident. They said it was an accident. Mother! Uncle Jacob said Mother slipped while walking along the canal. There was nothing near at hand to reach her he said. Perhaps she hit her head as she fell? He ran to the carriage to get Jim. Why didn't he help her? When they got back to the canal Mother was gone. The stone walls were too slick. Nowhere to grasp or climb. Clothes became a weight they said. Uncle Jacob kept repeating immigrants should teach their children how to swim. When they brought her body home I watched them lay her on the dining table as if Mother was asleep. Father rushed in. Wild eyed. I've never seen you like that Father. You held her. Sobbed. Under the table a dark puddle collected. I hate water. Cold. Unfeeling. Suffocating. Blackness.*

Samantha raised her eyes to her father's portrait as her hand clasped her mother's pendant. *You didn't leave her for days. What happened Father? You changed somehow. You seemed to lose interest. I tried. But I couldn't make you laugh like Mother did. Make you take an interest in the newspaper again. Like you loved to do. Even when we went on that British Isles tour the summer after Mother died. Almost five years now. It was sadness. Tears. You took us to Wales. To Mother's home. Before she came to America. You said she chose New York with intention. "Go where there are prospects to take care of yourself. Don't depend on anyone else." She was so pretty. You gave me her cameo pendant with her ivory profile. I never take it off.*

You and Uncle Jacob both loved her. But she chose you. Then she was gone. It was a month before my birthday. I was almost sixteen then. I remember coming down the stairs. What was the commotion? Jim carried Mother into the dining room. My fingers were stained with writing ink and tears that day.

Samantha stood looking out the rear window; the effect was unsettling. Like being trapped in a recurring dream. *After Mother died the days passed like glaciers. Uncle Jacob said your heart was not in the newspaper. You just stood by the window Father. Every morning. Looking into the garden. I sometimes wondered if you expected Mother to step out from the garden shed. Push her hair away with the back of her wrist. Leave a smudge of dirt on her forehead. And smile back at us looking out the window. Everything grew as before. Abundance. You loved the peonies with their large fragrant flowers. Mother always wanted to trim them. "Give them a haircut." You said no. Let them grow. She loved to bring the red and pink peony bouquets inside. Then dried them upside down in a closet. Like paper. Faded specimens still adorn the upper hallway.*

Samantha turned and studied the length of the large parlor room she stood in with mounting concern. The space in her childhood home stretched from the rear to the front of the house. *Two years later almost to the day Uncle Jacob said the spring influenza killed you Father. I wonder if it really did. Or did you let it? Not caring. Just let it in. Like a thief discovering an open door. Then you were gone too. I heard Uncle Jacob say he did not like children. Especially when they were not his. But how could he know? He has no children. No wife. Only employees he treats like children.*

"Samantha! Come here. I'm talking to you!" Jacob Swift barked. Samantha blinked. A large form stood silhouetted against the front bay window overlooking the street. Dark. Overbearing. "Come in here. The head mistress tells me you were expelled from that overpriced finishing school. She said you were caught with a young man in your room. Good God! You're not pregnant…or are you?" Jacob Swift demanded in his typically demeaning tone.

"No." Samantha answered her uncle's question before she crossed the parlor to a well-loved chair. *Why would I be?*

"Did you make a regular practice of giving yourself to men like a common tea cart girl?"

"No. Of course not." With rising anger Samantha took a seat. *Anyway…we were caught before anything happened.*

"What were you thinking…girl?"

Samantha Swift collected herself and inhaled a long breath. She was tall and fair. And exceptionally pretty—dressed in a wide-lapeled brown-velvet Spencer jacket that ended at her narrow waist. A soft-brimmed hat unsuccessfully tried to gather her unruly mane. The auburn hair strained to be let loose. She had striking sea-green eyes that complemented her outfit. Within the hour she was going to be cast out into the first great adventure of her life.

"I was thinking of this house." Samantha spoke in a wistful voice. "In the days when it was happy."

"Humph! Enough of that." Jacob Swift scoffed. "When your father died three years ago his will made me your guardian. I sent you to that woman's seminary for two years. Then this last year to the Chevy Chase School to be finished like proper ladies should be. Then I expected to find a husband for you. Now you're sent packing. Your reputation is in shreds…and our family's good name lies tossed in the gutter. What are we to do?" Jacob Swift began to pace. "Did you learn anything? Did I get anything for my hard-earned money? What subjects did you study…girl?"

"Spanish. French. Geography. Equestrian. My favorites were writing and ledgers." Samantha gladly summoned the list of courses.

"Writing? Ledgers? That's silly. Why try to teach a woman to understand words or figures? It's absurd. It's like trying to teach a cast-iron kettle to speak. Quite ridiculous. Maybe it's just as well you left that place." Swift huffed. "What a waste."

"Why are you living in our house?" Samantha asked.

Jacob Swift cleared his throat. "Well…now…I've been meaning to tell you…my dear. It's a bit complicated. But I will make it simple for you to understand." Swift stepped to a writing desk and selected a freshly-arrived Cuban Partagas Royal from a cedar case. Then slowly drew the cigar under his nose and breathed expansively.

"Let me start from the beginning. When your mother arrived here from Bangor in North Wales she was young. Beautiful. And without a penny. I saw her first at our printer's office. She was the tea cart girl. Served the clerks. Her last name was Thomas. Anne Thomas. That is how you got your middle name of course. That was when I began to drink tea. Horrid stuff. Even with sugar. Your father came with me one day to review the press proofs and I introduced Phillip to her. He began to accompany me more often. Then every edition. Even returned to see the galley changes! Soon he was actually showing them to her. Asking her opinion!"

"Did you court her too?"

Jacob Smith's pinkish-gray complexion reddened. "Don't interrupt me! Yes. I sent her gifts. Her favorite peony flowers. Embroidered handkerchiefs. Tried to pay for an omnibus to take her home to the boarding house. But she always said it wasn't proper…for a single woman…and all…to be in a gentleman's presence without a chaperone. Balderdash. She should have been interested in me. After all I was the older brother. Didn't seem to stop her when your father took a picnic and they went across into Washington Square. Or when the extra edition was late and he walked her home. After that first walk he announced he was going to marry her. What? Don't be stupid I told him! She's got no family. She's just out to get your money. Can't you see? But he didn't listen. Never did. Look where it got him. I suppose I never got over Phillip taking Anne away from me with this house."

Samantha blinked. "What do you mean?"

"Your father took out a large loan from the newspaper. He wanted to build this house on fashionable Bleeker Street and make it a haven for her. He did that. Called it Beaumaris after a castle on the Isle of

Anglesey somewhere near her hometown of Bangor. Spared no expense. Of course our newspaper was starting to be a success in those days. Even bigger today. All those shanty immigrants…you know…who knew they can actually read? Phillip dropped the price to a penny. Can you imagine?"

"Is that why they call it the penny press?" Samantha said.

"Phillip's idea. Sold like hotcakes…I must say. Naturally the *New York Sun* copied the price the next year." Jacob Swift muttered as Samantha's thoughts drifted away. *I remember that night. Father had an inspiration ahead of its time. Sell the newspaper for only a penny. It was brilliant. He told us at afternoon dinner. "I've got a radical idea." He held up the newspaper. Pointed to the price. "Six cents! Sakes alive…only the uptown swells can afford that." No paper charged only a penny. The competition would have a conniption fit. Mother asked: "What shall we call it? It's like a penny press."*

"That's it!" Father said. Mother's eyes danced as she looked up at you. I took her hand. "We'll hire an army of boys to hawk them on the street."

Father grabbed Mother and swung her around like they were at a picnic. "People won't even have to step into a shop to buy it!"

"The newsboys will love it!" And they did Father.

Samantha gave a longing sigh. "How can I forget. 1832. It was Christmas." Samantha smiled as she settled into her father's favorite armchair. "They loved each other so. You could see it. Hattie and Jim were peeking out from the kitchen. All smiles too."

Jacob Swift tapped cigar ash into the fire grate. "Before you were sixteen…your mother drowned." The blunt words revealed his bitterness. "Your father was never the same. He stopped going to the office. Then the flu killed him." Her uncle turned to face Samantha. "That's when I had to settle his affairs…make good on the loan to the newspaper. At my direction the newspaper paid off the mortgage on Beaumaris." Swift's tone made the outcome sound inevitable. Settled. "To keep the house in the family—and to be sure you had a home to return to—I took possession. Though I had to let Hattie and Jim go. No need to pay for live-in servants when it's just a bachelor living here. That debt settlement also ate up your father's interest in our newspaper business." Jacob Swift hooked his soft thumbs behind the lapels of his tailored suit jacket.

"That's why only your name is on the masthead now?"

Jacob Swift swelled. "That's right. I am the sole owner of the *New York Examiner* now. Yesterday street sales and citywide delivery passed fifty thousand for the week. My newspaper is the biggest in town. Far ahead of that second-rate rag the *Brooklyn Eagle.* The little people on the street love it. Sales are unbelievable. Give me a good murder. Or a trial. Or a fire. Children separated. A kidnapping. Cops and robbers. Those headlines sell newspapers. Now they are talking about pictures! Can you believe it? Woodblock engravings! Right next to the type! Use the same presses they say. But it costs money. Not to mention the riffraff competition will copy us again. You never know what stunt those clowns will try next at the *Eagle.*"

"So why did you want to talk to me…Uncle?"

"I told you to stop interrupting! How old are you now?"

"I'm twenty."

Jacob Smith turned and looked at Samantha as if he saw her for the first time.

Samantha Swift twisted uneasily in her father's deep red-leather armchair.

"Samantha." Her uncle fidgeted with his cigar. "Finishing school was to be the last step. But that's come to naught. Now that you're almost of the marrying age."

"I'll be twenty-one in April…only two months."

Jacob Swift stopped pacing. Adjusted his grip on his lapels and came right to his point. "It's time that you marry."

Samantha caught her breath.

"That's why…as your guardian and benefactor…responsible for your well-being…I've found a suitable young man. Good family. I've made certain arrangements."

"You've done what?" Samantha choked.

"You no doubt know the young man. Charlie Gray. He lives with his parents near Irving Park. Nice fellow. Good prospects they say. He is following his older brothers and his father into the *Examiner.* Buys newsprint for us. Newspapers always need newsprint. Understand… young Charlie is moving ahead. Works in the main office. Bit older than you. Twenty-eight…I think they said. The Grays say you would be a perfect match. I've always thought his father…Ernest Gray…

a solid sort. Middling fellow. Gets the job done. Suspect Charlie is the same."

"You old fool!" Samantha exploded. "First my mother picks Father over you. Now what is this? Are you taking it out on me? I can't believe it! You picked a husband for me? I don't want a husband! And if I did I'd pick one I loved! Not some boring…plodding…ordinary warehouse clerk somebody from your club suggested!"

"Don't talk to me that way…young lady!" Swift barked. "I've given this all the thought it deserves. I even wrote the announcement with Mr. Gray at the club this week. Told all the chaps. It's for your own good. You can't refuse. The engagement will be in the *Examiner* tomorrow. If you ruin this plan too…like you threw away your chance at school…you'll be a spinster forever! Not to mention my standing at the club will be damaged beyond repair. It's the only way. Get married…give parties…have children…what else can a woman do?"

"*What else?* For one thing I want to make my life in the newspaper business and carry on what Father began!" Samantha countered.

"The newspaper business! A woman? In the newspaper business! Don't be ridiculous. No woman can run a newspaper. Women's brains aren't made to hold all those figures. They would explode! All those decisions. Business is a serious matter! How would you manage without being allowed into the club? Why…a woman would dissolve into tears the first time she was attacked in print by a competitor. A woman can't do a man's job! Never. How absurd. And you have no right to the newspaper. That died with your father. I own the *Examiner* now. And I've decided you must marry Charlie Gray!"

Samantha jumped to her feet. A large gulp of air filled her lungs. The sensation was like bursting through the water's surface after a deep dive.

Her uncle continued: "I thought you might be troublesome. Headstrong! Just like your mother! That is why I've arranged the wedding to be in seven weeks. The date is already set…two days before your birthday!" Samantha's guardian exclaimed in a determined voice. "In the meantime…to give you time to come around to the wisdom of my decision…we have arranged for you and Mrs. Gray to assemble a *trousseau* and banquet favors. That will get this newspaper daydream out of your head. Show you your place in the world. You'll see it's for the best. The Grays and I will make all the wedding arrangements."

"No!"

"What? What do you mean 'No'?"

"I won't do it! I won't go with Mrs. Gray to put together my *trousseau*! I won't be engaged to Charlie Gray! I won't let you run my life!"

"You have no choice! Where could you go? What would you do? I have decided what is best for you! Your future is my responsibility! Either follow my plan or…" Swift paused. "Or get out of my house."

"You're an ignorant…old…angry man. No! I won't do it!" Samantha shouted.

"You won't?" Swift sputtered.

"I won't marry anyone you pick for me."

"Ridiculous! No one talks to Jacob Swift like that. This is my house. I am Jacob Swift! Owner and publisher of the *New York Examiner*. Kings bow to me. Titans of industry do as I say. I can make — or break — a president. No niece of mine is going to defy me!"

Jacob Swift fumed.

Samantha stood her ground.

"I didn't want it to come to this." Jacob Swift began a new tack. "But you give me no choice. You're no better than your mother. Look what it got her!"

Samantha shot back: "At least she had love…and Father."

"That's it! That's the last straw!" Swift bellowed. "You deserve what you have forced me to do!" Jacob Swift violently yanked open the drawer of the desk beside the bay window. With his other hand he barely stopped the cigar case from toppling off. From the drawer Swift grabbed a ribbon-tied blue packet. "This was my last will and testament. In it I left this house and all my fortune to you. But no more!" He ripped the papers apart and bulled his way toward the fireplace. "You will never return to my house. You will never inherit my newspaper. You will never speak to me in that tone again! I am in control here! To me you are now dead forever more!" With his final oath Jacob Swift pitched the papers into the fire. Samantha's torn future quickly burst into flames.

"Get out!" Jacob Swift growled as he watched the papers turn to curled ashes on the fire grate. "Go!"

⚔ ⚔ ⚔

Samantha Swift slammed the brownstone's heavy door behind her and tried to catch her breath. She had crossed her Rubicon. No question about that. She could never return to Beaumaris. Or trust Uncle Jacob. But where else could she go? Her feet led her down the worn limestone steps. Stepped around icy puddles on a bitter February evening. Slowly. Blindly. Her steps carried her along the street under the skeletons of winter trees. They brought her to a corner where there was a darkened news shop. Dozens of newspapers made appealing stacks in the display window. Before her Horace Greeley's *New York Tribune* and the *Brooklyn Eagle* were just visible in the darkening gloom. As she squinted between cupped hands at the nameplates arrayed beyond the cold glass an idea sparked to life. Her mother's words came to her. *"Go where there are prospects to take care of yourself. Do not depend on anyone else."*

Determination came into Samantha's voice. "You're right…Mother. I'll show them. I'll make my own way."

Samantha Swift gathered herself.

"But first there is something I must do."

CHAPTER 3

PATRICK HARP distrusted lawyers almost as much as he did landlords. Experience had taught him that painful lesson: neither were friends of an Irishman. But why had he been summoned by Israel David? And why meet at night at his cotton press office? Not at his money-lending offices in the Merchant's Exchange on Canal Street or his fancy house on Bourbon Street? *Something's not right.*

Harp signaled his four wharf rats to split into twos and watch the front door and the side entrance of the great cotton warehouse.

Harp reached for the gargoyle handle of the office's door then stopped when a disembodied steamboat whistle filled the night. The foreboding sound enveloped Harp and the darkened levee of New Orleans only a pistol shot behind him.

With his right hand on the leather-wrapped handle of the bullwhip at his left hip Harp stepped through the unbolted door and entered the devil's den.

☓ ☓ ☓

Israel David put a letter marked "Wildfire" into a folder and locked it in his private vault. "Come in!" The solicitor's voice boomed through the office.

Harp opened the oversized walnut inner door as the lawyer inside watched the ruddy-faced army private step into his office.

"Patrick Harp?" The stout lawyer stated his query in that manner his friends behind his back disparaged as a "jolly rotundity."

"Yes…sir." Harp responded stiffly as his blue eyes swept the room for possible exits.

Harp's sky-blue roundabout jacket and matching wool trousers with yellow side stripes and oval brass U.S. belt plate complemented his muscular frame. The artillery crossed-cannon insignia of the 5th Infantry on his forage cap was worn by a man more accustomed to giving orders than taking them. The Irishman's dense red hair curled past his collar. Israel David realized his spies were dead on mark. Harp was the embodiment of the legendary "Wild Geese." Those renowned Irish mercenaries of the century before who fought for foreign armies with the expectation they would bring their keen military skills back home one day. A day when the Wild Geese would cut down the British redcoats whose boots were forever on every Irishman's neck.

David shifted uneasily. Harp's eyes followed him with a hunter's instinct. The cold eyes of a man comfortable being paid to execute orders or kill.

"At ease…sir." David began his speech: "We are brothers of the same immigrant inspiration. My parents left the British Virgin Islands when I was eleven to escape that closed English society." David moved into the full light of the gas lamp. "We had not landed in Charleston a month before a slave rebellion led by that fiend Denmark Vesey left a scar on my memory. Can you imagine Africans rising against their masters? Terrifying for a boy. Still worrisome today. Even when I went to Yale the Puritans wanted nothing to do with a Jew like me. Someday you'll hear the trumped-up story of how they claim I was a thief. That's what propelled me to New Orleans eighteen years ago. Since 1828 I've made a name for myself in this town." The lawyer paused to allow his pedigree to sink in with Harp.

"I understand you got free passage to Canada with Her Majesty's army." David spoke his words offhandedly. "Then…shall we say… exchanged that uniform for the American Army."

Harp took measure of the portly lawyer. He admired his fashionable full beard and clean-shaven upper lip.

"Your information is mistaken…sir." Harp stood steady. "I mustered out of the British Army after seven years as a sergeant of artillery before I shipped to Mackinac in Michigan. It was two years before I joined the Americans—who said they were in need of experienced European soldiers."

David knew a court-martial would never give Harp a chance to prove that claim. But without blinking the cunning solicitor realized blackmailing Harp with threats he was a British Army deserter wouldn't be needed if Harp became troublesome. David took a familiar tone.

"Have you heard recently from your wife and son back in County Galway? Clifden town…if I'm not mistaken. I've heard reports that Clifden has been struck hardest by the famine in that troubled isle." David also knew the rugged coast of Clifden was famous for its smugglers. And rebels…and deserters.

Harp stiffened. No word had come for months. But not unexpectedly. Harp had not sent a single letter. He did not intend to. Mary and little Thomas were forever part of the old sod of Ireland…not his new world where he swore to grab the Golden Goose for himself.

"From your insignia I see you are under the command of the horse artillery in the Fifth Infantry. Now your troop is about to sail for Texas." David paused. "My colleagues tell me you are just the man we need."

Harp felt the first chill of discomfort. This smooth-spoken Jew knew more about his past than he had ever revealed. Even to his fellow gunners.

"Don't worry…Harp." David's words set the soldier on an even sharper edge. "As you see…we know a lot about you. That is why you are here."

In the close chamber the first icy rivulet of sweat ran over Harp's ribs.

"Can you enlighten me…sir?" Harp probed.

"We appreciate your enterprise…Mr. Harp. And we have a golden opportunity for you."

"We?"

"Yes…my associates and I. Their names are not important. You will know us as Wildfire. We know you have…issues…with several of the native-born West Point officers."

Harp's mind snapped to the scene where a Westie had pummeled an Irish recruit who had done nothing more than forget to button his cuff. The lieutenant ordered the poor fool to "ride the horse" — whereupon the boy had been set astride a high wooden sawhorse. His hands tied behind his back in the merciless sun of Corpus Christi. The private lost his balance. Without hands to break the fall he fell on his neck and broke that instead. Cold dead as a wagon wheel. "A lesson in discipline for the foreign croppies and Dutchies!" The Westie lieutenant had squealed in that high-pitched voice of his that got more tremulous when he was excited.

"Reports have it some officers treat you and your Irish brothers like cannon fodder." David warmed to his purpose. "They give Irish the worst duties. No leave. Even had many of your lads stand the barrel. Two hours on…two hours off…from morning reveille to final tattoo before taps."

"That lieutenant branded two of my mates with a 'W' for worthless." Harp hissed his outrage: "The bastard said another was a habitual drunkard and right nearly killed him with an 'HD' brand. Bullshit. Who's he to whine when most of the highfalutin officer bastards drink the corn juice from every sutler who is sellin'?"

"Where are my manners?" Israel David moved to his decanters and locked cigar caddy. "Whiskey? Cuban cigar?"

Harp pocketed four Partagas Royals for his boys and emptied the whiskey tumbler.

David feigned a toast. "Wildfire shares your feelings…Harp."

"What is it you want…Mr. David?"

"Speaking plainly…Harp. We will make it worth your while. Very worth your while…to help us defeat the American Army."

Harp stared straight into the face of the lawyer but now stood more at ease. "I've learned there is no place for shanty Irish like me in Polk's army. They promised me I'd regain my former rank of sergeant. All lies. I know now my first loyalty must be to myself and Ireland. That's why I'm here to soldier…so someday I can return to Ireland."

"You will be an honor to both yourself and your country when the abolitionists learn they cannot push men like you around."

David continued as he lit a Cuban cigar. "This trumped-up 'Army of Occupation' has many weaknesses…besides being outnumbered three to one. The Mexicans are veterans. Battle tested. They know how to fight…as they proved at Goliad and the Alamo. Plus the Mexicans know the land like their backyard. Most important they are fighting to defend their homeland."

Israel David moved a step closer to Harp and looked him in the eye. "The key to victory will be the first encounter at Matamoros. It is everything. Once the American Army tastes defeat…the abolitionists and expansionists in Washington will be split. While they dither in Congress and the summer fevers kill off Taylor's men on the Rio Grande…Mexico and the South and Wildfire will have time to establish the right of slavery in the western territories."

Harp listened.

"With more time we would have been able to divide Texas into three or four slave states…not just one. However we get them…more slave states mean the ultimate balance of power. In one stroke…Wildfire can command that power by defeating the Americans at Matamoros." David blew a cloud of triumphant smoke into the air and refilled Harp's glass.

"To ensure that outcome…Harp…we will pay you a handsome fee. Far more than the pittance of an army private."

Harp interjected: "As I said…What exactly do you want?"

"Do what you were born to do. Recruit as many foreign-born fighters as you can here in New Orleans to join the Americans. Make a special effort to find Irish men who are veterans of other armies."

"The army pays us a recruiting bonus for every regular we get to 'X' his enlistment papers." Harp tilted his empty tumbler and met David's eyes with an expectant look.

"For starters…Wildfire will triple that."

"And?"

"Place as many of your recruits to train in the horse artillery as you can. Learn every maneuver. Master every skill. We will depend on you to use your soldier's instincts to defeat this new flying artillery." The fat lawyer stopped in front of the fireplace. The hearth was already dead cold on this chilly February evening.

Harp sensed David was about to reveal a secret.

"As your ranks grow…seek out the foreign fighters like yourself. These men are the Achilles' heel of the American Army. Did you know foreigners number almost half of all the regular troops in Zachary Taylor's little force? Mostly Irish and German. Some British and Scots. When the time is right we have arranged for our Mexican friends to give you sanctuary for your efforts. True riches will be yours when your men cross over and join the Mexican cause. The money has already been deposited in Matamoros. Join us and you will get land. Money. Citizenship. And all the brown-eyed Mexican girls you and your men could dream of."

Land. Money. A new country that welcomed them. Harp knew that was everything his countrymen dreamed of from the Golden Door. The one that America had made clear was not open to the shanty Irish.

"Now you can realize your dream…Harp. You will be the commander of a legion of foreign fighters. Your actions will mortally weaken the American Army. You alone can turn the Americans' hatred of Catholics and foreigners around to bite them and their manifest aggression."

"What's in this plan for Wildfire?" Harp asked as he weighed his chances to even the score with nativist officers like those West Pointers and use the power of the Irish and German fighters for his own triumph. *If I'm going to fight…I might as well get paid well for it.*

"Our mission is simple. Defeat the northern army at Matamoros. Keep the territory west of the Mississippi open for slavery all the way to California. New Orleans will remain the jewel of the South. And slavery will cement the Crescent City's rightful place in the order of man forever."

"Wildfire can stick its holy mission for all I care." Harp spoke bluntly. "As for me…I will join the call to stop the Anglos and Protestants from stealing another land from my Catholic brothers. My love is to fight…sir. It's a happy day when the fight also gives a chance to kick bastards like that lieutenant in the teeth."

"Agreed."

David eagerly shook hands with Harp.

"I'm pleased our mutual interests have this opportunity to support each other." David rose and went to his safe. In a moment he turned with a pouch of Seated Liberty silver half-dollars. "Here is an advance payment to recruit the first twenty fighters to our cause. Famine ships are arriving daily on the levee in New Orleans. They offer good hunting. Wildfire's eyes are everywhere. They will report on your progress."

Harp knew the Irish neighborhoods. One called "The Swamp" festered where Girod Street met Tchoupitoulas Street two blocks from the levee in the American Sector of the Second Municipality. *My fortunes are looking up.* Harp tied the pouch of half-dollar coins to his belt. The trove hung in the hollow of his coiled bullwhip.

As he took his leave a mean smirk narrowed the Irish Private's eyes.

Patrick Harp knew frenetic wharves and tenements of New Orleans would prove to be fertile recruiting ground for more than soldiers.

CHAPTER 4

HARBOR/ABOARD SS *DECATUR*
CHARLESTON/SOUTH CAROLINA
23 FEBRUARY 1846/AT THE SAME MOMENT

"FULL STOP! One eighth back wash!" The captain of the *Decatur* shouted his orders. Not three boat lengths from the Charleston pier. "Pull up that line on the outboard side. So they can't see us from the wharf. Careful lads. That's not just any flotsam we've hooked." The deckhands pulled at the dripping rope. The deadweight at the end rose from the black surface. Tied by one booted foot.

The men lifted and dragged the mostly unconscious body onto the deck. The other foot was bootless. Sliced raw where a rope had seared the skin.

Natchez Jones took Dancer's limp body in his great arms. From behind he placed a large fist below Dancer's rib cage. Grasped the fist with his other powerful hand. Then jerked in and up. Once. Twice.

Like a cork popped from a bottle a rancid spew of water and vomit shot from Dancer's innards.

Sputtering. Coughing. Dancer sank to his hands and knees. Retched as if his life depended on it.

"He'll live…this time." The Captain rendered his judgment with flagrant disinterest. Propped against a cotton bale Dancer looked up at

Jones and choked. "Took your bloody sweet time."

Jones signaled to the steward.

"Take Belle's gift to mankind to my special cabin."

"Cabin Two. Yes…sir. Where the lady sent up everything but his suspenders before we cast off?"

"Yes…and put some liniment on that ankle."

"Right away…sir. And some 'Mrs. Winslow's Soothing Syrup' as a pain nostrum. It's patented…sir."

The steward took Dancer's right arm and placed it over his white-jacketed shoulders. Wrapped his left arm around Dancer's dripping waistcoat. Boot print. Footprint. Boot print. Footprint. Dancer wobbled across the deck as the steward steadied him. Once the steward gained the handrail he supported Dancer up the dark companionway to safety.

"Poor excuse for a secret agent. God help us." Natchez Jones spoke quietly under his breath.

"Full steam ahead…gentlemen!" The Captain again bellowed his order. "This mail is going to N'awlins!"

CHAPTER 5

**TRUST DEPARMENT/FREE BANK & TRUST
NEW YORK/NEW YORK
24 FEBRUARY 1846**

SAMANTHA SWIFT walked directly across the cavernous lobby of
the Free Bank & Trust of New York. Still wearing her short Spencer
jacket over her traveling dress she tried to look more confident than
she felt. Despite a too brief overnight at the Astor House. After some
minutes a clerk appeared who led her to the cloistered offices of
the Trust Department. The chief trust officer was busy. Very busy.
Most irregular. But Mr. Penrhos could spare a few minutes without
an appointment.

Swift entered a chamber surrounded by dusty records. Old ledgers.
Ancient files that looked as if they had not been touched since time
immemorial. Mr. Penrhos rose out of the clutter. His starched cuffs
pushed back above his wrists. In his dusty domain the trust officer
almost sparkled with fastidiousness.

Mr. Penrhos ushered Swift to be seated at a green baize-topped
desk the size of a billiard table. Another clerk materialized. Placed
a leather-bound ledger volume next to an oversized safe deposit
drawer. Swift introduced herself and Mr. Penrhos took a seat across the
large desk.

Swift did not dillydally. "How much am I worth…Mr. Penrhos?"

Unfazed Mr. Penrhos selected his favorite Thoreau & Company graphite pencil. Sharpened the red-cedar tip with his penknife. Opened the ledger volume. Copied some numbers. Totaled the columns. Checked his calculations.

"As of today…" He paused to review his figures. "As of today…you are a very wealthy young woman…indeed. As long as you don't do either of two things."

"How wealthy?" Swift asked as she tightened the drawstring on her beaded reticule purse.

"Current shares and valuations as of year-end 1845 indicate a combined account balance of just over…a quarter million dollars."

"And how many of those shares are invested in enterprises that pay profits or rent?" Swift pressed.

"Such as railroads or city real estate?" Mr. Penrhos's expression suggested surprise at the young woman's awareness of the new idea of investment capitalization. "A little over half…one hundred forty-four thousand. That annually yields an average of five-point-three percent combined. And that income is…in round figures…"

"Seven thousand six hundred dollars a year." Swift spoke the figure confidently. "Slightly over six hundred a month."

Penrhos's eyes twinkled. "Astonishing. You worked that out in your head?"

"Yes. Ledgers and figures come naturally to me."

"Remarkable. Quite remarkable."

"You said that was the balance unless I did not do either of two things. What are those?"

"Die. Or get married." Mr. Penrhos answered matter-of-factly.

Swift felt her composure weakening. "Why is that?"

"The way the trust is structured."

"The trust?"

"Yes. This monthly income has been paid to the trustee—Jacob Swift—for your welfare and education since your father's death three years ago."

Swift blinked. "So…I've actually been paying my own expenses… not Uncle Jacob?"

Mr. Penrhos replied: "That's correct."

"I've recently been discussing my future with Uncle Jacob… and from now on it is best if the money is paid directly to my personal account."

"When do you turn twenty-one?"

"In two months."

Mr. Penrhos scribbled a note. "I'll see to it as soon as you come to your age of majority. After twenty-one the trust gives you a great deal more control over your money. More than I approve for a young unmarried woman. I tried to convince your father otherwise. Yet he insisted." The banker pulled a long blue packet from a narrow metal drawer. "But wait…this is odd…"

Swift could see the packet was labeled "Codicil Document" and marked "Trust Revision."

For a long minute Mr. Penrhos scanned the papers.

"Most peculiar but appears to be in order…here is your father's signature." He pointed to the last page. "There was a change made a few days before your father's death. It says…to protect your assets from outside influence…a stipulation has been placed…on your trust."

"What kind of stipulation?" Swift leaned forward to read the paragraph upside down.

"If you marry or die…before your twenty-fifth year…all rights and assets of the trust will revert to the control of Jacob Swift as part of the settlement of loans made to your father by the *New York Examiner* newspaper."

"That's ridiculous!" Swift fumed. *That's why the snake tried to get me married off to Charlie Gray…so he could control my fortune!*

"Marriage? Death? In the next four years?" Swift muttered in a quiet voice as she balled her fist.

Mr. Penrhos looked at Swift over his half-moon spectacles. "There is one other course for you…Miss Swift. Are you aware of the legal term *feme sole*—which means an unmarried woman?" Penrhos tapped the codicil with his pencil. "In New York State it's not unknown for wealthy single women to shield their assets from husbands and creditors by establishing an 'equitable separate estate.'"

"What is that?" Swift asked.

"Under the laws of coverture…when a woman marries the husband gains full possession and control over all her assets and her income. That married woman is called *feme covert*—or literally a woman covered by marriage."

"As if she were a nonbeing?"

Penrhos nodded. "As a legally declared *feme sole* your assets remain your property even if you marry…and can be willed to a beneficiary upon your death."

"Wouldn't you think nowadays a married woman's property rights would be protected?"

The banker assented. "My wife agrees with you. That day may come soon…but in 1846 it is not here yet."

"How do I become protected as a *feme sole*?"

"Two ways. You can petition for private legislation in Albany to decree you as a *feme sole* by vote of the legislators. Or you can apply to a chancery court of equity for *feme sole* status. But there is a catch."

Always something to deny women their rights as citizens.

"To win *feme sole* status in the legislature or before the court a single woman must present…and prove…her ability to be independent and responsible…without the need of a husband's control."

Swift sat forward. "You mean I must prove myself?"

"Yes. Competent. Professional. Debt free. Proof—in short—that you are capable to navigate life as a man would. That includes…first: You must prove you can manage your financial affairs without loss of principal or incumbrance of debt. Second: That you provide proof positive of being self-sufficient at a profession or occupation."

Mr. Penrhos let these legal standards sink in before he asked: "Your twenty-fifth birthday is when exactly?"

"Fourteen April 1850."

Mr. Penrhos contemplated Swift's future. "That is four years and two months from now." *Much time for action…or mischief.*

"The advantage of going to court over legislation is the court proceedings are more confidential. Whereas the legislative course is very public and requires significant influence with lawmakers. On the other hand…some equity judges are fickle…especially when granting rights to a woman."

Swift moved to the edge of her seat as the idea that sparked to life after yesterday's banishment took stark clarity. *Polk's war with Mexico is coming. Newspapers will need correspondents. To avoid marriage—*

and prove my independence—that is what I must do. I must go to Mexico…and time is not on my side.

"I've resolved…Mr. Penrhos." Swift spoke clearly: "I have resolved to travel to the Rio Grande as a foreign correspondent."

"Amazing." Penrhos muttered his compliment even as his respect for Swift grew. "You will need newspaper credentials and a supportive editor…."

"To honor my parents I plan to use a penname. S. Thomas Swift."

"Your mother and father were most forthright. I always liked them." Penrhos appeared to warm to Swift's plan. "If I may…let me arrange for the *Brooklyn Eagle* on Old Fulton Street to expect your dispatches. There is about to be a new editor there in a week or so. A discerning fellow named Walt Whitman. I know his publisher always likes a competitive edge over Jacob Swift's *New York Examiner*. Dispatches from the front could be just the thing to sell papers."

"You've been most helpful…Mr. Penrhos. But there is one more thing."

Mr. Penrhos blinked. Then looked over his glasses at Swift.

"If you would be so kind…would you please make arrangements for my expenses at the Astor House? They were so kind last night to extend me credit when I mentioned I would see you today."

A twinkle came to the banker's eye. "You are a resourceful woman…indeed."

Swift began to rise.

"A young woman traveling alone in the frontier needs points of sanctuary if she is to survive…Miss Swift. Have you made travel plans?"

"That is next." Swift realized she had not given a thought to how she would travel to Mexico.

"Good then….You are best advised to take a packet steamship along the coast direct to New Orleans. You'll be in one ship all the way. One of the best in the business is the Southern Steam Packet Company. Just expanded its operations in the Gulf of Mexico. I understand the jewel in the line—the steam packet SS *New York*—is scheduled to depart shortly after its annual refit here. I will forward to your hotel several letters of introduction." Penrhos began a list. "Mr. George Kendall of *The Daily Picayune* newspaper in New Orleans. Great champion of Texas. He's a good one to know. Also a man named

Pepe Llulla in New Orleans who I helped many years ago. And…your uncle had some dealings with the American Consul in Matamoros Mexico…what's his name…oh yes…a Mr. John Stepptoe. Don't know him myself. But at least it will offer you a point of contact in a strange land."

"You are too kind…Mr. Penrhos. Now I must be on my way. So much to do and so little time."

"Wait. There is one more thing."

Swift sat back down in the chair.

"This is a bit of a mystery." The banker took out from the deposit box a small velvet jewelry case and letter. He handed the velvet case to Swift as he read from the letter addressed to Samantha in her mother's hand.

> *"To my beloved Samantha…I bequeath this signet ring. The ring is from Bangor in Wales and has been in my family for generations. I want you to have it with all my love. The ring is one of a pair. When pressed together the rings form a singular impression. Yours is of a raised design. The second ring — now lost — is a matching relief design. Find the mate to this ring and you will find the truth. Wear it always. All my affectionate love — your mother. Anne Thomas Swift."*

"What a strange tale. I wonder what it means?" Samantha Swift pondered her question as she slipped the mysterious gift on her left ring finger. The ring fit perfectly.

CHAPTER **6**

THE MIDDAY SUN warmed the skylight of the SS *Decatur*'s officer's quarters as Natchez Jones kicked the cabin door three times. Paused a beat. Then quickly tapped twice on the door. In his hands he balanced two steaming mugs.

"I'm not dead. Door's open." Dancer's response carried a tone of familiarity.

Stepping inside Jones offered his old friend an outsized mug of Creole *café au lait* fortified with one-third steaming milk. Dancer knew the last swallow would be an elixir of dark sugarcane syrup. Sweet enough to stand a four-hour watch without hunger. Just the way Jones drank it when they first traded rum together out of Jamaica.

Dressed in fresh clothes from his traveling cases Dancer lounged in the Captain's chair with his aching ankle elevated on the oversized bed. He lowered a short note he was studying. "Guess I owe you something for saving my life."

"Nothing you haven't done for me already." Jones dismissed his friend's observation without much concern. "My guess is you don't know Belle like I do. She's a helluva woman who likes her sport on her own terms and in her own time."

Dancer caught the eye of his friend whose packet steamship made frequent calls to Charleston and understood.

"Seems we both are beholden to the good lady for her favors." Dancer smiled.

Jones sniffed. "If she hadn't sent her boy to warn me you were being marched to the wharf I dare say I might have cast off with you still tied to that cleat…my friend. Good fortune for both of us."

Dancer shook his head. "You played it a little raw…Jonesy. The *Decatur*'s paddle box was coming a bit too close for comfort. I didn't know if I was about to be clubbed to death under the wheeler's bucket boards…or drowned before it mattered."

"Needed to get a bit of distance to make them think their mischief was a success." Jones explained his stratagem flatly: "We had worked out your escape beforehand. You made quite an impression on Belle. Not to say on her daughters too."

"Those twins are a piece of work." Dancer considered the scene at the Ashley residence. "You know I'm not one to stand in the way of a virgin's education but the little sluts jumped me. They were in it together for the sport! Pair of evil twins. Lucky to be here to tell the tale."

Natchez Jones took a long draft of his steaming *café au lait*. "So. To what do I owe the honor of this…unscheduled…visit?"

Dancer hobbled to the cabin door and double-locked the rim lock and slide bolt. Then returned to the roundback chair. In a low tone Dancer explained: "A State Department messenger sent by the President and his boys in Washington came to me yesterday. Gave me my orders to travel to Matamoros Mexico under cover as a war profiteer. My mission is to run down loan documents and one million dollars in specie and turn them over to the American Army."

Jones nodded. "Wouldn't give his name and said there was no need to wait for a reply."

"How'd you know?"

"The messenger came to me too. Told me you might need some help."

Dancer rubbed his swollen ankle. Took a drink of the sweet coffee. Then took the first of three more letters from a secret compartment in his traveling case.

"The messenger gave me this forged letter of introduction supposedly from Congressman Jefferson Davis." Dancer handed the letter to his partner in adventure. "The letter was supposed to be from the Congressman to contact Colonel Ashley in Charleston."

"Ah…yes. Davis." Jones paused. "He helped me out of a jam once bringing rum into Biloxi. Married Zachary Taylor's daughter against the old man's wishes in 1835…didn't he? But she died three months later from malaria. Davis just took his first seat in Congress in 1845. That was last summer if the penny press is not mistaken. They say Davis is raising a volunteer regiment of Mississippi Rifles now. They're headed to Mexico soon."

"When I realized Belle was the mistress of the house I made sure I got a billet of invitation…then dropped by a little earlier than expected."

"You're trouble…Dancer. As I said…you might need some help."

Dancer gave Jones a wry smile. "As for Ashley…it wasn't until later that I learned he was Belle's brother-in-law. The windbag is beyond his eyeballs in debt from his railroad adventures. He's fast becoming an evangelist for the peculiar institution of slavery. Dare say he sees abolitionists behind every one of his misfortunes."

Jones settled back into his built-in berth and put his heavy boots onto the table. "Seems like your cover held up. Go on."

"Ashley gave me this second letter of introduction to a Henry Kaufman in New Orleans. All regular and honor bright. Afterward Ashley gave me another letter. That's when it began to get strange." Dancer handed Jones the third letter addressed to Our Trusted Friend. "The letter introduced me to the American Consul in Matamoros. As you can see…it goes on about how helpful I will be to their cause…and how important people in important places say I can be trusted."

"That doesn't sound strange…except for their obvious lack of judgment." Jones's eyes twinkled at his lick back.

"Thanks." Dancer took a sip of strong coffee. "No. The strange thing is that there was no signature. No name on the third letter."

"So you don't know who wrote the letter that you're supposed to deliver to the Consul?" Jones leaned forward.

"Exactly. All I know is that it closed with a single word."

"What was that?"

"Wildfire."

"That's it?"

"That's it. What makes that strange is that Ashley told me his group—some kind of secret conspiracy—uses the code name 'Wildfire.' I suspect that's not a coincidence."

"What did the Colonel want you to do in N'awlins with this Henry Kaufman person?"

"He says Kaufman Brothers will set me up as a profiteer who is to trade with Zachary Taylor's army."

"Nothing new there. That's the cover the boys in Washington set up for you on this mission…if I understand the messenger in Charleston."

"Finding some willing partners with moneybags in New Orleans fits right into my mission—as you know. Just didn't expect them to fall into my hands on a silver platter." After a pause Dancer continued. "Wait till you hear what they really want. Ashley told me Wildfire shipped one million dollars in gold to Matamoros. That treasure was the principal on a loan to help Mexicans defend themselves against the United States. Upon the gold's delivery to a top Mexican general the documents were signed and sealed to establish the payment as a loan. The Consul has the documents."

"Sounds like a simple courier mission. What's the problem?"

Dancer swirled the last sweet drop. Downed the final swallow. "The gold has gone missing."

"That's the Mexicans' problem…isn't it?"

"Normally I'd agree. But President Polk's Inner Circle in Washington wants me to find the gold. And the loan documents. And turn them both over to the American Army."

"No easy task. But makes sense. The State Department doesn't want that Southern gold to buy Mexican bullets to kill our lads."

"And I understand Polk and the boys at State could use the money. Plus Treasury needs the loan documents to break up the slavery-driven powers behind Wildfire."

Jones nodded. "Discredit Wildfire as thieves and traitors."

"Exactly. Before Wildfire can carve more slave states from the disputed Mexican territories without firing a shot—and change the balance of power in America in favor of slavery."

At that moment the steamship pitched like a wild stallion as its bow lifted then slammed down into a large set of storm waves.

"Wildfire needs the loan documents to back up their forfeited-loan scheme to get their money back as a war claim. Wildfire figures it wins no matter what. They win if Mexico uses the money to fight the war against the U.S. Or when Wildfire gets the gold back so they can double their money when they cheat Washington out of the war claim. To sweeten their plot they said whoever returns the gold to Wildfire in New Orleans can keep one-fifth of the treasure as a finder's fee."

And Belle offered a special personal reward of her own.

"I played along with their plot to keep my cover…until Ashley's daughters played their little game."

Jones looked thoughtful for a moment. "Now that you made an enemy of Wildfire they'll be out to shorten your rope for good. From here on you'll have a bounty on your head. Not to mention Wildfire will send its agents to find the documents and gold before you do. They'll be hot on your trail going and coming."

Dancer winced as he pulled a boot over his throbbing ankle. "I thought they had me on the dock in Charleston…until Belle slipped that cleat rope."

"At least with Belle it appears your afternoon investment paid off." Jones rubbed his chin. Then drained his coffee mug.

Dancer leaned toward his traveling case. "I did too. At least…that's what I thought until I got this."

With that Dancer pulled a fourth letter from his kit. "This was in my luggage when I opened it this morning. I figured it was from Belle…."

Jones took the letter. "Not with that signature. That's not her handwriting." The Captain held the note to the light looking for a watermark. "Plus she only uses custom stationery from London."

"Something is fishy…Jones. The entire letter is only four words." Dancer's brow furled. "It just reads: 'Beware of Wildfire.' Signed… 'Mustang.' What does that mean? Is it a warning from my bosses in the President's Inner Circle?"

"You tell me." Jones did not wait for Dancer's reply. "But I know one thing. You won't be worth a fart in a whirlwind on an empty stomach. Let's get you some vittles. I have someone you should meet in the main cabin."

CHAPTER 7

WILLIAM BEACON came right to the point. "Let me see if I have this right…Miss Swift. If you do not prove your independence and capacity for business by your twenty-fifth birthday…all your money goes to your uncle?"

"That's how Mr. Penrhos reads the trust."

"Outrageous! Some publishers aren't worth the tobacco they spit. Sounds like when I told George Kendall I was going to New York to learn about the new daguerreotypes from Mathew Brady. You know — like me — Brady studied to be a painter. Then trained under the telegraph inventor Samuel Morse after Morse introduced the daguerreotype to America. I heard about this new photography invention from a Parisian friend in New Orleans. 'A perfect likeness in only one sitting.' Pictures of the famous and the common soldier right away make sense when you never know if waiting will be too late…as Brady says. He's a master promoter. 'Brady on Broadway.' Believe me…sweethearts and mothers love his photographs."

Swift smiled at the thought of Uncle Jacob's aversion to change. "Indeed…imagine photographs in a newspaper! Worlds better than those saccharine artist renderings."

Beacon rambled on. "One fool engraver called daguerreotypes a corrupting influence. Anyway I'll have the last laugh when I publish photographs from Mexico in my newspaper. You've seen *The Daily Picayune* in New Orleans?" William Beacon peered intently at Swift through his wire-rim reading glasses.

"Certainly. I love newspapers like my parents did. That's why I'm going to Mexico. Penrhos suggested I ask Mr. Kendall's advice when I reach New Orleans."

A gentle quiet surrounded the bundled travelers as they scanned the leafless silhouettes of the Virginia shoreline. Two hours had passed since the *New York* made an unexpected detour from the Atlantic to push up the Chesapeake Bay toward Washington D.C.

"Why—Mr. Beacon—do they call this steamship a packet?"

Beacon beamed with a flicker of pride at being asked. "Not long ago sailing ships waited until they were loaded with freight before they sailed. Or until the wind and tide were right. Some call it the spot market or 'tramp trade.' Never had a fixed schedule or published ports of call. That's why sailing ships carried mostly freight. Not passengers."

Beacon blew into his cupped hands and shrugged. "In the trade a packet ship is the opposite of a tramp sailboat. Packets travel non-stop…as long as the engines work. Much faster and more regular than sailboats. Predictable. Dependable. Packets like the *New York* win contracts to carry mail in peace time—and troops in wartime. Very profitable."

"I've read that Congress passed subsidies for steamships last year to give advantage to American ships over British ships."

"You've done your homework. The *New York*'s owner Charles Morgan has sold all his remaining interests in sailing ships and plowed the proceeds into a marine-engine works on the East River in New York between Eighth and Tenth. Guess he figures steam is the future."

"It shows on this ship. Polished mahogany walls. White satin-damask curtains in the main cabin. Stain glass windows decorated with the five-pointed lone star of Texas. Crystal glass and fine porcelain. Even the silverware handles are engraved with 'Steam Packet *New York*.' Not to mention the fine couch in my stateroom."

Beacon exhaled a cloud of white breath into the twilight. "That's true for the blue bloods in the main cabin. Then there are the standard cabins forward of the engine room. And the steerage passengers only get curtained-off berths belowdecks. We third-class tickets are allowed the freedom of the awninged decks forward…as long as our 'loud discourse' doesn't disturb the rich toffs in the main cabin."

Like a wooden-hulled plow horse the steamship pushed up the Potomac River toward Alexandria. There the port of the federal city was barely four months away from being retroceded back to the state of Virginia.

Beacon pulled a newspaper from his coat pocket. Snapped the paper open to the front page. "Abolition is one of the great issues newspapers must deal with today. Earlier today you asked my advice about being a newspaper correspondent. Where do I start?" The young artist inhaled deeply as he summoned the advice of his editor George Kendall. "Take on the great causes and reveal the truth. Tell it simply. Tell it in the voice of the afflicted. Do not be intimidated. The truth is greater than our personal wounds." As Beacon pontificated the *New York*'s steam whistle announced its approach to The Strand wharf at the end of Prince Street in Alexandria.

"What are the great issues that need to be revealed?" Swift asked as she tried not to let her inexperience show.

William Beacon led the way as they strolled toward the middle of the great steam packet sidewheeler. "Remember Ralph Waldo Emerson's words. 'What is man born for but to be a Reformer… a Re-maker of what man has made….'"

"…'A renouncer of lies…a restorer of truth.'" Swift finished one of her mother's favorite quotes.

The idealist nodded in agreement as the ship maneuvered perpendicular to the end of the wharf extension. "Take on the great causes Kendall says. America's impulse to violence and war. The theft of land they call 'Manifest Destiny.' The abomination of slavery. The limits on women's property rights…as you have seen personally. Temperance. The greediness and obsession with material wealth the Industrial Revolution has spawned. Wretched working conditions in our factories and mills. Then expose the ghastly housing of immigrants and the poor in our cities. Our madhouses. Girls driven into prostitution by hunger and male predators. You can start with the brothels of New Orleans! My…I do surprise myself sometimes. Imagine embedding all the correspondents in a real war…where we do nothing but send dispatches and photographs from the battlefield. Now that would be something!"

"What a novel idea." Swift's tone held awe at the possibilities. "Thank you. I'm sure I will never be wanting for a cause."

William Beacon permitted himself to glance at Swift's face before he shyly averted his eyes. "Just look about you on your travels to New Orleans. But most important remember one thing."

Beacon paused at the top of the companion staircase amidships. "Remember one thing…S. Thomas Swift. In Kendall's words…a story untold is only a dream. You must write. Give voice in your words. Write like your future depends on it."

"An excellent idea. Thank you. I won't forget."

Beacon bobbed his head in polite departure. Then descended the companionway to his bunk in the forward steerage quarters.

╳ ╳ ╳

In the late February cold the sound of the ship's steam piston laid a bass pulse into the air. Swift hugged herself for warmth. *Seems odd if this steam packet is to keep a schedule that our ship has taken a side trip into the Chesapeake Bay. And now the Potomac River.* Her mind held that question as she moved toward the railing on the ship's inboard side. There her gaze took in the deserted wharf where a solitary whale-oil lamp feebly glowed in the darkness. The cobblestone Prince Street led inland up into the darkness that enveloped the old town. Quickly the ship's boom swung the passenger stage to The Strand. At that moment the captain walked down the gangway to the dock. There a shadowy figure stepped forward. *Was that the glint of brass from a uniform?* After a brief exchange the captain returned to the ship. *What could be so important to make a special detour to Washington's port city in the dead of night…and take away nothing more than a leather case? Military dispatches? Orders from the highest level?*

No sooner was the bow stage withdrawn than the *New York* pivoted from the wharf. Caught the Potomac River current. And steamed back downstream into the darkness from where it had just come.

CHAPTER **8**

GRAND SALOON/THE *DECATUR*
RAISING SAVANNAH/GEORGIA
26 FEBRUARY 1846/THAT SAME EVENING

SIX HUNDRED MILES TO THE SOUTH the cotton trader snarled as he let the whiskey speak for him in the emptiness of the steamship *Decatur*'s grand barroom. "No…suh! What those migrants are doin' should be 'gainst the law…I say. 'Gainst the law." The man looked like an overstuffed sausage turned out as a carnival barker. Black patent-leather shoes. Golden spats over his insteps. Plaid pants. A green waistcoat vest set off by a yellow formal shirt. All this crammed inside a garish blue-and-white crosshatch morning coat that reached to his fat thighs. Dancer raised his eyes to the mercantile man before him. The impression was of a circus about to begin. On his arm was a saucy redhead that gave Dancer a look of interest.

Stepping forward Captain Natchez Jones opened both hands toward the trio in a gesture of welcome. "Allow me to introduce… Mr. Prospero Faubourg and Miss Fitzwilliam. May I present Mr. Jack Dancer of Charleston." Jones turned to Dancer. "Mr. Faubourg is one of the foremost cotton factors in New Orleans—and this is his traveling companion…Miss Josephine Fitzwilliam."

Faubourg extended a meaty paw to Dancer. Then with his other he downed his fourth shot of Jameson Irish whiskey. Miss Josephine's expression suggested to Dancer the evening was young.

"You were saying…sir."

"Ever since we recovered from the panic of 1837 — that was when the lily-livered N'awlins bankers stopped exchanging specie for their own notes. Bastards! Ever since — the cotton business has gone all to hell."

"How do you mean?" Dancer signaled the bartender for a fresh bottle.

"It works like this…son." The portly merchant arranged an assortment of objects on the gleaming mahogany bar.

"Over here are the big planters — this Kentucky apple-jack bottle — and the small growers — this shot glass. They grow the cotton…see? In bed with them are the storekeepers — this bowl of salted peanuts here. The storekeeps barter their dry goods in exchange for cotton from the big plantations and the small growers. They supply everything you can't even imagine a grower needs…or wants." Faubourg moved two nuts closer to the apple-jack bottle and pushed two empty shells toward the bowl. "Here in the middle are the brokers — honest commission factors like myself…suh." The fat merchant positioned a fresh Irish whiskey bottle in the center of his diorama. "We receive cotton from the grower and the plantation… or the storekeep." His puffy hands gestured a flow of goods from the apple-brandy bottle and shot glass and nut cup he had placed to his left on the bar. "Naturally I bring the cotton to market to sell to cotton buyers here." To his far right the broker placed a dice cup holding a half dozen Cuban cigars. "The buyers ship the cotton to New York or Liverpool."

"Sounds simple." Jones nodded. "Keeps the *Decatur* busy and that's fine by me."

"That's the problem." The cotton factor was blunt in his complaint. "It was simple. Neat. Tidy. Everybody knew how the system worked. Course…the planters bartered away every penny they hoped to get before they got it. So they kept coming to me to advance them money. To plant a crop. To endorse their notes in the city. To keep their *placée* mistresses in a grand style far from the home fires…if'n you git my meanin'."

The talkative factor poured another Jameson for himself. And took a long drink with one hand and held the bottle ready in the other. Then smacked his half-empty tumbler on the bar.

"That's the problem…Where was I?…Oh yes…the N'awlins banks that lend me the money…to lend to the planters…those banks want to git paid on time. That means the planter caint dawdle. Gotta sell cotton right after harvest. Banks caint wait. Planters git the going price regardless. Often enough—with everybody harvestin' at the same time—the planters are none too happy with the low price they git. Some try to take their cotton to market themselves. Foolish fellows. They soon discover they have to make a sale—at any price—before returning home. Course…we factors help 'em everywhere we can. That's why I own what used to be the largest warehouse on the levee. Course…N'awlins riverfront doesn't come cheap. But yah never know when buyers from New York or Liverpool will show up in town eager to keep their clients' mills runnin' back home."

Miss Josephine Fitzwilliam feigned a tired expression. "Big Daddy…all this cotton talk has me tuckered out." The mistress of the evening interrupted the trader with a voluptuous nuzzle. "I'm retiring now…sweet cakes. See you in the morning. Don't get up. I know my way around Master Jones's steamer. You just continue your manly talk." She breathed into the factor's ear: "This lady will see y'all for luncheon tomorrow…after my beauty rest in the morning. Mr. Dancer…a pleasure." Miss Josephine flashed Dancer her best riding-St.-George smile as she lightly touched the large diamond pendant almost lost in the bulge of her fulsome bosom. "Until later…gentlemen."

The gaze of all three men followed Miss Josephine's performance as the sound of her ruffled petticoats left the saloon.

"As ah was sayin'…we extend credit to the planters and take care of everythin' for 'em from supplies to slaves. Not to mention freightin' and weightin' and gradin' and storin' their cotton until it's sold. Course… it's our risk because we don't get paid until the crop is sold. We're businessmen too…you see. That's why all us factors charge a standard commission of two-and-a-half percent for our services…on top of the loan interest and advances during the year…naturally."

"Sounds to me like the banks and the factors are feeding from the same trough." Natchez Jones put in his two cents with unvarnished candor.

"That we are. That we are." The increasingly drunk merchant started to mumble his words. "We give credit to the planters when we provide 'em supplies…which we buy on account in N'awlins from the dry goods wholesalers…who in turn get their goods on credit from New York suppliers. Nice work when everybody pays. If the chain breaks anywhere along the line…then the New York suppliers are left holdin' the ultimate bill. But they've got the deep pockets in this system."

"What's your complaint…sir?" Dancer asked.

"I'll tell you what it is…it's those migrants…family of Austrians from Bavaria named the Kaufman Brothers. First there was Henry in '44…then his brothers Benjamin and Simon joined him. Nobody knows exactly how they do it…but I hear tell they get cash advances from cotton buyers in New York and Britain. Then use that cash to order supplies for their own store in N'awlins. They don't produce anything…just play the money side. Won't be long before they be buyin' warehouses and properties and even plantations…if I ain't mistaken."

Master Jones asked: "What's disruptive about that?"

"They are undercuttin' our prices. Cuttin' us out altogether. That's what's got me riled…suh. They is cuttin' out the honest factors like myself. We been the planters' best friends. For generations! Now these Austrian migrants go behind our backs direct to the planters with pockets full of notes. They're buyin' everything. Bigger the better. Prices are cheaper too because they go 'round us native-born American middlemen. These foreigners bring big money from New York. Lock up the planters before planting with promises to sell their cotton when the price is best…not when honest factors like myself must sell at harvest time to pay off my N'awlins bank loans. Leaves nothin' for us but the fluff off the bale…suh. It's not right. America should be for Americans…not a bunch of foreigners." The merchant leaned heavily against the bar. Raised a finger for another whiskey.

Natchez Jones steadied the corpulent factor. "Your tale has truth to it…sir. But a bit of sleep will make the world look a whole lot better in the morning." Together Jones and Dancer turned Faubourg toward the passenger accommodations. "We've got some weather ahead of us.

Best to batten down in your own cabin."

With that Master Jones guided the dejected merchant toward the bracing air of the companionway and the aft main cabins. "I'll bring this snifter for a nightcap…sir. On the house." The merchant sighed and numbly shuffled away like a bulging cotton bale being coaxed to its hold.

CHAPTER 9

JACK DANCER EMERGED in the darkness from the top of the forward deck companionway. He glanced toward the bow. There beside the anchor catheads he saw Josephine Fitzwilliam taking the air by the rail. Lit by the glow from the skylights beside her. She turned and smiled.

"The sea is so exhilarating. Or don't you find it so…Mr. Dancer?"

Dancer moved forward. Stepped beside her and breathed in the stimulating sea air and her expensive French perfume as he leaned into his hands on the rail. He felt her warm bare arm press close to his shoulder. Her breath near his cheek was fragrant with cloves. She was broad shouldered and full breasted. And he sensed how she liked the look of him. Never the type of man who falls in love Dancer took his tumbles when given the chance. The more often the better.

Miss Josephine was an Irish woman of the world. Dancer was bold. Always a man to shoot first and aim later. But it was a risk on the exposed awning deck. Unconcerned her fingers toyed inside the collar of his open-necked shirt. Dancer turned his head just as her lips met his. She smoothly guided his arm around her waist. Then laughed deeply throwing her head back. Giving Dancer access to her supple neck — which he nuzzled.

She purred seductively. "My instincts tell me you might enjoy a bed without cold sheets."

Dancer returned her kiss. Then without a word followed the factor's mistress down the forward companionway to her single cabin. She let him in first. Closed the door. And slipped the lock behind her back. As her light cloak fell to the floor. Dancer moved a step forward. Took her large breasts in either hand through her bedgown. Then stopped her gasp with his mouth. Without preliminaries she grabbed the bulge in his trousers with both hands. One of his hands freed a generous breast as he suckled it with his tongue. She toppled him onto her bed. Where they bounced about in rare style. First Dancer on top. Then the temptress. During one delectable pause astride her conquest Josephine Fitzwilliam shook out her red mane and gathered herself for a moment.

"Now darling." She breathed with feigned innocence. "What kind of a woman do you think I am?"

"One after my own heart…my dear. And one who knows what she likes."

Dancer kicked off his boots. Expertly released her fingers gripped on his chest. Felt her nails travel down his naked ribs. Then held her glorious melons for all he was worth as she rose to a gallop riding Saint George on top. The double-wide ladies' bed reserved for just this type of regular *Decatur* passenger was rigorously tested.

Into the night the steam piston worked in a steady throb. Both cylinder and shaft beat a rhythmic stroke down the coastal waterway. As the ship moved past Blackbeard Island a squall lifted the waves. The roll and thrust of the ship intensified. Yet the tempest in the forward cabin continued unabated well past the midnight bells.

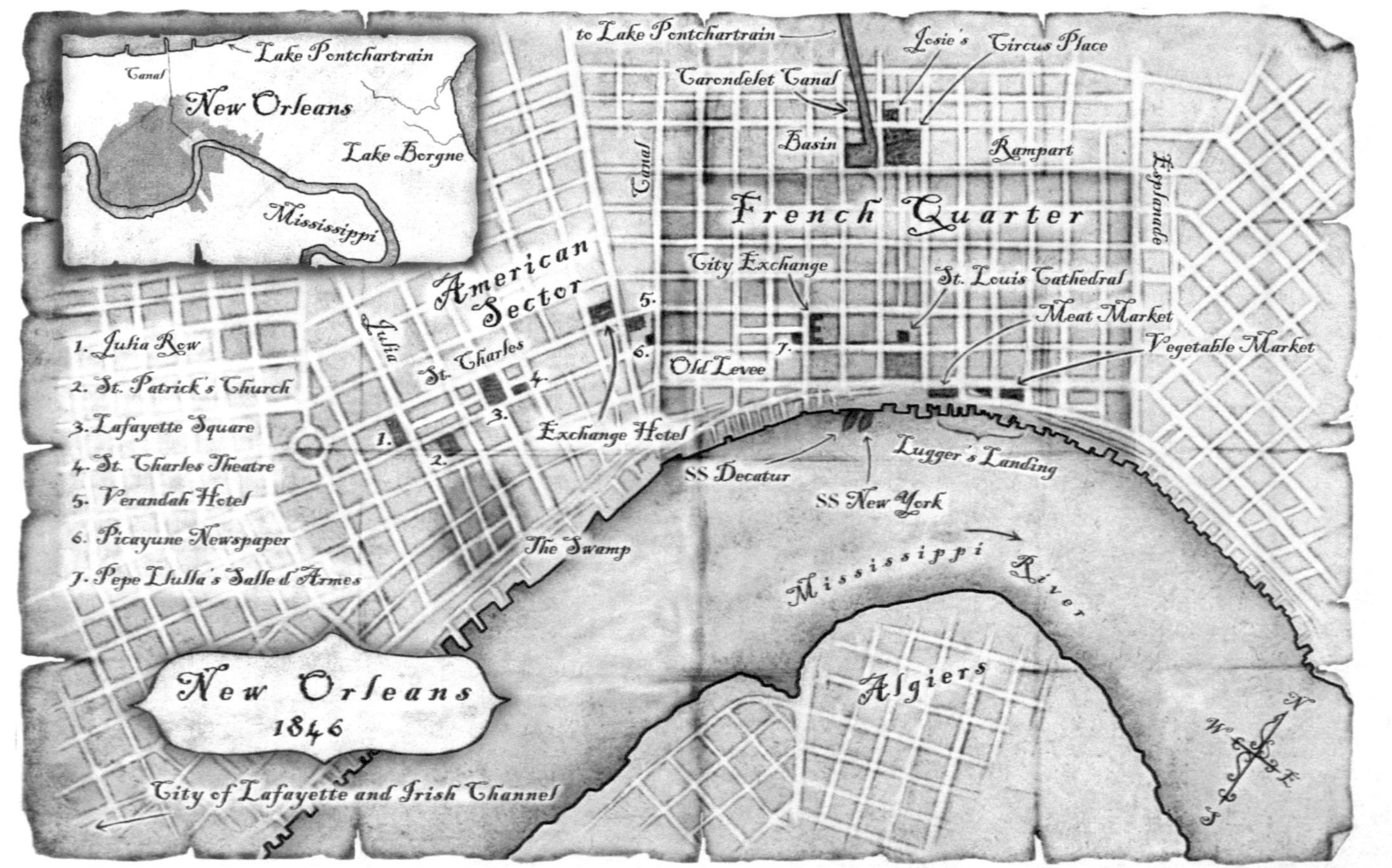

New Orleans
1846
French Quarter
American Sector
Algiers
to Lake Pontchartrain
Josie's Circus Place
Carondelet Canal
Basin
Rampart
Esplanade
Canal
City Exchange
St. Louis Cathedral
Meat Market
Vegetable Market
Old Levee
Exchange Hotel
St. Charles
Julia
The Swamp
SS Decatur
SS New York
Lugger's Landing
Mississippi River
1. Julia Row
2. St. Patrick's Church
3. Lafayette Square
4. St. Charles Theatre
5. Verandah Hotel
6. Picayune Newspaper
7. Pepe Llulla's Salle d'Armes
Lake Pontchartrain
Canal
New Orleans
Lake Borgne
Mississippi
City of Lafayette and Irish Channel
N
S
E
W

CHAPTER **10**

PROMENADE DECK/ THE *NEW YORK*
APPROACHING NEW ORLEANS
3 MARCH 1846

WILLIAM BEACON inhaled the heavy Louisiana air with gusto. Here he always felt at home. As he stood by the steamer's railing on the promenade deck he repeated a bittersweet saying from his mother. "You can always go back…but you can never return." *True. Every time I travel back to a place it is never quite the same.* He had been away in New York for six months practicing the new art of photography as a daguerreotypist. Times had changed. Or had he changed? As much as he sometimes wanted life to be the same as it was before he knew he could never return to yesterday.

"A penny for your thoughts."

Samantha Swift took a place at the rail beside Beacon.

"Not even worth a penny." Beacon's reply was less than candid. *One's inner thoughts are best kept to one's self.*

Swift ignored his blush and pointed to the rapidly passing bank on the starboard side of the steam packet as its great side paddles powerfully skimmed the downstream current of the Mississippi River. "Will New Orleans come into view as we pass this bend?"

Beacon smiled. "That's why they call it the Crescent City."

The steamboat rounded a curve and struggled against the oncoming current to make headway.

"There it is!" Beacon couldn't help himself. His love of America's third-largest city overflowed as the Gulf jewel rose.

"Show me. I'd be beholden." Swift was sincere in her request.

Beacon studied the young woman almost for the first time. Studied her as a portrait artist does. The morning sunlight made her face glow. And by now he knew the signet ring on her left hand was not a wedding ring. Beacon was half-surprised to realize Swift was exceptionally pretty. Her rich auburn hair swept back by the breeze as her customary English traveling cap was clutched in her hands. There was a sturdiness about her that was at odds with a touch of vulnerability. Was it a lack of confidence? Or perhaps just a lack of experience?

"Do you feel how the steamboat strains to stay near the bank to our starboard side?"

Swift heard the paddle buckets as they pushed the boat hard upstream against the muddy river. Instinctively Swift shuddered at the sound of water being sucked under the bow. She gripped the promenade railing and raised her gaze to the rising city.

"Far beyond the city the river returns to its mostly north-south banks. Upstream from here the river runs from west to east. There the plantations grow cotton mostly…but more sugarcane is taking over." Beacon pointed off to the west where dense stands of tall cane rose over the levee. "You can't see the cotton from here. It's too low. The movement of the river has deposited a natural levee on the northern bank that makes the highest land in these parts right at riverside. Water drains away toward Lake Pontchartrain to the north as much as it can. Upriver the great planters have their own wharves. Closer to the city the captains don't want to stop. So the planters arrange for their crop to be flatboated to the levee."

"Are those houses coming into view now? Near the edge of the crescent in the far distance?"

"That's the City of Lafayette beyond the border with New Orleans at Felicity Street. Some people call it uptown or the Garden District. On a clear day you can see the columned residences. You can't imagine the grand gardens. See those low structures near the bank?"

"Yes." Swift squinted against the low-angled sun. "Just beyond where the river bends…the houses look so small from here."

Beacon nodded. "They're small when you walk into them too." The next moment he continued. "That's the Irish Channel. From the river up Adele Street is the heart of the Irish Channel. That's where the lace-curtain Irish live." Swift gave Beacon a quizzical look. "They're the Old Irish. Scots-Irish mostly. Came to better themselves two or three generations ago. Made their way. Industrious. Took root and families sprang up like mushrooms. Now they're comfortable with homes and businesses and even curtains in the windows. The new shanty Irish arrive daily on the famine ships. Some call them the 'fever ships' for the typhus. The New Irish are illiterate peasants mostly. Displaced from miserable cottages and rotten potato patches. Rough and wild. Old Irish don't want anything to do with the New Irish."

"Why do they call it the Irish Channel?"

"Nobody really knows. The real Irish Channel is a strait between Ireland and Scotland where Irish privateers preyed on English ships since anyone can remember. Some say the new shanty Irish live in 'The Swamp' along Tchoupitoulas crammed into a couple blocks between Julia and Girod streets. But Irish in fact live in a swath along the riverside from Adele Street to Canal Street. Personally…I think the Irish Channel is a myth — or a state of mind. Ireland is wherever its people say it is. If you ask me…people think it's an Irish Channel because immigrants land here but don't stay. They move on to better parts of town — or move out farther west. The truth is as hard to pin down as a leprechaun." Beacon blushed slightly at his little joke. "No question…with wealth the Old Irish moved out of the tenements and levee shacks to build inland and above Canal in the Second Municipality."

"The Second Municipality?"

"That's the American Sector or what some people call uptown because it's upriver. Where the Business District is located. Beyond the old French Quarter — that's west or upriver from Canal Street — is the new section called the American Sector. All the names of the streets change when you cross Canal Street from the French Quarter to the American Sector."

"Is there a First and Third?"

"Only in New Orleans. You see in front of us now…the First Municipality is the Vieux Carré. The 'old square' or French Quarter. That section came first and is where the Creoles live…and a fair number of Old Irish. North of the quarter is the back of town called Faubourg Tremé. That section runs from Rampart Street north to Broad Street. The heart is a place where the Africans go to dance on Rampart. What whites call Circus Park and people of color call Congo Square. Near the Carondelet Canal Turning Basin. Closest to us now on the right — downstream from the French Quarter — is the Third Municipality. It starts at Esplanade and is more a village…mostly immigrants. Germans. Some Irish. Some *gens de couleur libres* — free men of color."

"What is that beautiful domed building?" Swift pointed upriver beyond the French Quarter.

"That's the Exchange Hotel on Saint Charles — one of the finest hotels in America." Beacon spoke with a note of pride in his voice. "That square gothic tower to the left is Saint Patrick's Church…built by the Old Irish immigrants near Lafayette Square."

"I've been told to stay at the Verandah Hotel."

Beacon gave her a sideways glance. "Must be nice to be rich." He said the words under his breath.

Swift ignored the comment.

Beacon continued. "Take Julia Street for example. It runs perpendicular from the levee and parallel to Canal Street. Near the levee on Julia are tenements and boardinghouses — especially between Magazine and the river along Tchoupitoulas. That area is called Connaught Yard — or 'The Swamp'…as I said. It's a jungle. Even the Charlies stay away from lower Julia Street."

"Charlies?"

"That's what they call the watchmen that masquerade as police." Beacon nodded as though to confirm his contempt. "It's worth your life in the Swamp to frequent Pat Duffy's on Girod…or Mrs. Gibbon's on Delord…or Mrs. O'Brien's on Julia. That's where the Irish toughs waylay other Irish. Beware of Noud's Ocean House…the Bull's Head Tavern…and the Isle of Man…if you want to live to tell. The alleys between the tenements are no more than six feet wide. Mostly pest-pots stinking with offal and refuse until the next rain carries the stink off.

In a dense fog the red lanterns hanging outside the shacks make the Swamp look like it's consumed by a conflagration from hell."

"Sounds awful."

"Worse than that. But then you go up Julia Street a few blocks from the river and you come to the 'Thirteen Sisters' between Camp Street and Saint Charles. Some of the finest side-hall row houses anywhere. That's where the elite live. There you'll hear the lilt of the elegant Irish mother tongue in its graceful brogue. Fine mansions are going up there. Not far from your Verandah Hotel."

"Now I see the French Quarter. What is that beautiful dome in the distance?"

"That dome farther upriver is the top of the City Exchange and Hotel on Saint Louis. It's the most elegant in the French Quarter. Archrival of the Exchange Hotel on Saint Charles Street in the American Sector. Under that dome are auctions for everything from slaves to livestock to furniture…You name it."

"And those graceful spires closer to us?"

"That spire and two corner towers are the Saint Louis Cathedral for Creole Catholics on the Place d'Armes. The superstitious Creoles don't allow funerals in the cathedral for fear the yellow fever will be spread. All their dead are serviced at The Mortuary Chapel of Saint Anthony on Rampart Street in the back of town about seven streets in from the river. The Creoles call the public square the Place d'Armes. But the Americans call it Jackson Square for Andrew Jackson and the Battle of New Orleans in 1815. The dockyards come right up to the foot of the square on Old Levee Street."

"How odd." Swift was amused.

"Not as odd as the politics. Each municipality is run by a recorder — sort of a mayor. Means each one hires his own Charlies as police and runs his own show. It's a wonder any streets are paved and canals get dug."

"I can't imagine the horrendous work that must be to dig a canal in this climate."

"Yeah…the Irish get those jobs — along with drayage and stevedore and sweeping jobs. If an Irishman dies the recorder just hires another for pennies a day. Nobody wants to risk a valuable slave on that canal work. Why kill your investment?"

"What about the young Irish women and girls?"

"The biddies?" Beacon asked. "They're maids and laundresses and nannies…if they're lucky."

"Lucky?"

"Not uncommon that the immigrant girls don't make it here as virgins. You see…the runners prey on them in Liverpool and Ireland. The fathers and brothers don't have a penny. In exchange for passage they sometimes sell their daughters or sisters to the runners who have their way with the biddies. Then in steerage during passage some desperate girls swap favors for food. When they get to New Orleans there are some landladies — so they call themselves — that offer 'employment agencies' to these girls."

"But they really are brothels?"

"You got it. Many of the girls are already abandoned or beaten…or both. A friendly word goes a long way in a foreign land…and a friendly bottle to the father or brother goes even farther."

This conversation fell silent as the *New York* advanced on the great port city. Before them the midstream channel was crowded with vessels. Some dropped down with the current. Others tugged up against it. Steamboats arrived from upriver. Some from the Gulf. Others departed upstream and down. Ferryboats crossed and recrossed at short intervals. Small boats shot in different directions. Barges — some full…some empty — floated lazily in the midst on the current.

Unexpectedly the steam packet's whistle blew two short blasts as the boat prepared to swing about to claim a gap at the downstream end of a cluster of steamboats tied to the levee. At the same moment the steamship *Decatur* overtook them traveling the same direction upriver. The Charleston steamer clearly intended to dock at the same opening.

Steam whistles pierced the air. Warning bells clashed. The *Decatur* pushed against the Mississippi River current while the *New York* came up parallel beside it.

Through his megaphone the *New York*'s captain shouted. "Steam packets have first rights…Captain Jones! Hold that skinny runt back!"

In reply Captain Natchez Jones shouted: "Carrying the mail makes you daft…Captain! Hold your steam while a real ship takes first honors!"

"Keep that floating tub upstream…sir. Before the *New York* sends it down the river forever!"

Almost within spitting distance the two captains glared at each other from their wheelhouses. Then something extraordinary happened. Both ships used the current to approach the quay at the same diagonal. With mastered grace the two captains nosed their crafts toward the levee as if approaching a single slip. In what appeared to be a practiced dance the ships entered a space just barely large enough for one. Boatmen amidships used poles to keep the steamers apart. At the bow heavy ropes were hurled simultaneously onto the levee. Two pairs of rough men dragged the lines and made them fast around anvil-shaped horn cleats. Fenders were dropped between the ships to separate the hulls.

Both captains released a long arrival blast from their steam whistles in mutual celebration.

Josephine Fitzwilliam watched this maneuver from the rear of the *Decatur*'s forward deck. When Dancer turned at the bow the madam made eye contact...a half smile of condescension on her face. With a blink the New Orleans madam slipped her arm through the crook of the elbow of her fat factor at her side. Mr. Prospero Faubourg preened like a strutting peacock displaying his prized feathers. Then the sound of escaping steam filled the air.

Shielded by the upper deck of the *New York* Samantha Swift followed the exchange on the *Decatur*'s deck below her.

Swift felt an odd sense of foreboding. Behind Fitzwilliam's false smile appeared a formidable woman capable of anything that defending her turf required.

CHAPTER 11

THE MAELSTROM of the New Orleans levee rose up and assaulted Swift's senses as she took in the scene from the upper deck. The *New York* had just passed a multitude of fine square-rigged long-voyage sailing ships moored abreast along the north bank to her right. Next: Scores of keelboats and flatboats nuzzled up to the levee like piglets to their sow within carrying distance of the markets at Lugger's Landing. Then came the *New York* and the *Decatur*. Beside them upriver from the cathedral square to beyond Canal Street steamboats from the river and coastal lines were clustered with their black funnels smoking. The steamers were trimmed in the most fantastic manner. Their paddle boxes painted gaudy colors. Finally in the far distance upstream smaller brigs and schooners and sailing sloops of the Gulf Trade lined the bank until their masts disappeared around the crescent bend.

On the spacious promenade that divided the city from the river hundreds of draymen readied their floats and jostled their dray wagons to haul away the flood of merchandise. A babble of tongues and calls came from all directions. Syllables with the familiar inflections of the

Emerald Isle stood out to Swift. The air redolent with fragrances as the fishiness and damp of the river blended with the smells of dung and industry.

Swift and Beacon leaned into the rail and gazed out at the breathtaking panorama before them. Pyramids of cotton bales. Rows of sugar hogsheads. Bags of rice piled in heaps. Barrels of pork and beef without number. All variety of goods shipped from the great river valley or foreign ports. And destined variously for European markets or distribution to the American frontier. The hum of labor and chants of stevedores mixed with the clatter of wheels and choking smoke from great boilers. Bales and boxes appeared in motion everywhere. Barrels bounced over the levee stones. Squealing pigs and cur dogs kept to the shadows. Mules passed huddled immigrants in rags. Yankees and toughs. West Indians and Negroes. Germans and Brazilians. Hard-looking women in calico and ribbon bonnets moved molasses barrels. Businessmen in brimmed planter hats idled with long stem pipes. Gamblers in claw-hammer frock coats mingled in the mayhem. Teams of men loaded and unloaded the ships. Sweat soaked homespun shirts. Woolen pants were held up by a length of rope.

Swift was mesmerized.

⊠　⊠　⊠

Jones and Dancer walked a gangplank like a tightrope between the *Decatur* and the *New York*—docked only an arm's length away. Jones gave the steam packet captain a big hug and introduced Jack Dancer.

"Jones has told me about you…Dancer." The captain winked. "Says beautiful women have their way with you."

Dancer faked a punch to Jones's gut. "Giving away my trade secrets are you?"

"Ain't no secret among the ladies." Jones smiled as he nodded toward Josephine Fitzwilliam as she descended the passenger stage from the *Decatur* to the levee. Seeing the trio Fitzwilliam raised a painted eyebrow toward Dancer and gave her Parisian parasol a contented turn.

A few moments later Samantha Swift followed the steward to the *New York*'s forward gangway stage. She thanked the steward and confirmed her trunk would be forwarded to the Verandah Hotel as she slipped him a gold Liberty Head two-dollar-fifty half eagle. Then gave

Jones and Dancer a polite greeting. "Good day…gentlemen."

As Swift waited with her small valise on the rounded levee stones the *New York*'s captain answered the unspoken question. "That's S. Thomas Swift. Correspondent for the *Brooklyn Eagle*. Says she's headed to the war in Mexico."

"Another innocent abroad." Dancer scoffed. "Let's see how long she lasts."

Without warning a ragged man ran into an opening among the bales in view of Swift. He stumbled. Unsteadily tried to stand. Quickly a gang of four levee mugs surrounded him. Dragged the man behind a mountain of cotton bales. A scream blended with the cry of a frightened team of horses. A scar-faced man came back into view. Wiped a bloody blade on his rope-belted trousers. And clapped a henchman on the shoulder. Without care the killer jerked his head toward a barrelhouse nearby. Where he knew empty kegs on the banquet indicated business was brisk.

Patrick Harp leaned casually against a gas lamp as they passed. The killer gave Harp a nod of recognition. Harp took note. A moment later a hand-pulled paddy cart jostled what could have been a body under a gunny blanket across the rough levee stones. The crowd parted. Then re-formed unconcerned and went about its business.

"Be a good boy. Go fetch our luggage…sweet cakes." Fitzwilliam purred to her protector. "I see someone I know." She kissed Faubourg on his pate. And turned him toward her bidding.

Fitzwilliam stepped near Patrick Harp and spoke in an offhand voice. "Good hunting?"

"Gets better every day."

"What was that about?"

Harp spat a stream of tobacco in the direction of a drunk slumped against a great hogshead barrel marked with triple XXXs. "The old sot sold us his biddy. Seems the brother didn't think two bottles of whiskey was enough for his sister. When we said no to a third whiskey…he threatened to spring a rattle for the Charlies. Seems my lads straightened out the misunderstanding."

"Where is the biddy now?"

"We've installed her at your plush house in the back of town near the Turning Basin. She seems to enjoy the Irishman's drink." Harp gave the woman a hard smile. "Or so my boys tell me. My guess is they enjoyed her as well."

"Can't you keep your dogs on a short leash?" Fitzwilliam snapped.

"You do your business your way…and I'll do mine." Harp sucked his tooth and reached to stroke Fitzwilliam on her ample hip.

The madam slapped Harp's hand. "Your job is recruiting soldiers for your little war. Leave the pretty goods to me."

"Thought you liked 'em broken in…and thankful." Harp smiled. "Makes your work easier."

"Damaged goods don't give the best service…but there are always more where they came from."

Fitzwilliam hiked her skirts above the filth of the levee. Moved toward the part of the city where her reputation ruled. A hand-cranked barrel organ struck up from a nearby showboat and called the denizens of the dock to experience a troupe of traveling players. Patrick Harp pushed himself away from the gas lamp as he eyed a cluster of immigrants nearby. The men were agitated. Argued loudly. Harp heard the desperation in their voices. Their desperation was directed toward a fellow son of Erin already established in the city. He had clearly slammed the last door of opportunity in their faces.

"Now what do we do?" They pleaded their helplessness in unison.

Harp made note. Easy pickings if any old veterans be among them.

CHAPTER 12

DANCER AND JONES made their way past the cheap levee lodgings. "Still building them from the rough wood of old flatboats." Jones offered his observation without further *adieu.* Concert-saloons. Dance houses. Bordellos. They all made little room for the tenements that grew on Julia Street near the levee. Without warning a raucous fight erupted on the second floor of a walk-up. Right in front of them a wounded man tumbled into the street. Beaten by a bat. Cut by bottles. Thrown downstairs. Clambering behind this excuse of humanity were two others. Tipsy as two tops. They lifted him from the dirt street in their unsteady arms.

"Barney McGee…you get what you deserve!" The husky voice of a voluptuous woman rose through the foul-scented air as she stomped down the stairs after her mark. McGee and his friends skittered farther into the street. They wiped McGee's bloody head with rags dunked in a horse trough. Out into the daylight came a frightening woman brandishing a broken whiskey bottle in each fist by the neck.

"Now Paddy." She pointed the jagged glass at McGee. "Look at that mule drinkin' over there. Ain't that a best example to you? See how he lays off when he's had enough? Poor creature's the most sensible of you both!"

"Oh…that's all well for you to say…biddie!" The tipsy Irishman offered his reply as soberly as he could. Which is to say: not very. "But feature this. What if there were another horse at the other side…and that horse said…'Here's to your health…me old boy!' Would he stop 'fore he drank the whole trough…think ye?"

"Someday your friends will bury you alive in a dead drunk… Barney my boy." Her assertion was uttered as much in jest as in anger.

"Buried alive? Nary true…my biddie love…nary true." McGee wrapped his arms around his companions' necks. "We have a sure test…me lads and me. Bring me a glass of the grog…and say to me…'Here's to you…McGee.' If I dun rise up to drink…then sure 'nuff…I'm dead and ready to be buried."

With that jest the woman took a feigned kick at McGee. And almost toppled herself into the muck-filled gutter. McGee and friends stumbled a distance down the filthy street before disappearing into an alley.

"Good riddance! Come back and there will be but one whole nose in the house…and that will belong to the tea-kettle!" The biddie sang out and dashed the bottles after the retreating trio.

Dancer and Jones sidestepped the flying glass.

Noticing the new prospects the woman volunteered: "Sorry gentlemen. Step inside and let me jerk you a beer to make up for your time."

"You're too good." Jones jested. "But when our business is finished you may be seeing us."

"Suit yourself. Just ask for Lulu at the Bull's Head Tavern. I know I can give you what you're looking for." She added a practiced leer.

Jones and Dancer moved down the street as an ice wagon made its rounds of the saloons.

CHAPTER 13

DANCER PATTED the letter inside his vest pocket. *Thank you… Belle…for keeping my traveling case dry.* "My first call is to meet this Henry Kaufman. His office is just down Commerce Street near the cotton press."

Jones nodded distractedly. "Once the freight is off-loaded my work begins protecting it from the wharf rats. Those vermin will steal anything in broad daylight if you don't post guards you can trust. Meet you later?"

"I need a word with Josie Fitzwilliam tonight. If I don't find her trolling the lobby and rotunda at the City Exchange on Saint Louis… I'll find her at her house on Basin in the French Quarter."

"Ah…looking to get lucky…are you?"

"We'll see. See you there?"

"Josie's it is. I'll bring my other cheek. In case any young Creole gentlemen want to test their fencing lessons from Pepe Llulla."

"*The Picayune* says duels are still as common as watermelons."

Jones punched his friend on the arm. "The dandies are all fools. But for them the fear of loss of honor is greater than the fear of dying."

"I know how they feel." Dancer assured his companion as the two men parted. "Sometimes honor is everything."

☓ ☓ ☓

Henry Kaufman studied Colonel Ashley's letter. Then he studied Dancer. "You surprise me…Mr. Dancer." Kaufman's words were thick with his heavy Austrian accent. "We had not expected an agent from Wildfire for some weeks. I see from your letter's date that you made haste to reach New Orleans so quickly." Dancer smiled politely. *If you only knew.* "Let's get down to business then…shall we?"

Dancer made himself comfortable. Let the sweet smoke from the financier's fine Virginia tobacco rise in the air of Kaufman's richly appointed office.

"As you know…Mr. Dancer…we have two dilemmas that we hope you can resolve for us. First: We must recover the documents that support the loans we made to the Mexicans—and locate the one million dollars if it hasn't already evaporated. I understand Congressman Jefferson Davis stands behind your reputation?"

"It's my honor and duty to serve Congressman Davis…as he served me once." Dancer spoke frankly then gilded the lily. "As Jeff says…'None but the brave deserve the fair.' Courage makes its own success…in my experience."

Kaufman studied Dancer. "If I may…what was that service Davis provided you?"

"Between us: I found myself with a shipment of rum bound for Biloxi that was not…how should we say…entirely certified with the authorities. The Honorable Mr. Davis was most helpful with the necessary certificates. And in a most timely manner." Dancer spoke offhandedly as he embellished his cover story.

"Ah." Kaufman smiled. "Not unlike our need for loan certificates now. As you may know…Davis and Wildfire work closely together."

Dancer leaned forward. "You said two dilemmas?"

"Yes. One is tied to the other. It is absolutely critical that we obtain the loan documents. But there is a second vital concern. My brothers and I expect to be the primary suppliers to Zachary Taylor's army in Texas. That's where you come in…Mr. Dancer. Congressman Davis has reached an understanding with Secretary of War Marcy in

Washington. If we can win the trust of General Taylor that we can supply everything his army needs…then we are guaranteed a handsome price for those supplies. But others will soon be on their way to Texas. It is paramount to get our supplies to Texas before any hostilities cut off that access. If we — if you — can reach Corpus Christi first…then any blockade to starve the Mexicans will also keep our competition at sea. That will guarantee a price Wildfire will appreciate."

Dancer gave Kaufman a hard look. "You talk about Wildfire. What or who exactly is Wildfire and what do they want?"

Kaufman deflected the question. "In good time…Mr. Dancer…in good time. For now all you need to know is that you will supervise the cargo that is being assembled now."

"You want me to be the commercial officer in charge on the *New York*? I've no problem with that." Dancer agreed to the supercargo assignment then upped the ante. "But I'll need an account to make the arrangements and contract the ship."

"We've arranged an account for you at Citizen's Bank of Louisiana."

"At Toulouse Street between Royal and Chartres?"

Kaufman's expression brightened. "You know your banks…sir. That's critical. Then you won't confuse Citizen's Bank with the Bank of Louisiana at Royal and Conti…or the Louisiana State Bank across the street…or the Union Bank at Royal and Iberville two blocks uptown toward Canal Street. Silly twits. They've all fallen in love with Gallier's Greek Revival architecture trying to outdo each other. Stone columns feed their egos…not their vaults. You've got credit up to ten thousand dollars in bank notes and one thousand dollars in specie as needed to obtain your supplies."

"I understand my contact in Matamoros is Mr. John Stepptoe… the U.S. Consul."

"Odd thing about the Consul." Kaufman pulled a pouch from the drawer of a corner pipe-rack nestled in a bookshelf. Selected a meerschaum from the tavern rack and thoughtfully pressed fresh tobacco into the carved-head bowl. Then tapped a document on his desk with the pipe's long stem. "This message came from Stepptoe yesterday."

"May I?" Dancer stood up and stepped to Kaufman's writing desk beside large floor-to-ceiling windows.

Kaufman handed Dancer a crude parchment map that looked like it had been folded in haste. Against the creases. Then smoothed flat as best it could. "What do you make of that? Almost looks like a half-finished sketch…but there's no context."

At a glance Dancer realized he may hold the key to a mystery. *Is this the map to the missing treasure of Matamoros?*

In the next heartbeat as he studied the shapes and lines Dancer decided to play it noncommittal. No words had been written on the map. Only a crude diagram. "You say Consul Stepptoe sent this? It may be the beginnings of a street map. This snaky line that looks like an 'M' could be the Rio Grande River. That box outline might represent…a plaza? This U-shaped building above it…maybe the Resaca House? See to the right that hollow square with a bump? That could be the Hotel Casamata and its Watch Tower." Dancer shook his head as if mystified. "Maybe Matamoros in Mexico?"

"Have you been to Matamoros…Mr. Dancer?"

"I've made some memorable visits." Dancer smiled to himself.

"Do you see any indication where Wildfire's one million dollars is located?"

Dancer scanned the wrinkled sheet a last time. "Nothing obvious."

"It's no use to us. You had best ask Mr. Stepptoe what he meant by sending this odd sketch."

Kaufman returned the map to its envelope and handed it to Dancer…who slipped it into his inner coat pocket.

"Is there anything else?"

"Yes…there is." Kaufman lowered his chin in reassurance. "You will not be alone on this mission. We have enlisted another agent to support you from here."

Kaufman rang a small bell on his desk. One second later the door of his office opened. In walked a short rotund man with a chin beard.

"May I present my associate…Mr. Israel David. Israel is a noted lawyer in New Orleans."

Dancer took David's outstretched hand and received a limp greeting. "I've heard your name…Mr. David."

"We have also arranged for another agent to work with you in the field. He will work from inside the U.S. Army. While you work from the outside with the Mexicans and the Americans as a civilian…for as long as that is possible."

"What is this agent's name?" Dancer asked both men.

Israel David dissembled the truth through narrowed eyes. "His name is Patrick Harp. He's attached to the Americans' horse artillery. We expect you will be most useful to each other."

"I doubt I'll need help from any enlisted boys."

"Never a bad thing to have a friend when you're swimming in foreign waters." Kaufman's comment came with an overtone of warning.

Unless that friend is a shark. Dancer's thought came unbidden.

David interjected: "This will not be an easy mission. The Mexican leaders are changing daily...."

Kaufman completed the lawyer's sentence. "...In the last twelve months the Mexican presidency has changed hands four times...the War Ministry six times...and the Finance Ministry sixteen times."

"One helluva way to run a country." Dancer gave them a wry half smile.

"I must impress on you...Mr. Dancer. It is paramount that you and Harp get Wildfire's loan documents securely in your possession *before* the first shots are fired."

"And locate our one million dollars if possible." David added. "After war breaks out...who knows what kind of madness will control Matamoros."

Kaufman handed Dancer a pouch of prized Virginia tobacco. "Remember...you and Harp are comrades — not enemies. You're both there to help each other...not hurt each other's chances. If you don't work together...we will not be able to achieve our mission...and the rewards for you and Harp will go up in smoke. Do we make ourselves clear?"

"With this map — and intelligence from Consul Stepptoe — you can count on me. I mean *us*...gentlemen." Dancer — having concluded his false assurances — took his leave.

As Dancer stepped into the afternoon light of the New Orleans levee a question gnawed at him. What is this Wildfire up to? *What's the real mission behind this scheme?*

CHAPTER 14

NEWSPAPER OFFICES/ *THE DAILY PICAYUNE*
CAMP STREET/NEW ORLEANS
4 MARCH 1846/MIDMORNING

SAMANTHA SWIFT found the offices of *The Daily Picayune* by asking a newsboy on newspaper row. No sooner had she opened the door than Swift stepped into the middle of a commotion. Two newsmen restrained a large scar-faced man who was shouting past them into the inner offices.

"You call this truth! You call this honor! I want the scoundrel who wrote those lies! I want Kendall now! We'll settle this here and now...if he is a gentleman! Any swine who printed these lies can't be called anything more than a horse's ass!"

"Now sir...Mr. Kendall is not in. You will have to come back later." One of the newsmen was insistent.

"Bring that bastard Kendall out here! Let him take my challenge like a man!" The belligerent ruffian was shouting.

"But we cannot do that"—the other newsman reasoned—"because Mr. Kendall is not here—as we said....You should leave before the police arrive."

"Do you think I care! I've killed more honorable men under the Oaks than this pissant you call an editor. Bring Kendall here! Now!!"

The bellowing man's hardened look gave an edge to his claims. With a mighty shove he freed himself from the grasp of the two newsmen. Quickly he drew the blade of a sword partway out of his walking cane. The steel made a chilling sound against the brass lip. Everyone froze.

"Gentlemen. Gentlemen." Swift said clearly. "This may not be any of my business…"

The man with the half-drawn rapier scowled. "Damn right… missy. Stay out of this. No place for a woman."

Swift persisted. "Actually…perhaps I can help. I have come for the interview."

"What?" One of the newsmen squeaked.

"The interview that is arranged." Swift spoke calmly. "The interview with Mr. Kendall and his friend and colleague…*Señor* Pepe Llulla. I understand *Señor* Llulla is to join us here at this time."

The belligerent man let his sword drop back into his cane.

"Llulla is coming here? Now?"

"Yes. Any minute. I'm Swift. Correspondent with the *Brooklyn Eagle*. Lately of New York City. I'm here for an interview with Mr. Kendall and his close friend…Mr. Llulla. I understand Mr. Llulla is a master with the rapier and the pistol…and he is the natural second for Mr. Kendall in any dispute."

"Llulla? Kendall's second?"

"Yes." Swift confirmed her revelation with an indefinable smile. "Is it not the role of the second to stand in for the challenged in the event the challenged is unable to serve?"

"Llulla is his second? That was never part of the deal." The scar-faced intruder backed to the door. He looked both ways before bolting down the street at a hurried pace.

"Well played…miss. Well played."

"Appears Mr. Beacon was correct. The name of Pepe Llulla carries weight in New Orleans." Swift mused then interjected with innocence: "Do duels happen often here?"

"More often than you'd think." The newsman's reply was not without candor: "We write anything in the paper and somebody takes offense. Some just write an insulting letter to the editor…usually with a pen name. But some send a hired thug to challenge the editor to a duel. No matter what happens…if the editor drops that line of investigation…or the editor leaves town…or the editor gets killed…the offended party makes their point without having to stand up for themselves. Makes being a newsman nerve-racking."

"Can't you just ignore them?" Swift asked.

"I see you don't know how the 'Field of Honor' works. To not show up to face the challenger means all respect for you evaporates. First it's the snickers behind your back. Then newsboys are robbed. Pretty soon advertisers don't pay their bills. Why should they? You're branded a coward and they dare you to come after them. You might as well fold your tent and leave town. Now…how can we help you?"

"I'm here to meet George Kendall. I'm S. Thomas Swift with the *Brooklyn Eagle*. I believe I'm expected?"

"Well…I'm afraid that's not possible. As we said: Mr. Kendall has recently gone to Texas to report from the western territory. But I believe he left instructions for you to meet with our War Correspondent… James Collingsworth Turner."

Into the front office stepped a tall thin-chested man in his shirt sleeves. Ink stained the cuff around his right wrist. His eyes peered through bifocal glasses that gave him a condescending expression. Swift took an immediate dislike to him.

Swift responded with a congenial indifferent smile. "Mr. Turner."

"Miss Swift. You look even more out of place than I imagined." Turner looked down at the hopeful correspondent from back East before leading Swift to Kendall's empty office.

Swift looked right and left into cramped offices as they walked. "What do you think makes a great newspaper…Mr. Turner?"

"Like the editors say: Make 'em pop. Vivid language. Direct style. Play to the man on the street. Make him feel there but for the grace of God go I. Sensational stuff. That sort of thing. Show him inside the lives of the famous. The rich. Make politicians uncomfortable. That's what sells papers." He answered in the voice of a lecturing uncle.

Turner directed Swift to a hard chair beside an overflowing desk as he rattled on. "I suspect up to now in newspapers like the *Brooklyn Eagle* all the stories came from documents—maybe a letter from a politician or a government report…if you were lucky. And—of course—the exchange news slips from other papers around the country. Great filler those slips. Cheap. My editors say your *Eagle* is always good for a slip or two." Turner sniffed.

Swift replied coolly: "You should try some actual reporting. In New York the best editors have this new thing. They call it an interview. Quote the people directly. Done right interviews make you feel like you were really there." *Instead of putting words into their mouths.* "Readers can't get enough."

Turner gave Swift a condescending look. "Being a war correspondent is not the business of a woman's life…and it should not be."

There was a slight pause and then Swift frowned. "I'm here not as a man or a woman — but as a journalist only. That is the sole standard by which anyone has a right to judge me." *And the sole ground on which I accept your judgment.*

Turner pontificated ignoring Swift. "Different classes want different news. Like the Irish all want to read about other Irishmen. Then you have crazies like that Thoreau up in Massachusetts refusing to pay his taxes. His taxes no less! Claims he doesn't want his money to pay for the war. As if his state taxes were spent on some foreign war! Are all Northerners such fools?" Turner had turned rhetorical. "Even Emerson said Thoreau is a fool."

Swift shifted the subject toward the war with Mexico. "And now this war talk sounds real."

"Old Polk up in Washington says he just wants to 'protect Texas.' Says sending Zachary Taylor and an army down there is just a defensive action. An 'Army of Observation.' Hah!"

Swift persisted. "If not to defend the Texas border…what do you think is behind this gambit…Mr. Turner?"

"You Northerners are truly hopeless…did you know that? Mark my words the real reason is to expand slavery into more territory. The planters just want more slave-driven states so they get more say in Congress. The slavocracy just wants the West for bigger pens to cram more slaves into." Turner warmed to his self-importance.

Swift listened as Turner spouted.

"Then you've got that ninny O'Sullivan over at the *New York Morning News* calling for 'Manifest Destiny' like it's some God-given right to spread the United States from here to California. Now he wants to add Cuba too!"

Animated by his own words Turner stood up abruptly. Paced furiously. Thrust his arms into the air. And shook his finger at Swift. "Did you see where those abolitionist bastards they call the 'immortal fourteen' in the House of Representatives — led by that old Whig has-been John Quincy Adams — is opposing the War Bill no less? They're right though to think everything is about slavery. Just peel back the layers. Anything else is just sleight of hand. But readers love the conjuring. Call it patriotism. Call it self-interest. Call it sensationalism. For great newspapers like *The Picayune* this war is a moneymaker."

Swift interjected. "Ever since Polk negotiated with the British last year to settle the Oregon border — and annexed Texas as a state last December — the drumbeat of war has been growing louder."

"Just you wait." Turner carried on as he ignored Swift. "The real winner in Mr. Polk's war will be sectionalism. Mind my words. Capture new territory…what have you got? More sections. More division. Next thing you'll hear is that Representative Wilmot character from Pennsylvania will want to ban slavery from any new territory we get — or take — from the Mexicans. The whole Mexican question has split both the Whigs *and* Democrats into pro-slavery and abolitionist camps. See what I mean? Now we have four parties at each other's throats — not just two! But that sells newspapers. And that's okay by me."

Swift pulled out Mr. Penrhos's letter to George Kendall and handed it to Turner. "Here is a letter of introduction…Mr. Turner. My intention is to report on the coming war in Mexico. But while I am in New Orleans I'm interested in reporting on an issue I've become aware of in my travels."

"And what feminine genre would that be…Miss Swift? Some children's literature…or soppy sentimental poesy?"

Swift let Turner's sarcasm slide off her impassively. "The issue is the exploitation of immigrant Irish girls and their being forced into prostitution in New Orleans."

Turner stopped and gave Swift a double take.

"Prostitution? New Orleans? Is this some kind of a stunt? You have no idea what you're talking about — or what you'd be getting mixed up with. That sword-wielding thug you met earlier was a kitten in comparison if you broke a story about prostitution in New Orleans.

Don't make me laugh…Miss Swift."

"I'm not laughing. And neither are those defenseless girls being raped and seduced and living in rags on the levee right now."

"You Yankees think you can step off the boat and fix everything.… Well maybe things don't need fixing. We can't help you."

"You mean you won't help me…don't you?"

Turner eyed the stubborn woman as if he was meeting a mother grizzly for the first time face to face. "We have important issues—like a war with Mexico—that need our attention. Not stirring the pot where some of the most powerful men in Louisiana get their honey. No. We cannot help you. But I have a suggestion."

"A suggestion?"

"Yes. If you want to see the underside of New Orleans…I suggest you get a guide. Why don't you ask someone who can keep you out of trouble? You'll need it. Who knows…maybe you'll learn something about the domestic sphere of a proper woman."

Samantha Swift rose. *The place of a woman? You've not seen anything yet.*

Swift politely thanked Turner for his suggestion. If not for his help. On her way out one of the newsmen who had held back Kendall's assassin greeted her with a grateful smile. And handed her a folded paper.

The address was simple: *Señor* Pepe Llulla. Salle d'Armes. Exchange Alley.

CHAPTER 15

LEVEE YARDS
NEW ORLEANS RIVERFRONT
4 MARCH 1846/MIDDAY

PATRICK HARP hunted with two prey in mind. The cunning strategy was simple. Harp worked the levee wearing his army uniform. He approached the women and girls. While their men "looked for work" in the barrelhouses these wives and girlfriends were often left on the levee wearing just their peasant rags. A gift of food opened the door to conversation. Bread worked best. Sometimes Harp brought a coarse but familiar meal. A small portion. Never enough. But always with a promise there was more where that came from.

The results were predictable. While the ragged women and girls devoured the food Harp explained he was in search of men who had served in the army. Perhaps their husband? Or brother? Or uncle? If there was a connection the destitute women were all too eager to retrieve their menfolk for Harp from revels at Noud's Ocean House or Pat Duffy's in Connaught Yard. Harp also made note of the young girls whose silence spoke of no protector. No one closer than a distant village or clan an ocean away. These steerage biddies received an extra portion of bread. Secreted with a lump of tallow wax passing as lard.

Harp moved in closer to his henchmen. "When a biddie shares the crust with a snot clinging to her skirt…you know you have a live one." His voice dropped into a hiss. "Bring those to me."

Flanagan was the meanest thug with a grotesque scar. As he fondled his cane-sword he gave the others a glare. "Take any man that can sign an 'X' on the papers. We get a bonus for every ignorant croppie we sign up. Every 'X' is a dollar sign for us."

"You do it your way…Flanagan. I'll do it mine." The smallest of Harp's gang they called Kelly the Weasel snickered. "The young sods light up when ya promise them glory…and all the brown-eyed women they can dream of."

Mickey O'Rourk piped in. "Keep your glory and women…Weasel. The grown men cave in for the three-month signing bonus. Not to mention the promise of a hundred acres of farmland in the West… or waiving the five-year wait to get American papers." O'Rourk had served in the army of more than one king. And had the flogging scars to prove it.

Flanagan lowered his voice as a sneer rose on his upper lip. "I had one the other day who thought he could get a job as a screwman in the cotton press and make a dollar a day. Hah! Let him try. Soon enough a private's pay at seven dollars a month will look pretty good."

"To these shanty Irish money to feed their broods is powerful." Harp's reply was unremorseful. "But lay it on. These Irish and Dutchies don't care about the drill of the army. They know the factory bosses don't want 'em — if there is a native-born man next in line. Mostly they spent any last penny they could borrow or steal to get here. And they know they can't get to the frontier without the free ride the army will give 'em. One poor bastard even believed me when I told him if he saved his wages every month for five years he'd muster out with seven hundred dollars savings to work his farm."

Flanagan laughed as he took a deep draft from a brown bottle. "You should 'ave seen his eyes get big as the moon o'er the Blarney stone! Signed on the spot he did."

"They may not think the army is their first key to grab the golden goose. But they know they don't have a better second choice." Harp confided to his cronies. "Boil it all down like Lulu's cabbage. Here's what you got: Offer the poor bastards land. Cash bonus. Or citizenship. And you've got yourself a nice-day's pay. If they don't fall for it…move on. There's another famine ship right behind them."

"And remember." Harp surveyed his minions. "Leave the biddies to me."

Flanagan broke in. "Who's to work up a thirst with me across the river in Algiers with a little bear and bull fight?"

"You lads go ahead. Here's a silver dollar to put on the bull for me." Harp flipped a coin to Flanagan. "I've got someone to meet while the sun is still with us."

CHAPTER **16**

SWIFT TURNED OFF CANAL STREET into Exchange Alley. She stepped into the other world of the Vieux Carré. The narrow half street between Royal and Chartres in the French Quarter had been designed by the architect of the City Exchange. More of an alley than a street the passage ran directly from Canal Street through to the hotel on Saint Louis. As Swift walked down the alley her view of the great dome at the far end was blocked. The view — as Beacon had told her — was filled by an unfinished construction site.

"That basement is all that is finished of the First Municipality building to be called Gallier Hall." She recalled all that Beacon had said. "The city ran out of money. So they put a roof over it. Made it the police station. And now they're trying to decide what to do. Rumors have it they may sell the property to the hotel. We'll see."

Swift paused at a small sign beside a narrow stairway that led upward: "Salle d'Armes. Pepe Llulla. Master." As she ascended the clash of foils echoed down from above. Next came a bass chorus of men's voices that cheered the duelists over the click and scrape of steel. At the top Swift stepped into a long room with tall windows flooded with light from both sides. She pulled up at the exact same moment the sounds stopped.

A distinguished man with a gray goatee gave a quiet order for the six pairs of young men facing each other to break. He came over to Swift.

"S. Thomas Swift…of the *Brooklyn Eagle?*" *Señor* Don José Llulla bowed slightly as he extended his hand and held Swift's gaze.

"*Señor* Llulla. I see my note preceded me. Thank you for seeing me."

"*Señorita*…please…call me Pepe. A ward of Mr. Penrhos is always welcome in my humble *atelier*. Barely six years ago Mr. Penrhos was most helpful to arrange my service with a merchant company that plied between New Orleans and Havana. Now I can return the favor. Please step into my office."

Swift followed Pepe Llulla's gesture and stepped into the sanctuary that filled the end of the airy hall. A place where the Creole elite exchanged a successful future for a decadent present. Swift took a seat as her gaze surveyed the extraordinary room. The space was hung with weapons of every variety. Round-bladed rapiers. Sharper triangular-bladed *colichemardes*. Brutal broadswords. Machetes. Murderous pistols in velvet-lined cases. The fine smell of rich Spanish leather and burnished metal honed with sperm whale oil filled the chamber.

The fencing master began: "How can I be of service to my friend Mr. Penrhos?"

"May I speak frankly?"

"Please do."

"As you may know" — Swift started in a clear yet subdued tone — "the terms of my trust require me to prove myself as a journalist and businesswoman before my twenty-fifth birthday…now just four years away."

The duelist steepled his fingers and nodded.

"Those terms have driven me here. Now I must prove myself." Swift tapped a balled fist into her palm. "Frankly…I've been appalled at the traffic of young Irish girls into the brothels of New Orleans. Many are raped. Others are destitute. All are desperate. I want to expose the practice in an article for the *Eagle*. To do that I need someone who understands the world of madams and can get me inside to talk with the girls."

Llulla's dark eyes sparkled. "That is easier said than done. Especially for a woman."

"Only a woman can get the girls to talk." Swift's reply was candid.

The Spaniard considered Swift's dilemma. "I don't doubt that. What is impossible is getting you inside in the first place. Those women are bound by a strange code of honor…If they speak to you it could cost them their lives. Impossible." Llulla dismissed the idea.

"I know my request is extraordinary. But I'm confident the girls will tell me their stories once I can gain their trust."

"And just how do you propose to earn their trust?"

"By the introduction of a man of honor." Swift paused. "By your introduction."

"Poff." Llulla again dismissed the idea.

"You are a man who has engaged in…what…twenty duels?"

"Some say thirty…but only two have died." Llulla added his observation matter-of-factly. "Most simply retreat to save their skins."

"Thirty duels?"

"And stood second more times than I care to remember."

"Those gentlemen you seconded are men who owe you a favor… am I right?" Swift asked.

"Many of them…yes." Llulla paused.

"And they are men of influence whose sons fill your *atelier*. True?"

"Go on." Llulla smiled at the thought of the dalliances of his clients and their offspring whose honor he had served by his presence.

"I understand there is a madam named Josephine Fitzwilliam. I've been told she is a leading force in the traffic of Irish girls. I want to learn how she does it — and expose her. That will give the girls cover to find a better life."

"It will also give you a short life — if Josephine learns of your little investigation before it is published."

"Time is running out before I must depart for Mexico. All I need is to talk to two girls…hide their identities in one combined generalized profile…and the story will be published in New York after I leave New Orleans."

"You've given this some excellent thought." Pepe Llulla turned to look out over Exchange Alley. "For the sake of my friendship with Mr. Penrhos…I will help you. On two conditions."

"They are yours to name." Swift held no objections.

"Pardon my directness — but…Miss Swift…you do not present in the person as either a hardened madam…or one of their wounded girls. That is a problem."

Swift blushed. "What can we do?"

"Our advantage is your face is not known in town. You have just arrived?"

"Yesterday. But how can that help?"

"Here is what we will do. On your honor keep your words about the girls…and do not write a word about their clients. Do that and you have a guide. After all…I will have to do business in this town after you leave."

"Agreed. You said there was a second condition?"

"I will arrange a room for you under the name of Kitty Carter at the Exchange Hotel on Saint Charles…diagonally across from the Verandah Hotel. Tell them you are just arrived from New York and here on business."

"Business?"

"Yes…You are the business manager for Fannie Flynn's house in the Five Points area of that city."

"She is known as the 'Irish Queen'…isn't she?" Swift recalled reading.

"Good. You are here to make arrangements to exchange suitable girls between your establishment in New York and a leading establishment in New Orleans. You must evaluate the girls to judge if any are suitable for your needs. Finder fees and commissions will be a most lucrative carrot for Josephine Fitzwilliam."

"When do we start?"

"I will arrange for midday calling attire to await you in your room. Meet me in the lobby of the Exchange Hotel beneath the great clock at ten o'clock tomorrow morning. Our outing will begin with a gentile *café au lait* near the Public Square on Old Levee — what the Americans call Jackson Square — opposite the Meat Market. Followed by a visit to Josie's pleasure house. That will open your eyes to how the oldest profession in the world works in New Orleans."

CHAPTER 17

SWIFT AND LLULLA stepped down from their cab. From the curbstone they studied the front of a three-story mansion on Basin Street. Carved in the stone were the initials "JF" in elegant script. The matching frosted front doors had a swirling "JF" etched in the oval glass. A discrete brass placard beside the bell pull spelled the word "Josie's." As Swift was about to put a foot on the first step she was surprised to see Jack Dancer coming out the front door. Swift immediately assumed the worst.

"Good day…*Señor* Llulla." Dancer greeted the fencing master with a bit too much bounce in his step to Swift's eye. "For all its size New Orleans is a very small town."

"*Buenos dias*…Mr. Dancer. May I present Kitty Carter…just arrived from New York."

Dancer ran his eyes over Swift from head to toe and back again in an instinctive assessment. *Kitty Carter? What happened to S. Thomas Swift?*

"What brings you out so soon after your morning adventures… Mr. Dancer?" Swift asked airily.

I know I have a reputation…but what is she playing at? Dancer knit his brow as he replied to Swift. "Business. We are mustering supplies for the army. Arrangements for the officers—and their personal beverages—are done best on Basin Street. And you?"

"Likewise…business." Swift responded smoothly in her guise as Kitty Carter—New York procuress. "Miss Fitzwilliam and I are discussing managing some property together."

"Be sure to count your fingers after you shake hands on any deal." Dancer's advice was more of a chide.

Swift's reply was clipped. "At least we aren't profiting from the tragedy of war."

"We'll compare notes someday…if you last that long." Turning to Llulla the smiling Dancer tipped his hat and strode down the banquette.

"Full of himself…isn't he?" Swift said to Llulla as Pepe opened "JF's" glass door for her.

Swift stepped inside and felt a thrill at entering a bordello. And yet a stronger thrill to launch her first ambush-journalism venture. The house was stuffed with too much of everything. *God awful. No accounting for taste.* In the foyer two sculptures of naked females flanked the entryway. *No doubt intended as an aphrodisiac.* Renaissance tapestries hung everywhere. The parquet flooring was immaculate. Tables were decorated with Turkish carpets. In the main parlor overstuffed and overcarved furniture filled the space. Among these furnishings ill-selected "art" and sculpture fought for attention. Outsized mirrors made the front room look larger and brighter. And gave the room a voyeuristic impression that allowed guests to watch while not being seen.

Josephine Fitzwilliam rose from a sofa in the side parlor. She looked imperious in a deep green shot-silk gown that changed hues in the light and was bordered with white Irish lace. The height of New Orleans fashion that season. The madam had dark red hair and large bright gray eyes. Perhaps one of the most commanding women Swift had ever met. Fitzwilliam was laden with diamonds put everywhere an inch of flesh could accommodate them. She acted the *grande dame.* In the small parlor her dominating presence—and her perfume—were just short of overpowering.

"*Señor* Llulla…always a pleasure to see you."

The fencing master took her extended fingers in the Spanish style and clicked his heels. Fitzwilliam tapped a small gong. "I sense our women's talk may be of little interest to a man of action like yourself... *Señor.* May one of our circus girls show you to the back bar?"

As Pepe Llulla withdrew Fitzwilliam motioned for Swift to sit on a velvet settee. "Miss Carter." Fitzwilliam began cordially with a masculine voice that rang with authority. But it did not lessen her femininity.

"I know who you are."

Fitzwilliam shot Swift a quick look in the mirror. Then turned to face the newcomer. "The people I pay for information tell me you are in need of a steady supply of girls for your establishment in New York. Tell me more."

Fitzwilliam spread her green gown as she settled into a large red sofa — uncomfortably close to Swift.

"Yes." Swift embellished Llulla's script as she started right in. "More than a year ago in New York I was caught up in a scandal of a sexual nature involving my banker and his son...but the details are not important. The upshot was my family cast me out. Having no possibility of becoming established in any work or business I searched for an opportunity. Having the reputation of a scarlet woman it occurred to me...I might as well use it to my advantage. Since that is the only direction society permits."

Fitzwilliam nodded encouragingly. "Not an unfamiliar story. Go on."

"An acquaintance with Fannie Flynn developed." Swift paused. "Do you know the name?"

"Fannie Flynn! That old strumpet...pardon my French. We worked the Mississippi steamboats together in the early years. Good to hear she's still in the business." Fitzwilliam tapped the small gong once. When two pretty young girls appeared she asked for refreshments. "Emily and Jane are in my circus. Please continue."

"As it happened Fannie Flynn had just opened a new mansion in lower mid-town. But she still had a property in Five Points that was too good to let go. She wanted a silent partner who could invest a little money. Take care of the business side. And keep an eye out among the girls — after hours."

"Like running a nursery…Miss Carter." Fitzwilliam gave Swift a half smile.

"Fannie handled the johns…and the political side of the operation. The Five Points area was doing well. And I knew others were investing in mid-town property. With some hush money from my banker — and profits from an import business — I put in thirteen hundred."

"If I know Fannie you collected the rent from the girls every week."

"Fifty dollars from every girl." Swift stated the tidy sum matter of fact — as Llulla had instructed.

"Fifty! That's New York City for you. Five bucks rent is the going rate here in the Quarter. But I get ten at Josie's. That's because we have the best clients and they leave the best tips. Our girls get two dollars a turn. Compared to a six-cent *picayune* in The Swamp or fifty cents on Gallatin Street in Lugger's Landing. Ten dollars a week for rent is nothing. Go on."

"Fannie had six girls so I collected three hundred a week. Because I had the business responsibility I kept one quarter and turned over three quarters to Fannie. In the first year I made over thirty-nine hundred just collecting rents. Fannie made almost twelve thousand. By the end of the first year we had a well-oiled system. But we had a problem."

"Probably counting your money." Fitzwilliam let her envy show. "Did John Law get his claws in you…or did your girls get better offers?"

"Neither. It may sound odd but because of the demand I rarely went out. If I wasn't keeping peace…I was keeping ledgers. That's when the problem hit me."

At that moment Jane and Emily reappeared each carrying a silver tray. Jane served Swift and Llulla iced drinks with sweetened lime juice and muddled mint. Emily with a curtsy presented the madam a straight up absinthe and rye Sazerac. Fitzwilliam savored a first sip then clapped her hands in disbelief. "Well I declare! The world works in strange ways. Are my informants right about you?"

"As you say — the key to our success is a stream of quality girls. That is why I want to establish a connection with the most exclusive and fashionable house in New Orleans. Someone who knows how to take raw girls. Clean them up. And teach them our trade. Someone who can send girls north — particularly Irish bawds — because we cater to the old line and they prefer immigrant girls. Lets the gents feel superior. Common — rustic — girls won't do. What we need are girls with style. Who know the business. And who want to make even more money. To share the wealth — in all fairness — we also have girls in New York that want to work in a warm place in the winter months."

"I doubt if my girls would suit you." Fitzwilliam bargained. "Most are right off the famine ships. Once a Jezebel…always a Jezebel."

"That may be." Swift paused. "But once you take the sharp edges off…we can finish them. Imagine. Dress them right with gowns and street dresses. A touch of glitter here…a touch of flair there. Teach them how to speak properly. You'd be amazed at the ladies we turn out."

"Wouldn't mind having some classy girls in the winter in these parts."

Swift set the hook and reeled in. "As the business partner of Fannie Flynn…we have one sacred rule that we never ever break."

"And what is that?" Fitzwilliam cocked a penciled eyebrow. *Here it comes.*

"We require personal interviews of every girl before we consider them. Simply put…that is my purpose today. If twenty-five dollars a week rent for each girl that passes our review is agreeable then perhaps we can do business."

"Make it thirty and we can talk. Profit is what this business is all about."

Swift nodded. "Only for the best girls….And if your extra *lagniappe* comes out of the girls' weekly rent of sixty-five…I can get Fannie to agree."

Fitzwilliam sluiced a long drink of her cocktail then groused about an old complaint. "Some johns ask why my girls are not more artful. Why do they not spend more time to please their clients. Those dimwits say we could develop loyal clients and keep them coming back. That might be true for horses or barbers or bartenders. But it requires a discriminating customer…one who makes it worth our while to spend more time with him. Hah! Johns here — and on the river too in my experience…johns here don't know the difference. As my friend Mary Thompson once told me in her 'cigar store' on Royal Street. 'The secret to turning johns is to keep 'em turning.' That's why your proposition is not up to me alone." Fitzwilliam stated her position firmly. "The girls must agree too. When do you propose to talk with them?"

"Tomorrow. Let's begin with just two." Swift leveled with the madam. "*Señor* Llulla has agreed to collect two of your most trainable Irish girls. He will bring them to my suite tomorrow morning at ten o'clock at the Exchange Hotel on Saint Charles. If they pass my interview…perhaps we can do business — at thirty a week."

Fitzwilliam rose to shake hands with Swift. *Too good to be true. Something doesn't sit right. This is work for Harp and his men.*

With the cunning of a venomous water moccasin the madam smiled to hide her misgivings. "Ten o'clock it is."

CHAPTER **18**

JACK DANCER stayed in the shadows as he followed the two figures. Thieves were bolder on the levee. More and more military supplies arrived daily. Mountains of goods were stacked in the open space roughly arranged for steamships to take them to Texas. Blankets stacked next to rifle crates. Salt pork next to black powder. Tents and wagon wheels mingled with shovels and shot between bridge pontoons. As more supplies arrived from river and sea and land the overworked quartermaster played a chess game of constant motion. Stores were marshaled. Rearranged. Then moved aboard ships bound for Corpus Christi in the north or Point Isabel in the southern disputed territory where the Rio Grande met the Gulf.

Dancer moved closer as a man pulled a young woman by the wrist. Took her among the stacks of cotton bales.

The man hissed as he twisted the girl's wrist. "Your father is dead. Your brothers are in the army. Now it's your turn to decide."

"You're hurting me." She protested as she tried to pull free.

He released his hold. "Nothing like what could happen to you if you don't look out for yourself." He leaned in. "You're a soiled woman.

The runners had you. The captain on the ship had you. And now my men have had you. You're a Jezebel. Your fate is sealed."

The girl began to cry softly. What option did she have? No work. No home. Barely anything to eat.

"Work takes references…little one. The only reference you have now is what's between your legs."

The brown-haired girl tried to pull herself up. "What they did to me has nothing to do with me…with who I am." She clutched her buttoned frock at the throat.

The Irishman struck a reasoned tone. "Miss Josephine Fitzwilliam takes care of her girls. You'll see. All you can eat. New dresses. You'll be protected in her house. No more nights sleeping on the streets."

"Maybe for a while." The girl softened. "Just to get some money. I'm so tired."

"Now you're talking sense. Miss Josie has several other girls just like you. It will be a whole new family. Josie's house has two bathtubs just for her girls."

"A hot bath…I'm so cold." She shuddered.

Patrick Harp took the shoulders of his newest recruit. Then turned her away toward the back of town.

"Do not move…Harp." Dancer gave his order as he stepped in Harp's path. "She's not going anywhere."

"What the hell?" Harp growled.

"I've been watching you…Harp. Your men killed this girl's father. And I know thievery has been your handy work as well. Let her go. No more recruiting on this levee."

Harp gave a sharp whistle. From out of nowhere four thugs materialized and surrounded Dancer.

Dancer grabbed two stevedore hooks from a nearby cotton bale and challenged the brutes. "Who wants his guts ripped open first?" Dancer menaced. "Be my guest."

The smallest wharf rat swung at Dancer with a shovel.

Dancer ducked and countered with a vicious arc of the sharpened hook aimed at the man's belly. The rounder jumped back at the last moment.

A second brute charged Dancer like a gorilla. The momentum spun Dancer around and slammed him into a wall of cotton bales.

Pain shot through Dancer's chest. Around his middle the roughneck tightened a crushing grip. As the hulk squeezed out the last breath Dancer placed his boots against the bales. In a blink his feet ran up the wall of cotton. Then Dancer pushed off and somersaulted backward over the man's shoulder. The movement toppled the brute to the ground. Dancer landed on top of his attacker. The other thugs closed in to finish Dancer off.

At that moment out of the corner of his eye pressed flat against the ground Dancer spotted Natchez Jones as he raced toward them from the riverfront. With one crushing kick to the brute's temple Dancer rolled freed. Jones grabbed the two bale hooks. The vicious points glinted in the tremulous gaslight. Jones pulled Dancer away. Kept his back to the high stack of bales. Moved to his right. The girl slipped behind them into an aisle. Jones filled the open space. Protected both Dancer and the girl. The light of a gas lamp overhead cowed the three thugs who kept back in the shadows like rats.

Harp hissed. "Let them go…men. There are more biddies in this world."

Realizing their advantage Jones shielded the girl and Dancer as they hobbled toward the landing. Back toward the safety of the *Decatur's* busy gangplank.

Harp shook his fist at the retreating trio. "Don't think you've seen the last of us…Natchez Jones. Nobody in this town kicks around Patrick Harp and lives to tell. Nobody!"

CHAPTER **19**

SAMANTHA SWIFT tapped her notebook. *So far so good. My first investigation is turning out nicely.* At a gentle knock Swift opened the door to her suite. Fitzwilliam's two girls—dressed in their best street clothes—stepped inside.

"Thank you for coming. I'm Kitty Carter…down from New York. I'm looking forward to talking with you both."

The taller girl—Emma—introduced herself with a soft Irish accent. She had a full sensual figure. *Rubenesque* Swift thought. Clear pinkish-white complexion under a pile of auburn brown hair. Soft and empty hazel eyes…not unlike a young heifer. Emma circled the posh suite drenched in morning light flooding the canary walls and bright floral fabrics. She traced a fingertip across the polished surfaces of each piece of furniture she passed. The smaller Irish girl had penetrating black eyes and a topknot of raven hair. Maggie's sharp movements made her birdlike frame seem to flit quickly from space to space. Her long fingernails nervously tapped in constant rhythm.

"Maggie and Emma…come sit in my view parlor. Ice water? Lemonade? Wine?" Both girls took a glass of wine and were drawn to the corner window looking northeast across Saint Charles Street.

"Look! You can see the river and…" Emma murmured as she looked past the Verandah Hotel on the far corner. Gravier Street framed her view as she squinted toward the levee to the east.

Maggie jumped in excitedly to finish Emma's sentence: "Look off to the right…Saint Patrick's. And the other way is the City Exchange and the Saint Louis Cathedral." She pointed breathlessly. "I've never been this high before."

Emma's gaze swept the horizon. "You can see forever."

"You'd make quite a splash on the street if you jumped." Maggie nearly giggled as she looked down.

Emma whispered to Maggie. "That girl…You know—the one from Dingle in the old country? She jumped from the Exchange Dome gallery they say."

"Not a bad way to go. Nice and quick." The dark-eyed Maggie gave Emma a surprise squeeze in the ribs that made her shriek. Together the girls looked down at the street five stories below.

Swift drew them back from the window. "Come join me here on the lounge. Josie tells me you're both recently from Ireland. Fannie Flynn and I have several Irish girls in our house in New York. As business manager I'm here to compare the practices of the houses…because we are looking for girls who want to work in New York in the summer months."

"I for one would love to leave New Orleans in the summer to beat the Yellow Jack fever." Maggie presented her offer straightforwardly. "I'd be interested…if the money is right."

"How much does an experienced girl get for each turn?" Emma asked. Her tone implied Maggie would be paid less.

Swift replied readily: "Johns in Fannie's house are ten dollars a turn to our girls."

"Josie only pays two dollars for riding Saint George on top." Maggie's exclamation only partly expressed her discontent. *And she charges ten dollars a week for rent.*

"Same for a screw as taking a flyer on a French job?" Emma pressed.

"At Fannie's one price gets all. No matter a screw…a French job…or a one-handed under the blanket standpipe.…It all costs the same at Fannie's." Swift leaned in to close her pitch. "Keeps it simple.

And keeps the johns coming back to try something different. That way Fannie's girls hit their mark faster every week. Weekly rent is only seven turns…sixty-five dollars every Monday."

Maggie and Emma's eyes met. Perched on the edge of the yellow-flowered sofa that faced Swift. Their body language said "pick me."

Swift settled back and touched her notebook on her lap. "Tell me then. Do you mind if I keep notes? I want to be sure I have all the details correct. Now…how did you both come to be employed by Josie Fitzwilliam?"

Maggie spoke first while she clicked her nails against her wine glass. "We was just off the boat from Liverpool. Been run off our cottage in Limerick when the potato-black rotted our patch…and all the neighbors' too. Nobody had nothin' to eat. Nothin' to pay rent. Mother died of the grip. My older brother went and joined the army. So my Poppy and young brother Johnnie and me shipped out. 'Human ballast' they called us. Made it here. Poppy and Johnnie found some work sweeping and odd jobs on the levee. The owner of the Bull's Head took me in as a beer jerk. Got a quarter for every pitcher I sold. Things were tough. Then one day this Irish fella came in. 'Name's Harp' he said. 'Patrick Harp.' Says he knew a lady named Josephine Fitzwilliam who had an employment agency. Fine Irish lady he said. I din' want nothin' to do with working the street or being one of those crib girls. He gave me her card and I went there to call."

Emma broke in. "Josie's is a class place. Not one of those mahogany halls with octoroons trying to pass as white."

"Josie didn't cotton to me. Said beer jerks don't rarely work out. But then she sez she needed a maid and laundress." Maggie smiled slightly at the memory. "At first that's what I did. At Josie's the girls give all their money to the maid who locked it in a strongbox during the evening. Didn't take long to see how much the girls were making."

"Real money. Like I'd never seen before." Emma's voice conveyed the admiration only the ring of coins might provide a working girl. "Maggie would do the wash up whenever a girl brought in a john." Emma sniffed. "The working girl…she'd get half-dollar tips from the customer. Which she shared with her wash-up girl. Pretty soon all the girls had Maggie do their wash up act…before and after."

Maggie giggled. "One night I walked in on Emma with a john…as if I was changing the towels or tidying up. I wore this little maid outfit with apron and ruffles and little white bonnet. Emma was washing off the john's prick with a washcloth. He said all important like: 'Don't you think your little maid should help out her friend?' We both laughed. Emma asked if I wanted to help — all polite and ladylike and everything — and held up the washcloth. I din't think anything of it. From then on they sold us as a two-for-one act…a proper lady and her maid."

In a told-you-so voice Emma added: "Sure was good for business. I was taking in maybe thirty dollars a week myself — and the other girls was getting more johns too. One time one of the girls had a john and was sucking him off when Maggie came in early. All proper in her maid costume. 'I can help with that.' So she sez. And they took turns."

Maggie chipped in enthusiastically: "I made a buck for my end of that one. Pretty soon I was doing my own face-making turns. Anyway…that's how I got started at Josie's. All because of Patrick Harp."

"It's like anything else." Emma examined her fingernails with a haughty look. "Like a kid whose father owns a dry goods store. You help in the store. Only Josie isn't selling dry goods…unless the girl looks like a sparrow."

Swift turned to Emma. "And how did you find your way to Josephine Fitzwilliam's…Emma?"

"My mother died on the ship coming over. Daddy was drunk all the time. To get bread for my little sister and brother I traded sex. The first night in New Orleans four gorillas trapped me on the levee. They were pretty juiced. They wouldn't let me go until I gave them all a French job. So I did. What could I do? I had no choice. But I'm not ashamed of what I done because I din't have much to do with it…No more ashamed of that than being a member of the human race. When the thugs left…a man came and gave me a dollar. All charitable like. That paid to feed my brood for two weeks. His name was Patrick Harp. Said I was different from the other girls. Said I was better. Not because…you know…I was so pretty or clever…but because I was a novelty — a white Irish girl."

"Even the not-so-pretty ones do not want to be around long

enough to get wore out." Maggie's snipe was not unkind…and did not go unnoticed.

"Harp told me I was a whore now and there wasn't anything else I could do about it…so might as well make the most of it." Emma accepted her situation.

"Harp has a way of making you see the bright side…din't he?" Maggie sang.

"Josie had me watch from behind one of those *portiere* doorway curtains that blocks boudoir scenes from view. She dressed me in a milk maid's dress to make me look like a country girl. Some johns like that. Others liked a lesbian warm-up act like those two underage trick babies put on for the back-parlor circus." Seeing Swift's quizzical look Emma translated. "Trick babies are children whose father is a john who paid their mother for a screw. Lots of the girls have children. Some of the babies work around the house until they get to be ten or twelve…when they can service johns regular like."

Maggie sniffed as she picked at her nails.

"These two trick babies did a dance in the back parlor where they played with themselves and then each other. When the john got worked up I took him aside and started to play with him. Those johns are done in almost an instant. Embarrassed mostly. So they try to cover it up with big tips. Pretty soon I had my own regulars. Josie calls them her 'private clients.'"

Emma almost cackled. "They sure like their privacy. Hah!"

"Were costumes supplied to you by Josie?" Swift asked.

"Miss Josephine always took care of us with new clothes." Maggie ran her hands over her smart dress.

"I have three gowns and six street dresses." Emma beamed. She was sure that was more than Maggie had. "It's been four months now since Harp brought me over. Already I got a stocking full of money."

Maggie elbowed Emma. "Remember the trick Miss Josephine pulled on that bitch Gypsy White? When they paid off the seamstress to make Gypsy's new dresses a full size too small?"

"You should have seen her!" Emma chortled to Swift.

"Who is Gypsy White?" Swift asked.

"She thinks she's better than us Irish. Runs four cribs off Basin Street on Custom House. Working-man tricks. Laborers. Girls sit out front and pose for the johns like an emporium store. Cheap trash—if you ask me." Emma flashed.

Maggie put in: "There you go...all high and mighty again. Anyway...One day when Josie saw Gypsy going to the dressmaker for a fitting Josie laid the bait. 'Why Gypsy...you're putting on weight. Must take better care of yourself...girl.' Josie even got some of us girls to say things on the street to Gypsy's girls. 'Gypsy's looking a little plump' or 'Gypsy must be eating well' or 'Gypsy's still packing it away...I see.' Some bitches will believe anything."

Emma finished the story. "After the dresses were delivered—every dress one size too small—we didn't see the old whore for a month or more. When she did make an appearance...she was gaunt as a scarecrow from purges and laxatives and enemas."

"Looked like death warmed over." Maggie hooted.

"When Gypsy found out...she sicced some mugs from the levee on us. But they thought it was so funny they never hurt us." Emma smiled.

"One last question. Tell me how Josephine Fitzwilliam does her business—I mean from the john's point of view. What's the setup?"

"Joshua...he's our Negro doorman. He greets the johns and announces the visitor if he's known."

Not to be outdone Maggie interjected. "The girls—maybe six or eight of us—lounge on sofas and chairs dressed in revealing *boudoir* clothes."

"*If* you have anything to reveal." Emma's words had a cutting tone that Maggie ignored.

"We'd rub up against them and tell them how handsome they were." Maggie was more than happy to provide an explanation. "If they were tall—the short girls would work them. If they were short—the tall girls approached them. Josie said it always worked."

Emma laughed. "And it did."

"Then we'd whisper in their ear what we would like to do." Maggie bragged: "We'd get them to buy us champagne or whiskey or wine. Never beer. That was too low-class at Josie's. If they liked the piano man's playing...we'd tell them to tip the professor."

"You can tell the experienced johns because they brought a pocket full of quarters and half dollars." Emma confided her insights into New Orleans economics. "If they only had a purse full of five-dollar half eagles some panel thief would snatch it and they would never see it again."

"We heard of one girl in Basin Street that had a trained raccoon that would pickpocket the johns…but I never seen it." Maggie beamed.

"You should get out more…Magpie." Emma punctuated her tease with a gentle elbow to her companion's ribs. "We gave the johns the impression they could expect something quite sensationally wicked in our little den of pleasure. Johns ate that up. Some of the girls are very theatrical."

"After a john selected you…Josie would say to the girl — pretend quiet-like…but so the john could hear: 'Now you take him and see that he has a *real good time.*'" Maggie filled her wine again. "Our routine never changed. But Josie thought it was good for business. Made the johns feel special."

"We took them upstairs to the boudoir where there was a four-poster and washstand. The girl took her clothes off right away and invited him to do the same. Then we would bring him to the washstand to wash his prick." Emma described the scene with blunt candor. "But first we would milk it — like Josie taught us — to see if he had the clap."

"One john was a doctor and he said we were better at checking for the clap than most physicians. Every john knows about this part of the routine. And they never complain. Just part of 'being safe' we'd say. They'd laugh." Maggie smiled as she boasted. "Then we'd put a few drops of some purple stuff into the water basin and wash them. Smelled foul."

Emma corrected…in a superior tone. "If you paid attention you'd know the druggist called it disinfectant." She resumed without taking a breath. "If we didn't do the maid act…we'd get the little lesbian girls to do it."

Maggie leaned in. Her voice a barely audible whisper. "Then we'd invite them to lie down on the bed. We'd come on top. Grind for a while…and then we'd have them. They'd let go right away. Never took more than a minute or two. Sometimes less."

"Ah…as the French say: *la petite mort.* The little death." Emma's tone was haughty. "Course — when we did the missionary — the better girls would feign the john had their passionate attention while they pumped away and that they were interested in seeing the john had a good time. But it wasn't necessary. Then we'd act just a little surprised when the john gave us money. Like we were so pleasured we had forgotten about that business detail."

Maggie made a joke. "One girl from Dublin had a special calling card printed. 'Doing a large business on a small scale.' Somehow she pulled it off."

"Some of us have pride in our profession." Emma tweaked Maggie. "Josie insisted I was never never to appear greedy or crass or uncouth."

Maggie continued unfazed. "Next we'd wash them again. Ask if there was anything else. Usually they would say 'Thank you...no... nothing else.'"

Emma jumped in. "Then I'd collect the money. Put on my robe and took them into the hallway. I'd give the maid the money. And she would escort the john down the back steps...."

"Never want to mix a done customer with an eager customer... Josie always said." Maggie smiled temperately as she chimed in. "Probably not a half hour had passed since Joshua the doorman announced them."

Emma added mischievously: "Heck of a lot easier for the gents than seducing some prissy young lady in their social circle. And cheaper to pay for a hooker—in the short run and the long run."

Maggie sat back. Arms crossed.

"Then we'd go downstairs and fish for another john."

Emma's expression suggested higher addition. "We'd have three or four johns a night. Sometimes five or six on Sundays. We worked almost non-stop in March during the Volunteer Fireman parades."

Maggie gestured for another refill. "Every morning all the girls and Josie gathered in the kitchen to talk—you know the way girls talk— and have breakfast. Auntie May fixed us—"

At that moment the double door of Swift's suite burst open like an explosion.

Swift rose out of her chair.

In rushed Josephine Fitzwilliam...followed by two of the meanest brutes the levee ever festered. Swift recognized the largest one as the scar-faced killer who threatened the editor of *The Picayune* to a duel.

Emma and Maggie jumped up. Squealed in fear.

"Get out!" Fitzwilliam ordered. "This interview is over!"

"But which one of us will she pick?" Emma stammered.

"You're not going anywhere. This Kitty Carter is a fake. She doesn't work for Fannie Flynn. Never did. Take the girls back to the house. Now!" Fitzwilliam snarled.

The second thug grabbed Maggie and Emma by the arm. Roughly pushed them out of the room and slammed the door.

Fitzwilliam squared on Swift. "Maybe you could hoodwink Pepe Llulla…my little pretty…but not Josephine Fitzwilliam." The madam moved closer. "You are not who you seem — are you?"

"Why…I do not know what you're talking about." Swift's mind raced to find a plausible explanation.

"Don't give me that damned crap. Just this morning a steamer arrived from New York. Guess who was on it? One of Fannie Flynn's girls — the *real* Fannie Flynn — and she says you're a spy…Miss Carter. Then Harp did some checking with your steamship captain. Turns out you're nothing but a rich little priss pretending to be a reporter because your daddy died and left you nothing. Hold her!" Fitzwilliam ordered.

Scarface grabbed Swift. Then yanked both elbows painfully back behind her. "No Pepe Llulla to protect you now…is there?" His tobacco-soured breath spattered her cheek.

"Make Miss Samantha Swift understand." Fitzwilliam hissed.

The thug wrenched Swift off the ground. Searing pain knifed through her shoulders. Her notebook dropped to the carpet without a sound.

"Get this and get it straight…S. Thomas Swift — or whatever your name is." Fitzwilliam growled as she picked up the notebook and shook it in Swift's face. "This interview is not going to be published. It is not going to be written. This little glory stunt of yours is dead."

Swift ground her teeth from the pain. "Get out of my room…"

"Hah! This is not a negotiation. You're done here. Let me make it clear to you…dearie. If one word of this information finds its way into print…your editor's life will not be worth the paper these lies are printed on…and your publisher will be in the poorhouse from the libel suits. We will find you wherever you are…and you'll join the bottom feeders in a canal just like your poor wench of a mother."

"You are a bitch." Swift's voice turned raspy as her anger resembled bravery.

"Are you finished? Most important — if you publish this story those two biddies won't last a day. Do you understand…Swift? Publish and it's their death sentence. You will have killed them. Have I made myself clear? No sources. No witnesses. Just your word against mine." For emphasis the thug grabbed Swift by the throat and drove his powerful fingers into her windpipe.

"Yes." Swift croaked a barely audible reply.

Scarface dropped Swift in a crumpled heap then moved toward the door.

Fitzwilliam towered over Swift. The Queen of Basin Street placed the ball tread of her buttoned boot on Swift's right hand. Shifted her weight. Ground Swift's fingers into the floor. Swift heard her knuckles crack.

"If one word of your stupid stunt is printed…they die first. Then you."

PART II

RUN-UP TO WAR

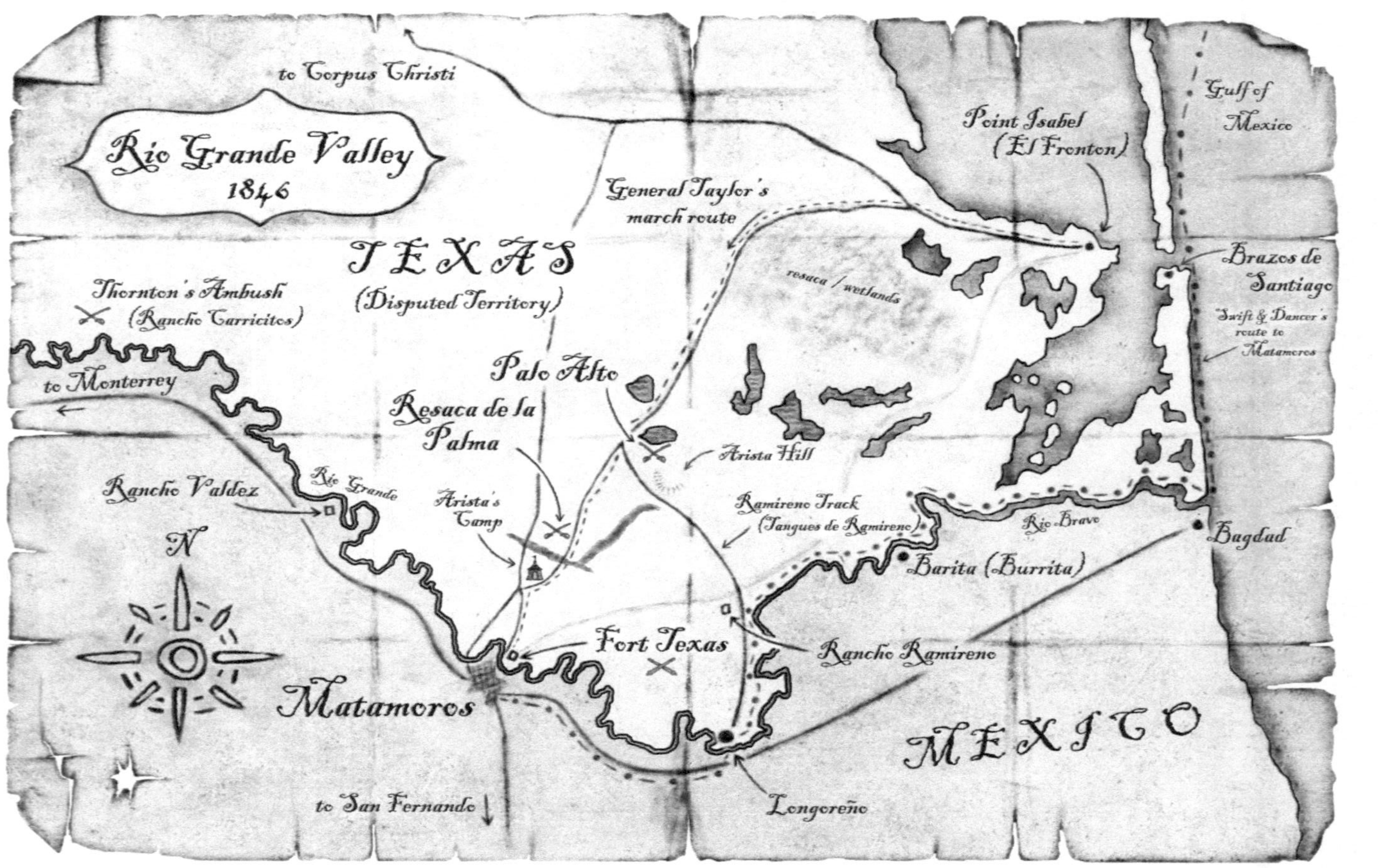

Rio Grande Valley
1846
to Corpus Christi
Point Isabel (El Fronton)
Gulf of Mexico
Brazos de Santiago
Swift & Dancer's route to Matamoros
General Taylor's march route
TEXAS
(Disputed Territory)
Thornton's Ambush (Rancho Carricitos)
to Monterrey
Palo Alto
Resaca de la Palma
Arista Hill
resaca / wetlands
Rancho Valdez
Rio Grande
Arista's Camp
Ramireno Track (Tanques de Ramireno)
Rio Bravo
Bagdad
Barita (Burrita)
N
Fort Texas
Rancho Ramireno
Matamoros
MEXICO
to San Fernando
Longoreño

CHAPTER 20

MAJOR GENERAL ZACHARY TAYLOR surveyed the New Orleans levee with satisfaction. Since July 1845 his Army of Observation had soldiered in Texas on the Nueces River near Corpus Christi. Endlessly they drilled. Trained. Marked time with camp life as always. When orders came 4 February 1846 to advance into disputed territory the General made ready. Then slipped back to New Orleans. The old warrior cajoled and called favors and procured three armed steamers. Two brigs of war and one cutter he knew were critical to patrol his supply line in the Gulf of Mexico. And form a blockade to protect his exposed depot at Point Isabel inside the Brazos Santiago. Just eight miles north of where the Rio Grande River met the Gulf. Now all was ready to push his Army of Occupation one hundred and fifty miles south into Texas. Taylor's objective was a point upstream on the north bank of the Rio Grande across from Matamoros Mexico.

My cannon will be a thumb in the eye of the Mexicans.

A little more than two months before — on 31 December 1845 — the Republic of Texas was officially annexed as the newest state in the Union of the United States. Taylor waited for Washington to make up its mind. *Winter is the only time to campaign in Texas* the General had warned the War Department. *Before the heat kills more of my boys than the Mexicans.* Polk wanted a war. Self-righteously marching into the territory both sides claimed as theirs — between the Nueces and Rio Grande — would do just that.

This old soldier will be ready.

As far as Taylor's gaze could reach steamships nosed against the New Orleans levee. Their great bowlines held them fast at the same angle — side-by-side — as the Mississippi River current pressed them together. Side decks were close enough for a man to step from ship to ship. Unseen by the bedlam focused on the levee. The side paddles and propellers and stern wheels waited for the steam to rise and put them underway. Long gangways extended like hungry tongues down to the landing — ready to swallow sacks of supplies. Barrels. Crates. Trunks. Separate stages deposited passengers near companionways that reached upper decks away from the sweating activity below.

Everywhere was a cacophony of activity. Men shouted. Teamsters cursed obstinate mules. Hogsheads rolled across cobblestone streets. Stevedores chanted heavy loads into place. Whips cracked in the air. The cacophony of harbor sounds rose above the base melody of steam engines at low boil. The sting of coal soot filled the air.

Two ships stood separate at the top of the line downstream. In second position was Captain Natchez Jones's giant *Decatur*. A worthy paddle frigate with two great sidewheels and three masts for sail. The *Decatur* flew the colors of the army command. Clearly the flagship. Nearer Lugger's Landing was the sleek *New York*. A smaller sidewheel steam packet with single auxiliary-sail mast yet its wooden hull more regal in gleaming white. The *New York*'s sleek presence set it apart as a passenger vessel more than a vehicle of supply. The steamer's promenade deck shadowed a walkway beneath where shuttered windows marked a row of staterooms. Like a throne for royalty at the highest point above the scene rose the *New York*'s wheelhouse. Its great wheel and latest devices ready to alert the engine room amidships of maneuvers and speed. Some said the *New York* was the fastest ship in the Gulf. Its best time from New Orleans to Corpus Christi — 18 hours 42 minutes — was the unspoken standard for the elite Gulf captains.

No one knew of a better time.

CHAPTER 21

S. THOMAS SWIFT massaged her bruised right hand. As well as her shaken confidence. At her feet was a modest valise with an engraved brass nameplate. She waited patiently amidst a gaggle of war correspondents to board the *New York*. The same sidewheel steam packet that brought her to New Orleans. Her fashionable French hunting suit with close-fitted jacket and matching trousers looked out of place. A woman in a man's world.

"Your husband let you carry his bag I see." One of the assembled writers eyed Swift's valise. "S. Thomas Swift. S. Thomas Swift. Do I know that name?"

"Not yet." Swift smiled mildly. "That's a byname."

Taken aback the correspondent opened a new avenue of inquiry. "Who does your husband write for?"

"I write for the *Brooklyn Eagle* mostly. But there is no 'he.' I'm here to report on the war…just like you." *Stand tall Sam. Believe in what you say…and make your mother and father proud.*

"Pardon the assumption…Swift." The newsman from the *Boston Courier* shook Swift's hand enthusiastically. Swift winced as he squeezed her writing hand. "Guess this whole thing is new to most of us. They say this is the first war where the press is allowed to come along."

At that moment — as a dark cloud blocked the sun — who stepped up to Swift and the Boston correspondent but James Collingsworth Turner of *The Daily Picayune.* "So you're still here?" Turner smirked. "Must say I'm surprised. Sounds like your little ambush stunt with Josephine Fitzwilliam didn't work out so well…did it?"

"How'd you hear about that?" Swift shot back as she tried not to let her misgivings show. *What was I thinking that I could expose Fitzwilliam's world in one interview?*

"This is a small business. Word travels fast when you have your ear to the ground."

"You mean to the gutter — don't you?" Swift retorted.

"The lesson is clear." Turner sniffed. "A true woman's role is to be obedient and silent."

Swift smiled without humor. "Then your understanding would be expanded by the editorials of Jane McManus Storms with the *New York Sun*…or Margaret Fuller's 'The Great Lawsuit.'" *Although — with Storms's pseudonym 'Montgomery' and Fuller's* New York Tribune *columns only signed by an asterisk — I doubt a jackass like you would get the point.*

Turner continued oblivious. "The boys and I have a little bet as to how you'll do when some Texas *hombre* tells you not to write about him.…My money is on the Texan."

Turner handed Swift one of his ever-ready calling cards. "Here's a name to remember. James Collingsworth Turner. Also use a bushel of *noms de guerre* when needed." He strutted pompously. "But we're here to cover Polk's war. Sure beats editing the newspaper exchange slips…or captions for those gaudy hand-colored fashion plates in some lady's magazine. I say 'we' because that's my illustrator over there on the bales. William Beacon. Old line Southern family. He doesn't miss a detail. Artist. Cartographer. Lithographer. Just back from New York. Now a daguerreotypist — of all things. Man of a thousand pictures…and few words. Best in the business. Sees everything in pictures."

Swift fluttered her fingers in the direction of the friendly face from the steam packet. Beacon touched his sketch pencil to his temple in recognition.

Turner pressed an impertinent question. "Did your paper send an illustrator with you?"

"No. I'm covering the war on my own."

Turner replied: "Not surprising. Only the top papers know how to do it right. What did you say your paper was?"

"The *Brooklyn Eagle*." Swift repeated the name with a sense of pride.

"Is that one of those police-report rags that sell for a penny on the street?"

Swift bristled. "The *Eagle* is an evening daily. Sells for nine cents a week by subscription—or three cents a copy on the street. You may be mistaking it with the *New York Examiner*. My father owned the *Examiner* before he died."

Turner flicked lint off his sleeve with a dismissive gesture. "I'm surprised that tenement riffraff can even read. Maybe the penny press finds its true calling in the fish shops." Turner muttered under his breath as Swift moved out of hearing: "…Or the privy."

☒ ☒ ☒

Just then a great scatter from hooves and carriage wheels rose from the Rangia clamshell landing. In a show of gallantry and brass General Taylor's command arrived to board the *Decatur*. Captain Jones beckoned them forward. Positioned at the end of the passenger gantry on the *New York* a newly hired steward introduced himself to the arriving war correspondents. Then personally escorted them to their staterooms.

He allowed no surprise when S. Thomas Swift turned out to be a woman. *Best be placed in the lady's cabin forward the engine.* A spacious accommodation assigned for special guests of the captain. "Your cabin enjoys a better breeze from two side windows." The steward rattled through his oft-repeated welcome as he deposited Swift's small valise on the high bed. Then gestured toward Swift's heavy portmanteau trunk forwarded from the Saint Charles Hotel and placed in the lady's cabin. The upright hinged trunk—with its hanging compartment and drawers—almost came to Swift's shoulder. "Dinner at sunset. About six o'clock. Breakfast at dawn…ma'am. About six thirty. The captain's bell will announce. Most of the rooms are empty because the General is on the *Decatur.*" Swift tipped the steward generously. He took his leave.

Wanting not to miss a detail from the promenade deck Swift locked the inner door behind her. Then closed the outer louvered door as she left her cabin.

With triumphant blasts from the steam whistles and black smoke billowing from the soot-covered smokestacks the stevedores levered the great tethers off their wharf spindles. One by one the steamships backed away from the levee. As their great engines pulled them into the Mississippi's current the ships swung downstream. Quickly picked up speed. Soon the great dome of the Exchange Hotel grew smaller in the distance behind them. Some time elapsed as the ships passed the English Turn. Then threaded their way more than ninety miles through the delta. At every moment pilots kept a sharp eye for incoming traffic to America's second-largest port. Once the steamships forged into the Gulf of Mexico the tailing current of the river no longer multiplied their speed. Shortly they settled into a rhythmic hum across the gentle Gulf waves.

Above the horizon a spectacular orange sun beckoned the small flotilla toward a land that appeared to be on fire.

CHAPTER 22

THE CAPTAINS of the *Decatur* and *New York* received an order to slow to a meager pace. Just enough to steady them. Gradually the two ships converged in a brief courtship like two whales nuzzling. Soon crew held the lines at bow and stern to keep them together. After a brief consultation General Taylor and his entourage moved from the *Decatur* to the *New York*. Their personal equipage smoothly followed under the direction of Captain Jones and the steward. In short order all came aboard the *New York*.

"What's the song and dance?" One of the correspondents had grown curious.

As the supercargo in charge on the *New York* Dancer invited them to gather in the grand saloon. All would be made clear.

The two ships were cast apart to rejoin the flotilla's formation.

The correspondents filed into the saloon…where they were met by a kindly looking gentleman who appeared to have just left his plantation. White cotton duck trousers. An open collar shirt. Wide-brimmed straw hat on the table beside him. Behind him stood a phalanx of braid and brass and blue. A stark contrast of military rank and insignia.

Dancer began. "Gentlemen…my name is Jack Dancer. As a representative of the New York Steam Packet Company I'd like to welcome you. Please be seated."

A general scuffling for chairs and position broke out until all found a seat.

Dancer stepped to the front of the saloon. The great mirror and redwood bar aligned from port to starboard across the wall behind him. "Let me start by saying — " He had barely begun before his words were cut short.

The forward cabin door to the saloon opened to his right. In stepped Samantha Swift. Still dressed in her casual hunting costume now accented by a plumed Cavalier-style riding hat and kid gloves. All heads turned in Swift's direction. There was a commotion as the entire body of men attempted to rise at once. As if they were snapped to attention by the commandant of West Point — though he was already seated in the room.

"They say you salute the uniform not the person." General Taylor spoke under his breath but could not hide his amusement. "Bully for you."

In the silence the only sound to be heard was the grinding hum of the ship's paddles. Swift gave a slight nod to General Taylor.

Taylor introduced. "Mr. Dancer…this is S. Thomas Swift with the *Brooklyn Eagle.*"

"We've met." Swift and Dancer spoke in unison with some mutual annoyance in their voices.

All eyes returned to Swift. She passed up the opportunity to accept the favor of every previously occupied chair in the saloon. Instead Swift lifted a chair hung on its wall hook. Moved it to the table nearest General Taylor. And took her place.

The crowd settled back like disturbed geese upon a pond.

Dancer continued. "As I was saying gentlemen…and Miss Swift. We are fortunate to have an opportunity for the press to meet with General Zachary Taylor…commanding General of the Army of Occupation in Texas. If you have any questions the General has agreed to share his thoughts."

Zachary Taylor kept his seat and cleared his throat before he spoke.

"As you may know…this is the first time we have welcomed the press to join our expedition. Let me say it is an experiment. The War Department has instructed me that with the proper cooperation we may both be useful for each other." Taylor paused. "When that understanding is no longer true…there will be changes." The General thumped the table lightly with two fingers.

With that caveat the General opened the floor. "Now ask me what is on your minds."

"Why did you change ships after we left New Orleans?" The correspondent from the *Boston Courier* did not hesitate in launching his interrogation.

"That was Dancer's idea. Seemed like a good idea to keep them guessing…and I agree."

"Why are we going to war?" This next question came from the *New York Sun.*

"We are not going to war." Taylor's answer was spoken calmly. "We are an army of occupation on a mission to hold the new state of Texas…and to establish the rightful borders with Mexico. This is intended to be a defensive mission."

The correspondent from the *New Orleans Delta* shot a hand into the air. "We all remember the Alamo. Do you expect hostilities to open soon?"

"If it comes to war"—Taylor did not remove his gaze from the correspondent's eyes—"I won't be the one to fire the first shot."

"We understand you have been ordered to build a fort across the Rio Grande from Matamoros in Mexico. Is that fort to be called Fort Taylor?"

"No. It is simply a camp. My name is not to be attached to it like some street or boulevard to commemorate dead generals." Taylor seemed content to have clarified the issue.

"We will call it Fort Texas then." Turner from *The Daily Picayune* did not wait for the General's approval. "Is there a timetable for the war?"

"First off…there isn't a war. Just a defensive occupation of our territory. Anyway…missions like this never have the same timetable the planners in Washington expect. One thing I can tell you is that our contingents of volunteers—rather than the regular army troops—will end their twelve-month enlistment at the end of May. We'll see if this whole business can be concluded before then."

From the correspondent with the *Brooklyn Eagle* came the next question. "Can you share with us some of your background…General Taylor?" *As Father said…"Always tell us something about the man… the job…the world. Give us something revealing to grab on to. Readers need details."*

"Thank you…ma'am. Myself…I've been doing this for nearly forty years. Military camps are my life. I was born in Virginia. Raised in Kentucky. And currently live on a plantation in Louisiana…if I ever get a chance to get there." A general reassurance rose from the officers that it may be sooner than he thinks. "I served in the War of 1812. The Black Hawk War in thirty-two and the Second Seminole War in Florida. When was that? Took forever. I reckon between thirty-five and forty-two."

"We understand you own slaves at your plantation." *The Picayune* reporter probed into the heart of the matter. "Are you proslavery or an abolitionist?"

"As for politics…I can tell you I do not have any. Never been home to vote in my entire life. As for slavery…if you are asking if slavery is behind this operation — the answer is no. We are here to occupy our new state. Not to spread slavery to the territories." The General's gaze swept the room. "First we have to win this thing. My personal hope is that folks in the territories move directly to establish their own states and constitutions. Do not get hung up with all the territorial shilly-shallying mess because that *will* give the slave interests time to sink their teeth into some other outcome. No…sir.…We must win this contest. Then open the gates to the people."

A lull came in the questions as pencils scribbled.

"Thank you all for your attention. While dinner is being set up let's move to the promenade deck — where we can have a cigar or bowl. I pray someone will share some Virginia leaf."

CHAPTER 23

THE ASSEMBLY MOVED to the outer deck in the sunset-intensified twilight. Without warning the tranquility was shattered by a sudden commotion of bells and whistles from the direction of the *Decatur.* All eyes turned toward the ship. In an instant they realized the thick black smoke from the twin stacks had turned into red jets of flame.

At that precise moment a huge explosion blasted from the midship boiler room. Giant chunks of railing and decking and cabins were catapulted into the air. Commands were shouted from the forward wheelhouse of the doomed vessel less than one hundred yards away. Flames spread quickly along the remaining deck toward the bow cargo hold.

"My God! The powder!" Lieutenant Ridgely of the artillery watched as helplessly as all the others from the *New York.*

Dancer jumped into the breach and took charge. "Captain! Bring her about!" Dancer shouted at the boatswain. "Drop both lifeboats! Now!"

Like the wind the flames raced to engulf the *Decatur.* Men jumped into the sea. The heat of the fire was felt on the faces of the correspondents. And General Taylor. A roar grew of crackling fire and sizzling timbers as they hit cold water. Flames leapt higher toward the forward hold where the powder magazine was stored. Without warning the second boiler exploded. Its great smokestack launched into the air like a spinning Hale rocket. The black funnel hung in the air for a moment. Buckled. Then fell back into the fiery debris. Next came a stupendous explosion—black powder...ammunition—that blew the remaining ship to smithereens. A man's leg flew into the air. His torso cartwheeled the other direction until it splashed into the water near the *New York*. Spray wetted the spectators looking aghast at the hideous wreckage they were witnessing.

Dancer leapt into the first lifeboat. The men pulled toward the smoldering wreckage. Bumped into blocks of flotsam with every stroke.

"There!" Dancer pointed. "There's a man over there."

The boat shot forward toward the floating debris where a man kept one arm weakly over the wreckage.

"It's Captain Jones...sir."

"Bring him in. Be gentle." After giving his order Dancer stared down at the dark oily water. *How can this be?*

The bloody blackened body was singed and broken almost beyond recognition as they lifted the poor soul over the gunwale. It was Natchez Jones.

"Jonesy...what happened? Did a boiler blow?" Dancer asked gritting his teeth. *Be strong Dancer...for Natchez.*

With a bloody hand Natchez Jones gripped his friend's outstretched palm and thumb to gain strength. Jones shook his head. "Bad boilers...before they blow...give white steam out the stack...not black." Jones pulled himself closer to Dancer. "Not a boiler. That was a ball of fire. An explosion."

"What could have caused it?" Dancer asked his dying friend.

"Somebody vandalized the doctor...the feed-water pump that refills the water supply to the boiler..."

"How?"

Jones fought unbearable agony. Gathered himself with his last ounce of strength and willpower. "I smelled it before it blew. Somebody put coal oil in the supply tank...When I topped up the boiler... *bam!*...Then the powder went...nothing we could do..."

Natchez Jones pulled himself closer to Dancer's ear.

"Dancer…promise me…"

"Anything my friend."

"Promise me you'll get the bastards that did this…."

With those last words Jones fell back lifeless onto the hull of the boat.

"I will. I promise you." Dancer felt his friend's grasp loosen and slip away. *You have my word…Jonesy. On my honor…I will find the bastards. The same as I will find the snakes that murdered my brother Jace.*

CHAPTER 24

ABOARD THE *NEW YORK* after it was checked from stem to stern for any works of havoc General Taylor came to the wheelhouse where Jack Dancer was alone with the captain.

"May I have a word with you Dancer? Alone."

The two figures stepped outside to the wheelhouse railing and faced a black starless sky. A cold wind rose from the west.

"First I must thank you for bringing my command to the *New York*." The General ran a gnarled hand along his upper arm to stop a slight shiver. "You saved my life. And my whole command. I won't forget it."

"Something wasn't right...sir. But it was Natchez Jones who suggested the transfer. All that powder and all."

"I'm sorry about your friend. He was a good man."

"Damn bastards." Dancer pounded the railing with his palm. "A fair fight straight up is one thing. But when those murdering sons of bitches hide a bomb that kills everybody aboard. They deserve to be strung up by their ballocks and burned alive....Who would do such a thing?"

"There is a larger enemy in this fight than the Mexican Army." Taylor paused. "It's a monster of evil and opportunity. All want the western territories. All want the same thing but for different reasons."

Jones…why you and not me? Dancer asked himself.

Taylor permitted himself to look beyond the horizon. "Some want more slave territory to trade and sell more slaves — and that means the wars in Africa will never stop. Still others want that slave territory to counter the political growth of the abolitionist North. Others just want land from the Atlantic to the Pacific to be the United States. They see money building that country. Greed is behind them."

Dancer turned thoughtful. "Then there's the immigrants and second sons and settlers and farmers…and the common men who just want a break…a chance to make a fresh start."

"Not to mention the great European monarchies that put their fingers on the scale to push our fledgling republic into defeat during our first foreign war."

Dancer scoffed with a note of sarcasm. "Wouldn't want to leave the impression that a democracy by the people was a workable notion for their citizens."

"Like those immigrant soldiers and classroom officers they send me." Taylor snorted almost to himself.

"Sir?"

"Here I am going to meet one of the best fighting forces the Mexicans have ever assembled. Half my men are foreigners. Who knows if they will fight? And my West Pointers have never maneuvered units larger than companies despite the months of drill in Corpus Christi. 'Academy Turks' the press calls them. My ass! Give me seasoned veterans any day. Not to mention we have no maps." Taylor ground his teeth.

"No maps? What do you mean?"

"Just that. Here we are waltzing into the enemies' backyard and we do not have a single map of the terrain north of the Rio Grande. Or more important — no map of Matamoros or the Mexican territory to the south. We're as helpless as a blind man in a cage with a bear. How am I supposed to fight a war without maps! God help us."

"Can I ask you something…General?"

"Certainly. By all means."

"Have you heard of someone or something that calls itself 'Wildfire'?"

Zachary Taylor gave Dancer a quick glance. "Yes." He paused as he considered his words carefully. "Wildfire is a group of desperate men. But it's bigger than that. It's an idea…a movement. They want to spread slavery to the new territories. Wildfire doesn't have a leader…no one single man. But they are a ruthless…like a many-headed snake. They'll stop at nothing. Slavery is a battle to the death for Wildfire."

"But you own slaves…sir."

"I own slaves. And I do not apologize for it. But to tell you the truth whether you buy a slave — give them food and shelter and clothes — or if you hire an immigrant for two dollars a week. The cost is the same."

"And the moral cost?"

Taylor considered the idea. "That is a question no planter from Virginia to Louisiana would ever ask."

"Do you think Wildfire could be behind bombing the *Decatur* and killing Jones?"

Zachary Taylor leaned over the railing. Looked down beside the bow in the place where moonlight usually illuminated the foam turned over by the ship's progress. Now beside the bow there was only blackness.

"I don't have any proof…but I wouldn't be surprised. I'll let you in on a little secret…Dancer. President Polk doesn't trust me. Thinks I'm too informal. Not military enough. Says he thinks I may turn out to be a Whig with ambitions. Tarnation! Never held public office. Never want to. Soldiering is what I know." The General's expression turned confidential. "Word from Washington tells me you're a man to be trusted…Dancer."

Dancer shot a look at Taylor. But kept quiet. He knew the old General was looking for information. Revelations. Clues to understand this secret agent he had taken into his confidence.

Taylor continued. "The War Department doesn't usually get everything right. But I trust they are right in this case."

Taylor gripped Dancer on the forearm.

"Thank you…sir."

"Not withstanding that little episode in Charleston with Belle

Ashley…" Taylor smiled. "Dangerous to mix pleasure with business."

How'd Taylor know about that?

"The War Department tells me you're to be one of the primary suppliers to the army in this contest." Taylor paused. "Patronage contracts aren't uncommon in times like these. Count on me—and the Department's money—to see that will happen. But orders or not…if my quartermasters find a single short count you'll be in the fire instead of the frying pan. Is that clear?"

"Yes…sir. How can I return the favor?" Dancer offered.

Taylor cleared his throat. "Dancer…there is one thing you could do for me."

The two men turned to face each other square on.

"My command and I need an agent like you who can move naturally between both sides of the Rio Grande. Somebody who appears to be a profiteer…buys from the Mexican locals…supplies the American Army. Independent. In it for the money. But also a man that can give me intelligence on the Mexicans and those bloody foreign volunteers they keep sending me. What you see and what you hear could be very helpful. Very helpful indeed. Could you do that for me?"

"You've got my word…sir. I'll do whatever I can."

Dancer's mind flashed to Colonel Ashley's impossible mission…and being a double agent for Wildfire. *Before Belle dunked me in the Charleston Harbor.* And the strange note signed by "Mustang" that was slipped into his luggage. *Wildfire? Mustang? Who are they? How the hell am I supposed to find a million-dollar treasure. Grab some documents…and clear out before the shooting starts? And now without Jones at my side. This is crazy!* Dancer kept any mention of his instructions from "Mustang" to himself.

"I thought you could." Taylor clapped Dancer on the shoulder before he eased his old bones down the companionway to the staterooms' deck.

Dancer stared hard into the black sky as storm clouds snuffed whatever stars could give the *New York* a dead reckoning. It was dumb luck he hadn't been killed. Washington expected him to solve a mystery behind enemy lines. Natchez Jones was dead. Jonesy's killer no doubt would be happy to hit Dancer next. And there were Stepptoe's baffling map scratchings.…

Spy? Double agent? Treasure hunter? What kind of a mess have I gotten into this time?

CHAPTER **25**

BREAKFAST WAS CLEARED as S. Thomas Swift finished her eyewitness dispatch on the *Decatur* bombing. The *Brooklyn Eagle*'s first report since her aborted exposé on Josie Fitzwilliam went nowhere. Riveting details enriched Swift's pages. One by one the officers and correspondents drifted into the small morning saloon. The mostly West Pointers were dapper in their dark-blue frock coats. Visored campaign caps. And red-leg trousers. The aroma of New Orleans coffee stylishly brewed in glass French Balloon pots mixed with the smoke of cigars and pipes.

"Morning…Miss." Lieutenant George Meade nodded politely. "May I join you?"

"Good morning…sir. Please do." Swift locked the lid on her glass inkwell. Stowed the dip-pen holder and steel nib in the narrow tray of her mother's traveling writing box. Then took out a pencil and opened her notebook to a blank page.

"Have you given any thought to which way you plan to tell the story of this war?" Meade opened.

Swift cleared a newspaper from the chair beside her. "Tell me from your experience what approach you would suggest."

"Any army on the march is like a big many-faceted centipede. Infantry. Cavalry. Artillery. Skirmishers. Scouts. Topographical Engineers like myself. Fortifications. Then of course there's the command and officers and men. Not to mention the regulars and the volunteers and the fringe with all the teamsters and sutlers and camp followers. Where do you plan to start?"

"Well…to be honest…I'm sure I'd appreciate your advice." *State the facts. Get the details. Be a keen observer. What more is there?*

Meade spoke in a confidential voice. "Take it from me — stay close to the command. They're the only ones that see the big picture."

"What exactly does a Topographical Engineer do…Lieutenant?" Swift asked.

"Topogs?" Meade answered. "We're a select corps. Only forty-four of us in the whole army." He paused then fortified his answer: "We're the eyes out front. We map the land. Survey for natural and man-made features the military needs to know about. Often topogs work alone. We ride out into the countryside and record what we see. Dangerous business. Mostly head work…ma'am…not the guts and glory that fires Major Ringgold there. In a way we're much like explorers. Appraise the unknown. Find a creative response to the enemy's response. Then put it down in detailed notes. We can talk the talk with generals and scientists and engineers. What we know is precious to them all."

"Do you have maps of the area?" Swift asked.

"Not a one…ma'am. Puts us at a severe disadvantage. But that's why the topogs will make the day in this contest. Mark my words."

From the next table Major Samuel Ringgold piped up. "Don't listen to old George…Miss. The real action is the flying artillery."

"Flying artillery?" Swift said. A vision of hot air balloons carrying cannons came to mind.

Ringgold moved his chair closer. "Every infantry regiment has ten companies." He counted off the top ten cards from a deck on his table. Arranged them in a row. "One of these companies is light artillery — what we call field artillery — with fast horses to take them wherever they're needed." Ringgold touched a card in the middle. An ace. "Artillery is always out front of the infantry companies." He moved his ace forward. "Otherwise you'd be galling your own men with your flat-trajectory set at the enemy lines. If my artillery does its job right…the infantry just waltzes forward and mops up the havoc we have wrought." Ringgold thumped the ace with his fingers and displayed the distinctive ring of a West Point graduate.

"If the bastard foreigners don't take a potshot at your back." A sullen Lieutenant Bragg hissed in his high-pitched nervous voice from the corner.

Lieutenant Ulysses S Grant looked at Bragg from across the table. "You've been riding the new recruits pretty hard…Bragg."

"Leave my training methods to me." Bragg's tone was derisive. "Only thing those Irish country sods understand is the whip and the rail. Sure I'm tough on 'em. But without driving discipline and protocol down their throats we won't have an army…least not one that fights on our side."

Grant nodded. "You can be a mean sonovabitch…Bragg."

"You could take a lesson…Grant. Might turn your immigrants into fighting soldiers—like the artillery does." Ringgold poked fun—at Grant's expense.

"Now hold your hosses there…boys." Captain Charles May deemed it necessary to put in his two cents. His knee-high cavalry boots were polished to a mirror shine. "Your guns have their place…not sayin' they don't. But the real hammer that can turn the enemy's flank or slip behind their battle lines and win the day is my dragoons." May swept three jacks forward from the end of the row of cards. The Captain's wheeling maneuver separated his dragoons from the infantry cards still sitting behind Ringgold's ace. May turned to Swift. "Miss…if I were you looking for the real heroes…I'd follow the mounted infantry. As dragoons we're destined for glory. No question."

At that moment Lieutenant Jacob Blake of the Topographical Corps leaned back in his chair. But being nearsighted misjudged the distance to the saloon wall. The chair tilted too far backward. Blake's head smacked the wall with a hollow thud. His chair wedged under the wainscot. Blake was stuck. Suspended in an awkward place—unable to lean forward but held from crashing to the floor. He blushed crimson. Finally fellow topog Meade gave Blake a hand to help extricate him out of his predicament.

Lieutenant Randolph Ridgely of Ringgold's flying artillery cuffed

Blake on the shoulder. "Whatever you do…Miss…give Blake a wide berth. He's not known as 'Dipsy Doodle' for nothing.…Are you Blake?"

Swift broke the embarrassing moment. "Thank you…gentlemen… but I have a different question for you. Tell me. Why should a war correspondent report only from the American side?" Swift asked.

Bragg almost choked on his coffee. Mugs hovered in midair. A murmur fluttered from the officers and the other correspondents. Then a torrent flew.

"Why it's the only patriotic thing to do!"

"Unthinkable!"

"What a hair-brained idea."

"New England readers want New England heroes." The correspondent from Boston chimed in with what he evidently thought needed no explanation.

"The guerillas and *rancheros* would eat you for lunch." This from another mocking reporter.

"If I even asked the question"—yet another correspondent scoffed—"my editor would think I was joking."

James Collingsworth Turner sniffed. "We all need the couriers to take our dispatches to the port. The Mexicans wouldn't be so helpful."

The Philadelphia correspondent almost shouted. "My editor would skin me alive if I did a story about the enemy. 'WHO YOU TRYING TO AID AND ABET!?!' would be his last words."

"There's a good reason no one has ever done it. We know who pays the piper."

Several correspondents nodded in agreement.

"Might be some good sketches on the Mexican side." The shy illustrator from New Orleans injected his comment quietly. Just loud enough to be heard by Swift.

"Imagine a Mexican reporter inside the Alamo." Colonel William Worth—who had been at the mission just after it fell in 1836— seemed to be smiling sympathetically at Swift. "The Texans would have pegged him for a spy before he took out his pencil."

The Picayune's Turner asked: "You're not truly considering reporting from the Mexican side—are you…Swift? If you are…you could have the shortest career in newspaper history!" *If the Mexicans don't kill you that corset will in the Gulf heat.* Turner's repartee brought snorts of laughter from the men who surrounded Samantha Swift.

"I haven't decided." If the correspondents were willing to play charades Swift was game. "I can see the disadvantages—as you say. I just wonder if there are any advantages." *Like a vantage point none of you men have? If I report from Mexico that doesn't mean I'm a traitor. Does it?*

"Believe me…in this war you'll be able to find all the real correspondents in one place." Turner could not resist getting a last laugh at Swift's expense. "That's in the American camp saloon drinking American whiskey with American heroes. Count on it."

⟂ ⟂ ⟂

Within hours the *New York* reached Corpus Christi. General Zachary Taylor assigned a quartermaster to relieve Dancer of his supercargo duties. Then the General went ashore with his command. Followed by the correspondent corps. Already Taylor's orders to advance had been translated into Spanish. Sixty copies of the directives were distributed into Mexican territory. That afternoon the American Army sent forward its first contingents into disputed territory. Major Ringgold's light artillery. Captain May's cavalry. Brigades of infantry would follow.

In Mexico's eyes the American invasion was an act of war.

Later that evening a small flotilla commanded by Major John Munroe steamed toward Brazos Santiago and Point Isabel. With Munroe traveled a siege train of wagons and mules. A field battery of heavy guns. Engineers and ordnance officers. And the army's payroll department. The battle group was covered by revenue cutter *Woodbury*. One of the three ships Taylor had requisitioned in New Orleans to guard his Gulf of Mexico supply line.

Aboard the *Woodbury* two civilian passengers spent a long night as the ship beat an irreversible course toward their fate. But Samantha Smith's anxieties regarding her future sounded as loudly in her restless dreams as Jack Dancer's snores sounded in his rich and peaceful sleep.

CHAPTER **26**

SWIFT'S CABIN / CUTTER *WOODBURY*
RAISING BRAZOS SANTIAGO / MEXICO
9 MARCH 1846 / FOLLOWING MORNING

IN THE LONG HOURS that night aboard the cutter Samantha Swift spent every moment debating her dilemma. In the darkness before morning she jolted half-awake. Damp from a bad dream. Tired from sleeplessness. Something in the darkness frightened her. Out there beyond a terrifying fork in the road. What lurked up ahead? Hidden in the blind blackness? Swift's eyes squinted at a black blotch on the ceiling above her head. An ugly cockroach stared back. When the insect's antennas twitched Swift let out a startled gasp.

The nightmare still gripped Swift. Was it too late to go back? Should she go on? If she did not turn around should she report from the American camp or the Mexican side? The decision had shaken her to the core. Desperate to find her bearings Swift took up her night notes. Scribblings. Pros and cons.

What good is it to go to Matamoros? I'd be isolated on the other side of the river…everything in Spanish…nobody to help me…no one to watch my back. I'd be trapped. A river between me and safety. Cut off from the American camp. I won't know what's going on. I'd be a castaway on a desert island. Worst…I'd be telling the enemy's story. What if the Mexicans win?

I'd have helped our defeat. What benefit is that?

At that moment the cockroach dropped on Swift's bare shoulder. She muffled her scream as it skittered into a crack. Through her shuttered window the night turned from black to gray.

Swift was wide awake.

If I make the wrong choice…everything I've set out to do… everything I must do…will be lost. With the American Army I'll have resources. Couriers to file my stories. The Eagle *newspaper wants heroes. Our dear boys…braving the odds…standing by their brothers. Readers want to know how they lived. Not just how they died. Swift struggled. The competition will be fierce. I've never done this before…not like the working reporters. They're old hands at deadlines. Dispatches. If I stay close to the Army…I'll be in camp with the other correspondents…Maybe I can learn from them…except that pompous ass…James Collingsworth Turner.* Swift clenched her teeth.

What would Father think? Is it too dangerous? Would he not even let me close to the front? Or…would he give in to Uncle Jacob? Marry me off to the first "right" man.…

She shook her head to get rid of the negativity. *Both Mother and Father would be proud of my independence. I can feel them with me. They would tell me it is too late to cut and run. I must finish what I have started.*

A calmness came over Swift. And with that she fell asleep — again dreaming of herself as a war correspondent. But from which side?

CHAPTER 27

THE *WOODBURY* LEFT the Gulf of Mexico behind by midday. Steamed slowly through the Brazos Santiago gap at the southern tip of San Padre Island. In the near distance was Fronton San Isabel—or Point Isabel.

Jack Dancer came up to stand beside Swift as she watched the barrier island slide by and the lowlands of Mexico take shape ahead.

The secret agent didn't give Swift a glance before he gestured toward Point Isabel. "This is where I say goodbye. We'll be landing soon—and the last correspondents who didn't get off in Corpus Christi will go ashore to wait for the army to arrive. The cutter will take me to Boca Chica at the mouth of the Rio Grande. I'll take a lighter over the sandbar and from there head upriver to Matamoros."

Swift gripped her notebook. Absently tapped it against her chin. Her eyes fixed beyond the distant horizon as far as she could see ahead.

"Been a pleasure making your acquaintance. Maybe we'll see you again." *Unlikely given what's in store for this valley. Anyway...I must tackle finding this treasure...and avenging Natchez and Jace.*

Swift shifted uneasily. Struggled with a life-altering decision. Her restless night had proven unsettling. But now she had more clarity than ever before. *Honor my parents…and honor my calling. I must do my best for my father and win back his newspaper. And stand up for myself as Mother showed me how to do. That means get the story for my readers with the best reporting possible from the frontlines.*

A moment later Swift found her voice and spoke with what she hoped sounded like conviction. "I'm going to Matamoros." *There I said it. I'm committed now. And it doesn't sound nearly as dangerous as I suspect it will be.*

Dancer looked at her. His gaze saw the young woman as if for the first time. He was surprised to see she was tall. Almost as tall as he. The smooth skin of her face would tan well in the sun. *You've got spunk. But people surprise me sometimes. Like Jace and Jonesy. Hope this isn't your best worst decision. Who knows? Maybe we can help each other somehow.*

Swift knew from that moment nothing would be the same. Yet she didn't know exactly what to say. To think. To do.

In short order the military and the last correspondents offloaded at Point Isabel. Swift waved to William Beacon who stood apart on shore. He waved back with confidence as he gripped the field bag that held Swift's *Decatur* dispatch for delivery to the first courier. The cutter *Woodbury* cast off into the shallow Laguna Madre. Within minutes the cutter steamed through the Brazos Santiago narrows and chugged south toward the mouth of the Rio Grande.

Within two hours the *Woodbury*'s launch navigated the sandbar opposite Faro Baghdad eight miles south where the Rio Bravo del Norte—or Rio Grande River—emptied into the Gulf. The two Americans boarded a river packet that pushed upstream toward Matamoros. The low banks of Mexico snaked by on the port side of the packet. An identical wall of green brush hugged the starboard side of what President Polk considered Texas. Muddy meanderings of the river in the narrow channel made slow going to Longoreño: the last deep water twelve miles short of Matamoros.

As they stood at the bow of the packet neither spoke. Swift's thoughts continued to race. *What have I committed myself to? How will I prove I'm not a spy to the Mexicans? Will all this even work?* She gripped her valise with its letter of introduction from Mr. Penrhos to the U.S. Consul in Matamoros even tighter.

Dancer finally broke the silence. "Well…nobody should show up in a new town without knowing somebody. If you allow me…I have a friend in Matamoros. Knew her way back in Savannah Georgia… Made quite a life for herself on the Rio Grande…Operates a 'Ladies Hotel.' Her name is Michelena Anoche. Or at least she went by that name last time I was here. Can I give you an introduction?"

Swift looked at Dancer. With a frank gaze she tried to place who he reminded her of. *Dancer is a multitude of things. A man of action. Independent. Clearly a rake unrestrained by morality.* His hands reminded her of that young man at the finishing school before she was expelled. Swift closed her eyes to shake the comparison.

"A 'Ladies Hotel'?" Swift asked in a bemused tone. *I wouldn't expect anything else from you.* "Yes. Thank you. I guess that will save me asking the American Consul." *Maybe Dancer can be more useful to me than I thought. Reporting from the Mexican camp might just work.*

╳ ╳ ╳

As the afternoon sun rose higher the travelers boarded an old mud-wagon stagecoach at Longoreño. Its rolled up canvas side-curtains let in any available breeze—and maximum dust. Soon Swift and Dancer bumped along the rutted track that avoided the tedious crescent-shaped oxbows of the Rio Grande that ran the distance to Matamoros.

Swift tried to imagine what lay ahead. "Dancer…level with me. Do you think my going to Matamoros is a bad idea?" *Maybe some useful advice?*

Dancer answered frankly: "One of the dumbest ideas I've ever heard. But you've made it this far…so who knows? Maybe you'll catch a weasel asleep." *No more chance than a cat in hell without claws. A city princess survive on the frontier? Needy? Desperate? Chaste? I may be wrong…but I doubt she'll last a week.*

"Somehow I'm not reassured." Swift frowned as she rubbed her mother's signet ring with her thumb. *Presumptuous. Arrogant through and through. I must believe Dancer is wrong.*

In the silence that followed the land stretched out flat in every direction. Only the dense chapparal of mesquite and thorn trees blocked their view for miles.

Swift paused then turned to Dancer. Using what she imagined was her new correspondent's voice she asked a simple question. "So Dancer…where are you from?"

Dancer raised his eyes to glance at his companion. "Started out in Charleston. Both my parents died in a Charleston factory fire when I was ten. My younger brother—Jace—and I were raised by two of the toughest…gentlest people you'll ever meet. MayBelle and Tony Holmes. They had about a dozen of us—give or take—at times. All orphans."

The spring air was heavy and smelled foreign. Abruptly the stagecoach jolted. Swift and Dancer both slid hard across their facing bench seats against the side-curtain struts.

When they righted themselves Dancer continued. "It was 1829…or thereabouts. Jace was thirteen. I was fifteen. We all had jobs to support the home. I made a penny here…a dime there. But even the desperate efforts of a dozen urchins couldn't sustain us."

"What did you do?" Swift flexed her hand and remembered Fitzwilliam's threats.

Dancer continued his story without smiling. "I traded working the rich toffs of the Peninsula for the poor riffraff of the Battery. Discovered highfalutin city people can't be trusted like working people who don't get everything handed to them on a silver platter."

Swift bit back a rebuke. *Like some city people whose uncle will steal everything…unless she takes it back.*

"After a few scrapes with the law a magistrate placed young Jace and me with a distant uncle-in-law. Widower. Bitter. Disciplinarian. Commandant of the Charleston Arsenal. I tried to stay out of his sight. That's when I learned soldiering. Horse riding. Marksmanship. Fencing. Explosives…And fell in love with his housekeeper. Sally was French Acadian."

Dancer's face darkened.

"Wasn't long before I pulled a prank on the old man. Embarrassed him in front of his troops. He threw a conniption. Blamed Jace. The old bastard pressed Jace into the army on the spot. Arranged for my brother to be shipped to Louisiana. Then Texas." *I should have objected. Taken the punishment myself.*

Swift could see the anger—the shame—in Dancer's face and clenched fists. His guilt was palpable.

"I was angry as hell. Signed onto the next coastwise steamer leaving the wharf. When I came back…I learned Jace was missing in Texas. And my uncle had married Sally…in fact took her as his mistress. Clearly I had no future in Charleston. So I went to Texas to find Jace. To bring my little brother back…make him safe. Like before. But I was too late. Santa Anna had executed Jace—along with several hundred 'rebel prisoners' at the massacre of La Bahia near Goliad."

"And that is what drives you…Dancer?" *Your hate? Your shame? Your loss of Jace and Sally?*

The double-agent dissembled as he finessed his cover story. "On the trail I saved a Texian from an ambush. Turns out he was Sam Houston—leader of the Texian militia. Scouted and soldiered for Houston and Texas for maybe nine years. Then I returned to Charleston in December 1845. That is…until I got an invitation to do some business in Matamoros."

"Spoken like a true war profiteer."

"War is just an opportunity to buy low and sell high." Dancer lit a fine cheroot. "Think of me as just a wandering prodigal son looking for his fortune…and a little adventure along the way."

"We may have more in common than one would think." Swift turned her gaze as the open-sided coach passed the first peasant dwellings…and then occasional brick buildings…and shortly came to rest outside the gateway of what looked like an old fortress.

CHAPTER 28

MICHELENA ANOCHE clamped Dancer in a bear hug that almost leveraged him off his feet.

"Well…if that don't make a stuffed bird laugh. Jack 'Honey Buns' Dancer. My my my. Just when we thought there wasn't goin' to be any partying in this old town no more. Where you been? What brings you here? How long you stayin'…dahlin'? My…I do have a smite of questions." Anoche stopped short when she saw Samantha Swift come through the cantina door and hesitate.

"Now…Jack…who's this? She's too pretty to be your sister. Is this the little missus?"

"Michelena Anoche let me introduce Samantha Thomas Swift—war correspondent for the *Brooklyn Eagle* newspaper. Miss Swift is here from New York to report the news. She has decided to be based in Matamoros."

"Ah…that is good news." Anoche let her hand slip down Dancer's back past his belt—where her palm paused for a lusty squeeze before she stepped toward Swift.

"Pleased to make your acquaintance…Miss Swift." Anoche held

out her hand in welcome.

"Thank you…and please call me Samantha." Swift's eyes smiled as she shook Anoche's hand.

"Hell…I'll do better than that. How about 'Sam'? My name is Michelena. But everybody calls me Mitch. In this territory you got to make it like a man…or yah don't."

Dancer stepped forward. "Mitch…I promised Miss Swift an introduction because she needs a place to stay. I thought you might accommodate her."

"Absolutely. Know just the room. One of my *señoritas* ran off with a Texian last week. What a waste. But don't get me started. Got just the perfect quiet corner for you…Sam. Got any luggage?"

"Just my valise and *portmanteau*." Swift gestured toward her valise and trunk.

Anoche's gaze inventoried Swift's closely tailored Spencer jacket and corset-sculpted silk dress. "Good. We'll see what we can do about that wardrobe too." Anoche's head gave an appraising tilt in anticipation of the project. Then called out over her shoulder. "Big Tim! Would you carry Sam's bags and show her to the balcony room in the front corner next to mine?"

Out of the cantina's corner came the largest man Swift had ever seen. When he reached down for her valise only two of his huge fingers filled the space where Swift's hand used to be. He hefted the traveling trunk under the other arm.

"Thank you." Swift smiled warmly to the giant man that towered over her.

Big Tim turned without a word. Led Swift past the left end of the cantina's bar. Down a short hallway. Past what looked like a fortified strong room on the left. Then into the bright central courtyard formed by the rectangular building. The sun glared off every surface of plastered adobe over brick. On three sides a colonnade supported a *portale* that faced the open courtyard. Shaded doors to cloistered rooms — each with a slot window — lined the long sides. Barracks style. To Swift's left an arch allowed the colonnade to extend to both corners. From the courtyard the stone Watch Tower stairway ascended the arch to the walled parapet above. Sentries once patrolled the *casamata* arsenal from the rooftop of the one-time frontier fortress.

At each corner of the *portale* colonnade a set of steps led up to a gallery. The walkway served a second level of living quarters. At the far end of the courtyard a passage sheltered what appeared to be stables on both sides. Beyond a heavy iron door Swift could see passersby in the bright sun beyond the square opening. A rooftop embrasure sturdily fortified the gateway overhead. There within recent memory a battery of light artillery pieces had defended the entrance. The courtyard was large enough for a two-horse carriage to turn about easily in the space. The sweet smell of horses infused the air even though the sand had been raked clean recently.

The stairs to Swift's left creaked as Big Tim lumbered up. He emerged at roughly the middle of the gallery. Farther along the walkway a single ornate door led to the only other room. Big Tim made an about-face at the top. Took several strides and put a key into the lock of the room at the front corner of the second level. Swift followed. From that vantage point Swift could see across the courtyard. But not past the opposite rooms and stone battlements that overlooked the *Plaza de la Independencia* beyond. Her view barely revealed the domed Custom House that stood next to the prominent towers of a fine cathedral. Beyond the twin spires a modest bell tower of an old church completed the Matamoros skyline.

"Room." Big Tim stated the fact flatly. "Key." He held it in his outstretched hand.

Big Tim went inside. Put the luggage in a small dressing alcove. Passed the wash basin. Navigated around the foot of a large bed. Opened wide the front balcony's north-facing double doors. Swift marveled at the view of the Rio Grande beyond the wetlands. A knot of nerves again gnawed at her stomach. *Hard to believe. Mexico. Matamoros.* Next Big Tim opened another large window…now in afternoon shade on the eastern wall opposite the door. The incoming light turned the colorful Mexican rugs vibrant in the cool space. Even cheerful. A small table stood between the large window and a conical fireplace with a white painted adobe hearth in the far-right corner. Big Tim saw Swift glance at an arched door on the right wall with carved designs in the native style. He grunted. "Mitch room. Locked."

Swift moved a few steps into the center of the pleasant room. "This will do nicely."

When she turned to thank Big Tim…he was already gone.

Her circumstance struck her. *You know no one here. No one knows you. You are on your own. What would Mother do? No. You must sort this out yourself. Get settled. Figure out Michelena. And Big Tim. And maybe Dancer…if he hangs around. Make something of yourself.*

Swift lit two candles. The waxy smell was comforting. Took out her writing box. As a new moon appeared in the black sky the nocturnal notes of a solitary mockingbird came from the riverside. Its melancholy ballad seemed to mimic Swift's loneliness.

With determination S. Thomas Swift worked into the night to set down her first report from Mexico…about arriving in what promised to be enemy territory.

CHAPTER 29

DANCER RAISED HIS HAND to knock on Anoche's door. Only to find it opened to his touch. Dancer walked into the central sitting room. He turned to the familiar bedroom door on his right. Over the stable.

Anoche was seated on a padded stool. She brushed her rich brown hair before a dressing-table mirror. She was draped in an imported Japanese kimono of transparent white silk.

"Hello…stranger." Anoche breathed quietly as Dancer's gaze admired her supple body and the sensuous curves of her waist and full hips. Anoche's ample breasts stood clear of her light robe. As Dancer locked the door behind him his eyes met her arresting face in the mirror. Anoche glanced up and down at Dancer's reflected image. He slipped off his traveling boots. Shook off his shirt. And stood naked to his waist before her gaze.

Dancer made a slight bow. Then came up behind Anoche. Before she could speak Dancer put one hand beneath her chin to tilt her head back. He kissed her full on the mouth. His other hand rounded her breast then slipped down her smooth belly with passion.

Anoche arched her back. Moved on the bench with smothered endearments…and then began to quiver. Dancer felt her hand reach his neck to push her tongue deeper into his mouth. He lowered himself to one knee by her bench. Smiled tenderly into her face. Then stole a kiss on each breast before he swept Anoche up into his arms as he stood.

Dancer carried her to the great bed. Positioned Anoche's back and hips near the edge while he held her body easily with a hand under each buttock. Anoche locked her strong legs around his waist and pulled him into her. "Ahhh!" Anoche arched her back and grabbed at the bed sheets in passion. "Oh…yes." She moaned as Dancer artfully worked away. "Oh…Yes! Oh…YES!" Quickly the proprietress of the Hotel Casamata succumbed to the touch she longed for. "YES! YES! YES!" She released as passion soon devoured her in breathless bliss.

After the first romp both knew it would not be the end of the evening.

Dancer needed the distraction. *Mustang. Wildfire. Stolen gold. Loan papers. Useless maps. Now that newspaper woman has complicated everything. Not to mention a real shooting war any day. What next?*

The touch and scent of Anoche brought him back to the moment. Pleasure first.

CHAPTER 30

SWIFT STEPPED onto her river view balcony. Her gaze took in the sweep of Matamoros in the morning. Beyond the earth-colored town promenade along the river's cut bank the land sloped away across green flats to the Rio Grande River. The Mexican olive trees virtually sparkled in the brilliant early morning sun. Swift inhaled the air spiced with mesquite and wood smoke. Yet the river was a foreboding green. Somehow dangerous. Swift shivered with dark thoughts about her mother's death. Then unlocked her gallery door. Stepped onto the walkway. And went downstairs. At the bottom step she faced a hallway marked "Saloon." Swift turned left. Walked under the stairway arch toward the far side of the courtyard. Several saddled horses and a two-seat covered phaeton carriage now occupied the yard. Swift ran her fingers along the rough adobe and turned right into the main building under a sign that read "Cantina."

"Sleep well?" Michelena Anoche smiled with an extra bounce in her step. "You will need to be rested for the day Dancer has planned."

"Why thank you…yes. The room is lovely." Swift clutched her notebook and pencils to her chest. *If I'm going to report from Mexico I need background. Sites. Scents. Food. Characters.*

Anoche directed Swift to Dancer's table. Over sweet Mexican coffee and hot tortillas with honey and grated green chilies Dancer outlined his plans.

"Today I have army business for General Taylor at Rancho Valdez…family home of Don Carlo Juan Baptiste. He is the wealthiest landowner in Northern Mexico — and someone I think you will enjoy meeting. The rig and team are ready. We should get started soon. It will take most of the morning. Will you join us? Mitch will be coming. And Big Tim will be here with the supply wagon any minute."

Anoche nodded to Swift's silk dress. "Leave some of those New York petticoats here…Sam. You'll appreciate it when the sun hits midday."

Swift downed the last sugary swallow from her porcelain mug. Hurried to her room to shed some layers. *Dear Reader…your special correspondent's next dispatch is in the works.*

CHAPTER 31

RANCHO VALDEZ was an oasis of fields and pasture and leafy willows that had used the life-giving watershed of the Rio Grande River for over a century. Dancer slowed the horses on the last crest to point out the vast lands below. The *hacienda* itself sat nestled on high ground. Rancho Valdez faced west over a wide plain carved over time by the sudden floods of the river. Swift could only see numerous outbuildings. The main structures were shaded by spreading cottonwoods carefully fed by the *acequia madre*—or mother ditch. From that source a series of intricate irrigation channels enveloped the property like a glittering spider web.

Don Carlo Juan Baptiste was expecting his visitors. Two of his three sons were in the *hacienda*'s greeting courtyard to meet the incoming carriage.

"Welcome to Rancho Valdez…*mis amigos.*" Don Carlo greeted Dancer as he hopped out of the carriage. The older son helped the two women from the carriage. Big Tim navigated the large supply wagon around the carriage and rumbled on toward the *rancho*'s storehouse. "I pray your travel was uneventful. There are reports of guerillas moving in the countryside. War is in the air. Ah…*Señor* Dancer…who do we have here?"

Dancer gestured. "Don Carlo…let me introduce Michelena Anoche…mistress of the Hotel Casamata."

"*Señorita*…welcome. Word of your service to Matamoros precedes you." Don Carlo touched the brim of his hat.

Anoche curtsied and responded graciously. "Thank you…*Señor.* And thank you for the handsome escorts. Your second son — Luiz — has been a welcome guest in our humble hotel…along with his friends."

Don Carlo turned toward his sons. "Yes. Luiz is now twenty-one…and I fear at times more interested in himself than his place. Next to Luiz is my youngest — Roberto — who is nineteen now."

The little brother sat awkwardly in his saddle and blushed as he touched his riding whip to his hat brim.

"My youngest — Roberto — follows his brothers like a shadow." Don Carlo smiled. "My oldest son is away. He missed being with us for his twenty-eighth birthday two weeks ago. But we pray that Diego's travels will bring him home soon."

Dancer gestured toward Swift. "And this is Samantha Swift — correspondent for the *Brooklyn Eagle* newspaper. She's just arrived."

Swift stepped forward and extended her hand. For a moment Don Carlo Juan Baptiste paused. His glance took in the tips of tight-laced boots. The forest-green silk high-neck dress set off the young woman's clear smooth skin already growing golden from the sun. Her visage was surrounded by severe swept-back auburn hair straining to be released. The whole effect was set off by a broad-brimmed bonnet. Although a practical sunshade the bonnet looked comically out of place in this frontier outpost.

"*Bienvenida*…*Señorita* Swift." Don Carlo took her hand in both of his warmly. "Pardon my hesitation. Your presence brings back fond memories of my wife…rest her soul. For a moment there I thought… But enough of old memories. Come inside and refresh yourselves."

The *hacienda* of Rancho Valdez was a long domino of adobe rooms added over the years. The *rancho* faced onto the central yard bounded on the far side by the mother ditch that carried water from the river toward the fields. Large trees rose from the far slope of the fast-flowing channel. The valley fields spread out beyond—into the middle distance.

Don Carlo led the visitors through the estate's double doors. Painted white and trimmed in turquoise. The entry's upper half already opened to the inside great room.

"To the left is my library." Don Carlo gestured toward a peaked-arch doorway. "The Rainbow Room is named for its diagonal *latillas*—those decorative peeled branches in the ceiling above the *viga* beams—that were painted by my wife. She insisted the windows be low to give the best view while you are seated reading." Their host paused as he envisioned a happier time. "To the right from the great room are the stairs to my rooms above. Beyond the study and through those inner doors are the guest rooms where you will be staying." Don Carlo pointed past the stairs. Two fireplaces were the centerpieces of the great room. One in the center wall of the great hall in the native conical style and one at the far end opposite the rainbow library in the squared-mantel style of Spain. Four great pillars of spiral-carved tree trunks supported the massive *vigas* with a dark patina of hospitality. Fourteen feet overhead a skinned-Aspen wood ceiling topped the room with a blond crown.

"This way to the dining room. Watch your heads." Don Carlo led the party down three semi-circular steps to a large below-grade room with red and black alternating pattern floor tiles. Several heavy communal tables were ready to welcome guests. The largest one in the center under a bronze chandelier was set for twelve. Three others for eight. And a round table of four filled an alcove on the right nestled beside a cozy fireplace. Two lace-covered ground-level windows flanked the chimney. "The ceiling *latillas* are painted in earth pigments to be like a woven Indian blanket." Don Carlo pointed overhead. Silver sconces with fresh candles accented the whitewashed walls. The kitchen door at the far corner framed three ladies with large smiles and healthy appetites who gauged the new arrivals. Don Carlo led his guests through the outside double doors to the left. They all stepped onto a flagstone patio shaded by a high pergola covered in green grapevines and red blossoms of bougainvillea.

During the tour Swift took notes in her head. *The nib pen will come later.*

As his guests and two sons took seats Don Carlo made an expansive gesture. "Much has changed in Mexico since Christmas…and much remains the same." He addressed Dancer but the group as well. "As you know little has changed with the Indians—who are now about four million of our seven million population. The *mestizos* of mixed Mexican and Indian blood are now half that—about two million. There are only about one million of us…of pure Spanish lines. As you may know…we sons of the highest *gachupine* are Spanish-born—and own the land. Alas…few of our noble class of *Hidalgos* these days want to dirty their soft hands with real work. That is why political power has drifted away from us into the hands of the *Creoles*—who are mixed Spanish and Mexican blood. So much so that almost every Mexican president in recent years has come from a cadre of *Creole* generals. The latest—Paredes—is one of these."

Don Carlo continued. "These greedy rulers—and their liar priests—have created a privileged elite for themselves. Now both the army and the Church enjoy *fuero*…what you call immunity from the authority of the courts. They think they are above the law."

Unbidden the kitchen ladies served pitchers of chilled lemon water and carafes of red *sangria* wine. Swift asked in Spanish: "Do you think…Don Carlo…there must be…" She hesitated as she searched for the exact Spanish word. "…War?…Fighting?"

Don Carlo nodded gravely and continued in English. "Mexico can live with its own. But the colossus to the north is the bane of our tribulations. Alas…as one of our poet's writes: 'So far from God and so close to the United States.' Now your country sends soldiers into our land. And we are bringing soldiers to Matamoros to meet them… as we must."

A silence fell over the group as a large cloud darkened the entire *rancho.*

Don Carlo broke the silence. "But first we must attend to this afternoon's work." He looked at Swift. "I see you are a student of our language. With practice I suspect the words will come easier for you. Let me ask: *Señorita* Swift…are you familiar with riding a horse?"

"Yes. I rode as often as I could at school. But that was mostly English saddles I fear."

"Good. You will find our Spanish saddle a much more comfortable fit for a full day's ride."

The patriarch addressed his sons. "Luiz. Roberto. Bring around three horses. The large black for *Señor* Dancer. The palomino for *Señorita* Anoche. And the red quarter horse for *Señorita* Swift."

Roberto protested: "But that was Mother's horse."

"Do as I say. We will meet in the courtyard in one hour."

Don Carlo turned back to Swift. "Before we join the *gauchos* in their branding and calving we must get you properly outfitted. Would you all please follow me? I will show you what I have in mind." Don Carlo led. Swift. Anoche. Dancer. And Josefina. The largest of the kitchen ladies. All trooped up a flight of open steps from the patio to their host's private chambers above the dining room.

CHAPTER 32

DON CARLO JUAN BAPTISTE'S BEDROOM had once enjoyed a woman's touch. But now was a man's room. Part bedroom. Workshop. Office. Tack room. Armory. The room's walls gave off a complex aroma. Leather. Tobacco. Gun oils. And hard-ridden horses. Before the large fireplace two chairs were placed. Beside the smaller winged chair of chintz florals were two tables. One with a woman's glasses and sewing accessories. The other with a lady's riding gloves and books of poetry and patterns. Swift went to the table and picked up a small framed watercolor of a serious young woman in wedding attire.

"That is my late wife. Maria." Don Carlo's voice was grave.

"I'm so sorry." Swift's condolences were offered in a quiet tone. "I lost my mother in a drowning accident and my father of a broken heart."

Don Carlo commiserated. "Without my sons…I do not know how I would have carried on."

"How did she die…if I may ask?" Swift studied the watercolor.

"She was returning from a visit to her cousin — the Baroness de Pontalba of New Orleans. On the road from Point Isabel to her family's *hacienda* at Rancho Ramireno on the north bank of the river… The circumstances are not clear. They told me her party was attacked by a band of highwaymen — or Indians. She did not die immediately. They found her body in the chapparal the next day…after the coyotes had started. It has been three years now. But word has come to me from some *rancheros* that there were Creole military men with the band. I have my suspicions.…" Don Carlo's words trailed off into his inner thoughts.

"1843? That was the same year my father died." Swift put the painting back into its honored place. *If you can't take notes remember details with association or a picture. Use all your memory tricks.*

"Yes. In anticipation of my wife's return…I had gathered a wardrobe of presents for her. A welcome home surprise…you might say." Don Carlo turned to Samantha Swift. "You would do me and our family a great honor if you would accept a gift from this wardrobe. As I can see…*Señorita*…you are the same size as my Maria. It would be a great honor to her memory if this wardrobe would finally be put to use. Please — let me show you."

With that introduction Don Carlo opened the lid of a large leather-strapped sea trunk. Out of this magnificent vault Josefina lifted a riding ensemble…after working outfit…after *fandango* gown… after dress upon dress. Hats. Boots. Shoes. Scarves. Bags. Slippers. Even jewelry followed. A veritable hope chest of the finest fashions: Spanish. American. Parisian.

Josefina held up a working outfit with *gaucho* pants and subtly embroidered suede vest before Swift. Maria's favorite helper beamed with an idea. Inspired by the armful of clothes she took Swift to an anteroom. When they emerged Swift turned a quick circle. She had been transformed into a horsewoman of the Spanish gentry. All admired the perfect fit of the elegant yet simple working outfit Josefina had selected. Even the polished-leather riding boots were comfortable. Before the mirror Swift settled the black flat-brimmed *cordobes* riding hat over her long auburn hair. Now on full display across her shoulders.

"*Perfección.*" Don Carlo beamed.

Swift stepped closer to Don Carlo. "I'm sorry she is no longer with you…and I'm sorry you have to live without her."

"She is with me always — and now you bring that memory to life.

You're as beautiful as my Maria." Don Carlo's gentle tones seemed to linger in the room as he stood admiring Samantha.

"Thank you for these unexpected gifts." Swift returned. "But I am a different woman…not that memory. I am not Maria…nor will I ever be."

Don Carlo took Swift's hands in his. "I know…my dear. My Maria would agree with you. Now there is work to do."

CHAPTER 33

DON CARLO JUAN BAPTISTE'S SONS led the string of riders and horses in a fast canter. They moved toward the herds. Smoke from the branding fires scented the breeze. Young boys drove the cows with calves into holding zones ringed by *vaqueros* with their white sombreros and lassos. Swift and Dancer worked their horses among the stock. Separated the male calves from their mothers as needed one by one. The experienced cow ponies knew almost better than their riders what to do.

It was hot and important work. To improve the herd all cows were only bred to a pair of prize Iberian bulls. Magnificent huge meat-bred specimens imported from Spain. Spring was the time when the young male calves became steers before they came of breeding age.

Other *vaqueros* lassoed the calves with their lariats and dragged them bawling to the branding fires. One wiry *ranchero* with his pigging string in his teeth tossed the calf on its side. Then deftly with a knee and one hand gathered into the air one foreleg and both back legs. Faster than Swift could follow he looped the miniature lariat over the foreleg. Then—one-handed—bound all three legs together and finished the last half-hitch knot with a flourish. The wrestler kept a knee on the calf's neck. While another *ranchero* pressed a red-hot "B" brand onto its hip.

Next another *ranchero* cradled the scrotum of the male calf in his left hand. Then flicked a razor-sharp blade upward away from his fingers in a single stroke…which released the testicles into his left hand. With a slight pull he quickly cut the tubes. Dropped the pair into a bucket of bloody water. A fifth *vaquero* slathered the incision with a dark tar substance. Then yanked the pigging string loose. And the steer calf with its eyes bulging in terror skittered off in search of its mother.

As the sun crested high in the sky Swift and Dancer were spelled from their calf-cutting duties. They moved closer to watch the men working near the fire. The branding *ranchero* asked if they wanted to try their hand. Swift stepped up. The cowhand gave her heavy gloves. Had her test the hot brand against a log. Then against a hide used for judging the heat of the irons. Half in Spanish. Half with gestures. Swift learned to apply steady pressure to burn off the hair…watch how the smoke rises quickly then stops…hold for a moment to scar the hide…then release just as the singe turns to sizzle.

Dancer took his turn at castrating the calves. "This hurts me more than it hurts you…little waddy." Dancer winced. He quickly learned to wait a beat while the terrified calf settled before he stuck the sharp blade between his cupped fingers. Outfitted with a leather apron Swift moved in to wield the tar brush. Calf after calf after calf passed through the process. Everyone stepped into a different position in an unspoken rotation. Into this circle Anoche appeared. With clean expertise she worked the blade. Quickly the bloody bucket filled. Together Swift branded and Anoche did her part. Shortly Anoche beckoned Swift to change places. Swift took her turn with the knife. And soon discovered her initial squeamishness dissolved into the precision of repetition. One by one the spring supply of new calves finished their ordeal.

At day's end everyone gathered by the buckboard supply wagon. Washed. Smoked. And quietly talked of the next day's work. With the low western light off their right shoulders the entourage rode back up to the ridge. There they admired the silver beauty of the Rio Grande as it slipped silently through the green valley hugged by willows at water's edge. Then meandered through meadows and pastures and planted fields beyond.

The magpies sang their tranquil evensong as the string of riders rode in silence toward the *hacienda*—now bathed in red-orange twilight.

Yet the coming conflict with the Americans prowled like a wolf somewhere beyond the horizon. A somewhere for Swift and Dancer that felt worlds away.

AL FRESCO PATIO
RANCHO VALDEZ
10 MARCH 1846/THAT EVENING

JOSEFINA AND THE KITCHEN LADIES prepared a special feast. While Swift jotted hurried notes before a perfumed sponge bath. And Dancer rested and shaved for dinner. A great table was set for all on the patio with candles and lanterns giving the scene a glow as warm as the evening air. Special savories and new tableware and utensils delivered by Dancer's supply wagon decorated the banquet table with goods from New Orleans and foreign lands. Don Carlo arranged for Swift to be seated to his left. Dancer to his right. The second son — Luiz — took the other head of table. Anoche sat to his left.

Grilled beef. Spitted lamb. Slow-roasted rotisserie chicken were complemented by *mole*. A distinctively spicy sauce with puffed corn and whole kidney beans. Served with rice. Tortillas. And large squares of steaming cornbread. The bread then topped with a mouth-watering relish of diced red tomato. White onion. Green serrano chilies. And cucumber. All fused into a unity by sharp cilantro leaf. Lime. And Josefina's magic touch. A dollop of honey.

"What do you call this?" Swift spread a double thick layer on her cornbread.

Josefina laughed. "*Salsa picada.* Good…yes?"

Don Carlo smiled. "Red. White. Green. The colors remind us of our Mexican flag...Others call it *pico de gallo.*"

Dancer brought laughter from the group when he told them of the avocado's reputation as an aphrodisiac. "Does anyone know what they call avocados in New Orleans? There the folks call these 'alligator pears.' Whether that is from a mispronunciation of avocado — or it's skin-like exterior — no one is sure." *Either way…it may lose something in the translation.*

Swift found herself confronted by another mystery dish served onto her plate. When she caught Dancer's eye he whispered: "Those are Rio del Norte oysters. Lightly breaded and fried. Very good. Especially with salsa. Somewhat of an acquired taste though."

"Well…I guess we aren't that far from the ocean. A local specialty?" Swift ventured.

"You could say that." Dancer raised an eyebrow as Don Carlo and his sons watched.

Swift sliced the oval-shaped specialty in half. Speared it with her fork. And withdrew the tines slowly from her mouth.

"Hmm…tastes like an oyster. Or a spicy sausage. But seems a bit chewier than others I've had." Swift's expression searched for a connected memory as she worked the morsel in her mouth before swallowing. Then reached for her wine glass. "Where were these caught?"

The boys — unable to hold their mirth another second — split into uproarious laughter. Luiz slapped young Roberto on the shoulder. Michelena clinked both their glasses. Dancer about rocked his chair over backwards he howled so hard.

Swift looked up. Baffled.

"My dear." Don Carlo's voice conveyed warmth even as he was eager to reveal the truth. "We call those Rio del Norte prairie oysters — or *criadillas* — because they *do* taste like oysters. But they are not caught in the river. This delicacy comes once a year…from those calves today."

Swift almost choked. In that instant she realized the joke was on her. *Calf's testicles.* Then turned to the ornate Talavera platter with fork raised. "When in Mexico do as the Mexicans do." She speared another whole oyster and popped it into her mouth with gusto. Followed quickly by a chaser of wine.

Over the glass Swift considered her role in Mexico. *Guest. Correspondent. Invader. Will my presence lead to other roles?* She glanced across the table at the men before her. Don Carlo. Luiz. Roberto. Dancer.

Cheers and toasts and camaraderie rang around the table. And continued into the evening. Before the lanterns dimmed Don Carlo made a gift to Swift of the red quarter horse. "For your stay while you are with us. Maria would have wanted it so." Don Carlo spoke with true warmth.

Swift glowed with thanks. "If I may…I want to name her Peony. In honor of my mother's favorite flower. You are most kind…Don Carlo." Swift rose in her fine boots and encircled the patriarch in an affectionate hug.

CHAPTER 35

LONG AFTER DINNER was enjoyed Don Carlo and Dancer closed the door to the rainbow library for privacy. Important business that held the destiny of the American Army was at hand.

"Don Carlo." Dancer began in a business-like tone. "General Zachary Taylor—the American commander—has sent me to ask for your help. An agreement could be vital to the outcome of this conflict. May I speak plainly?"

"Please do."

"As you know the Americans have established a supply depot at Point Isabel—twenty-three miles away on the Gulf...and will soon build a fort across the river from Matamoros. Taylor's force fields almost three thousand men. As you also know—General Ampudia will soon replace General Payaso in charge of the Mexican force in Matamoros. That command is being reinforced with troops from Monterrey and the south. The estimate is about three thousand men."

"That figure is now closer to four thousand." Don Carlo confided the information soberly. "And is growing daily...soon to be six thousand I understand."

Don Carlo directed Dancer toward a pair of carved walnut high-back Spanish throne chairs that flanked a cold fireplace. Dancer accepted a brandy and sat down on the painted leather seat.

"To transport and feed their men the Americans need mules and oxen and food supplies—especially cattle and sheep—as well as grain and beans. The policy is to purchase those supplies at market prices—not resort to foraging from the local population…with whom the Americans don't have any dispute."

Don Carlo touched steepled fingers to his chin. "The Mexican Army must eat too when they arrive. And they are my countrymen. If I sell to the Americans…my countrymen may see me as a traitor. My honor and my country are paramount. You can understand my position…I'm sure."

"Only if we let them know." Dancer paused. "I have a suggestion. Today when we branded the calves I saw your brand was a 'B.' Brands can be changed. If we added a backward "Ɔ" to your brand it would become a "ƆB"—which stands for Dancer Brothers…my company." Dancer handed Don Carlo a business card with a large "ƆB" embossed in bold letters. "Dancer Brothers—Purveyors of Fine Mercantile—Jack Dancer (Principal)—New Orleans/Louisiana"

The patriarch turned the card in his hand. "Go on."

"We want to contract for enough mules and oxen to pull four hundred supply wagons and cattle to feed three thousand men for a month. In time more supplies will be coming by steamship…as will more men and equipment. But these items are needed immediately. That is why the Americans will pay a fair but premium price. Plus you avoid the *alcabala*-like excise tax on goods sold in the public market."

"We have that much stock—or I can arrange for it within days—if we can come to an agreement. As you know the *alcabala* is an onerous internal tariff that is sent directly to the corrupt national government…whoever that is at the moment. To avoid the *alcabala*—and be able to sell our livestock locally at a premium…rather than hide them and risk cattle rustlers—begins to make your offer interesting. My true concern is for my people. They will lose their sons—and bear the pain of this conflict—more than the wealthy and the landowners. If we were discussing guns and powder that could be used to kill my brothers then I would end the discussion here."

Don Carlo selected a fine Cuban cigar from the colorfully illustrated cedar box delivered by Dancer. With his gaze fixed on the American Don Carlo lit a Ramon Allones creation that featured the prized tobacco of the Pinar del Rio region in Cuba.

"If the Americans win…I have done business with the victor." Don Carlo exhaled. "If the Mexicans win…then I have traded with the enemy. Either way I must protect my interests…and my family and my *rancheros*. What can you offer to help me decide…*Señor* Dancer?"

Dancer lit one of his fermented black-Oscura cigars. "You mentioned your wife's family land—the Rancho Ramireno and *hacienda* north of the river. I understand Rancho Ramireno is the forty square miles that surrounds what will be Taylor's Fort Texas?"

"Yes. That land will be lost if it is confiscated by the Americans. It has been cultivated by Maria's family for more than a hundred years— back to the times of New Spain…before this Mexican Republic."

Dancer gently placed his Oscura in the holster of a smoking tray to let the accumulated ash insulate the burn. "First…many Americans have invested in the Mexican government. As part of any treaty those Mexican debts will be paid in full to the bondholders by the American government. We will make arrangements for you to be paid in full for the land's value…plus twenty-five percent as a reparation payment. Believe me—you won't be alone in those arrangements. Moneyed interests from Texas to New York already buttonholed Congressman John Slidell to include that provision in the minister's first offer to your government."

An outline of a deal began to take shape.

"Second." Dancer continued. "The Americans will arrange for you to 'acquire' the land now held by General Payaso that is adjacent to your property to the east. I understand Payaso has not always been such a good neighbor."

"That Creole snake. Once—in heavy rains—the river shifted course. Payaso claimed what used to be my land was now his land by the 'right of natural contiguity.' More than three hundred hectares! Almost seven hundred American acres! He got his lackeys in the government to seal a large colorful document that confirmed it. I had no recourse in the court because Payaso is in the army and beyond the law. I also have my suspicions…Payaso may have been involved in

Maria's murder."

Don Carlo returned to the business at hand. "Now you are getting somewhere...Dancer."

"Third." Dancer played his last card. "Payment will be in silver and gold coin...not printed money or notes of promise."

"Good." Don Carlo allowed an expression of interest. "But let me ask you. How will you be paid...*Señor* Dancer? And how do I know I can trust you?"

"Don Carlo...you and I are of one mind. We must watch out for our own interests. Not the American interest. Not the Mexican interest. But to watch out for ourselves. To show you my good faith I promise not to collect my commission until the dust settles on this little war. I propose you separate and secret my payment in a place known only to a trusted third party of your choice in Matamoros. That will ensure no collection will be made until the last shot is fired. If the Mexicans win...you get it all. I must trust you—and trust in General Taylor— or I will never see a penny."

"*Señor* Dancer...you have addressed many of my concerns. And shown me how to avenge the injustices of General Payaso. Something I have wanted for three years. If we move quickly—before General Ampudia's regular Mexican Army arrives in the weeks ahead and his quartermasters come calling—I can honorably offer my countrymen whatever livestock I have left."

Don Carlo gave a conspiratorial smile and flicked his extinguished cigar into the hearth. "There is no one more trusted in Matamoros than the good Father Thomas—and his old church provides many secure places to hide a treasure...if you agree."

"Agreed. We will put our trust in the arms of General Taylor—and in the sanctuary of the Lord's house."

Don Carlo stood up. "And make delivery during the calm before the storm. Here is my hand. May both of us earn the outcome we hope for."

Dancer pumped Don Carlo's hand with emphasis. "Don Carlo... I trust neither of us will be disappointed. I certainly didn't come here to go back empty-handed." *General Taylor and Mustang will be very interested in what I've heard tonight. Very interested indeed.*

Two copies of the secret agreement and payments were drawn up and signed. One for Dancer. One for Don Carlo. Only the location of Dancer's payment was omitted. If all went according to plan both men expected the arrangement to remain their personal secret.

CHAPTER 36

CHURCH TOWER
OLD CHURCH/MATAMOROS
28 MARCH 1846/EIGHTEEN DAYS LATER

FATHER DANIEL THOMAS watched from his church tower as the American Army arrived on the headland across from Matamoros on 28 March 1846. Colors streamed and bands played. The Army's march had followed the road from Point Isabel. And halted opposite the northside of town at the Paso Real ferry crossing. Here the Rio Bravo del Norte—as Mexicans referred to the Rio Grande—swept due south. The town hugged the western bank. Within view of the Hotel Casamata the river again bent back 120-degrees to the northeast. This riverbend created a peninsula that presented an ideal promontory for an invader's camp. Protected on the west and south by the river. Partially bordered to the east by a lagoon where the river once flowed. Less than 150 yards separated the American camp and the northeast corner of Matamoros. Virtually point-blank cannon range.

Father Thomas mused the name of his old church was consecrated in the distant past...when the town was called Villa del Refugio. Before it was renamed Matamoros in 1826 after Mariano Matamoros—who was a hero of the Mexican War of Independence from Spain. His church was only a few blocks from where the river flats to the east rose to meet the town. The first buildings sat back behind a rough promenade that followed the bank's natural edge. Today this *paseo* promenade quickly filled with sentinels and townspeople. Curious spectators on numerous nearby rooftops looked across the river. The mood was nonchalant. A midday outing. Yet all the small boats that typically landed on both banks of the river had been taken to the Mexican side.

As both populations watched from opposite sides three young women from Anoche's hotel strolled across the flats to the riverside. Being inconspicuous was not what the girls of the Hotel Casamata had in mind. Without hesitation the girls dropped their clothes at the water's edge. Waded naked but carefully into the stream. As if the numerous spectators on both banks didn't exist. Their playful laughter and splashing soon turned even more heads.

Among the bathing young women was Dolly O'Hara. The tall voluptuous girl was born with blazing green eyes. Dolly stood waist deep in the gentle sideways current. She shook out her long red hair like a cascade over her pale shoulders. In a splash she dunked under the water. Then rose again like a phoenix. With both elbows raised and her supple breasts lifted heavenward the water sluiced over her wet white skin. The glistening maiden slowly…methodically…twisted her dripping locks like a rope behind her neck. Then gently bounced the damp cascade with her hands. Elbows high. She let gravity and the noontime air turn her dancing locks into a personal pendant. A mare's tail that gently swept her back reaching low on her shapely form.

Cheers erupted from the American boys. Some climbed on the shoulders of comrades for a better view. Whistles. Waves. Shouted exhortations of lifelong love were offered. Driven to action three young Irish volunteers pulled off boots and pants and plunged into the river. The trio propelled themselves madly across the current. Like lost lovers committed to unite with the dreamlike vixens on the far side.

Their enthusiastic progress was halted by a demonstration from the Mexican guards. Shouted orders and shouldered rifles forbade them to cross the center of the river. The volunteers blew kisses and threw gestures that the damsels had captured their hearts as the boys returned to the American side of the river.

Exhilarated by their successful foray two of the tawny temptresses excitedly gathered their clothes into their arms. Then retreated with girlish laughter into the bushes on the Mexican side. The third saucy damsel of the red hair and milky-white skin took her moment lazily. Maddeningly slowly she stepped into her skirt. Then shimmied it over her lovely hips. She then lifted her blouse high over her head. Paused. Then shivered into the thin cotton shirt as it clung to her damp arms and breasts.

Dolly flounced her fiery tresses one last time to the delight of the smitten throng. Satisfied. She strolled toward Matamoros. Stroking the lush greenery with a playful touch. Then with a last glance. And a kiss tossed toward the broken hearts on the far bank. The beautiful vixen disappeared into the willows with a come-hither smile as beguiling as her intention.

✠   ✠   ✠

General Francisco Payaso — commander of the Matamoros garrison — was furious. He knew his superiors considered the Americans' invasion through the Mexican state of Tamaulipas to the banks of the Rio Bravo del Norte an act of war.

Before the Yankees' fife and drum had stopped Payaso ordered a breastwork constructed near the Paso Real middle ferry. There a battery of 12-pounder cannons could rake the front of the American camp.

Taylor responded with a forward battery of light artillery pointed straight at Payaso's emplacement.

With an energy that concerned the Mexicans the Americans began furious work on an earthwork fort. Rapidly — as only three thousand men can work — the walls rose with six angled *redan* bastions. Each triangular bastion defended a corner. Two more projected from the middle sides. Dark and airless bombproofs hugged the inner walls below the sheltering bastions. Personal ratholes were dug where a man or two could dive for instant cover. Outside the growing walls of Fort Texas — beside a lagoon — the Americans' main camp settled into a routine of frantic construction and watchful waiting. Tension in the army camp grew with every shovelful of earth. Nearby the Americans occupied the empty buildings of the Rancho Ramireno.

CHAPTER 37

NIGHT AFTER NIGHT laughter and revelry and music rang from
the Hotel Casamata. Dolly O'Hara especially enjoyed men's attentions
at the *fandangos* put on by the ladies of the hotel. More and more
Americans made it across the river under cover of darkness as word
spread of the ladies' lovely charms. None more lovely than those of
Dolly O'Hara. The red-haired Irish goddess — as the Americans called
her — seemingly known by every soldier on both sides of the river after
her bathing demonstration.

Before Anoche's *señoritas* entered the saloon their mistress gave each
a careful adjustment one by one. Victoria received a filagree
tortoiseshell *peineton* comb for her black hair that gave an air of wealth
and flamenco energy. Teresa's deep neckline gained a lariat drop
necklace in the focus of her lusty *décolletage.* "A secret is more
compelling than the truth…my dear." From a delicate chain of gold
draped an Our Lady of Guadalupe medal around the revealing neck of
Sharice — a latte-skinned Haitian from Port-au-Prince…and many
other ports. Anoche tied a traditional woven sash of blazing reds and
yellows and oranges around the wasp-like waist of Gabriella. The waif

twirled merrily to show off her billowing skirt and sky-blue ribbons that ascended her brown calves from her woven-leather *huarache* sandals. Even Dolly—who sometimes hesitated…oddly unsure of herself when not on stage—blossomed with a relaxed air when Anoche gathered her red waves with a simple bow of white ribbon behind her neck.

Anoche smiled at her successes. "Tonight we entertain soldiers from both sides of the river. They are here as our guests on neutral ground. Treat them well. Dance with them all. Drink with them all. And bed them all. Everyone will leave happy. Tonight we dance…and share love."

Two *señoritas* locked eyes and hiked their hems to each reveal an ankle in a mock flamenco dance. Everyone giggled in anticipation.

"Thanks to Dolly's brief swim"—Anoche nodded as Dolly took a congratulatory curtsey—"we will be busy. Remember my golden rule: Business first. Pleasure second. Take your places…ladies. Big Tim… open the door. Let the games begin!"

With that the girls took their positions. Struck their poses. And the door swung open like the dropping of a steamer's stage.

The string *son jalisciense* band with high-pitched *vihuela* guitar and deep-bodied guitarrón—joined by violins and harp—launched into a fast tempo *cumbia* folk-dance rhythm. Sharice undulated from her island roots. Mexican regulars and American volunteers poured inside from the settling darkness.

Anoche took Swift aside.

"Is this your first *fandango*?"

Swift nodded.

"Good. You'll enjoy it. Let me give you a tip. Watch Dolly. See how she works the crowd. Engage. Beguile. Move on. Keep it light with laughter. Do not get cornered with one man. Let them all get a nose of your perfume. Dance with everyone that asks. Favorites will come later…after the drinks are sold."

"Anything I should watch out for?" Swift asked with half attention.

"Only one. Avoid the Irishman name Patrick Harp. You'll recognize him by the bullwhip tied to his belt. Dolly is soft on him. But he's a mean one. He'll try to make Dolly jealous by ignoring her. And pretend to give his attentions elsewhere. Works every time…far as I can see. Just avoid Harp."

Swift looked the stunner in a white Mexican blouse and white cotton skirt hemmed with red embroidery. In a mirror she pulled the blouse down to expose her shoulders. High on her head her luxuriant auburn hair was gathered in back. Held fast by a small white-pearl *peineta* comb. While the main torrent fell loosely across her tanned shoulders. Swift's bright sea-green eyes were delicately accented by a light skin wash that diminished her freckles. *Gives me a natural look…at once confident yet unpracticed.*

Anoche adjusted the neckline of Swift's blouse back above her shoulders.

"You're my guest — not one of my girls. I don't want any of the boys getting the wrong idea. Keep Big Tim in view…and enjoy yourself."

Both women smiled as they gave each other a warm hug.

CHAPTER 38

THE BARROOM quickly filled with thirsty men. Soldiers. Teamsters. Some merchant types. And a few sons of solid citizens. Chairs and tables were moved toward the walls. Dancers took the floor. Anoche hovered near the bar. Big Tim stood sentry beside the front door.

In one corner two Mexican *caballeros* sat with Luiz Juan Baptiste. They drank tequila and admired the *señoritas* dancing together. Through the door walked four American deserters. The last one dripped wet. Without conviction he told Big Tim that his kit slipped during the short swim across the river. All four made a beeline to the bar.

"Whiskey…and keep it coming." The tallest—in an Irish lilt—barked his order at the bartender. A nasty scar ran a raw path from his nose to his ear. His mates closed in around him. The wet one left boot prints across the dusty floor and a puddle by the bar.

Dolly moved in immediately.

"I see you boys like to swim as much as I do." She practically cooed her charming observation.

The foursome turned as one toward the sensuous voice.

"Yes…ma'am." The American stopped—mouth agape. "Aren't you the…the red-haired goddess? I recognize the—hair." The soldier stuttered…unable to take his eyes off Dolly's cleavage.

"If that's the only thing you remember…we need to get you some glasses…soldier." Dolly's greeting delighted the other three soldiers. "I'm the one…and only." Dolly dipped a fey curtsy. "What's a girl to do to get a drink around here?"

"I'll buy." The scar-faced leader was quick to tend to Dolly's offer.

"What do you want?" The other American was close on the leader's heels.

"First one's on me…ma'am." The third soldier saw little harm in following suit.

"Have this one." The wet soldier offered the drink he held.

Dolly smiled. Moved inside the group. Swept her hair—as if in indecision—to spread her alluring scent. She closed her eyes for a moment. Then Dolly slowly recited as she touched each soldier in turn. "Eeny…meeny…miny…moe. Catch a tigger…by the toe. If he hollers…let him go. Eeny…meeny…miny…moe." To draw out the game Dolly added another line. "Out goes one. Out goes two. Out goes another one…and that is you!" She opened her playful eyes and looked up at the tall deserter. "You…sir…shall have the honor to buy me the first drink. But I won't forget a single one of you boys. No…sir. Not tonight."

The tall deserter asked: "What will yours be…little darling?"

"Strong—like you." Dolly batted her lids with a smile. The bartender poured her a house blend of tea and water. For disguise he added a whiff of whiskey from the bottom shelf. Then collected full price from the soldier.

✠　✠　✠

The band hit its stride with another fast-paced *ranchera* dance tune. Instantly wavering *grito* shouts trilled the air. "Aaaayyyyeeee!" Soon the floor filled with a new mix of couples. Some did a *ranchera* step. Part folk dance. Part whatever you wanted. All the girls danced. Swift noticed a solitary young man seated in the corner. William Beacon the illustrator gave her a friendly nod.

"Evening…Mr. Beacon." Swift smiled. "I see you are capturing the *fandango* in a sketch."

Beacon half rose from his chair. Swift settled him with a gesture.

"May I?"

Beacon mouthed something undecipherable. Pulled over a chair for her.

Swift leaned close over his sketch pad as Beacon inhaled the smell of a woman for the first time since leaving New Orleans.

The artist's pad revealed a swirl of dancing figures. The movement was sketched around the edges in continuous lines without the pencil point leaving the paper. In the center was a detailed portrait.

Swift immediately recognized herself in the sketch. *How extraordinary to be the focus of attention.*

"Much better looking than the original."

Beacon blushed.

"Thank you." Swift gestured at the sketch pad. "That's very nice." *Mitch said to enjoy myself. And I think I am. But I'm not here to get a man. I hope that is clear.*

The two correspondents sat side by side in silence. Comfortably. Not needing to feign idle conversation.

"I've been working at a daguerreotype studio across from the American Consulate. If you would ever like to see how we photographers capture real life with the magic of light…you'd be most welcome."

"Be my pleasure." Swift's reply was to the point. *Words and photos are going to make history in this war. Might as well see the future.*

"My pleasure too." Beacon's reply was said in earnest.

Swift gave him a smile. The artist touched his heart to say thanks.

"Perhaps someday soon." Swift smiled to confirm her intent.

☒ ☒ ☒

Dolly and the *señoritas* danced and worked the crowd for drinks. One by one the women drifted off with a man to her barrack's room under the courtyard gallery. Patrick Harp joined the group of four deserters.

"You boys made the right choice. Put that pagan army behind you and come over to a true Catholic nation. How many came with you?"

"Us four and six others I know of tonight." Their leader with the grotesque scar reported this information.

"Good start." Harp nodded. "I'll see you're well taken care of. Let's make sure word of your warm reception by the Mexicans gets back to the others that I expect will be joining you soon."

Dolly matched up a *señorita* with three of the deserters. Well into his drink Gabriela half-carried the damp fourth soldier toward a courtyard room. Her woven sash flipped sassily with every step.

Harp grabbed Dolly's arm roughly and took her for himself.

CHAPTER 39

S. THOMAS SWIFT finished transcribing the insurance copy of her Rancho Valdez dispatch she had written before dawn. Sealed both copies with her signet ring pressed into hot wax. Then inserted the dispatches into separate leather pouches. *Frontier life on a Mexican rancho…dear Reader. You won't get that from James Collingsworth Turner or his other scribblers.*

"What you doin'?" Big Tim asked.

"I'm writing a newspaper story."

"What's that?"

"A newspaper story?"

"No…what's writin'?"

"Let me show you." Swift patted a seat next to her in the cantina but Big Tim remained standing. Unsure.

"Writing is putting letters next to each other. Letters make words. Words tell the story. A writer puts words together to tell a story. Like a bricklayer puts bricks together to build a wall."

Big Tim drew the back of his large paw across his mouth wondering what this meant.

"There are only twenty-six letters. Letters make words. Watch while I write your name."

Big Tim leaned closer to see the magic.

"First is the letter 'T'—like this." Swift wrote a "T" in large careful strokes.

"Next is the letter 'I'…It looks like this."

Big Tim furled his brow. Mistrustful.

"Last is the letter 'M.' Together they write your name: T-I-M. Tim. That's your name in writing."

Big Tim stood holding the paper with his name written large. He asked her to say the letters again. Tried to follow along. Swift gave Big Tim a pencil. She twisted his large fingers around the pencil to show him how to hold it. Then showed him how to put another paper over the first and trace his name in letters.

"People say me stupid." Big Tim blinked.

Swift shook her head. "That's not true. *Those* people are stupid. You know why…Big Tim?" Big Tim stared at the paper with his name on it. "Because those people don't know how really smart you are. *I* know—with practice—you'll be able to write your name…if you want to. I bet those people who said that aren't smart enough to write their names. Not like you…Big Tim."

Big Tim straightened. What passed for a smile came over his face as if an angel had touched him.

"Big Tim…would you do me a favor?"

"Sure. You my friend."

"Would you take this note and these two pouches to the American camp? Do you know Jack Dancer?"

"Sure. He Mitch's friend."

"Find Jack Dancer. Give him the note and both pouches. He will know how to get these into *The Picayune*'s express pouch."

Big Tim set off on the mission before Swift could thank him properly.

Just then Dolly O'Hara entered the cantina. Even heavy powder and combed-over hair couldn't hide the black-and-blue welts and a badly swollen eye. Michelena Anoche confronted her. Dolly yanked her arm free from Anoche's grasp. Vicious words flew between them until Dolly ran away to her room. Tears streaked her defiant face.

⊗ ⊗ ⊗

Outside the hotel in the streets of Matamoros Big Tim made his way through a growing Mexican Army. An Army that itched to defend its homeland against the American invaders.

CHAPTER 40

RESACA HOUSE
UNITED STATES CONSULATE IN MATAMOROS
5 APRIL 1846 / THAT AFTERNOON

U.S. CONSUL JOHN STEPPTOE barricaded himself in the Resaca House like a rat in its hole. When Dancer knocked abruptly at the consulate door Stepptoe nearly peed in his pants.

"*Quién es?* Who's there?" Stepptoe squeaked. "Consulate is closed. *Cerrado.* Go away!"

"This is Jack Dancer. Wildfire sent me."

Stepptoe slid aside the wooden guard over the peephole in the door. Judged that Dancer was alone. Then spotted the food basket he carried. Quickly he unbolted the heavy second-floor door at the top of the stairs.

"Get in here before they see you." Stepptoe mumbled while he pulled Dancer inside. The Consul shot a wary look toward the courtyard below. Then slammed the door. Two dead bolts and a safety bar were thrown into place.

"What took you so long?"

Without another word Stepptoe snatched the basket from Dancer's hands. Ripped away the cover napkin. Gnawed a tortilla-wrapped egg and bean mixture before Dancer's eyes adjusted to the darkness inside.

Stepptoe was a small man with a long nose. Pointed chin. Nearsighted squint. He downed the first tankard of beer. The stink of his unwashed body and slept-in clothes made Dancer recoil. The second-floor consulate clearly had served many uses for weeks. Stepptoe's office. Bedroom. Kitchen. And toilet. Stairs in the corner led up to a third floor.

Dancer gave Stepptoe the letter from Wildfire. The Consul swallowed hard. Took the letter and moved furtively into a corner to read by what light came through a crack in the secured shutters.

"I've been expecting you...Dancer." Stepptoe looked away then back in Dancer's direction. "Did Kaufman give you the map?"

Dancer studied the little man. "I have it. But the chicken scratches you sent to Kaufman in New Orleans don't help."

Stepptoe tittered as he made a quick jig step.

Dancer looked at the frightened creature through narrowed eyes. *He's as mad as an abandoned castaway.*

Stepptoe nervously giggled again as his eyes bulged slightly. "What did you expect? A pirate's treasure map?"

"What's going on...Stepptoe?"

Stepptoe moved along the wall. Paused before he reached two barred French doors inside stout bolted shutters that led to a balcony. Then scurried quickly past the sliver of light.

Dancer struck a calm tone. "Wildfire says they sent you a one-million-dollar loan payment...and they want the documents in return."

Stepptoe's eyes darted from Dancer to a painting on the far wall. A canvas large enough to conceal a hiding place. Then back to Dancer.

"A million dollars? They told you it was a million dollars?" Stepptoe's voice rose to a higher pitch. "Bullshit. It was only one hundred thousand! A million? Shit. No wonder the Mexies want my ass...or yours."

Dancer stared at Stepptoe. "They told me it was a million dollars in gold half-eagle coins."

"Well...it wasn't...my friend. Whoever 'they' are sold you a bill of goods if they told you that." Stepptoe chewed at his thumbnail. "A hundred thousand fits in four strongboxes. Hell. A million dollars would be ten times that. Forty boxes of gold. But that's Wildfire. Send a hundred thousand. Claim it's a million-dollar loan. Then when it's only a hundred thousand dollars…they accuse you of stealing the other nine hundred thousand. You're screwed no matter what."

Dancer shrugged and kept his voice low. "So…what really happened?"

"I'll tell you on one condition." Stepptoe bargained in a thin whisper.

Dancer replied: "Try me."

"I'll tell you what you need to know…if you help me get out of here. I'll make it well worth your while. The Mexicans have watched me now for two months. Feels like house arrest. I haven't eaten since day before yesterday." Stepptoe gobbled down another tortilla like a ravenous prisoner.

"As you know…I've got people who can get you out of here." Dancer stayed calm. "And I'll do that if you level with me right now."

Stepptoe nodded once. Then surreptitiously checked the window overlooking the courtyard. The same dusty courtyard where the American Consul typically kept supplicants interminably waiting. Not a soul sat on the circular stone wall surrounding the large Mexican olive tree. The courtyard was empty. Except for a figure that entered the daguerreotypist's new studio under the *portale* on the far opposite corner.

Stepptoe paced the room nervously. "I knew it wouldn't work. I told them. The whole thing was preposterous. They didn't listen."

"They? What are you talking about?" Dancer demanded.

"My days are numbered." Stepptoe whimpered. "They have me trapped in the consulate."

"Tell me something I do not know."

Stepptoe began to wring his hands. "With that puppet Payaso in command…and now with his *ranchero* henchmen here.…They came to see me about a month ago. They think I know where the gold is hidden. But I don't…you see?"

"Who came to see you?"

"Payaso and that killer of his. Malvado. Antonio Malvado." Stepptoe's small frame gave an involuntary shudder.

"Tell me what happened." Dancer was determined to press on. "I can help you."

The man collapsed into a side chair. "The gold was delivered in early February." Stepptoe began haltingly as he took another gulp of beer. "I kept it here in the consulate. Stood guard the whole first night. But somebody came to break in. I'm sure I heard them. Sounds on the stairway. Tried the door." His frightened eyes twitched then glanced toward the room above. "So next day I moved the four strongboxes to the Custom House…It's the only safe place for that much money in Matamoros."

"What happened?"

Stepptoe's words tumbled out faster as he grew more nervous. "Later that day I heard the teamster who delivered the gold was missing."

"What happened?"

"They say he must have been ambushed driving back to Longoreño. Never found the body… Maybe the vultures ate it…who knows? All they brought in was his head with one ear cut off."

Dancer frowned. "Do you think Payaso sent his cronies after him to find where you kept the key to the strongboxes?"

Stepptoe shrugged unconvincingly. "Your guess is as good as mine."

The little man opened another beer. "The next day I went to check on the gold. I just wanted to be sure it was safe and sound." Stepptoe tilted his head as he paused. "When I got there all four strongboxes were gone!" Stepptoe fell back—exhausted and beaten. "I demanded an explanation from Payaso. That loan was for the Mexican government not the local *commandante*…I told him! He laughed at me. But he stopped laughing when I said there wouldn't be any more money paid on the deposit unless I had the official loan documents. That got his attention. Greedy clown." Stepptoe spit the words.

Dancer shook his head. "So you let them keep the four strongboxes—if they gave you the documents verifying a million-dollar loan?"

"What could I do? It was supposed to be a loan. The money was delivered. At least I'd have the papers to show for it."

"You think Payaso and his men stole the money?" Dancer pressed.

"Think? I know it!"

"How do you know?"

"Because they showed me where they hid the strongboxes! You know the cathedral the Creoles built between the Custom House and the old church?"

"Of course. They say the Creoles wanted to humiliate the old Hidalgo church with a grand monument to their power. Looks like they did a fine job. No expenses spared."

Stepptoe jumped at the sudden noise of a wagon passing outside. "They built a passage…a tunnel."

Dancer settled into a leather chair to encourage Stepptoe to keep talking.

"That's how they did it. That's how they stole the money from the Custom House. I do not mean just Wildfire's hundred grand. I mean hundreds of thousands…maybe millions. The Creoles forced the merchants and ranchers to pay an excise tax."

"The *alcabala*." Dancer's tone was soft. Knowing.

"Right again! The Creoles were siphoning off the tax money. That's why they needed the cathedral. Not because they were worried about saving souls. Holy shit…no. They used the construction as a cover. What they really built was a passage to get the money out of the Custom House."

"That's why they built the cathedral next door." Dancer nodded.

"Exactly! What better cover than a cathedral when what you want is a damn tunnel? Anyway…I bluffed. I told them they could kiss the rest of the million dollars goodbye unless the four strongboxes were recovered. That's when they showed me the passage — and where they had hidden the chests in the catacombs of the cathedral. Payaso gave me the loan documents in exchange for the key to the strongboxes."

"Then you went back later to see for yourself?"

Stepptoe cracked his knuckles nervously. "Anyway…I went back two days later while Payaso and his officers reviewed their troops at Fort Paredes. Used a secret second key."

"The same secret key that got the teamster killed?"

Stepptoe's face reflected indifference rather than remorse. "I opened the padlocks on each strongbox. But the boxes were empty! The money was gone! Poof! One hundred thousand dollars gone…I tell you! I didn't know what to do."

"Sounds like the robbers got robbed."

Stepptoe stole a glance out the window. Cowered away from the light. Then pulled the curtains closed. "But that's not the strange thing."

Dancer waited.

Stepptoe paced back and forth like a hunted animal. "I don't understand. The money was gone. But all four strongboxes were still there! Still locked!"

"Why would Payaso or the thief take the money and leave the strongboxes?" Dancer asked.

"To frame me...of course! They must have known about the second key! I swear to you. It wasn't me. I didn't steal the money. I almost fainted. You could have knocked me over with a feather." Stepptoe choked.

"I bet the Mexicans had something else in mind besides a feather when they found out." Dancer leveled Stepptoe with a look. "Who *did* steal the gold...you?"

"Do I look stupid? You don't want to mess with Payaso's boys over gold. But that's just it. I don't know! It could have been the Mexican generals. The bandit *rancheros*? It could have been Wildfire. Who knows? The point is...the Mexicans think I stole it! But I tell you — somebody else stole it. You've got to believe me." The Consul pleaded pathetically.

"You're a marked man."

Stepptoe wrung his hands and shot Dancer a pitiful that's-not-funny look.

"So when did you make this map?" Dancer took out the parchment base map of Matamoros that Kaufman had given him.

Stepptoe's eyes narrowed. "When the gold arrived....I made that map to confirm receipt and that I put the gold in the Custom House. Then sent it to Wildfire in New Orleans by steam packet. I figured I needed some proof in case something happened to the loan documents."

Dancer considered the Consul's story. "Now Wildfire thinks you stole the money...because you made this crazy map. And Payaso thinks you stole the gold...because you're the only one with a second key to the strongboxes."

Stepptoe chewed another already-raw fingernail.

"But this map is useless." Dancer shook the creased parchment at Stepptoe. "All it has is shapes. This 'M' could be the Rio Grande. Who knows? These scratches could be streets. Or buildings. Or landmarks.

Or—anything. But there aren't any directions. No words. No clues." Dancer's anger was evident.

Stepptoe hesitated. He dropped his voice to a knowing tone. "That's because there is a second map."

"What?"

Stepptoe led Dancer to the farthest corner...away from any window or door. "I made a blind overlay map before I sent the base map to Kaufman. Then—after seeing where they stashed the money in the catacomb passage—I revised the overlay map. It's an old diplomatic trick. As you can see—that base map is drawn on parchment. The overlay map is on transparent tracing paper. The second map has the legend. The symbols. The keys you need to read your base map. Without the second overlay map the first map is worthless...and vice versa."

"So where is the overlay map?" Dancer asked.

Stepptoe's eyes flitted toward the large painting. Then toward the upstairs room. "Let's say it's in a safe place...along with the second padlock key and the loan documents."

Dancer nodded. Kept his voice low. "Something tells me your two maps and the mystery of the keys aren't the whole story."

"When I returned from Point Isabel after dispatching the parchment map to Kaufman I discovered the consulate had been broken into. Not exactly broken into like a burglar. I mean somebody had been inside who had a key....Nothing was missing—but I could tell some things weren't in their right place."

Stepptoe's eyes shifted toward the frame on the wall. Then stared disconsolately at the ground. "Payaso only knows I have the loan documents. But nobody knows about the overlay map...or the second key."

"Sounds like we have something somebody wants...."

"What do we do?"

"Whoever we're dealing with...something is holding them back." Dancer's reasoning seemed incontrovertible. "Payaso can't come for you because that would expose his tax money racket. The Creoles want more payments. Varmints like Malvado or Wildfire's henchmen don't know where to look...nor exactly what they are looking for. That's why they didn't take anything when they were here."

Dancer answered the question in Stepptoe's expression: "You sit tight. Try to act normal. Put on a little show of business as usual. Show the flag. I'll make arrangements to get you out of here."

"You can do that?" Stepptoe sounded hopeful.

"Business as usual. It may take two or three days. You'll be okay. I'll send word as soon as everything is arranged. You've got my word." *For whatever that's worth in this godforsaken rattlesnake pit.*

U.S. Consul John Stepptoe almost cried with relief.

CHAPTER 41

PRIVATE PATRICK HARP did nothing but watch as the lieutenant ordered Harp's fellow Irishman stripped half-naked and tied to a cannon wheel.

"Let this be a lesson to every one of you Micks and Dutchies!" The officer screamed mercilessly as he addressed his charges. "A soldier's discipline is the Lord's will. Every misstep will be punished until you do as I command! This man fell asleep on guard duty last night...*and* he was out of uniform." A sergeant held up the victim's jacket cuff. Many knew it had been ripped while scrambling up the riverbank to reach yesterday's *fandango.* The West Pointer pointed triumphantly at the jacket. "This is why he will get twenty-five lashes. Do you understand?" The lieutenant's face turned a peculiar shade of purple as he shrieked.

The assembled troop of foreigners in U.S. Army uniforms stood rigidly at attention. They knew the example would be followed by days of wretched rations. Anything to drive home the lieutenant's sadistic point. The sergeant at arms uncoiled the lash. Deep brown from the dried blood of previous floggings. A drum roll began.

The officer ordered: "Lay into it with a will...Mr. Lancaster."

Even the rising drumbeat could not muffle the anguished screams of Kelly the Weasel as the cat-o'-nines sliced his back into a bloody hash. Until he lost consciousness.

Patrick Harp made a promise. *I'm going to kill you...Lieutenant. I don't know where. I don't know how. But you will die for this...and it will be painful.*

Chapter **42**

S. THOMAS SWIFT counted the days. Imagined the map. Nine days had passed since Dancer sent her first true frontline dispatch from Matamoros on a relay race to New York. The war news traveled with *The Daily Picayune*'s express rider to Point Isabel. Then steamship to New Orleans. Next by steam packet to New York City and hand delivered to the *Brooklyn Eagle*. The exclusive news from Mexico would electrify the streets. *If my story makes it there first.* Swift's gaze was drawn beyond the Rio Grande and into the far distance.

"Read all about it! War news from Mexico! *Eagle* Exclusive!"

Swift imagined multiple editions snapping off the presses that same day. Newsboys sold out. Empty-handed the enterprising street sellers raised the call of the next edition coming within the hour: "News from Mexico! Special Edition! Get it here first!"

Battle Lines Drawn On Rio Grande
Mexican Preparations For War
Enemy Galled By Stars & Stripes
General Taylor's Reply: Fort Texas
MATAMOROS MEXICO — 28 MARCH 1846. General

Zachary Taylor and the Army of Occupation arrived today on the banks of the Rio Grande River (locally referred to as Rio Bravo del Norte) to establish Fort Texas and the American position on the north bank. Your correspondent watched from the rooftop of a hotel as the American colors flew in the morning breeze and strains of the regimental bands playing "Yankee Doodle" reached across the 150-yard river that separates the two nations.

In the afternoon General Taylor composed a communication to General Francisco Payaso — his Mexican counterpart — and ordered his second in command Colonel William J. Worth to carry the message to General Payaso.

Colonel Worth and five aides proceeded to the American bank under a white flag. When the Mexicans saw the signal they sent a party of two cavalry officers and your correspondent as an interpreter in a small boat. (For — dear Reader — this correspondent has placed your intrepid scribe deep within Mexican territory to faithfully bring you the war news firsthand.) What transpired next is set down as conversation exclusively for the Brooklyn Eagle *readers as best memory and history can recall.*

When the Mexican officers returned to their side with word that the American second in command wanted to deliver a letter from Taylor to Payaso the Mexican General refused. Payaso was affronted because his honor would agree to nothing less than a commander-to-commander meeting – not to receive a letter delivered by a subordinate.

Instead Payaso allowed his second in command — Brigadier General Romulo Diaz de la Vega — to meet with Colonel Worth.

Thus summoned Worth and five aides crossed – this time to the Mexican side. As the only war correspondent on the scene your reporter recorded the parley.

With courtesy and respect de la Vega received Worth… who exhibited Taylor's dispatch intended for Payaso. Worth requested your correspondent read the letter aloud to de la Vega — but took care not to hand over the document.

From the outset the positions of the antagonists were clear — and opposed — as one would expect of the American and Mexican views.

Speaking for Payaso — General de la Vega told Colonel Worth the Mexicans regarded Taylor's march through the Mexican State of Tamaulipas — the disputed territory between the Nueces River and the Rio Grande — an act of war and demanded the Americans withdraw immediately.

For the Americans — Worth responded his government considered the Army to be occupying its own territory and would remain there "whether rightfully or otherwise" until ordered by superiors in Washington to withdraw. The question of disputed territory and borders was one to be settled by the two governments…according to Worth.

Worth then added that he was sent as a messenger – not a negotiator – and if he could not deliver his message in person to Payaso that he would withdraw the letter. "I have allowed it to be read to General de la Vega as a simple courtesy." What happened next this author recorded in notes only minutes after the exchange — when the scene and words still rang in recollection.

General de la Vega bristled. "If Mexican troops marched into United States territory how would the Americans view the matter?"

Worth deflected the charge by quoting an obscure proverb. "'Sufficient unto the day is the evil thereof.'" General de la Vega ignored him — or didn't understand the words. Worth then added the Americans would deal with such an occasion when it occurred.

Worth continued to press de la Vega on other points.

"Is the American consul at Matamoros under arrest?" Worth asked.

"No."

"Then I demand to see him."

General de la Vega made no reply.

"Has Mexico declared war against the United States?"

The General replied with a single word. "No."

"Are the two countries still at peace?"

"Yes."

"Then I demand to see the consul of my government."

At that point de la Vega sent a messenger to Payaso with Worth's demand. He soon returned with a rejection of what Payaso called a "request."

At this impasse the parley ended. Worth invited the Mexicans to send a courier with Payaso's reply—who he promised would be received by General Taylor in person. General de la Vega then complained at the sight of the Stars and Stripes flying over Mexican territory. Worth said the American flag would remain and that any incursion by Mexican forces on the north bank of the river would be considered an act of war.

Worth and his party returned to the American camp. With only the shallow Rio Grande separating the two armies the tinderbox of war only needed the first spark.

S. Thomas Swift

War Correspondent

Special to the **Brooklyn Eagle**

PART III

AMERICAN BLOOD
ON AMERICAN SOIL

to Resaca de la Palma
to Point Isabel
Mexican Mortars
Chapparal
Mexican Artillery
to Rancho Ramirene
Fort Texas
Rio Grande / Rio Bravo
Middle Ferry (Paso Real)
Payaso's Battery & Breastwork
Ringgold's Battery
Upper Ferry (Anacuitas)
resaca / wetlands
Matamoros 1846
Fort Paredes
Resaca House
New Cathedral
Paseo Promenade
Old Church
Hidalgo Plaza
to Gulf
Cabildo (Town Hall)
Hotel Casamata
Presidio (Payaso's Headquarters)
Custom House
Plaza de la Independencia
Palacio de Armas (Arista's Headquarters)
N
Hotel Casamata
1. Gateway
2. Stable
3. Courtyard
4. Barracks
5. Portale Steps
6. Tower Stairway
7. Watch Tower
8. Cantina
9. Saloon
10. Strong Room
7.
8.
9.
10.
6.
5.
5.
4.
3.
4.
2.
1.
2.

CHAPTER 43

BELL TOWER
OLD CHURCH/MATAMOROS
7 APRIL 1846

FATHER DANIEL THOMAS lived life through his Matamoros parishioners. To all and sundry who would listen he poured forth their woes in a constant homily of reassurance. "For the *rancheros*" — Father Thomas was fond of repeating — "they all have two homes. Their hovel and the church." Over the previous four weeks Swift had grown fond of Father Thomas. Life in Matamoros slipped into an almost comfortable routine — as the years in Mexico had done for the Welsh priest.

As a poor youth in North Wales Daniel Thomas was first apprenticed to a woodblock printmaker. When that master died Thomas apprenticed to an Irish watchmaker. Then Thomas discovered the Catholic Church and his true calling in the priesthood. That service took the Welshman to Mexico.

Father Thomas's old church was complete although never truly finished. Yet the great cathedral of the reformed Creoles overshadowed it. The cathedral's two brick towers rose high over the narthex foyer. Combined with the opulent dome of the Custom House next to the cathedral the two buildings defined the Matamoros skyline. All three structures—the Custom House…the cathedral…and the old church—faced the open Hidalgo Plaza to the west. To the east only a block or two of adobe structures and a row of warehouses separated his church from the *paseo* promenade along the riverbank—where his flock strolled under a line of trees after Mass on Sunday.

Father Thomas was a small man who at times was almost hidden at Mass behind the Holy Altar and its giant Bible and golden chalices. Always dressed in the heavy cowls of his calling his shining eyes gave the impression of a much larger presence. After their first meeting it occurred to Swift that Father Thomas reminded her of a favorite fairy tale by the Brothers Grimm. A story her mother read to her every time she insisted. Like the hardworking shoemaker in *The Elves and the Cobbler* Father Thomas busily scurried about. Always cut the leather for tomorrow's work. Always surprised to find the shoes completed. With little to give the cobbler always clothed the elves for their help. Father Thomas's generosity and lack of elves always left him behind—and always in a hurry to catch up.

The Welsh priest made things worse by carrying three pocket watches. One timepiece set each day with the noon sun showed the hour in Matamoros to officiate Mass. One displayed an hour Father Thomas imagined was the time in Rome—to be closer to the Holy Father. And a third kept a time the priest fancied was a match for the Bangor Cathedral in Wales with its church mice carved in the woodwork. This last timepiece allowed Father Thomas a perpetual touch with his home clan in County Gwynedd.

The priest was forever mistaking one watch for the other.

✠   ✠   ✠

Samantha Swift enjoyed the coolness and peace of the Matamoros church. She admired the detail in the sculptures that created the Stations of the Cross. The carved oak altar and the filigreed side screen were works of grace. From above great transcendent ladders of light traveled down to the fitted limestone pavers of the nave. The shafts with drifting particles of dust appeared to the scatter of prayerful believers as a celestial stairway—faithfully substantial—that someday would take them to a heavenly peace high above their world of toil.

"My child." Father Thomas spoke to Swift in Welsh-accented

English. "Welcome again. May our Lord be of service?"

Broken from her reverie Swift turned to greet the small priest with the bright eyes.

"Father. Good morning. I was hoping you could help me gain a better understanding of the people of Matamoros…if you have time."

"My child…time is all we have. Come. Let me show you our old church and give you a perspective on our town from its bell tower."

They climbed the rough wooden stairs that grew narrower and steeper as they rose toward the bells. Ever higher Father Thomas guided the correspondent. With every step she learned more of the place where history was soon to be made.

"In the boom times ten years ago the population swelled to fifteen thousand…but taxes and disputes over Texas independence withered our fortunes. Those troubles reduced the residents to only seven thousand. Now with the American Army arrived many have fled south. Today the residents number" — Father Thomas guessed — "maybe two thousand. Yet their numbers are quickly being taken by the arriving troops of the Mexican Army…if troops can be considered residents."

When the pair pushed the bell-tower trap door open the diminutive priest led Swift onto the carillon platform. The small space was dominated by three huge iron bells. At the stone balusters Swift scanned the lands before them that surrounded Matamoros.

And opened a fresh page in her notebook.

To the north the winding path of the Rio Grande River flowed west to east as it worked its way toward the Gulf of Mexico. Three blocks to the east the *paseo* promenade meandered along the right riverbank past the *resaca* bridge that led down to the middle ferry of Paso Real. There the road to Point Isabel was now crowded on the opposite left bank by the Americans' Fort Texas. About three miles upstream — to their left — the upper ferry known as *Las Anacuitas* was defended on the Mexican side by Fort Paredes. Recently renamed to honor the latest Mexican president.

Father Thomas pointed with both arms beyond the river into the space between east and north. "The two roads from the Matamoros ferries travel through the lands of the Rancho Ramireno. Three miles from the river the two tracks converge like an 'X' about a mile south of a place called Resaca de la Palma. From the crossroads the left-hand road runs north all the way to Corpus Christi."

"That was the path the Americans used coming south?" Swift noted.

"Yes. From that crossroads — if you follow the right-hand road northeast through the Resaca de la Palma and past a pond called Palo Alto — you will come to Point Isabel in about twenty-three miles. Just before Palo Alto another track strikes off southeast past the Hacienda Ramireno to Longoreño on the Rio Grande — perhaps twelve miles as the crow flies from Matamoros — where you came ashore with *Señor* Dancer."

"How do you know how I arrived…Father?"

"It was the talk of the town. Many Mexicans trade openly with the Americans. Among them are spies. These spies regularly report on the American movements and strength. I am amazed at the detail of their knowledge. They laugh at the Americans for being so naive."

Swift's gaze focused on the river separating Matamoros from Fort Texas. "Sometimes I think I'm missing the real story in the American camp. I'm so isolated over here. It's like living in another world. I wonder if my work is valuable…or even if my dispatches are getting through to my newspaper. Every time I think of that *Picayune* reporter beating me to the real news…it makes me worry even more."

"My child…sometimes barriers in life are more in our minds than our Lord's creation."

Swift looked north of the church tower…past the Resaca House and the U.S. Consulate. Then her eyes swept northwest to the rows and rows of tents and Mexican military activity that surrounded Fort Paredes. The scene seemed to stretch to the horizon.

"That land to the west near the river is held by General Payaso." Father Thomas paused. "I think you know…farther upriver — beyond that cluster of large cottonwoods — is the Rancho Valdez of Don Carlo Juan Baptiste.

"Yes. We visited Don Carlo. A very generous man." Swift stroked the suede riding vest that had become her favorite.

Father Thomas continued: "Matamoros contains two churches. This old mission…and the grand cathedral you see next to us."

"Who built the cathedral?"

"The backs of the *rancheros* and townspeople." The Father's voice was laced with a touch of bitterness. "They were virtual slaves. 'For the good of God' they are told. But the people were used as slaves to build the church—or if they refused as conscripts for the army."

"But who was behind the building?" Swift probed. "Surely your old church is enough for the people."

"Our church was built decades ago by the Hidalgos. The pure-blood Spanish-born nobles. Then the Creoles—the mixed-blood Spanish-Mexican usurpers—wanted to build a larger cathedral that sent a message to the people. The Creoles wanted to humble the Hidalgos before the people. That jealousy is what built the fine cathedral."

Swift took notes intently. "Did the money come from the excise tax? What did Don Carlos call it? *Alcabala?*"

The foreign priest gave a slight nod of his head. "That is why construction went so quickly fifteen years ago. The Creoles used some of the money for bricks and timbers. Some said men from America supported the early work...but one cannot be certain. See there—beside the cathedral nave to the south. Facing the plaza. That dome is the Custom House—where the taxes are held."

Swift looked down at the glistening Custom House beyond.

Father Thomas continued. "Most of the houses in town are built of cane stalks. Plastered with mud. And thatched with grass. I fear the roofs are nothing more than kindling waiting for a flame. As you see Matamoros has few gardens...and those are without fruit of any kind. The scarcity of rain is to blame—and the difficulty of getting water the great distance from the river."

Swift's gaze strained to follow the road west from Matamoros toward Monterrey 180 miles away. One of the most heavily fortified cities in Mexico.

"How has the arrival of the Mexican and American armies changed the city?" Swift asked.

"Sometimes I am baffled." The small priest frowned. "Of course the soldiers will someday meet in battle. But on the streets for weeks now there has been peace...uneasy as it may be. Especially the Mexican *rancheros* and the American volunteers seem to find common ground. Not so much the regular soldiers in their proper equipment and uniforms. Often the American volunteers are attired in the most curious clothing. Many affect varieties of palm-leaf hats. I suppose in honor of Taylor's famous straw hats." Father Thomas smiled to himself. "Both armies are made of simple men."

"I've seen they put the sugarcane to more use than just making roofs." Swift smiled to herself as she scribbled.

"Yes. Despite the heavy taxes the authorities put on its sale…cane liquor has Satan's appeal. It twists their senses. I've seen this demon swing the *rancheros* from drunken furies to tearful sentiments as if their souls were unhinged. Some unfortunates forayed beyond their groups. Where their numbers gave them safety. They wandered into the darker byways where the outlaws—like Antonio Malvado and his cutthroats—took them one by one into outlying areas…where some became food for the wild dogs and carrion crows."

Father Thomas gestured south and west—where the hovels stopped and the thorn scrub began.

"We are blessed that the soldiers are behaved in my old church. What is most remarkable about the Mexican men is their respect for women. Which is part of their culture. The American volunteers are sometimes a different story." Father Thomas shook his head sadly.

Swift agreed. "I have seen that for myself at the Hotel Casamata. Men need women it seems. Yet among those girls I have met…many have the fondest hope to catch one of their suitors before the army retreats so they will be taken to the United States more or less married."

Father Thomas chuckled as he gestured to descend the rustic bell tower steps. "True. I understand the Americans love to dance and call the girls their *señoritas*."

Shortly the correspondent and priest stepped into the north aisle facing the Ladies Chapel.

"As much as I love engravings and watches…they are just things. Beautiful…but just objects. My true mission is the people. That is what drew me to the Church…and doing God's work." With that Father Thomas gave a soft laugh—as if he smiled at himself with humility and irony. At the tower doorway the priest reached inside a locked tithe box to get a richly colored lithograph print.

"Must run. There is a lad that has dropped out of school." Father Thomas recalled his task distractedly. "He is talking about joining the army…and I must take him a special print of the Blessed Virgin…and comfort his mother…before it's…" Father Thomas looked at one of his watches. Then slipped the colorful gift into his sling pouch. "After all…before I became a priest I was a watchmaker…and before that…a printmaker. Both—when done well—can give timeless pleasure." With that mission Father Thomas prepared to take his leave. Then paused as he absently fingered a ring hanging from his wooden cross.

"Oh…by the way…Father." Swift raised a finger as the good shepherd turned toward her. "Could you help me with one last request?"

"Any way I can…my child."

"I want to interview General Payaso. Do you know how that could be arranged?"

"Payaso is one of the Creoles who built the cathedral. A needlessly proud man. He sometimes comes to Mass here. I may see him tomorrow morning. He will ask me your purpose."

"Tell him I want to tell his story. The story of this dispute from the Mexican point of view. No one has told the Mexican story…and it needs to be shared with the world before—"

"I understand. Before the horror begins. I will do what I can." Father Thomas nodded quietly to convey his promise. "May I send word to Mitch's hotel?"

"You know Mitch?"

"My child." Father Thomas spoke with a mischievous twinkle. "The privacy of the confessional is the heart pulse of Matamoros." With that the robed priest quietly padded past the confessional booth and out the north door on sandaled feet.

CHAPTER 44

UNKNOWN TO SWIFT Dancer had entered the church. Alerted by voices from the bell tower he saw the priest and Swift descend the last tower steps. Not wanting to be seen by anyone Dancer slipped into the back of the confessional — where the priest normally sat — before Swift and Father Thomas turned that direction.

Swift tried to sort the information from her interview with Father Thomas. Feeling the need to quiet her thoughts — and be alone — Swift stepped into the parishioner's confessional booth to have a talk with herself…with only God as her witness. Silent thoughts tumbled through her mind…The break with Uncle Jacob. *Something was not right about his explanations. His anger. It was too strong. Too sudden. Did he deliberately arrange my marriage while he hid the change to my trust? Tried to divert me from passing its test before my twenty-fifth birthday?* The journey alone across the country. New Orleans. The *Decatur* explosion. *Why was I spared?*

"What am I doing here?" Swift asked…not realizing she spoke out loud. "What made me come to the Mexican side? I must be crazy. What a silly twit. Maybe Uncle Jacob was right? Perhaps a woman isn't suited for a man's work. No. I do not believe that. What should I do? God…this is difficult. Sorry. Not you…God. You know what I mean. At least I hope you do. Am I doing the right thing? Everybody has been great. Mitch. Big Tim. Don Carlo. Even Dancer. Now there's a case for you. I know he doesn't have any family and is out to make his fortune. That's all dandy…but I can't figure him out." Swift paused. "But Dancer is not the issue. The real question is should I stay in Matamoros…or should I get out while I can. Before the shooting starts. Oh…what would Mother do? I feel so alone. So lonely sometimes. There I go again…feeling sorry for myself. Nobody got you into this mess but yourself…Swift. So nobody can get you out but yourself."

Swift reflected on her situation. "You're right. You can do this. You've made it this far. Keep going. As Father always said…stay out of judgment and stay in curiosity. Listen with more than just your ears. That's what makes a good correspondent…and good things will happen." Swift lifted her chin. Slapped her knees with both hands. Resolved. "Thank you…Lord…for listening. That's what I'll do."

Swift opened the confessional and stepped out. Her spirits much lighter.

Dancer waited for Swift's footsteps to recede across the stone floor. He didn't budge until he heard the concussion of the heavy main door close.

More power to you…Swift. You'll need it in this viper's den.

Then secret agent Dancer continued his search for the perfect place where a golden treasure could be hidden.

CHAPTER 45

INTERIOR COURTYARD
HOTEL CASAMATA
8 APRIL 1846

PATRICK HARP mocked General Taylor the next afternoon. Surely the old man had blundered and put his small American force in harm's way. *Although I doubt the Mexicans on this frontier can whip the Americans.* Harp was content to muse to himself. *Who's to know they can't gather ten thousand men willing to defend their hovels. The Americans will be cut off…with no retreat and no supplies at Fort Texas. Mexican victory is a true possibility. The longer that fool Taylor fails to make some pretext to take Matamoros…the sooner Wildfire will get its wish.*

Dancer tethered his horse in the stable at Hotel Casamata under the gateway. Before he stepped out of the shadow he heard two men's voices coming from the gallery above. He paused in the darkness to listen.

"You know those two dragoons that were captured at Arroyo Colorado on the Americans' march from Corpus Christi?" The first voice asked the question in a stark and gravelly tone.

"Sure. The Yank prisoners that were returned with Colonel Worth's parley at the river?" The second voice spoke without interest.

"You wouldn't believe how they went on and on about their royal treatment by the Mexicans!" The enthusiasm of the first voice's report was unrestrained. "Attractive *señoritas*. All the food they wanted. They crowed like true believers. The Mexicans even paid them half wages! Better money than the Americans have seen since New Orleans."

Dancer recognized one voice. It was Patrick Harp.

The second voice muttered: "Lots of the lads signed up just to get work…to get away from the hole they were in…or to get a free ticket out west."

"Who can blame them? Food's bad. Camp is worse. Now some of 'em are going to stop a Mexican ball…or end up on the wrong end of a pig sticker. Sorry bastards."

"What's that to you…Harp?"

"Not to me…to this bloody war. I'm still with the Americans. But not for long. I've seen 'em from the inside. They bluster and bugle and drill—but they are vulnerable…Very vulnerable. The Mexicans outnumber them three to one…soon to be four to one. The Americans are in a foreign place. They don't know the first thing about the terrain on either side of the river. Don't even have a map. Nothing. But it's the Mexican's backyard. They will fight to save their land. Plus the Americans are isolated. Fort Texas is miles from their supply depot. I saw them take in a herd of cattle and sheep. Quartermaster Cross told me they expect a delivery every three days. Without it they'd starve in a week."

"What are you sayin'?"

"I'm saying…here's how the Americans can be defeated. We strike at their weakness. The volunteers and foreign-born. We get as many as possible to desert just like you did…Flanagan. The rot of camp life is bad enough. Facing canister and grape from Mexican cannon is something else. Sure as hell ain't worth a piddling signing bonus—or weevils in your biscuits."

"What do you plan to do?"

Harp lowered his voice. Confided in his confederate. Dancer moved into the light. Dangerously closer to hear the whispered words.

"The time is right. Most of the twelve-month volunteers will muster out at the end of May. Not even seven weeks from now. Nobody wants to be buried in this place only days before they're discharged…with or without pay. So here's the plan. We work them to desert. Fake sickness. Get lost. Anything. Give them a reason not to fight. Whatever it is. That way we reduce the Americans to be even weaker than they are…and spread the word of the paradise that awaits them in Mexico. The Americans won't stand a chance in hell. Victory will be ours. And the Mexicans will be beholden to us. We'll be heroes in a new land. This is our chance to put famine behind us forever. Land. Riches. All the *señoritas* you want to dance with will be ours."

Excitement came into Flanagan's scarred face. He licked his lips slowly.

Harp spoke freely. "I met with the garrison commander… a General Payaso. A local man who kisses any ass to keep his place. They say he may be replaced. But until then we'll use him. Many of the American boys are Irish. Some are German. Others British. None of them give a fart about this war. All they want is a break…and a new start."

"And better food." Scarface piped in as he cottoned to the idea.

"For now…I'll work from inside the American camp. As the deserters come over…you gather them together in one camp. I'll persuade the Mexicans' new commander to give every man acres of land plus free passage papers and support wherever we go in Mexico." Harp warmed to his scheme. "We'll leave old puff and fraidy Taylor blowing in the wind." Harp spit over the balcony.

The second voice laughed coldly. "Ole Taylor been playin' army camp so long he forgot how to general…if'n you ask me."

"Payaso liked this foreign legion so much he gave us a name… *Legion de Estrangaros* — Legion of Foreigners. Top secret of course. But he promised the Irish will get our very own battalion." Harp paused as Dancer strained to hear. "They call us the Saint Patrick's Battalion. Sounds even better in Spanish: the *'San Patricios Batallón.'* I like it. That name will be our badge of honor."

The second voice tried to roll the Spanish words around his mouth. But the idea of better food wouldn't yield a place for the foreign phrases.

"Payaso liked the circular I worked up…and I know just how Kelly and I can spread it around to the boys. Won't take much to start a stampede…I reckon." Harp smacked the balcony railing. "I'll beat the Americans at their own game and take back my old command. In the meantime…I've got a message for you to deliver to that little runt

Stepptoe at the consulate. And then that newspaper girl could be very useful too. Very useful."

Dancer stayed hidden as heavy boots traversed the wooden gallery. Then descended the steps and entered the saloon. *Got to warn Swift… and get Stepptoe out of town tonight as planned with the Texas Rangers. I gave Stepptoe my word. If Jones was with me we could split up. Warn them both…before it's too late.*

CHAPTER 46

GENERAL FRANCISCO PAYASO'S OFFICE
GARRISON HEADQUARTERS/PRESIDIO
8 APRIL 1846/AT THE SAME TIME

IN THE PRESIDIO at that very moment Payaso handed Swift a broadside circular printed side by side in English and Spanish. The headline foretold the message.

Catholic Irish — Frenchmen — and German of the Invading Army!

The text made a grandiose case for desertion:

> *The American nation makes a most unjust war to the Mexicans and has taken all of you as an instrument of their inequity. You must not fight against a religious people — nor should you be seen in the ranks of those who proclaim slavery of mankind as a constitutive principle. The religious man — he who possesses greatness of mind — must always fight for liberty…and liberty is not on the side of those who establish differences in mankind — making an unhappy and innocent people earn the bread of slavery. Liberty is not on the part of those who desire to be the lords of the world — robbing properties and territories which do not belong to them and shedding so much blood in order to accomplish their views — views in open war with the principles of our holy religion. The*

> *Mexican people wishes not to shed the blood of those who profess their own religion and I in the name of the inhabitants of the State of Tamaulipas invite you to abandon them. You may be respected in all the towns and places of the states where you happen to go — and all requisite assistance shall be given to all. Many of your former companions now rest content in our ranks. After this war is over the magnanimous and generous Mexican nation will duly appreciate the services rendered and you shall remain with us — cultivating our fertile lands. Catholic Irish — French — and German!! Long live liberty! Long live our holy Religion!!*

⊠   ⊠   ⊠

Garrison Commander Payaso glanced sidelong into a large gilded mirror to admire his gold epaulets and many glittering medals. An ostentatious double sash strained under the weight of more honors over his forest green tunic. *He looks like a besotted peacock.* Swift thought.

"General…do you think this San Patricios strategy will succeed?" Swift quietly poised her pencil over her well-turned notebook.

"It already has."

The Creole General spoke in careful English. Payaso paused to be sure the American writer recorded every one of his important words. "The ones that came over first…are also helping those that follow… in a brotherhood of our holy religion. Those who wish to join our forces…find they are given advancement…especially the officers. Supplied only the finest uniforms…boots…and equipment. With the 'safe conduct' documents we give them…they obtain lodging… employment…even food and handouts of money. My idea is like a worm rotting the apple that is the American Army from the inside. We are helping that worm escape."

"How many of the men of the American Army are foreign born?" Swift asked.

"Our spies tell us out of every one hundred…about forty are Irish. Fifteen German. Maybe only twenty are Americans. That means as many as half will welcome our offer. The rest are from many other places. Oftentimes…how do you say…these men are refugees. Men without a country. We give them a new motherland." The General swelled with a prideful swagger. His smile seemed false. Painted on.

"What do you think drives these men?" Swift asked.

"How do you say in the United States? It is 'Manifest Destiny'—as your newspapers say. Yes…I read your newspapers. What is Manifest Destiny? Nothing more than opportunity. Self-interest. Look out for yourself first. Be your own man. Rugged. An individual. That is what they want. Not some distant notion of a nation. They want to break the ties of tyranny. Not serve another master. That is why they left their countries…and what they do not find in the American Army. They want their own personal liberty. Do you see? They do not want to die. These men are driven to come over to us. That is the great genius of my brilliant strategy."

"You mention slavery in your circular. Isn't your system of contract labor—where *rancheros* are treated no better than slaves—just the same?" Swift demanded.

"It is interesting you ask that question…*Señorita* Swift. Perhaps you have not traveled much in your country." Payaso fussed condescendingly with a loose thread. "Slavery is behind this war. First Texas…a slave state now. Now your president wants to conquer more lands for slavery and the slaving-owning class. The motivation is quite clear. Slavery is what controls America. Even though the old white heads in your Congress may protest…it is true. Americans are the barbarians. Not the Mexicans."

Swift closed her notebook and prepared to take her leave.

"This has been most enjoyable…*Señorita*. Allow me…if I may…before you leave…to compliment you on your boots. If I am not mistaken those are the finest work of the bootmakers of Barcelona. World famous. I see you have taken up some of our ways."

"Thank you…General. These boots were a gift." Swift stopped as she realized she should say no more.

"I pray this is not our only visit." The General's voice exuded a smooth elegance. "When we have victories—as we most certainly will in the coming demonstrations—may I invite you to return? As you say…the Mexican story and my heroic role must be told. As always it is a delight to have your assistance. In gratitude…please take with you this gift. It is a document of safe passage that carries my seal as commander in chief. As you pursue your work you will undoubtedly find it useful. You see…we can both be useful to each other!" Payaso let his last words hang in the air. Then ended the session with a soft clap of his hands and a large smile.

Swift rose from her chair. Certainly the safe passage document could be useful. But she also knew she must tread softly. How to balance an exclusive source with the need to be truthful to her readers? *Beware a deal with the devil.*

Outside the Presidio Swift mounted the buckboard as Big Tim steadied the wagon. The *Brooklyn Eagle* war correspondent realized her heart was pounding. The image of Payaso and his false smile loomed in her mind. Swift was reminded of a sly cat that hovered near a mouse burrow for his own amusement.

CHAPTER 47

SWIFT LEFT the General's presence and met Big Tim where he waited for her outside the Custom House. The suffocating late afternoon heat weighed like a blanket on every breath.

"Maybe there's still time to visit the consulate." Swift touched her pouch where she held Mr. Penrhos's letter of introduction to Consul John Stepptoe. Big Tim snapped the reins and wheeled the buckboard toward the Resaca House. When they maneuvered into the consulate's courtyard Swift met William Beacon as he left the daguerreotypist's studio.

"Hello…William…Good to see you." Swift bit off a joke about always attending dances but never dancing.

"Are you here for your 'magic of light' demonstration?" The daguerreotype photographer displayed a hopeful look.

"You are too kind. No. I came to present my credentials to the Consul." Swift continued in a friendly tone: "Is the consulate open? I know it's coming on evening."

"Suppose so." Beacon's reply matched Swift's cheeriness. "When I was here three days ago I saw Jack Dancer leaving the consulate. Must be somebody there."

Swift smiled. "Thanks…William."

"Seems odd though."

Swift turned back to face Beacon. "What's odd?"

"The smoke. When I arrived early this morning I noticed there was smoke coming from the consulate chimney. It's stopped now. But why have a fire — or burn papers — on a warm day like this? Just seems odd."

Swift faced the consulate stairway with a growing sense of foreboding.

╳ ╳ ╳

When Swift and Big Tim climbed the stairs to the consulate office they found the door ajar. "That's strange." Swift kept her voice low. She gently pushed the door open. Inside their eyes adjusted to the shuttered darkness. At first nothing seemed out of place. Then Big Tim gestured to the broken painting and a lighter-colored area of the wall where the door of a safe stood open. *Whatever was locked in there is gone now.*

Swift called out. "Hello? Consul Stepptoe? Is anyone here?"

No answer.

Swift flashed back to her arrival to New Orleans. She went cold with the memory of the poor Irishman on the levee who was killed before her eyes. A sudden shudder ran through her…she touched Big Tim's arm to warn him of the danger she felt.

Tremulous Swift listened for the slightest sound. From the upper room came a low thumping.

When they turned toward the third-floor steps Swift sensed something — or somebody — upstairs. Slowly she ascended the stairs. Big Tim close behind.

Swift stepped through the door at the top of the stairway. They entered the foyer area of the private apartment of the consulate. In the far room Swift could hear the sound again. Steady. As if a heavy weight thumped against another object.

She pushed the door of the far room open. Swift entered the space. Then stopped short. Horrified at what she saw in the dim early-evening light. Big Tim came up beside her.

As she raised her eyes toward the sound Swift saw a mutilated man's form hung from the chandelier hook. A rope tied both his wrists to the ends of a wrought-iron curtain rod. And a noose bound his neck to the bar. His half-naked and crucified body swung back and forth. Lazily. Moved by the breeze through the open balcony doors. The curtain rod rhythmically bumped against the plastered brick. The body faced the far wall. Suspended above where he once reigned from behind a heavy writing desk. Flies congregated in swarms on the corpse.

Big Tim recognized the dead man. "Stepptoe."

As Swift came around the corpse she gagged at the putrid stench spreading from the body. With horror she realized what the killers had done. There on the Consul's chest was a vicious gash of bloody singed flesh. The smell of burned hair reminded Swift of the acrid odor from the Rancho Valdez. Stepptoe's chest had been branded with a letter "W." A drying pool of blood collected under his bare feet.

Finding a reserve that surprised her Swift surveyed the room with an objective eye. The reporter noted the scene. The details. The time. The circumstances. Swift's gaze attracted her toward the writing desk. There amidst the jumble was a sheet of stationery. At first the page appeared blank. Yet when turned toward the light Stepptoe clearly had pressed some message into the clean page. The indentation of his last words was faintly visible. *Did Stepptoe write this with the end of his pen handle...when he heard his killers coming?*

"Bring me some ashes from the fireplace...Big Tim."

Dabbing her handkerchief into the retrieved ashes Swift rubbed them gently across the sheet. From the gray smear three words emerged in ghostly letters. Swift read them out loud.

"Payaso...Tunnel...Wildfire."

"What mean?" Big Tim asked.

Swift bit her lower lip uncertainly. "I don't know. Dancer was here three days ago. But this happened today. The warm ashes. The fresh blood. Maybe it was Payaso — or his hired gun...Malvado? Then again I wouldn't put this past Harp and that scar-faced deserter of his. But I know one thing. Whoever did this is dangerous. They will kill. And they are likely in Matamoros."

At that moment beneath the carpet — under the writing desk — Swift felt something through the sole of her fine Barcelona boot. She bent down. Lifted the rug. Kicked — or hidden — under a ripple in the carpet was a key. Swift held the key up to the light. "Too small for a front door key. Too large for a desk drawer. Maybe this opens a padlock?" Notwithstanding she dropped the key into a pocket inside her correspondent's pouch.

With a sudden upwelling of understanding Swift realized she was reporting this war from the enemy camp. Surrounded. She must be careful. *No false steps. Or they could be my last.*

◌ ◌ ◌

Much later as night settled into the river valley the town was released from the grip of the unseasonal heat. A Gulf breeze stirred the trees of the *paseo* riverfront walk. Matamoros glowed with the soft light of lanterns. Seated just inside her balcony doors in the Hotel Casamata S. Thomas Swift inhaled a deep breath. Then her pen quickly turned out an exclusive eyewitness report of the murder of U.S. Consul John Stepptoe.

On that same spring evening fourteen American deserters swam the Rio Grande to the Mexican side…with no intention of returning.

Harp's handiwork had taken hold.

CHAPTER 48

GENERAL ZACHARY TAYLOR'S HEADQUARTERS
FORT TEXAS/ARMY OF OCCUPATION
8 APRIL 1846/AFTER DARK

MAJOR GENERAL ZACHARY TAYLOR fumed at his commanders. "At this rate we won't have enough men to make a stand when the Mexicans find their backbone! Put a bounty on the deserters! For every deserter captured from now on…there will be a thirty-dollar reward for the man who brings him in. That's three month's pay! Colonel… every night I want you to post your best sharpshooters. If another fool tries to swim the river…shoot to kill. We will put a stop to this *fandango*."

The American commander crushed the Mexican circular he was holding and tossed it roughly into the campfire.

⊠　⊠　⊠

Desertions continued. Ever harsher discipline increased the grumbling among the foreign soldiers. Some whispered of ways to take revenge on particular officers. As war ticked closer even Taylor paced the question if this motley collection of men the War Department called an army would stand and fight…and on which side?

The next night two deserters were shot dead in the river. Their blue uniforms floated lazily in the slow current toward the sea.

Correspondents noted in their dispatches that the first shots fired in the war with Mexico were fired by American troops on their own men.

CHAPTER 49

CAPTAIN SAMUEL WALKER felt contempt for all things Mexican. Off the field his conduct—and his fellow Texas Rangers—were the despair of General Taylor. They were frontiersmen. Knew each other like brothers. And carried with them the memories of the Alamo and the fight for Texas independence against Mexico.

"These Texans bring their old enemies with them." Dancer shared his firsthand experience with the General.

Walker and his Rangers were tough. Hardened by the cruelty of frontier warfare. Irregulars they were called. Seventy-seven in number. All volunteers. Even the regular dragoons admired the Ranger's horsemanship. Organization was loose. They listened to orders. And did what they pleased. Walker and his Rangers knew what they were there for. Topmost in their sights was Antonio Malvado and his brutal *ranchero* guerillas. The "Chapparal Fox" and his band were known to be operating in the area.

Walker's and Dancer's tents were side by side under the shade of a large cottonwood at the edge of the army encampment. Beyond a plowed field that was soft under foot to the west the white army tents were precisely ordered in formation. Behind the tents the timber and earthen walls of Fort Texas rose higher by the hour.

"Thunder tarnation! What did he think he was doin'?" Walker accepted a bottle of Kentucky bourbon from Dancer.

"Who?" Dancer asked.

"That darned fool…Colonel Trueman Cross. Just because he's the deputy quartermaster general and an experienced veteran he thinks he can go off for a horseback ride from camp. He left in a hurry today. Hasn't come back. Went off with Private Harp."

"You mean that Irishman with the horse artillery?"

"That's the one." Walker nipped at the whiskey again. "Harp came back without him. Says Cross wanted to keep goin'."

"Maybe somebody should go out and look for Colonel Cross." Dancer was only half-interested in the dilemma.

"The whole camp is obsessed with his disappearance. If it was somebody else…maybe one of my boys. I'd say odds are good he is in Matamoros enjoyin' the warm company of one of those hotel sluts." Walker snorted. "But not Trueman Cross. Probably went lookin' for some wildflowers to add to his collection…or somethin'."

"He's a regular trooper. He can take care of himself."

"Not with the enemy out there. Particularly Antonio Malvado… the Chapparal Fox. And his *rancheros*. All out for blood. Tamaulipas is Malvado's home country. Based in Camargo upriver. Came out against Paredes early on. But he came back into the fold when Paredes won. Takes orders — for the moment — from Payaso…I understand. Knows the lay of the land hereabouts like a wolf knows his den." Walker sucked tobacco from his teeth. "Nope. Cross don't stand much chance. Not much chance at all."

Walker poured another snort. Then smacked the cork back into the whiskey bottle. "What the devil?…I'm goin' to see old man Taylor. Maybe offer my services."

Dancer looked up. Remembered the rare adventures he had had with Natchez Jones. There was something about this Texan that appealed to Dancer's nature. Does whatever it takes. Stays calm. Unshakeable. Follows his own rules. "You can't do it alone." Dancer joined Walker as they left Dancer's side-walled tent.

When Walker and Dancer came up to the commander's tent a knot of officers gathered in front were arguing over some point of order.

"Cross is a colonel. Should be a colonel...or major at least...that goes for him." The tall colonel smacked a fist into his palm emphatically as if the answer were obvious.

"Trueman was a friend of mind." A second officer was firmer in his observance. "We're both from New York State."

"Gentlemen. Gentlemen." Taylor quieted the dispute. "For now we must focus all our attention on building Fort Texas. The fort is more important to this mission than one man. Colonel Cross is on his own. Perhaps he will show himself. God willing. If not...then in some days' time Lieutenants Porter and Dobbins will form two parties of ten men each. The troops will make a search of the area east and west of camp." Taylor addressed the two officers: "Stay on the north bank... gentlemen. Do not give chase across the river. We wouldn't want to start a war now...would we?" All the officers took the joke with general amusement. Most of them itched for action.

Far beyond view of the Americans three wide-winged shapes lazily circled high above the chapparal scrub in the far eastern sky. Their heads low. Each appeared to await their turn.

CHAPTER **50**

MAJOR GENERAL PEDRO DE AMPUDIA had made sure all the church bells of Matamoros rang as he entered the town. And equally sure that His Excellency was followed by a guard of two hundred cavalry. Upon Ampudia's signal a 21-gun salute sounded. The roar could be heard by the Americans across the river…as intended. Obligated to attend the procession along the southern road from San Fernando the people of Matamoros stood in the shade of buildings. Then mechanically applauded the green uniforms that the riders filled.

Word leaked to Swift that not all citizens were enthusiastic to see Ampudia. Payaso was an incompetent. But at least he was local. People knew what to expect from their strutting Creole. Three days prior a contingent of town leaders led by Don Carlo Juan Baptiste gathered in secret council. The result was a letter to President Paredes. They expressed their gratefulness for the reinforcements scheduled to arrive in seventy-two hours and to replace General Payaso. But Ampudia was another matter.

In private some called Ampudia the "Butcher of Tabasco." While others called him the "Assassin of Sentmanat."

Don Carlo argued before the secret council. "Two years ago—in 1844—Pedro de Ampudia was stripped of his rank when he brutally put down an insurrection in Tabasco State on the southern shore of the Gulf of Mexico."

Another elder testified. "Ampudia personally ordered the throats slashed of the principal leaders. Then had them shot to finish the job. For Francisco Sentmanat—the foremost rebel leader—Ampudia reserved special treatment. The General ordered Sentmanat's severed head to be fried in oil."

Don Carlo finished the story. "In Ampudia's own words…'The better to preserve it for display.' Then the butcher exhibited his gory warning on a stake in the public square of San Juan Batista."

The city elders knew Ampudia to be an opportunist. Don Carlo pointed out that Ampudia was only restored to command because he had seconded Paredes's *pronunciamento* at San Luis Potosi last December. That declaration propelled Paredes to take over the presidency.

"Ampudia rode that horse into power." Don Carlo's words concluded the secret gathering.

With delicacy the Matamoros patriarchs wrote to Paredes to ask another general be sent. The letter hinted that General Mariano Arista might be the man.

In his first official act upon arrival Ampudia promoted Payaso to be second in command. In fact the local Creole was still no more than commandant of the Matamoros garrison.

CHAPTER 51

AMPUDIA WAITED three days for reinforcements of three thousand men to arrive in Matamoros under the command of General Torrejón. All the while he secretly made preparations to attack the Americans the day after arrival of the reinforcing troops. In the interim the new Mexican commander busied himself with tweaking the American General. Ampudia's first broadside demanded General Taylor and his army withdraw within twenty-four hours.

Ampudia wrote:

> *"To Don Z. Taylor…I require you in all form—and at the latest in the preemptory term of twenty-four hours—to break up your camp and return to the east bank of the Nueces River while our governments are regulating the pending question in relation to Texas. If you insist on remaining upon the soil of the Department of Tamaulipas it will certainly result that arms—and arms alone—must decide the question; and in that case I advise you that we accept the war to which—with so much injustice on your part—you provoke us.…"*

Taylor responded. Polite but without doubt of his resolve:

"I regret the alternative which you offer; but at the same time wish it understood that I shall by no means avoid such alternative. If it should come to war let it be known that it will not be the United States that fires the first shot."

⊠   ⊠   ⊠

As a precaution Taylor ordered the 2nd Regiment to move to the far northeast side of camp—outside the fortification. This put the battlements of Fort Texas between his force and the reach of the battery of Payaso's guns at Matamoros.

Dancer moved his tent into the same vicinity that afternoon. Then sent an urgent note to Swift in town by a camp follower's boy. "Last river packet leaving Longoreño soon. Send dispatches now."

⊠   ⊠   ⊠

Late next morning Taylor summoned Walker and Dancer to his tent.

"Gentlemen…there are important orders I must get to Major John Munroe in Point Isabel. Every man is needed here to complete the defenses of Fort Texas. Dancer…I know you have commercial interests in Point Isabel. Walker…they say you know the terrain. This expedition will show me your value as scouts and guides. Can you both leave for Point Isabel within the hour?"

Walker slapped Dancer on the back delightedly. "I'd just about do anythin' than sit around this camp all day…bein' no good to nobody…and just tuckerin' myself out doin' nothin'. Plus it'll be good to take the measure of my Rangers in Point Isabel. No tellin' what mischief they've been into."

"Anything to assist…sir." Dancer agreed but knew this distraction took him away from his real business in Matamoros.

"Good." Taylor closed the session. "Take this pouch to Major Munroe with all speed. Wait in Point Isabel for further orders. And Walker…have your Rangers do what they can to help Munroe protect his supplies…not drink them. If we can blockade all shipping on the Rio Grande then the Mexicans will soon see their supplies running low to feed their army. That will force the action."

Walker surveyed the sky. "Looks like a storm's brewin' in the Gulf…General. If the rains move inland…they could be heavy upstream. That means the river will go through some changes."

Within the hour Dancer and Walker swung into their saddles. The twenty-three miles to Point Isabel could be a comfortable outing. Or it could be a race with death. The disappearance of Colonel Cross was all too fresh.

"I figg'r once we get beyond the camp we stay off the road." Walker's figuring was Dancer's command. "We'll ride fast for a mile or so among the scrub like rabbits. Then slow to a trot. Stay low. Like as not our horses won't make a sound in the sand. That way anybody out huntin' rabbits will be disappointed." What rarely passed for a smile crossed Walker's determined face.

Walker and Dancer rode hard and avoided Malvado's *rancheros*. By late afternoon the pair reached Point Isabel without trial. Upon arrival they learned the bad news.

Unknown to Taylor the storm that raged in the Gulf drove his only two brigs of war out to sea. The *Lawrence* and the *Flirt* were useless. Left with nothing but his own invention to muster a blockade Munroe improvised with a chartered merchantman called the *Alert*. Just in time the hastily mustered vessel single-handedly established a blockade at the mouth of the Rio Grande—near Faro Bagdad. Within days two American schooners from New Orleans—the *Equity* and the *Floridian*—loaded with flour purchased by the Mexicans appeared. Both were warned off and sent packing by the *Alert*.

The flame beneath Polk's caldron pushed war toward a boil.

CHAPTER 52

LUIZ JUAN BAPTISTE smoldered under the anger of being the second son. His older brother Diego would inherit everything. Luiz would always be beholden to the patronage of Don Carlo. Then the wealth of Diego.

Luiz clenched his fist. "The second son is the forgotten son…until the day when the elders are moved out of the way."

Notwithstanding a show of empathy Payaso fueled the fire of Luiz Juan Baptiste's anger.

"You know what they say…neighbor." Payaso feigned cordiality. "The first man gets the oyster. The second gets the shell." Payaso paused. Then baited his trap. "But now — while Diego is away — you are rightfully the elder son…is it not true?"

Luiz straightened at the idea.

"I understand you have a document for me that may hasten the day when you take rightful control of the Rancho Valdez and all the riches that entails."

"We can help each other." Luiz saw no reason to be anything other than blunt. "I will help you find this treasure of Matamoros before someone steals it again — or Dancer finds it. In return…you will reveal to the authorities the treasonous dealings of Don Carlo — and make it impossible for Diego to return."

Payaso smiled. "That is our arrangement. What did you bring me?"

Luiz Juan Baptiste drew a document from his case that he had forced Josefina to reveal. The two conspirators huddled over a small table in Payaso's office.

"You may only read and copy this letter. This original must be returned to my father's library before it is found missing."

"Agreed." Payaso scanned the contract between Don Carlo Juan Baptiste and Jack Dancer to supply the American Army.

"Excellent." Payaso rattled the document in his fist like a snake. "Simply the existence of this agreement is enough to condemn Don Carlo for treason. When the time is right…the proper authorities will be more than interested."

Vindication rose within Luiz Juan Baptiste.

Payaso pointed to the last paragraph. "I see here that Dancer's commission will be hidden in a secret place…and only collected if the Americans win. Where is this place?"

"It is the church of Father Thomas. No one knows exactly where but somewhere in his old church is the hiding place."

Payaso smiled again. "As for the treasure…I'm sure I can find ways to have the little priest tell us where it is hidden. Count on me."

Payaso finished a copy of the agreement and returned the original to the second son.

"Tell me…*Señor* Payaso." The aggrieved Baptiste was not reluctant to broach delicate matters. "Stories from our *rancheros* have come to me.…Someone of authority has been dipping into the *alcabala* taxes for himself. The *rancheros* talk about an underground passage between the Custom House and the new Cathedral? They say Consul Stepptoe learned of this passage — and that hastened his end. So unfortunate. Has this story reached you too?"

Payaso stiffened. "Those rumors have been spread by some men who call themselves Wildfire. The stories are lies. Propaganda. A secret plot? Ridiculous. Nothing more than desperate gossip by guilty traitors. They fear their secret plot will be revealed…that is why they try to paint their plot on powerful men like me."

"What *do* you know?" Luiz Baptiste insisted.

Payaso held the rolled copy in his fist like a bludgeon. "What I know is that there is far greater treasure to be had for both of us — in just reward for our patriotic service — when we spring our little trap."

On that final word the two confederates went their separate ways. Baptiste to return the stolen contract to Rancho Valdez. Payaso to his thoughts of how he could implicate Luiz Juan Baptiste at the same time he took down his lifetime enemy. Don Carlo.

With betrayal and revenge in mind Payaso bided his time.

CHAPTER 53

CHAPPARAL
EAST OF CAMP/FORT TEXAS
18 APRIL 1846

LIEUTENANTS PORTER AND DOBBINS each led separate patrols of ten men in search of Colonel Cross a week after the quartermaster's disappearance. Dobbins found nothing indicating Cross had been to the west. His patrol returned safely to the American camp.

Meanwhile Porter's search party continued to thread its way through the underbrush. At that moment the newly arrived Ampudia sent a message to Taylor denying any knowledge of Colonel Cross's disappearance.

East of camp Porter noted a kettle of circling buzzards. He followed the sign toward a wood where the road north from Longoreño met an old Indian trail. The road meandered northeast from the crossroad. Past the wetlands along the Tanques de Ramireno. Toward the main road at Palo Alto. Beneath the buzzards Porter's patrol soon came upon a body. Or what was left of it. Cross's stripped corpse lay in a grotesque twisted position half-hidden — or dragged — under a thorn bush. There were no signs of flight or defense. Cross's spare frame and a peculiar tooth — together with a colonel's shoulder strap found near the spot — placed his identity beyond question. Cross's Colt revolver…pocket watch…

and horse were nowhere to be found.

Cross had been ambushed and murdered. His skull crushed by a blunt instrument. "This is no accident." Porter snapped his judgment to his sergeant major.

"Probably a horse pistol or musket butt." The sergeant muttered his inference to Porter.

The Lieutenant ordered Cross's remains bundled behind the saddle of one of the corporals.

"No place to be after dark." Porter called out. "Men…return to camp."

As the patrol worked through the thicket Porter's search party came upon an encampment of Mexican *rancheros.*

"Kill the bastards!" Porter shouted in a hoarse whisper. His patrol charged with revenge on its mind. Firing right and left the Americans rushed into the midst of the *rancheros* sitting around a fire. The Mexicans scattered in every direction. Riderless horses reared. Raced into the bushes. The Mexicans' campfire was trampled. Sparks scattered. Sizzling tortillas fell limp on the sandy soil. Three *rancheros* lay dead. One trooper emptied an extra bullet into a lifeless *ranchero.*

Lieutenant Theodoric Porter beamed to himself. *I can see the newspaper story back home.*

> *Lieutenant Teddy Porter (he hated his given name)—son of the late Commodore David Porter of the United States Navy…who had fought with the Mexicans in their courageous battle for independence from Spain only 25 years before—heroically recovered the remains of his fallen comrade—Colonel Trueman Cross—on a daring mission in enemy territory.*

Too far from Fort Texas as night fell Porter's men made a cold camp in the scrub. Later that night angry *rancheros* encircled Porter's small group with a force of 150 men. At the signal of a dove call the guerillas attacked the search party. In the chaos and darkness all ten soldiers escaped but one. Lieutenant Theodoric Porter was killed.

⊠   ⊠   ⊠

Summoned to an interview sometime later at the Palacio de Armas headquarters Samantha Swift made a discovery. Major General Pedro de Ampudia had newly acquired an ornate pocket watch. From a description given to her by William Beacon she recognized the watch as belonging to the unfortunate Colonel Cross. The same day in the Palacio courtyard Swift recognized Cross's horse. Now claimed by a Mexican officer.

Three Americans had fallen at the hands of the Mexicans. Stepptoe. Cross. Porter. Swift heard whispers among some American troops how the dastardly acts inspired a call to avenge the murders. Among these men sympathy for the Mexican people — whom some felt had been unjustly treated — evaporated.

While others whispered their opinion that getting killed any day now was not worth the price of enlistment.

CHAPTER 54

PAYASO'S OFFICE
GARRISON HEADQUARTERS/PRESIDIO
24 APRIL 1846

SAMANTHA SWIFT reckoned the entire Mexican Army was in the streets of Matamoros. The mood of relative calm since she arrived six weeks before had given way in the week since Lieutenant Porter's death to surly distrust. Fierce black clouds gathered in the east. *Perhaps another gale coming out of the Gulf?* This time to garrison headquarters she felt safer riding Don Carlo's spirited horse — who begrudgingly by now accepted Swift's calls of Peony. Reflexively the correspondent touched the pouch where she kept Payaso's safe passage letter.

As Swift kept to the broader *avenidas* she ruminated over a story that morning in the *Matamoros Gazette*. The paper claimed forty-three deserters and six runaway slaves had crossed the river in recent days. *Possible. But why are they counting?* Swift's misgivings included not knowing why she had been summoned to an interview by General Payaso.

"Madam…please…sit here." The officious little commandant gestured to a lone chair opposite a battered desk. "I will come directly to the point."

Swift took her appointed seat.

"As you may know…madam…many foreign-born members of the invading army have chosen a better life and have come to the Mexican side. We welcome them."

Swift took out her notebook.

"To show we are a generous nation"—the commandant uttered his words as if he expected them to be transcribed—"and to exhibit to all the world that Mexicans are not a barbarous people—we announce today a special inducement for all foreigners who want a better life in Mexico."

Swift took down the words. Then waited.

"Our noble Presidente and our national Congress…in their infinite wisdom…are now offering…" Payaso paused as he pulled himself up to greater importance. "We are now offering any foreigner who assumes citizenship of Mexico a full three hundred and twenty acres of land to have as their own to start a new life and prosper."

Swift noted the number.

The General struck a pose as if presenting an Independence Day declamation. "To those who have soaring spirits…a trait shared with many Mexicanos…and to those who now know that advancement in the American military is only a lie reserved for officers with political influence…and to those who joined the military because they were shunned by the factory bosses of your cities…and to those who came to our fair land simply because the American Army provided convenient transportation…" The commandant stroked his thin mustache as he watched Swift's pencil catch up. "…And to those who find their service is distasteful to the life they honestly wish to lead…we welcome them. If they wish to remain in military service…we have a special *Legion de Estrangaros*…the Legion of Foreigners…where the newcomers can join the already swelled ranks of men from many lands…even though they have been temporary Americans."

"Today the *Matamoros Gazette* reported forty-three deserters and six slaves crossed the river. Can you confirm those numbers…and over what period?" Swift asked.

"I'm sure those numbers are correct…and growing." Payaso put on an air to hide his lack of information. "Personally I can tell you that General Ampudia predicts fifteen hundred foreigners will desert before our inevitable victory is complete." The commandant leaned so close to

Swift she almost gagged from his sickly cologne.

Conspiracy-prone Payaso continued in a low voice. "I can also give you my personal word that I have sent a letter to Ampudia where I predict to see most of the Seventh Infantry…at what the Americans call Fort Texas…to embrace Mexico at the first sound of our cannon because most of those unfortunates are Irish and Germans."

Payaso straightened. Quite proud of his importance. And clasped his lapels triumphantly while he waited for Swift's reaction.

"You are very informed…sir." Swift flattered. The commandant swelled. "We have reports that General Mariano Arista will soon replace Ampudia. As the new commander of the Division of the North does General Arista share this same expectation?"

"I am certain of it." The little commandant dissembled his assertion with certainty.

"Even though it is only thirteen days since Ampudia replaced you…General? Will Ampudia remain second in command — as is the custom?" Swift asked in a matter-of-fact tone.

"Certainly. And myself…loyal as sworn…will be third in line and will remain *commandante* of Matamoros as well." Payaso paused with pride. "When Arista arrives tomorrow the lesser officers will be informed as well."

"Of course. As the garrison commandant you must be informed of these important changes. It is only proper." Swift's tone was one of complete understanding. "And General Torrejón mentioned he has special orders too?" Swift put her notebook away.

"Yes. Isn't it exciting?" Payaso burst enthusiastically. "Torrejón received orders yesterday to take sixteen hundred cavalry northwest and cross the Rio del Norte some miles upstream at La Palangaña basin — before the rains swell the river. Surely he will move east to cut the road to Point Isabel. That maneuver will trap the invaders in a vise from which they most certainly will not escape!" Sensing he may have said too much the commandant of Matamoros stopped.

"I have taken too much of your valuable time…*Señor* General. Thank you for your kind assistance helping me understand the generous Mexican offer of lands to foreigners. My newspaper will be very interested to know of your nation's noble spirit."

Payaso clicked his heals proudly — and bowed crisply — as Swift moved toward the door.

As if in an afterthought Swift turned. "Oh…one small question… *Señor* General. What light can you shed on the deaths of the three Americans? Consul Stepptoe? Colonel Cross? And Lieutenant Porter?"

Payaso blinked twice. "Why…Cross and Porter were obviously killed by *rancheros* angry at the American invasion of their land."

Swift nodded. "And Consul Stepptoe? As you know I was the one who found his body. It appears his killers were also thieves who emptied the safe. Do you know what they were looking for?"

Payaso almost choked. "Looking for? Why what do you mean?"

"Apparently Stepptoe had placed a large sum of money in the Custom House. That is under your command…is it not? And that money is now missing. Can you comment?"

"I know nothing about…well…there was a report." Payaso stammered. "…Something about all four strongboxes missing…but I must investigate. It is too early to be certain. Records in wartime are sometimes slow.…" Payaso forced an excuse.

"Do you know anything about a secret passage?"

"Passage?" Payaso squeaked like a mouse caught in the open. "What do you mean? Me? No. Nothing. Of course not."

"Or something called Wildfire?"

Payaso shook his head. Frozen speechless. Swift's steady gaze saw the commandant's swelled pride deflate into the look of a deer in a floodlight. *He's hiding something.*

"Thank you again…*Señor* General. You have been most helpful." With that Swift closed the door behind her.

☒ ☒ ☒

Back at the Hotel Casamata Swift asked Big Tim to take an anonymous message to General Taylor as fast as possible. Swift closed her correspondent's pouch where she kept Payaso's safe passage letter. *With Payaso no longer in command…if some* Guardia Civil *stopped me now…how much will this paper protect me?*

CHAPTER **55**

THE OLD GENERAL read Swift's anonymous note. *Well done to keep the source quiet.* Immediately Taylor realized his predicament. The time for mere saber rattling was past. Taylor gathered his command.

"Gentlemen…we now know the Mexicans will have a third change of command in just thirteen days. First it was Payaso. Then Ampudia. Now General Mariano Arista. Arista didn't arrive until today. That will leave them unsettled for a mite longer. What is most troubling is a pincer movement Arista ordered toward our vulnerable supply line to Point Isabel." Taylor stabbed a blunt finger onto a crude sketch hastily drawn by Meade and his topogs.

As Taylor put Swift's message into his planter's jacket he glared at his commanders. "Irregular *rancheros* are one thing. A significant force of Mexican regulars crossing onto the north bank of the river is another matter. In Washington they will read this affair as an invasion…a true act of war."

Taylor issued his orders. "Captains Thornton and Hardee…we have reason to believe a large force of Mexican regulars will soon cross the river upstream. Perhaps fifteen or twenty miles as the crow flies.

Near La Palangaña. Your orders are to take the Second Dragoons on a reconnaissance patrol. Ascertain if the enemy has crossed the river. Report on his position and force. Avoid attack…gentlemen. I repeat. We want you to return in safety with the information. Do not engage the enemy. Is that clear?"

"Yes…sir!" Captain Thornton responded. He was an overconfident veteran—a fellow native of Virginia. Who had fought with Taylor in the Seminole War in Florida.

"Good. Take my personal guide—Chapita Sandoval. He knows the back country. I have instructed Chapita to work ahead of your patrol two or three miles. That way if questioned he can claim to be an innocent traveler on his way upriver to see his people."

"I doubt the Mexies will cross over." Thornton spoke with bravado. "If they do…they will learn the hard way that one Yank is worth twenty of their kind…sir."

Taylor concluded his orders. "Captain Hardee is second in command…and Lieutenants Kane and Mason will support. Captain Ker has swept the country to the east downstream and reports no contact. I repeat: Gentlemen…reconnoiter and bring back the facts. Do not engage. Understood? Do not engage. Those are your orders."

Taylor thought to himself. *Even bravery can have its limits when you are outnumbered twenty-five to one.*

CHAPTER 56

RANCHO DE CARRICITOS
UPRIVER/DISPUTED TERRITORY
25 APRIL 1846

UNDER DARKNESS after midnight the dragoons rode out of the nervous camp near Fort Texas. Their jingling harnesses and metal trappings wrapped in leather to deaden any sound and darken any glint off polished brass as the moon rose in the sky. Thornton's sixty-four dragoons rode through the night a dozen miles or so upriver. Then halted until daylight in a cold bivouac.

After Chapita Sandoval rode upriver another eight miles by mid-morning the guide raced back to meet the dragoons.

"*Señor*…they are here!" Sandoval cried out. "A farmer told me so…and another traveler who came from the west confirmed it. Do not proceed. You will be taken and killed…*Señor*."

"Sandoval…you're an easily frightened old fool." Thornton dismissed him. "The Mexicans would never cross into our territory. And if they did…they will not fight…rest assured. You will be safe with us. We will continue."

"No…*Señor*. I cannot. If they catch me…I will be hanged as a traitor. Do not go…*Señor*. It is too dangerous. I will wait at the farmhouse you passed a mile back."

Thornton signaled to his troops to follow him forward. "You'll miss all the glory…Sandoval."

The dragoons worked their way through the thorn scrub for a few miles. Captain Hardee of the 2nd Dragoons—a native of Georgia… and a West Point graduate only eight years before—was the first to come upon a man working a plantation field. When the fieldhand saw Hardee the man disappeared like a jackrabbit behind a chapparal fence. Hardee's gaze noted how pairs of posts had been sunk every six feet or so. Rows of heavy timbers and thorn were closely compacted to fill the gaps. Over the seasons tough dry vines with barb-like thorns had grown over. And through. And created a natural wall six to eight feet tall. *Not jackrabbit proof but that will keep the cattle in…or the wild dogs out.* Hardee knew these thorn fences were nearly impossible to take hold of—even with the greatest care—without being wounded by the barbs. The Captain saw the fence surrounded the remote plantation beside the river. Its impenetrable wall outlined a space as strong as a box canyon.

The only entrance to the central compound was nearest the river. Hardee rode up to the gap. Stopped short of the two poles drawn across the opening. The inner space had the appearance more of a trampled stockyard than a front courtyard. Hardee's gaze traveled to the far end of the barren compound—perhaps two hundred yards from the gate. There a cluster of buildings faced the open yard. The West Pointer dismounted and withdrew the two poles that closed the gap.

Lieutenant Mason fell in beside Captain Thornton. Thornton brushed aside Mason's query if a guard should be placed at the gate. Without hesitation Thornton led his troop single file into the enclosure. When the file scuffled to a stop before the buildings several troops dismounted…and scattered to find a *ranchero* or owner. They found only an old man. Who seemed to be alone on the plantation. Thornton tried to communicate with him. But deciphered only that the plantation was known as Rancho de Carricitos.

Hardee was the last to enter. As he brought up the rear Hardee thought it odd the Captain did not pass down orders to post a sentry at the gate. As he reached the dragoons at the far end of the compound Hardee's horse joined the nervous light cavalry. All milled about— awaiting Thornton's feeble gestures to communicate with the old man.

In frustration the Captain raised his voice. Shouted louder. As if that would make the old man understand English.

Then something happened that would change history. "Look!" A trooper shouted the imperative. At that exact moment a musket shot split the silence of the yard. All eyes looked as one toward the plantation gate. Where moments before there was a gap in the fence…now it was blocked by Mexican infantry. Beyond their rapidly filled ranks were regular Mexican cavalry in green tunics and shako hats. Then from the entire chapparal fence on all sides came puffs of smoke and flash. Instantly the crackle of musketry filled the space.

Next to Hardee a dragoon screamed when a ball slammed into his chest. The bullet knocked him off his horse. Another ball zipped past Hardee's ear.

Thornton bounded forward. Bellowed. "Charge! Give 'em hell!" The Captain regained his saddle and advanced at full gallop. His saber pointed toward the enemy. Hardee screamed like the rest. Spurred his horse to follow. His stallion leapt over the bodies of two troopers and their fallen mounts. Hardee desperately searched for an opening in the encircling thorns. The more he searched the more Hardee felt like a rabbit caught in a trap.

Into his mind flashed a recent memory. Had he heard a woman's voice? *Didn't that lovely* señorita *at the* fandango *tell me I was as generous as a saint?* His mind careened wildly. *And what saint would that be? Saint Jude—she said—the patron saint of lost causes. Then she danced with another man.*

"Saint Jude…help me now!" Hardee muttered. In leaping bounds Hardee forced his horse forward. Sweat cooled on his forehead in the wind. Thunderous volleys of muskets roared from all sides. The Americans were pummeled by the muzzle loads. Several lead balls hit the horse beside him. The beast somersaulted headfirst. Threw its trooper into the sand beneath it. The soldier's neck broke with a dull snap. Hardee galloped into the teeth of hell. The Mexicans took dead aim from their positions inside the gate to the left and right. The kneeling front rank bristled before a standing second. Muskets flashed in cruel volley. Reloaded with discipline. Fired again.

Hardee's mind took in the glint of bayonets that protruded from the smoke and fire like crooked spikes. The barrels now poured death into the melee. Mexican cavalry lined the exterior fence like the center ring at a circus. Two dismounted American troops knelt to return fire. As if condemned before a firing squad both were thrown down by deadly volleys.

When Thornton saw the gate filled by a mass of Mexican regulars he wheeled his charge clockwise to his right. Skirted the interior of the fence. Their leader desperately searched for an escape. What remained of Thornton's company followed him. The charge splintered. Separated into a state of disorder.

Hardee intercepted Thornton. Shouted over the din. "The only hope is to find a hole in the fence!"

Not stopping his horse. Nor the men behind him. Thornton bellowed. "Do it!"

As the enemy moved closer inside and outside the chapparal walls the green tunics steadily grew in greater numbers. Hardee judged the entire fence now was lined with Mexicans. Without mercy they poured thunderous close-range fire into the desperate Yankees. With a glance at the entrance Hardee realized escape by what had been the only exit was utterly hopeless.

An unhorsed trooper from C Company tried to return fire. But the horses abandoned by screaming dragoons thundered in every direction. Their frantic hooves were as much a deadly threat as the onslaught of musketry from every side.

Captain Thornton drove his terrified horse forward and shouted. "Get out any way you can! Every man for himself!" In the tumult with that last exhortation the Captain spurred his horse to full speed. Raced toward a low area of the hedge. Cleared the compound with a huge leap. And disappeared headlong into the scrub beyond. His command left to fend for themselves.

Two troopers landed hard on the sand when their horses were shot dead beneath them. They pitched within the reach of some Mexican infantry. Before they could recover a half dozen Mexican bayonets drove into their bodies.

As they faced certain destruction the Americans were without possibility of resistance. From every quarter of the chapparal came a murderous fire that ripped into the reconnaissance party. Hardee wheeled his lathered horse to his right. Shouted. "Follow me...men!"

Do or die Hardee made one last effort to escape the snare in which they were fatally entangled. His horse raced for a far corner of the lower field — toward the river.

Miraculously — over a small gape of fencing — Hardee cleared the barrier. Perhaps two dozen men followed. Hardee was suddenly in command. He led the way toward the riverbank. Could he swim the Rio Grande or place his troop in a position of defense? That plan was soon dashed when the riverbank proved a boggy quagmire. The river itself wide and swift. Hardee's last avenue of escape was rejected.

By now Hardee had rallied his men into a ragged line of battle. Perhaps one-third of the total force. The captain coolly took stock. Examined their condition as destructive fire roared in the plantation compound. Only minutes had elapsed since the entire ambush exploded. Quickly he realized almost every dragoon had lost a saber. A pistol. Or carbine. Every man looked at Hardee. Hardee knew his men would sell their lives at as dear a cost as possible. They would fight to the last extremity.

The Mexican skirmishers slipped like venomous shapes between the riverside trees and scrubs. Disappeared. Then appeared again. Hardee made his decision.

He moved forward. Found General Torrejón...who by this time had his whole force collected in the field. "The Americans will surrender." Hardee addressed the Mexican commander. "If we — as prisoners of war — can secure good treatment entitled by the rules of civilized warfare." As the pungent smell of gunpowder filled his nostrils Hardee heard a great cheer go up from the plantation. He realized the day belonged to the enemy.

Between Hardee's troop and the men captured in the compound Torrejón held forty-seven prisoners. Among them Lieutenant Kane. Hardee was told eleven soldiers were dead. Six dragoons wounded. Few if any casualties were taken by the Mexicans. Among the American dead was Lieutenant Mason...who had fallen in the first charge. Mason's spurs were later seen in the possession of the enemy.

Thornton was nowhere to be found.

CHAPTER 57

GENERAL ARISTA'S HEADQUARTERS
PALACIO DE ARMAS/MATAMOROS
26 APRIL 1846

SAMANTHA SWIFT noted the date. Almost one month since the American Army arrived across the river from Matamoros. She knew the two-story full-block brick headquarters of General Arista was where the American prisoners were taken in Matamoros. And that she alone had been summoned as the only correspondent at hand.

Even though Swift and Arista had just met the newly arrived red-haired General spoke to the prisoners with exaggerated graciousness. In fluent English. "Gentlemen. Let me introduce S. Thomas Swift of the *Brooklyn Eagle*. She will record your story. Beginning with the officers." Then excused himself.

Hardee and Kane reported lodging at Arista's "hotel." Eating at Arista's dining table. Hardee spoke candidly to Swift. "General Arista's frankly agreeable manner and generous hospitality almost made us forget our captivity."

As she moved among the prisoners of war Swift quickly assembled every detail of the Thornton debacle. Her dramatic dispatch almost wrote itself.

Within the hour Arista returned to address the troops personally.

He chose his words intentionally for Swift to hear. "I know my nation has been regarded as barbarous. But—as you see—I wish to prove to all that it is simply not true." To emphasize the point Arista grandly promised the officers would receive half pay while they were his guest. "And the men will get ample rations." To show good faith Arista presented every man with an American twenty-five-cent piece. A sum Swift realized was greater than many had seen from their own paymaster in weeks. "We intend to supply all their needs. All their wants." Arista was more than happy to boast of his largesse to Swift.

"Such a remarkable victory over the American invaders will fuel the imaginations of the Mexican nation." The General crowed proudly. "We can see true visions of numerous future triumphs to come."

Arista distributed his effusive letter—addressed to Your Excellency General Torrejón—and made sure a copy reached the Mexican newspapers. The commendation was also hand-delivered to the only American war correspondent in Matamoros. Who translated it verbatim.

> *This has been a day of rejoicing to the Division of the North. It having been known this day of the triumph achieved by the brigade which Your Excellency so worthily commands. The rejoiced country will doubtless celebrate this preliminary of glorious deeds that her happy sons will in future present to her. Your Excellency will communicate to your brave soldiers that I have seen with the greatest pleasure their valiant behavior and that I await your detailed dispatch to elevate it to the knowledge of the supreme government. So that the nation may learn the triumph of your arms.*

⊠   ⊠   ⊠

Within the hour Swift dusted the ink on her exclusive dispatch. She knew her news carried word of what would become known as the Thornton Affair. With urgency she implored Big Tim to speed the dispatch to Fort Texas. Her words would be carried by the next express pouch to Point Isabel…and the first steamer to New Orleans. Before the other war correspondents on the American side of the river even heard the standard military reports. Within days she envisioned S. Thomas Swift's exclusive dispatch would reach New York. The electrifying news would rouse a slumbering patriotism with blazingly large headlines.

Swift breathed deeply on her balcony overlooking Fort Texas. With satisfaction she knew it could be weeks—at the earliest perhaps 9 May—before Washington would receive Taylor's formal military reports that Mexican regulars had attacked...captured...and killed American troops in American territory.

Meanwhile in Matamoros the clock of war ticked on.

CHAPTER 58

**TAYLOR'S HEADQUARTERS TENT
AMERICAN CAMP/FORT TEXAS
26 APRIL 1846/THAT SAME DAY**

MAJOR GENERAL ZACHARY TAYLOR was furious. Not only had Thornton disobeyed orders not to cause a fight but now—although presumed dead—Thornton was very much alive. And a prisoner of the Mexicans. Along with Hardee. Kane. The others.

"He would have deserved his fate if he *had* been killed." Taylor growled.

⊠   ⊠   ⊠

Almost two weeks would pass before Eastern nabobs and politicos quibbled over the nuances of who actually fired the first shot in the ill-fated Thornton Affair. Liberal supporters of Mexico claimed the Americans provoked the incident. Thornton's aggressive confrontation and charge on Mexican troops—while they defended their own territory against invaders—was at fault. Conservative leaders countered that Torrejón's troops in fact fired the first shot at Thornton's benign reconnaissance patrol.

⊠   ⊠   ⊠

Headlines screamed:
Rush to the Rescue!
America Cannot Stand Idle!
Taylor's Army in Danger!
A Call to Battle!

President Polk at last had the provocation he wanted. On 11 May—to Congress…and to the nation—he would proclaim: "American blood has been shed on American soil!"

War on Mexico would be declared in Washington on 13 May.

Back in Matamoros Swift studied her words as she made an anxious entry in her journal. *26 April 1846: Out of the frying pan…into the fire.*

CHAPTER 59

JAMES COLLINGSWORTH TURNER demeaned Swift's Thornton dispatch as beginner's luck. Nothing more. *This little shooting shindig will be well over before that damned woman finds out her luck didn't last. Indeed. Her dispatch deserved special handling before my* Picayune *express left for New Orleans.* In March—when Taylor arrived in Matamoros—Turner immediately reintroduced himself to Old Zack—as he called the General beyond earshot—to be sure the commander knew Turner's name. And could recognize him on sight. "Presenting yourself to the village chiefs before a fracas always pays dividends." Turner had so lectured the other war correspondents several times.

Turner considered himself an expert dab hand. He knew Swift had taken an instant dislike to him. And the feeling was mutual. Turner was a flamboyant character. A great storyteller around campfires. He mingled easily with officers. Dispatches flew off his pen. Mostly uninhibited by the facts. Rivers of words flowed as Turner reported anything he heard…even the slightest camp rumors. Which were especially rife among the foreign recruits.

Turner made it a practice to offer *The Picayune's* express pouches to all the correspondents. His control of the express service to New Orleans allowed Turner to post letters faster than the army courier for officers and volunteers as a personal favor. Weeks later—when the recipient back home received these notes in the regular post—they often wondered why the seals were broken. Why envelopes appeared opened. As if the letters had been read. An official-looking woodcut stamp—"Inspected—Military Censor"—provided a plausible explanation. Meanwhile the readers of *The Picayune* already had read the gist of them. Disguised as an observation. Anecdote. Or an anonymous tip gleaned by "your devoted correspondent."

Turner burned through the writing paper with his long dispatches. Sometimes cribbed from the slips of other newspapers in *The Picayune's* exchange network. Other times simply recopied over his name. As he scribbled Turner made a vow to himself. *S. Thomas Swift…you will get your just desserts.*

Mexican Terrain Second Enemy
Topographicals Explore Fields of Honor
'Manifest Destiny' Threatened by Cordgrass
FORT TEXAS—27 APRIL 1846. Success on the battlefield—as your faithful correspondent has seen—depends not only on valor and bravery but also on the ability to use the landscape to advantage.

In the recent march of the American Army from Corpus Christi in Texas to Matamoros in Mexico no more important role fell to an elite corps—known by all as the Topographical Engineers. This modest scribe is privileged to share valuable references from the private reports of two such extraordinary soldiers: Lt. George Meade and Lt. Jacob Blake. Herewith are excerpts of their critical observations for the coming conflict.

In modern warfare—as Meade related—visual contact with the enemy is paramount. "Artillery to strike the enemy must be positioned in the open for a clear line of sight. As well they must be sure a necessitated rapid change of position not bog down the gun carriages in prairie muck."

According to Blake's observation: "Charging cavalry must quickly decide if this prairie brush sufficiently conceals their movements to maintain surprise…or if that bog ahead would impede maneuvers and must be avoided."

The prairie of Tamaulipas—dear reader—as the department north of Matamoros on the Texas side of the Rio Grande River is known—is as monotonously flat as a flood basin. As Lt. Blake told your trusted reporter: "Meander scars left by tributary channels abandoned long ago by the ever-shifting Rio Grande as well as seasonal floods relieve this monotony."

Meade confided recently: "Some of these old channels retain water most of the year and are locally called resacas. In other places large depressions—sometimes as great as thirty acres or more—can create a pond of fresh water for horses and oxen and men."

Saber-Like Cordgrass

In this part of Texas a slight change in elevation can affect the vegetation on the battlefield. Where land is lowest—and drainage poorest—a zone is formed called the salt prairie. Blake told The Picayune: "One can almost taste the salt if you licked a dry stone." Very little woody vegetation survives here beyond sword-like yucca plants and scattered mesquite trees.

Blake further told your correspondent: "Covering this salt prairie is a blanket of cordgrass. This coastal grass is a torment for our infantry. The razor-sharp and spine-tipped blades of cordgrass can slice through the toughest uniform."

Meade and Blake reported perhaps a quarter of the terrain north of Matamoros supports stands of virtually impenetrable mesquite—especially in and alongside the resacas. "In these stands visual pursuit is quickly lost. The ability to 'track' one's enemy by their spore is essential. At night – even in the brightest moonlight—opposed forces can pass close to each other without detection…as long as one passes in silence."

About the salt prairie low rises occur that can stand 10 feet and are called motitas in Spanish. The mounds often support a mesquite thicket. In the rainy season motitas can become veritable islands surrounded by water. "This season has proved *wetter than usual." Meade entrusted the latest reports to his local sources.*

Roads and Tracks Critical

Travel through this terrain by foot or horse or wagon — or for livestock — as you can imagine — made the necessity of roads and tracks critical. The three all-weather routes or ferry roads to Point Isabel from Matamoros and Longoreño are of great tactical importance.

Upon these prairie fields and sandy byways will be decided the trial of fire and the fate of Manifest Destiny.

James Collingsworth Turner
Senior Mexican War and Foreign Correspondent
Exclusive to The Daily Picayune

CHAPTER 60

WATCH TOWER/HOTEL CASAMATA
MEANWHILE AT FORT POLK/POINT ISABEL
28 APRIL 1846

SWIFT. ANOCHE. FATHER THOMAS. BIG TIM watched from the hotel's rooftop Watch Tower with a dark presentiment. The Americans opposite Matamoros threw every resource and three thousand men into a manic effort to complete Fort Texas as rapidly as possible. Four blocks north along the *paseo* promenade on the right bank the Mexicans labored day and night to construct riverside batteries. Payaso named the breastworks to oppose the Americans: *Fuerta Guerrero*—Fort Warrior. His engineers put up a circular redoubt overlooking the middle crossing. The strength of this parapet was reinforced by cylindrical *gabions* of wickerwork at breast height. Then extended downstream with a long entrenchment. These Mexican works were further expanded along the riverbank by a triple-arrowhead redoubt pointed at Fort Texas. Each embrasure point had three or four cannon emplacements. Wickerwork connected the parapets with bundled sticks called *fascines*. Swift made a rapid sketch.

Meanwhile miles away at Point Isabel Major John Munroe commanded a support detail. Quartermasters. Engineers. Medicals. Ordinance specialists. The depot barely mustered five hundred bodies for morning roll call. Nowhere enough troops to defend the army's stores and supplies and wagons and livestock at what war correspondent Turner had dubbed Fort Polk. Only twenty-three miles northeast of Fort Texas Munroe knew his small unit was as isolated as any frontier outpost.

Renegade Antonio Malvado had tasted the blood of Cross and Porter. Now the Chapparal Fox hunted in the vicinity of the Tanques de Ramireno road between Palo Alto and the Rio Grande. And looked for easy pickings.

To make matters worse: After the exhilarating rout of Thornton at Rancho de Carricitos Torrejón had moved his sixteen hundred Mexican regulars east. Unknown to Walker and Dancer in Point Isabel these disciplined troops now sat at the junction below Palo Alto — where the Point Isabel road from the east met the Tanques de Ramireno road that ran from the south — at the Longoreño crossing on the river.

Munroe fretted to Walker and Dancer. "We're in a desperate fix. The navy is far out to sea patrolling the mouth of the Rio Grande. We have our backs to the Laguna Madre bay and the Brazos Santiago narrows. There's virtually no fortification to block any advance from the west. If the Mexicans bring a force — even the size you say trapped Thornton — we won't be able to hold them off." Monroe paced back and forth as he clutched a ledger in his hands like a Bible. "For God sake this is Point Isabel…not Fort Isabel." Even his West Point education and decades in the army had not rid the vestiges of a Scottish lilt from Munroe's words. "We've got to get word to Taylor. How in the world did we get into this position…?" He cradled his bound accounts.

"Don't you fret yourself…Major." Walker spoke up confidently. "Me and my boys are gettin' a bit rusty just sittin' around here watchin' the sunsets. Fishin' ain't our style no how. And we ain't doin' much good to you…sir…nor for Texas. No…sir…not much good at all for Texas."

"You Texians are something else…Walker. A real piece of work. Truth be told — with all due respect — your irregulars have a way about them that seems to attract trouble. It would suit me just fine to have a few less of my men get the worse end of your bar fights."

For days Dancer's mission relentlessly gnawed at his gut. Obtain the loan documents. Find the treasure. Turn it over to the army before the shooting starts. *How the hell can I do that stuck here in Point Isabel?*

Walker and Dancer stood up to take their leave.

Munroe made a decision. "Here's a dispatch I need taken to Taylor as fast as possible. Tell him we can't defend Point Isabel." Then the Major added—more for emphasis than actual fact: "And tell him the Mexicans are coming our way sure as hellfire."

CHAPTER 61

CAPTAIN SAMUEL WALKER gathered his Texas Rangers. He laid out the mission. Asked for volunteers. To a man the Texians carried more weapons on their person than any regular soldier. The latest carbine rifles. One always at the ready. A second loaded and waiting in a saddle scabbard. A black-powder revolving Paterson Colt pistol hung from each hip. A personal Deringer secreted under their belt. A twelve-inch razor-edged Bowie knife just behind the right holster with its grip turned forward. Ready to be snatched by a left back-handed grab. While the right hand kept any prey at bay with the five-shot Colt. Several of the Rangers also favored a medium-sized cavalry saber. As versatile at cutting wood as cutting off an enemy's hand. Or whatever appendage presented a good target. Their dress was as unique as their armaments. They presented a fearsome appearance. More like a frontier raiding party than a troop in the United States Army. Known to the Mexicans as *Los Diablos Tejanos* or "The Texas Devils." Munroe thought: *Heaven help us.*

The entire troop stepped forward. Walker counted them off by twos. Selected the odd numbers.

"We'll parallel the road but stay off the track." Walker addressed half his Rangers who would accompany them. "Work our way through the mesquite. Run silent…boys. If you see or hear somethin' give the call of the snakebird and we all halt. Hand signals only."

The Rangers mounted and fell into single file behind Walker and Dancer. They worked the low depressions. Climbed the occasional *motita* to scan the twilight for trouble. Steadily the lonely column of thirty-six men wove its way southwest toward Palo Alto. Nothing untoward disturbed their passage. At first.

That evening the Rangers halted and made a fireless cold camp in the shelter of a cluster of three *motita* dunes. Out of sight of any prowling enemy. Or so they thought.

Walker drew Dancer aside.

"When we bed down use an old Indian hunting trick Kit Carson taught me. Don't be in the center of the camp. Find a spot at the perimeter. Sleep with your pistol in your hand and your carbine primed. Tonight we won't unsaddle the horses." Having cautioned Dancer appropriately Walker concluded: "I'll tell the men."

A slight coolness came into the breeze as night stars moved across the heavens on that moonless night.

It wasn't long before something startled the horses. They were uneasy. Muzzles sniffed the air. Ears worked the night sounds. What was it? A coyote? The blades of a dense cordgrass colony rattled in the breeze.

From out of the darkness roared an explosion. The flame of muskets and pistols rent the night. Accompanied by a bellowing Mexican voice: "*Ataqué!*" In that instant Dancer felt a heavy thud beside him: A Ranger dropped in a grotesque heap in the salty sand. Next came the sound of his last life wind from where a ball left a hole the size of a fist in the Ranger's chest. Out of the darkness death flashed from the muzzles of a Mexican patrol. Rangers fired back blindly at the flashes. Screams split the air when a ball struck home. Horses reared. Spun in circles. Their shoed hooves a threat to the men who knelt beside their bedding as they fired into the musket flashes. Battle cries came out of the darkness. The sound of a saber being drawn from its metal scabbard filled Dancer's ears as he looked up.

Two Mexican regulars loomed over him. One charged at Dancer's form. A musket at his hip with a fifteen-inch bayonet affixed to its muzzle. Dancer pulled his pistol from under his blanket. Fired pointblank into the soldier's face. The visage evaporated in a bloody mass as the body fell forward. The bayonet drove into the sand. Inches from Dancer's thigh. Dancer turned to his second attacker. Then a carbine roared from behind Dancer's head. The second Mexican's body jerked. Stopped in midstride. A look of astonishment appeared on his face as his saber fell from his hand. And he toppled backward in a twitching heap.

Dancer looked behind him. Walker reloaded his carbine in an instant. Then shouted. "Take the top of the dunes! Use the dunes… boys! Use the dunes!"

Fire ranged at the shapes in the darkness. Walker's men turned. Scrambled. And pushed their mates to the top of the dunes.

Walker shouted to Dancer to follow him. Then he grabbed the three Rangers nearest at hand.

"Stay low. Fire low. Move into them. Now!" Walker spat angrily.

The five men formed a wedge that moved beyond their camp. Fired at anything in front of them that moved. Or made a sound. They poured a devastating fire of death into the Mexican troops ahead. Made their way between two *motita* dunes. The rises to left and right gave them a momentary advantage. Like moving down a corridor. As if the walls were sheltering friends.

Abruptly from a third dune to their right bullets zipped past their heads. Splashes of sand raised around their feet. The Mexicans had taken the elevation. And emptied their flintlock Brown Bess muskets at the five men. Walker's wedge wheeled right. Poured its concentrated fire at the enemy's dune.

Just as abruptly as it had begun the firing slackened.

Walker acted instantly. He raced back toward the camp site. Now a macabre scene of moaning and lifeless forms. Walker shouted to his men. "This way lads. We can get out this way!"

His men heard his call. The Rangers still standing pointed their fire at the shadows in the scrub brush at the far end of camp. Rangers on the dunes above kept up a steady covering fire. The Rangers below dropped back. Covered the progress of their walking wounded. And carried their dead. Behind the dunes the Rangers recovered their horses.

All hitched to a large rope corral to forestall a stampede. The Rangers mounted. Then retreated into the night. Walker and Dancer came last.

His men regrouped. Walker counted his losses. Five dead. Four wounded or taken prisoner. The losses marked an emboldened new aggressiveness on the part of the Mexicans and Antonio Malvado. More blood lost. American blood.

"Bastards." Walker spit. "Thunderin' bloody bastards. Jump us in camp. In the middle of the night. This won't be the last those coward *rancheros* see of us. Malvado is my guess. Just wait. Mark my words."

Walker and his men — including Dancer — made their way in darkness. Took a circuitous route around the outskirts of the mesquite woods south of Palo Alto. To their right in the near distance they discovered the campfires and pickets of Torrejón's main Mexican force. The band of Texians kept a wide berth. Covered by occasional mesquite and brush they walked their horses in silence. Presented a lower target above the scrub until they struck the Tanques de Ramireno track.

The Rangers continued south along this road a short distance. A moment later Walker aroused the sharp cry of a Mexican sentry.

"Who goes there?" The Mexican guard's challenge was succinct.

"*Amigos.*" Walker replied using the Mexican phrase.

Not expecting the enemy to approach from the same direction as his main camp the sentry was satisfied and replied carelessly. "Advance friends."

Walker knew it was a picket guard in the darkness. But how many? Decisiveness was key. Hesitation would spell disaster.

Walker drew his Colt revolver slowly. Thumbed the hammer back. Touched the folding trigger…now in firing position. Every man behind him silently followed his lead. Behind Walker the force advanced directly into the sentry camp. By the light of the small campfire American pistols cracked at anything that moved. Five Mexican sentries fell immediately. A sixth writhed in agony from a bullet in the shoulder. He was silently dispatched by a Bowie blade thrust into his throat.

The knife now christened with the revenge of Mexican blood was wiped clean on the sentry's tailcoat.

CHAPTER 62

SAMANTHA SWIFT returned to her room after writing in her journal on the Watch Tower parapet. When she went to straighten her bed she discovered a letter. Secreted under the blue indigo cotton coverlet. *The door was locked when I came in. Whoever left this note was a friend…with a key.*

The cryptic message read simply: *Torrejón sits Isabel Road at Palo Alto. Need road clear. Spread rumor snipers wait Arista at Longoreño.*

No signature or seal indicated the writer. Except one hint. Swift recognized the watermark. A piece of stationery with the header sliced off from the steam packet SS *New York.* Swift smiled to herself. *Dancer.*

Swift left her room quickly. Locked the door behind her. Found Michelena Anoche and Father Thomas in the cantina. Quickly they hatched a plan. Together Anoche and Swift quietly worked the saloon and lunchtime cantina frequented by Mexican soldiers. Anoche told what she knew to one. Swift asked another if he had heard the news. Together they repeated to newcomers the misinformation. Father Thomas spread the word to soldiers in the street. And among officers who entered his church. *Did you hear?*

Like a spark fanned in tinder a rumor spread. The Americans expected the Mexican Army to cross at the Longoreño ferry tomorrow. An ambush is set. An elite corps of sharpshooters. Led by that scum they call Texas Rangers. Invisible as Indians. Many had taken up positions opposite the ferry. Their long rifles can drop a javelina pig at three hundred yards…much less a man. Explicit orders. Target officers. Assassinate Arista. Kill our most brave commander in chief. As he leads his gallant warriors across the river to defend Mexican honor against the northern invaders. One version of the rumor claimed a bounty of fifty American dollars to the man who made a confirmed kill. Soon the Arista bounty became one hundred fifty. Officers' bounty hit seventy-five. From rapid repetition the misinformation turned into truth. Then truth into fact. And finally into an explicit intercepted order direct from Taylor himself.

This critical intelligence raced directly to the Mexican commander's ears.

Arista blinked. A truly worrisome development. The Mexican commander rushed urgent instructions to Torrejón.

> *Disregard original orders to wait for Arista to reinforce your company at Palo Alto. Displace your position astride the road at Palo Alto upon receipt. March with all haste to the north bank of the Rio Grande at Longoreño. Attack entrenched riflemen.*

Swift and Dancer's ruse had worked.

The Point Isabel-Matamoros Road was open again.

If only for a brief window.

CHAPTER 63

THE AMERICAN GENERAL called a council of war. Zachary Taylor read Munroe's message out loud. Walker's and Dancer's encounter with Torrejón's camp at Palo Alto had clarified the situation. Now the anonymous message from Matamoros—delivered by Big Tim— put the last piece in place.

"We know Torrejón and his force of about sixteen hundred regulars moved from Palo Alto down the Tanques de Ramireno track to the Longoreño ferry yesterday." Taylor began to trace the developments on the same crude sketch surrounded by his top commanders. "Word has come to us that their intention is to protect the north bank…while Arista brings his entire force across the downstream narrows at Longoreño. The Mexicans expect to surround us. Then lay siege to Fort Texas. Cut off our supplies from Point Isabel."

Taylor let the facts of their position sink in before he continued. "Gentlemen…this is where we stand. At Point Isabel we have a supply depot without defense. At Fort Texas we have an army and defense without supplies. If the enemy traps us here at Fort Texas they can pick us to pieces on two fronts at once. No supplies will get through—

and Munroe won't hold out for long." Taylor's steady gaze studied his command.

"Your opinions...gentlemen."

An uncomfortable silence filled the tent.

Finally Dancer spoke. "Walker and I have just come from Point Isabel...General. From what we've seen — sir — Point Isabel is a port... not a fort."

Taylor nodded. Faced the other officers. "How long do you judge Fort Texas can withstand a siege?"

"How many men would defend her...sir? And what guns could be spared?"

"Major Jacob Brown and the Seventh Infantry musters about five hundred. We can spare two batteries with eight guns. Lowd's four eighteen-pounders...three six-pounders...and a mortar with Ringgold's field battery."

A pessimistic veteran of the Alamo debacle spoke first. "If they shell us and attack at once...we're outnumbered three to one. Most of these Irish and German troops have never faced gunfire before. No telling what they can stand."

Major Brown offered his assessment with lukewarm conviction. "On the other hand...if they only bombard the works — and that's a big 'if' — we may be able to hold for a week...ten days at the most. That's assuming the water well holds up...or we can still draw water from the river. Powder and ball will need to be husbanded."

Taylor moved toward the front of the command tent. His hands clasped behind his back. To the other commanders his visage could have been that of an elderly planter surveying his lands.

"We must act." Taylor turned to face his command. "Strike camp immediately. Decamp at fourteen hundred hours. Take all three hundred supply wagons. Leave Brown and the Seventh Infantry enough for two weeks. We are going to Point Isabel...God willing."

⊠　⊠　⊠

Smart salutes. The officers bounded past their general. Spirits high. Conscious of being on the march. Not only for supplies... and to strengthen Fort Polk. But also for a fight. The army came alive. In short order The Cottonbalers — as the 7th was known from its heroic defense of New Orleans under Andrew Jackson in 1815—hunkered down inside Fort Texas.

Outside the hastily raised walls their comrades decamped as the eye of the storm swirled around Fort Texas.

CHAPTER 64

PATRICK HARP AND SCORES OF MEN used the chaos of the army striking camp to slip away. Before they deserted Harp made special note of the walls of the fort—where Bragg's four-gun field battery was stationed. *Your time has come…bastard.*

That afternoon Harp gathered the men of the San Patricios legionnaires. Then presented his troop to Arista's headquarters. Harp was shown into the commander's ornate chambers. There all three generals who had occupied the rank in quick succession gathered.

"Mr. Harp…Come in…come in." Arista purred. "My congratulations on joining the just fight of Mexico."

Harp clicked his heels and gave a smart salute. "Reporting for duty…sir. Today I present the command of the San Patricios battalion to your service. I have assembled a hundred and fourteen able men—with more to come—thanks to your generosity…General."

"Yes…many more to come…certainly." Ampudia chimed his appreciation.

"Perhaps we will need a regular ferry." Payaso toadied his observation.

"Tell us about Wildfire and your orders." Arista bluntly stated his order.

Harp handed over a letter from Israel David he had concealed for weeks. He stood at ease. Then explained. "In New Orleans I accepted the assignment to recruit foreign-born soldiers. My mission was to convince as many of my brothers as possible to serve in the Mexican cause."

Arista came right to the point. "And in the meantime our friends in Wildfire tell us you have become a student of the Americans' new artillery."

Harp studied the three generals. "That is correct…sir. I became an expert in artillery—particularly what the Americans call their horse artillery."

Payaso cut in to upstage Harp. "They call them 'flying artillery'… General Arista."

Arista pressed the deserter. "What is the weakness of this 'flying artillery'?"

Harp answered simply. "The horses…sir."

"The horses?" Payaso scoffed.

Harp responded coolly. "Yes. The cannon are light six-pounders designed to be unlimbered and fired quickly. The carriage that pulls the cannon includes a caisson of shot and powder. What makes the horse artillery different…is the gunners ride on the horses that pull the carriage."

"Ride on the same horses…not on separate mounts like real soldiers!" Ampudia shot off. "How demeaning! Mounted horse guns will never succeed on the battlefield."

"That is the great advantage—and the great weakness—of the flying artillery." Harp explained further: "Kill the horses and you kill the artillery. That is the secret."

"Ah…yes." Arista's remark was telling. "Without horses they cannot fly."

All three generals laughed at Arista's joke.

"And the horses are the largest target." Payaso noted the obvious.

Harp directed his words at General Arista. "The way to defeat the horse artillery…is with similar units…or with skirmishers and sharpshooters."

Ampudia wet his lips. "With the right long rifles it will be hard to miss these flying wagon trains."

"A turkey shoot for our *cazadores* marksmen." Payaso laughed.

"That is what we have learned." Harp drew his conclusion quickly. "The San Patricios stand by today to deliver the blow that will neutralize this so-called innovation."

Arista. Ampudia. Payaso. All three moved away slightly beyond Harp's hearing. They conferred in hushed Spanish. Soon facing Harp again the generals probed.

"How do we know you are not a spy?" Ampudia demanded warily.

Harp gave the answer he had rehearsed. "Because I am a man in search of a country…a country of justice and tolerance…and a country that shares my Catholic beliefs."

"And a country that pays well." Payaso discreetly spoke his remark under his breath.

Harp finished his answer. "Saint Patrick's Battalion gives us the opportunity to right the injustices of certain American officers that have mistreated my men."

Arista nodded. *So it is personal. Revenge is in his heart.*

Harp turned to Arista. "What service can we be to the Mexican cause…General?"

"Now that you have told us how to defeat this horse artillery — Mr. Harp — be it known among us that you will be given your command and the rank of lieutenant. Your San Patricios Battalion will report to General Payaso in the Matamoros garrison. Specifically your orders are to man a siege battery on the bank of the river opposite the American fort. Share your knowledge with our artillery commanders to reduce the American works to a mound of mud… as quickly as possible."

Harp came to attention. "My men will take positions immediately…sir."

"My orders will give the San Patricios their assignments." Payaso's words were officious.

Arista cut off Payaso in a belittling tone. "No…General Payaso. You will follow my orders…as will Harp's expatriate troop. San Patricios will take the central forward position."

"But they are foreigners!" Payaso protested.

Arista waved Payaso away with disdain. "What's more—the San Patricios will have the honor of firing the first shot upon my orders."

"That honor is rightfully mine! General Francisco Payaso is commander of the Mexican Department of Tamaulipas and Matamoros!" Payaso blustered.

Arista rounded on the little man to humiliate him. "You forget your place…Payaso. Never make that mistake again. Now Your Excellency is giving the orders. Is that understood?"

"Yes…Your Excellency." Payaso's surrender was spiteful.

Arista turned now to face Harp. "When Taylor attempts to relieve what remains of his little Fort Texas…you and your San Patricios will join me as my personal field advisor to ensure the defeat of Taylor's army at Palo Alto. Is that clear?"

Lieutenant Harp stood straight before his new commanders. "Consider it done…sir." Harp saluted proudly. Then Lieutenant Patrick Harp pivoted and left the General's chambers.

Payaso closed the door behind Harp.

General Mariano Arista adopted a confident expression. "Now we have a war to win."

He smacked his white leather gloves into his palm.

"Tighten the noose around Fort Texas."

CHAPTER 65

ARISTA'S HEADQUARTERS
PALACIO DE ARMAS / MATAMOROS
2 MAY 1846

GENERAL ARISTA took the rapid movement by General Taylor's army as a precipitate retreat. Within hours the Mexican Army prepared to cut off Taylor's return to Fort Texas. Yet another victory of Mexican arms was anticipated. The General summoned the American correspondent S. Thomas Swift.

Since their last meeting after the Thornton Affair Swift had gathered background on Arista. Although now the Army of the North's commander in chief—Arista—had shown a decided tendency to change allegiances to further his career. Off again. On again. He was at times an ally—or rival—to General Santa Anna. He reviled the exalted victor of the Alamo. Arista during one banishment for a two-year period between 1832–1834 had been sent packing to Cincinnati in Ohio. While there his proudest accomplishment was to perfect his English. Upon returning his military career flourished. By 1839 he was named commander of the Tamaulipas Department. Even his resignation in 1841—over accusations that he participated in a separatist movement—did not tarnish his reputation. Now Arista was back in command in the north. Much more familiar with the territory of war than the newly arrived American General Taylor.

Seated in a plush armchair upholstered in grand Spanish brocade Swift scanned the first paragraphs of the General's communiqué. Arista's self-important words were crafted to create an impression of the invincibility of Arista's army. Especially among the Mexican soldiers. As well as in the mind of the government in Mexico City.

Americans Abandon Matamoros
'As Fear Has Wings' Retreat to Point Isabel
Cowardly General Taylor Sacrifices Fortification to Save Himself

General Taylor dared not resist the valor and enthusiasm of the sons of Mexico. Did he foresee the intrepidity with which our soldiers would rush against the usurpers of the national territory? Did he know the many injuries which were to be avenged by those who had taken up arms—not to aggrandize themselves with the spoils of the property of others—but to maintain the fierce independence of their country? Did he know that the Mexicans would be stopped neither by trenches or fortresses or large artillery? Thus it was that the chief of the American forces—frightened as soon as he perceived from the situation and proximity of his camp— that our army was preparing to cross the river—left with precipitation for Point Isabel—with almost all his troops. And most of his supplies.

Arista indicated Swift should continue reading out loud as he struck a pose before the grand fireplace. Swift noted he inserted his right hand into his buttoned vest. Perhaps with illusions of how Napoleon might have looked.

The terror and haste with which the latter fled to Point Isabel—to shut themselves up in it and avoid a conflict— frustrated the active measures of the most excellent Señor General Arista—which were to order the cavalry to advance in the plain and to cut off the flight of the fugitives. But it was not possible to do so—not withstanding their forced march during the night. General Taylor left his camp at 2 o'clock in the afternoon and—as fear has wings—he succeeded in shutting himself up in Point Isabel.

Arista gave a sniff of pride at his eloquent turn of phrase. The text continued:

> *Why did the Americans not remain with firmness under their colors? Why did they abandon the ground which they pretend to usurp with such iniquity? Thus an honorable general would keep his word. Had not General Taylor said—in all his communications—that he was prepared to repel all hostilities? Why then does he fly in so cowardly a manner to shut himself up at the Point? The commander in chief of the American Army has covered himself with opprobrium and ignominy in sacrificing a part of his forces who he left in the fortifications in order to save himself. For it is certain that he will not return to their assistance—not that he is ignorant of their peril—but he calculates that this would be greater if he had the temerity of attempting to resist the Mexican lances and bayonets in the open plain.*

Arista clapped his hands in triumph. Strutted back and forth before the fireplace. The General especially liked the charge of cowardice against General Taylor. His mind put aside a similar charge years before that had worked against him—wrongfully—and led to his exile in the desolate Ohio Valley.

"Congratulations…General. Your victory seems complete." Swift honeyed her flattery.

"You have been most considerate—and helpful—*Señorita* Swift. Surely through your correspondence the world now knows America is the barbarian in this contest…and Mexico is the humble victim."

"I look forward to reporting your progress…General." Swift was forthright in her reply.

"As it should be." The General answered in a low voice…like someone confiding a secret.

At that moment the most unexpected thing happened since Samantha's uncle Jacob Swift banished her ten weeks ago. Nothing would ever again be the same in Samantha Swift's life.

"*Señorita* Swift…Soon the siege of Fort Texas will begin—as we all know. Shortly I will lay our trap for General Taylor and his cowardly army when they return from Point Isabel to relieve Fort Texas—as they must."

Swift listened intently. *Where is he going with this? Am I about to be arrested? Locked away in the Palacio to waste away at some giant treadmill as they do in the New York City jail?*

"It would suit the honor of Mexico and me personally if you would accompany me to the battleground as a special correspondent. You would have full access—as you have enjoyed already—and a front row *parterre* seat to report our victory to the world."

Swift stared at the General. "You are inviting me to come with your army now…and report on the battles from the field?"

"Precisely…*Señorita*. From that vantage point you will be able to write dispatches that no other American correspondent can equal—not even James Collingsworth Turner."

"You know my rival's name?" *Best tread softly here. Could Turner have shown the Mexicans my dispatches? But how?*

"There is more I know about you than you think…*Señorita* Swift. Be that as it may." With that surprising revelation Arista's entire countenance changed. The graciousness left his eyes. Swift saw it replaced with a cold-blooded look capable of anything.

Arista deliberately withdrew his parade saber from its position on a side table. "Do you know the difference between a correspondent and a spy…*Señorita* Swift?" His voice was low and threatening.

Swift sat forward on the edge of her chair. *Do not panic. Do not look afraid. Add a small smile.* "What do you mean?"

"Let me instruct you. Correspondents report what they see and what they are told by the authorities in control." Arista selected his words carefully. "If I ever learn you are seen on the American side…or exchange secret messages with the Americans…then I will know you are a spy."

Swift's mind froze. Speechless.

Arista stepped within the length of steel he held in his hand. "You know how we deal with spies?" Without warning Arista's blade sliced the air. Stopped short of Swift's elbow. Red pulp splattered Swift's notebook as the blade split a melon in two.

"That is the head of a spy when we catch them." Arista noted the splatter of red matter-of-factly. "No mercy. Instant. The justice of war. Do I make myself clear?"

Swift nodded. Attempted a smile as a trickle of red juice lodged in her notebook's center hinge.

"Good." Arista relaxed. Kindness and benevolence returned to his face. "I look forward to working with you in my camp as my personal guest. You will be as comfortable as I will be when we defeat the American invaders. Do we have an understanding?"

Swift swallowed and looked up…amazed. "I accept…General. An invitation such as yours is not received often." *Refusal is not an option…but what did I just do? Betray my country?*

"Excellent. Now that we are agreed you will be placed at the center of things for my next great victory! Go now."

Swift took her leave. Payaso followed her. At the bottom of the Palacio steps the little commandant pulled the correspondent aside.

"We have them!" Payaso swelled with self-importance. Convinced of Arista's victory. "We have split their forces! The simple earthwork they call Fort Texas has few supplies. Even less water. Now all we must do is tighten the noose! Yes…the trap is set!" Payaso's eyes blazed with triumph. Empty braggadocio and overconfidence overshadowed any concern to share Arista's plans. After all…victory was certain. The invaders were all but defeated. "We will crush the fort before Taylor can return. Ampudia will encircle the fort on the north and east. To the south and west is the river. And there my batteries complete our impenetrable iron ring. Arista will take the main body of the army under his personal command and lay a trap along the Isabel Road. You will see. All we must do is wait for Taylor's attempt to save those doomed in their pathetic fort. We have them!" Spittle formed at the corner of his lips.

Swift excused herself with the guise she needed to make preparations to join General Arista in the field. Peony waited impatiently for her in the Palacio courtyard. The pair passed through the heavy-gated entry. Swift's mind danced with dangers. Real. And imagined. Fortunately the bright little quarter horse knew the way to the Hotel Casamata stable.

For a Saturday night the streets were eerily empty. At least for a garrison town that teetered on the abyss of war.

CHAPTER 66

ACROSS THE RIVER Captain Joseph K. Mansfield of the Corps of Engineers guided Dancer and Walker as they took stock of their new abode. The works were Mansfield's engineering genius. Fort Texas was well situated on the high lip of the river's cut bank. The roughly oval six-sided earthen fort overlooked the Rio Grande upstream and down. The fort's western wall stopped only yards before the river flats began. And overlooked the middle Paso Real ferry that crossed to the Point Isabel road.

Mansfield pointed with pride as they walked the fifteen-foot wide parapet. "At each corner where the six walls meet is a protruding *redan*—or bastion—designed like a four-sided arrowhead. From point to point the two southern walls are one hundred and fifty yards long. The other four sides are one hundred and twenty-five yards. The two long south walls face Matamoros and the whole works stands perpendicular west-to-east from the river."

Dancer made an observation from his youth at the Charleston Arsenal. "Each *redan* offers a field of fire that dominates the open ground before it. The inner angles protect the walls from ladders of assaulting troops."

Mansfield nodded. "You know your works…Dancer. The fort commands the town of Matamoros to the southwest. Fort Texas has an eight-hundred-yard perimeter in all. The wall is ten feet high and fifteen feet thick at its base."

Outside the fort an eight-foot deep and twenty-two-foot wide ditch surrounded the walls. From here—explained Mansfield—the earth had been removed to pack the walls between its timber outer skins. "On the south side the riverbank cut gives eight more feet of added height to the bastion wall."

"What is that forward platform outside the southern face?" Walker asked.

"That is where our field guns bear directly upon the public square of Matamoros. The six-pounders are within good range to demolish the town. These works are secure against twelve-pounders…the largest guns the Mexicans have." Mansfield was confident as they walked the parapet. To the north a boggy lagoon where the river had once coursed partially protected that side from assault. Between the northern side of the fort and this lagoon was a cultivated area where the American camp had been. Now a rutted empty mire of mud and wagon tracks.

"The main entrance to Fort Texas—gentlemen—is on the northeast wall." Mansfield pointed toward a narrow opening the width of a gun carriage. Here between bastions No. 1 and No. 6 a wooden bridge spanned the ditch. At the end nearest the wall a fulcrum drawbridge could be tilted up or down like a seesaw. "The only other breach in the walls is a single-file opening in the western *redan* closest the river. That sally port gives access to water and the ferry landing." Mansfield saluted with some pride as he completed his tour.

Dancer used his cover persona as the army's primary purveyor to make sure Walker visited the bombproof built to protect the most precious supplies. The largest shelter was of special design. Relatively protected by the large southern arrowhead bastion. Yet situated beneath the great flagpole soon to be targeted like a gunsight by Mexican artillery. Dancer guided Walker inside. To enter this burrow one passed through an opening. Along an intricate passage. Then through a second door into a space that served as warehouse. Bombproof. And powder magazine. At the far end nearest the bastion a second entrance led into the shelter. In the middle a long room was crudely furnished with hardtack-biscuit crates as furniture. Several boxes clustered under a small hole in the earth-and-timber roof. A shaft of white light shot straight down upon the playing cards strewn on the largest crate below. *Deliverance or damnation.* Dancer smiled as the vision recalled Father Thomas's church with its light shafts beckoning believers to heaven.

Walker pointed to the earthen wall…where an illustrated weekly lithograph of a cheeky young woman was pinned. "Is that your sister…Dancer?"

"Your boys say it looks more like your mother."

The duo continued through the earthy space. Walker ducked his head to navigate the low ceiling. Five carbines rested parallel on pegs. Equipage hung on handy twigs from the log roof. Campaign hats dangled from roots in the walls. A window slit ran the length of the bombproof. The opening gave much-needed air. And a boot-level view of the killing ground in the central fort. Dancer's gaze took in several dozen cannonballs stacked in a pyramid just outside. They marked the second entrance several paces away — near the eastern end of the bombproof.

As they reached the second passage Walker's gaze was drawn to a living area arranged among the stores beyond the entrance. Separated by a blanket curtain. A broad bunk almost filled the space perpendicular to the earthen wall. Over the double bed a cleverly designed vent let in air and cast light on the cozy scene.

"Room for special guests…I see." Walker smiled.

"Someone has to guard the officer's stores." Dancer gave an innocent look as his toe grazed a case marked "Product of France."

Dancer liked the humid smells of earth. Men. Sweat. And fresh-hewn timber. When he closed his eyes the dank closeness reminded him of a happier time. Hidden in the root cellar of the Charleston arsenal. With his uncle's Acadian mistress. Sally.

PART IV

DESTINY'S CLOCK

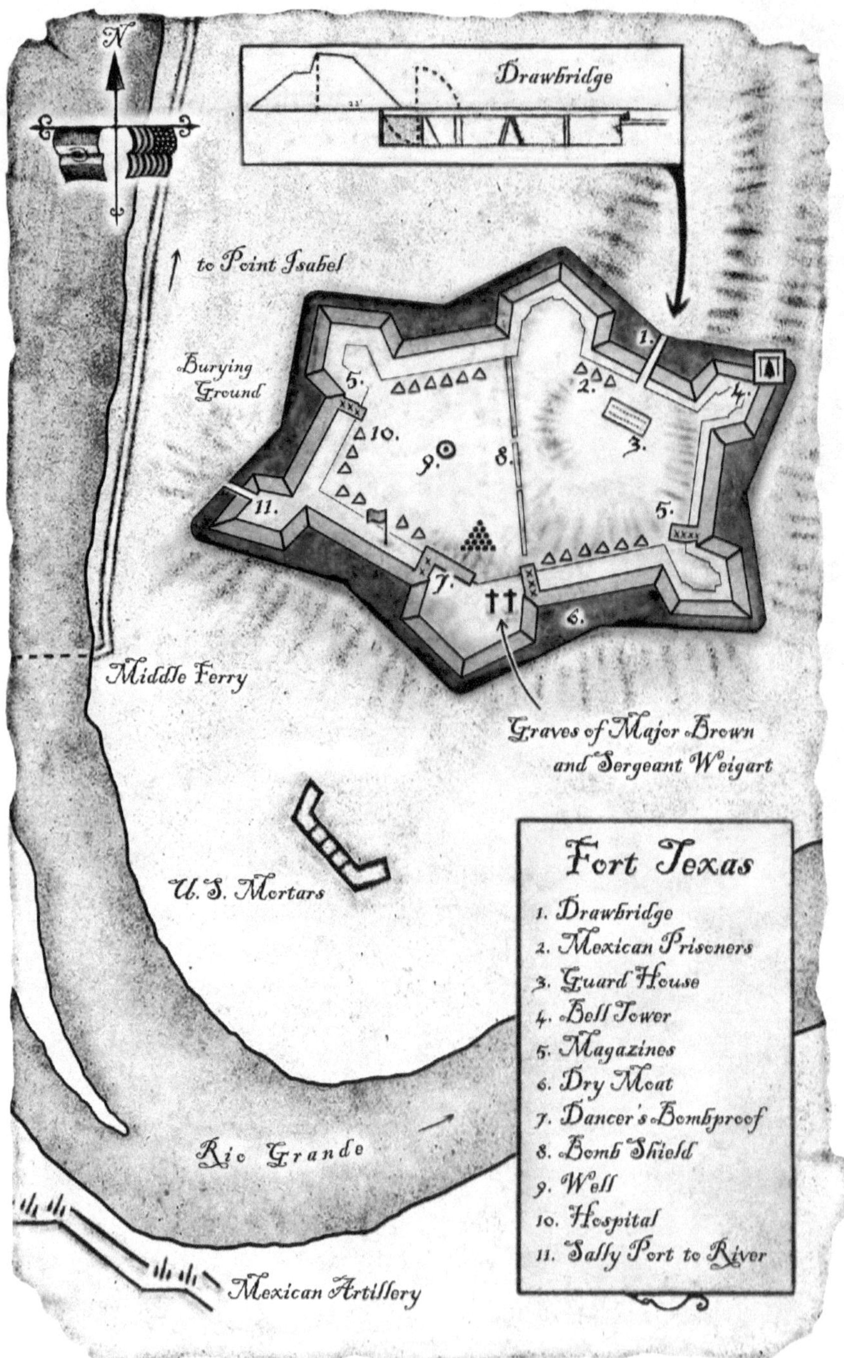

N
Drawbridge
to Point Isabel
Burying Ground
1.
2.
3.
4.
5.
5.
5.
6.
7.
8.
9.
10.
11.
Middle Ferry
Graves of Major Brown and Sergeant Weigart
U.S. Mortars
Rio Grande
Mexican Artillery
Fort Texas
1. Drawbridge
2. Mexican Prisoners
3. Guard House
4. Bell Tower
5. Magazines
6. Dry Moat
7. Dancer's Bombproof
8. Bomb Shield
9. Well
10. Hospital
11. Sally Port to River

CHAPTER 67

**AWAITING THE INEVITABLE
INSIDE FORT TEXAS
3 MAY 1846/NEXT DAY**

SARAH BORGINNIS was a formidable woman. Yet she knew she was a sucker for a uniform. After all she was married to a soldier. Or had been once—or perhaps twice—at one time. Which made her presence at least officially acceptable in the record as a military wife. The soldiers accepted "Borginnis." As that was her name after a recent husband. Though no such soldier still appeared on the duty roster. Keeping her names straight was not easy. Whispers claimed the bawdy laundress and cook had changed husbands freely. Cheerfully. Frequently. And informally—as occasion presented.

Borginnis stood six feet. She was a muscular woman. Who took no insult from insinuating soldiers. Few joked that she could whip any man in the regiment. In fact months earlier—in the original camp near Corpus Christi—a brash country boy named Private MacKenzie learned the hard way. New to the 7th Infantry he was overheard by Borginnis when he spoke of her in a leering brag. The poor devil took a beating within an inch of his young life. Ever since that incident politeness became the order of the day toward Mrs. Borginnis.

The men gave Borginnis a nickname of which she did not

disapprove. They called her "The Great Western." After a famous steamship that never slowed for either storm or gale. Her "damn their eyes — full speed ahead" confidence made sure the nickname stuck.

Despite her powerful strength and pugnacious personality Sarah Borginnis was a pleasure to look at. A pleasure the men took with liberty. And her approval. Borginnis was proud of her dark wavy hair and gray-blue eyes. Yet often showed her tender heart when the situation called for it. By caring for her boys. In addition to Borginnis perhaps a score of civilian men and a half dozen camp women now huddled inside Fort Texas. Everyone in the camp knew the month before Borginnis had refused the offer of easy passage by sea from Corpus Christi to Point Isabel. Instead she traveled overland with the army. "Because my boys need me beside them."

Her sentimental frailties and moments of tearful joy were notorious. Most knew her moods sprang from a deep well of goodness. The Great Western attracted more than one correspondent's attentions and pen. As one scribe wrote:

> *Born in 1812…or thereabouts…now 34 years old. She is probably as celebrated for her personal appearance as she is for her deeds. With an erect and majestic carriage she glories in working among the troops. Offers succor here. Water there. Always with a playful scolding or ribald joke. Her presence is enough to boost the morale of every soldier nervously awaiting the inevitable.*

CHAPTER **68**

SUNDAY MORNING REVEILLE
BOMBPROOF/FORT TEXAS
3 MAY 1846

DANCER HALF LISTENED from his bombproof as the Reveille bugle call mustered Sunday morning at Fort Texas. When from out of the sky a Mexican cannonball whistled over the American works. Fired from the San Patricios battery six hundred yards across the river.

The angry ball gave notice that war had commenced.

And with it Dancer's chances to escape in one piece from his earthen rathole were dashed. Much less accomplish his mission in Matamoros. What hope did he have now to find the treasure in enemy territory? Secure the loan documents? Turn them over to the American Army? Little or none.

The opening shot was rapidly succeeded by others. Faster they came. Thick as a deadly hailstorm. Major Jacob Brown ordered his command to their posts. Within minutes the American 18-pounders roared in reply. Payaso's circular wicker *gabions* and the Mexican town itself were American targets.

Michelena Anoche. Big Tim. Father Thomas. Samantha Swift. Again they huddled on the fortified rooftop of Hotel Casamata. Their gazes compared the smoke of the opposing guns. Then the flash. And then came a terrible boom. Quickly a sucking sound followed as shells punctured the morning air. From their half-mile distance the contest had the surreal aspect of a sandbox battle between play soldiers.

Swift saw from their vantage point how the deep thunder of the 18-pounders from the fort took aim on the lower Mexican battery with practiced execution. Outside the walls the advanced light battery of field pieces sent a higher pitched crash into the air. But the smaller 6-pounders fell short. The enemy beyond their range. Brown's orders ceased firing to husband shell and powder. The forward guns were leveled low. Ready to meet an infantry assault at close quarters when it came.

"We got one! We took out one of their guns!" The soldier's shouts resounded from western bastion No. 3 above the sally port. The 18-pounder *redan*.

Anoche pointed to the Mexican redoubt. There a gun had been dismounted and silenced. Quickly an elite battalion of *zapadores* engineers lifted the heavy iron barrel. Righted the undamaged carriage beneath it. Soon the gun roared back into action.

Through the morning the four observers saw the American soldiers work like ants to complete the works of Fort Texas. Under constant fire the Americans kept feverishly employed in shoring up the exterior walls to a height thought to be more secure. Swift made careful notes.

At first the Mexican cannonballs flew high over the fort to the fields beyond. Other shots fell short…plowing into the muddy flats below the walls. Steadily. Inexorably. More and more shells found their marks.

From the flag parapet above his bombproof Dancer watched as more shells began to drop inside the fort. Some round shots bounced and skipped and bowled across the central ground like Satan's marbles. The next arced shell buried itself in the ground. Eyes watched from a distance as the shell's lighted fuse fizzed. Then with a rending explosion blew shrapnel like a geyser of deadly shards high into the air.

Sergeant Weigart was taking a smoke directly below the parapet where Dancer watched that first Sunday. To his surprise a shell fell into the fort no less than twenty feet from the Sergeant. Instantly exploded. A fragment of shot sliced Weigart's head. Half severed his neck. The soldier crumpled in a pile as the sand turned muddy red under him.

"Help me!" Sarah Borginnis shouted to two other men near at

hand. She grabbed Weigart's legs. Each man lifted the body by an arm. Together they struggled toward the hospital tent under the western wall where all the sick lay who could not march.

Sergeant Weigart was dead.

His corpse was laid at the end of the hospital tent on a bare plank. Separate from the sick or malingering.

Not minutes later Dancer watched as another shell from the lower Mexican battery ripped the canvas of the hospital tent. The bomb buried itself directly under Weigart's plank. With a deafening explosion the shell burst. And blew Weigart's skull and brains in every direction. Yet the blast did not injure another sole nearby on the tight-packed cots.

Shortly after midday the remains of the unfortunate Weigart were gathered. Piece by piece. Then placed in a rude coffin. Pallbearer Jack Dancer helped bury the Sergeant near the American flag in the southern No. 4 *redan* that faced the enemy across the river.

The drums and fife ended. Dirt shoveled. Men returned to their posts. Not long after a third shell flew agonizingly slowly across the blue cloudless sky. The sentinel warned: "Look out!" As if directed by fate the mindless killing piece arced high over the riverbank. Then descended toward the parapet. The bomb buried itself in the soft earth of Weigart's grave. Not far from the oversized American flag. With all eyes turned to the scene the shell exploded. Dancer shielded his eyes from the blazing Texas sun. Watched from the door of his bombproof not twenty yards away as the air rose in a spray of earth. Followed slowly by Weigart's coffin. The box twisted in the air. Then landed heavily in the smoking earth. Its grizzly contents spilled out onto the pulverized ground.

History noted the honor of Fort Texas's first fallen fell to Sergeant Horace B. Weigart of B Company 7th Infantry. He died in glory… or so the correspondents wrote.

For on that first day of war Sergeant Weigart was killed three times.

CHAPTER 69

BOMBS BURST IN AIR
FORT TEXAS UNDER SIEGE
3 & 4 MAY 1846

DANCER HUNKERED inside the bombproof as the fierce exchange of shell and shot continued without pause until sundown that first day. As twilight deepened into darkness Captain Walker raced as a silent solo figure away from the fort. Through the night a few straggling shots were thrown at the Americans in Fort Texas. Sleep was impossible.

Early the next day the cannonading renewed its furor. The heat from the American guns made the morning air hot on the men's faces. Sentries watched for the flash from the guns of Matamoros. Then shouted for all to hear. "Look out!" Seconds later a shell slammed into the fort. The men began to use the phrase as they left their bombproof for sentry duty: "I'm going on lookout."

All the way from Point Isabel Taylor could hear the distant thunder of the 18-pounders. And the answering Mexican guns. *No one can withstand that bombardment for long.*

In the afternoon of that second day Dancer spotted Walker and six or seven of his men as they raced across the open flats toward the fort's north gate. "Drop the drawbridge!" Dancer shouted a moment before the horses' hooves pounded across the wooden plank bridge. Soon

Dancer and the American officers gathered around Walker.

"When Taylor heard the bombardment…he ordered the army to march to the Fort's assistance." Walker began his tale between swigs from a canteen. "But then he countermanded the order. Seems reinforcements of Louisiana volunteers are expected to arrive soon at Point Isabel from New Orleans."

Walker addressed Brown directly. "Taylor says Fort Texas must stand alone."

✠   ✠   ✠

Meanwhile in Hotel Casamata an extraordinary discovery was made. Father Thomas had seen Swift's signet ring. During a lull in the bombardment—while the Mexican guns cooled—Father Thomas drew Swift aside.

Father Thomas's eyes twinkled. "I see you are—or at least your ring—is from North Wales. Bangor…if I'm not mistaken."

Swift touched the ring gently. "It is an heirloom from my mother. How did you know?"

"That is my home country too." The kindly priest asked: "May I see it?"

Swift slipped the ring off her left little finger and handed it to Father Thomas.

"Do you know the origin of this symbol?" Father Thomas asked.

"No. All I know is that it is a signet ring. I was told there is another ring of matching relief. My mother said if I found the second ring… I would find the truth."

"Perhaps that truth is not so mysterious." Father Thomas touched the flat head of Swift's ring with the tip of his little finger. "Do you see here? This symbol?"

Swift looked at the ring closely for the first time.

"This symbol is the head of a mouse—or more correctly…an incomplete mirror-image of a mouse. It is patterned after the mice carved in the wood decorations in the Bangor Cathedral by an anonymous woodcarver who they nicknamed the 'Mouseman.' Bangor—as you may know—is the town on the Welsh mainland across the Menai Strait from Beaumaris on the Isle of Anglesey."

Swift leaned forward. Her brow knit in close concentration as

Father Thomas continued. "To the whole world your signet symbol is meaningless…by itself. If I told you these are its ears. And this is its nose. You would think me daft."

Swift sat transfixed as the meaning of her signet ring was revealed. "You see…when your ring is pressed into sealing wax the intaglio—the in-cut engraving—leaves an unintelligible symbol. But when the ring is joined with its raised-image partner…and they are pressed together with paper in between…they leave the embossed impression of a mouse."

"Amazing. I never realized…" Swift whispered.

"You say your name is Swift?"

"That is my father's surname. My full name is Samantha Thomas Swift. My middle name is my mother's surname."

"Not Anne Thomas from Beaumaris?"

"Why yes." Swift's face opened in astonishment. "How do you know?"

"What a small world." Father Thomas chuckled. "My mother married the son of a Robert Thomas. Robert Thomas was the brother of an Anne Thomas. Could this mean we are second cousins?"

Swift blinked in amazement.

Then something happened that was truly exceptional. Father Thomas reached inside his cowls and withdrew his wooden crucifix. From the simple cross hung by a leather thong was a ring of gold. Father Thomas held up the round ring next to Swift's signet ring. The signet rings were a perfect match.

Swift threw her arms around the priest. Gave him a spontaneous hug. "Cousin?" Then gave Father Thomas a kiss on his bald forehead.

"My…my." The priest blushed. "We have discovered our ancestors and an important truth…but the mystery of these rings is not yet clear. What can this mean?"

Both Father Thomas and Swift looked at each other. Then at the rings. Speechless. From the riverside the deadly Mexican artillery harassed the fort constantly.

CHAPTER **70**

LIKE A MOUSE IN A TRAP
FORT TEXAS
5 MAY 1846

DANCER DISCOUNTED the war stories of hairbreadth escapes. Safe inside the Fort Texas bombproof a young recruit embellished his story. "It was during the heaviest incoming fire." His voice rose excitedly. "Captain Lowd directed us to return fire. Out of nowhere a musket ball grazed the top of his cap. The cap flew off his head without injuring the captain…or even disturbing his balance! I picked up his cap and stuck a finger through his 'holy cap.' Now that's a close call!"

Major Brown dispatched Walker and a small patrol to carry word again back to Taylor. Brown instructed: "Tell the General the fort is secure." Then the Major added a second sentence with some bravado. "Tell him all is well."

Only minutes elapsed after Walker left the fort before Dancer spotted Walker racing back toward its safety. Behind his dust — as Walker broke at full speed from the clearing before the fort — Dancer saw twenty or thirty Mexicans in full cry and close pursuit of Walker's small band. "Fire at will!" Brown shouted. The crash from a salvo of musketry gave the Mexicans pause. That gave Walker the covering fire to clear the drawbridge.

When Walker caught his breath he reported. "We proceeded two or so miles on the road north…at a *motita* I took a lookout. Tarnation if the enemy cavalry in force blocked our path. We tried to return to the fort. But was cut off by a party of Mexicans. They had taken a shortcut trail known only to them."

Dancer listened as Walker described what happened next.

"With no other choice…we charged the patrol in a fury. Must have surprised them because we burst through. I guess they followed us. Reckon the 'All's well' message to Taylor will have to wait a spell."

Within the hour of Walker's narrow escape the northern side of the fort was surrounded by Torrejón's advance skirmishers and marksmen. Their fruitless search for entrenched riflemen at Longoreño turned up empty-handed. Soon Ampudia's full force joined these regiments. The Mexican regulars rattled a steady fire of musketry into the American fort. "Looks like preparations for an assault." Or so Brown told his men. Between not knowing when the next bomb would fall—and what moment the Mexicans would attack—sleep was out of the question for a second night.

⊠　⊠　⊠

Later through the moonless dark Texas Ranger Walker—in a solitary dash—evaded the enemy that patrolled the chapparal in packs like cur dogs. Walker reached Taylor unscathed before midnight with the word that Fort Texas's flag was still there.

CHAPTER 71

SARAH BORGINNIS carried a plate of food she was about to serve when it was shattered from her hand by a Mexican shot. Yet she kept frantically busy during the siege. The Great Western took care of the men. The sick and wounded. And the camp women as well.

The interior of the fort was entirely open ground. Nothing to shelter under or behind…except a low bomb shield that split the middle parade. This ground became a no-man's-land few dared to cross. Shells fell now with much greater precision. Bombs killed several horses. Their bloated carcasses grew rank piled near the drawbridge.

By the third night Dancer could differentiate the deep bass of the cannons' round shot. Explosive canister shells were an octave higher… more of a whistle. These bombs were the bane of the defenders — as well as the Mexican cannoneers.

Each canister shell surrounded a powerful charge of powder. Jammed with a mix of balls and iron shards. The deadly Mexican shells exploded by a lighted fuse. First the propelling powder charge was rammed into the cannon and wadded. Then the fuse of the canister shell was lit. And the lighted bomb rammed in the barrel on top of the base charge. At the ramrod's signal the cannoneer ignited the main charge. Which sent the lighted canister sailing toward its target.

"What could possibly go wrong?" Dancer remembered his arsenal instructor's words. Words that gave many a new artillery recruit in Charleston anguished moments in the beginning of what could be a very short gunnery career. When—as No. 4 crewman—they pulled the lanyard on the match-like friction primer in the touch hole. Only to discover they pulled too hard. Or too gently. Without discharging the cannon. Inside the cannon's bore the lighted canister shell progressed toward double detonation. Not to dive for cover—as instinct suggested—but to reconnect the lanyard...or reset another copper-tube primer in the vent as quickly as possible. That was the point of the training. To this ventman's drill every raw recruit gave his rapt attention.

Harp's battery was now expert. Ideally the canister shell exploded closely over the heads of the enemy. And threw shrapnel and ball in a deadly spray across a cluster of men. If the fuse was timed too short...the shell exploded harmlessly far before it reached its target. If cut too long...the shell bounced around its destination or buried itself in the earth. Thus announced its arrival. The burrow would smoke for a few seconds. As the fuse finished its deadly work. Then the shell exploded. A buried shell blew straight up with a thump through the hole it had made. More or less harmless to defenders. Who calmly waited. Then went about their business. Still other shells that came to rest on the surface exploded. And scattered their murderous destruction of shards and balls to deadly effect. Dancer saw men save their own lives by throwing themselves flat on the ground when a shell landed among them. Unexpected shells slammed inside the fort. And burst in deafening explosions. Death lurked everywhere. Only the fetid bombproofs offered a respite from the constant bombardment.

Dancer stirred in his bunk as dawn approached. He became aware of the warm smell of a woman as she slipped under the light sheet. Borginnis touched his lips with a gentle finger.

"Hush...my dear. If we are to die today...we may as well die happy."

Dancer felt the weight of her body move on top of him. Her rich hair was silhouetted in a halo of early light from the vent overhead.

Borginnis pulled Dancer's shirt over his head. And began to undo the drawstring of his sleeping drawers.

Without warning the shrill call of incoming fire reached the dank bombproof. "Look out!"

At that moment a vicious enemy ball whistled high over the bastion. Hit the stack of cannonballs outside the bombproof. Split the balls asunder like a pyramid-pool break. Then—with the devil's destiny…as if the Mexican iron had Dancer's name on it—the explosive shot ricocheted across the sand. Bounced through the air-slit opening. Caromed off an ammunition case. Skipped across the packed earth floor. All the while the fiendish ball's timing fuse flipped sparks like a mad pinwheel. As the perfectly timed explosive rolled under the blanket curtain.

"Fire in the hole!" A sentry bellowed his warning as he dove for cover outside.

Dancer turned his head as much as he could under the weight of the Heroine of Fort Texas. The shell smashed through a biscuit crate only a foot from their bed. Splattered Dancer and Borginnis in flying splinters and debris. And wobbled to rest with a smoking hard thud against the base of Dancer's boudoir bunk.

Dancer saw the sparks of the fuse fizzing fiendishly…then disappear inside the shell. Borginnis froze. Dancer tossed the woman aside. Strained to extend his reach. Grabbed a bottle of champagne from a basket near the shattered biscuit crate. In a last desperate act Dancer smashed the neck off the champagne bottle. Inverted the foam onto the fuse hole. Finally he threw his body over Borginnis. In a vain act to shield her from certain destruction.

Before Dancer's mind's eye passed all that he yearned to accomplish…but would not.

In a frozen moment the demonic shell sparked. Vibrated. Then spouted a final fizz. The end had come!

But instead the shell lay still.

Nothing.

Dancer raised his head. Borginnis peeked out from under his naked chest. They stared at the dead shell.

Numb with speechless terror Borginnis managed to find her voice.

"They were right…Dancer. You attract trouble."

Dancer exhaled. "Sorry to waste a good champagne on a bad bomb."

Borginnis choked in realization. "You protected me. You would have died for me!"

In one motion Borginnis flipped Dancer on his back. Began to cover him with kisses. Kisses everywhere. "You were going to die for me. No one has ever done that. Die for me! It's true—my dearest… you do love me!"

Borginnis continued to devour him in kisses. She did not stop until she had rewarded her savior—and herself—several times with the ecstasy of the living. In a moment of lassitude between romps both lovers drained another bottle of champagne that Dancer held in private reserve. Tucked into an earthen nook just within easy reach.

Outside their shelter the daybreak cannons continued their deafening contest.

CHAPTER 72

SIEGE OF FORT TEXAS
MATAMOROS
6 MAY 1846

EXACTLY WHEN the Mexicans would storm Fort Texas was the only question that animated conversation among the American soldiers.

On that fourth morning the one-sided cannonading from the Mexicans continued with undiminished vigor. To Harp and the Mexican officers as they scanned the American fort with their spyglasses it seemed a defeated encampment opposed them.

"The Americans no longer respond."

"Are their guns smashed?"

"Are they all dead or dying?"

"Who could survive such a bombardment?"

Unknown to Harp the Americans had expended two-thirds of the 150 rounds for each 18-pounder. The only four guns used to advantage. Major Jacob Brown's orders were clear. "Gentlemen… reserve your ammunition for the point-blank work of the assault… when that surely comes. Fire your large artillery only at intervals during the day. Show spirit…and signal Taylor's camp that Fort Texas still holds." Out of earshot the battery officers cursed the question. Why over the last month had a larger magazine of rounds for the

18-pounders not been laid up? The question was raised most often by those who expected the worst from an assault.

Later that morning Major Brown walked across the central ground to inspect the bombproof where the fort's supplies were sheltered. Through the window slit Dancer saw Brown turn his direction. The Major's approach interrupted Dancer's thoughts. *How the hell can I find the missing gold and documents now in the middle of the Mexicans' camp?* Dancer patted the ample rump next to him. "Rise and shine… Borgie. Time to work on that inventory. We've got company coming."

Without warning a canister shell screamed over the southern wall. Landed only yards from Brown. The shell exploded with deadly timing. Slammed into Brown. Shrapnel from the blast tore his left leg into shreds.

In agony the Major was hurried to an empty powder magazine. Now a makeshift surgery. Confined by space and want of fresh air the sawbones worked in the intense heat. Nothing could be done. For the splintered remains of the leg amputation was the only recourse. Afterward the medic shook his head. "Not good." There was little hope for recovery. The Great Western made it her personal mission to do all that could be done to comfort the Major in his miseries. And stop the wounds from claiming the second death at Fort Texas.

Then nights and four days blurred into one continuous hell. Harp and his Mexican gunners sharpened their skills from the target practice they worked. Their guns were well suited as stationary emplacements that faced an immovable target. The heavy Mexican siege weapons rocked on carriages that took three yokes of oxen to transport. Murderously — with infinite patience and deadly effect — Harp taught the Mexican artillerists to tap and adjust the wedge *quoin* that set each gun's elevation. With science they weighed their shot. Precisely measured their powder. Deadly became their accuracy. Shell after shell found its mark. Harp watched as every blast chewed away ever larger bites in the American defenses.

� ✗ ✗

Meanwhile in the cathedral's unfinished catacombs a sinister plan took shape. Payaso paced back and forth past the open door of a six-foot tall armada chest his men had just bolted to the stone floor. Beside the reinforced safe sat Stepptoe's four strongboxes. Two burning torches illuminated the arched alcove in the extensive darkness of the catacombs. "How could this have happened? Who could have done this?" Payaso muttered as much to himself as to Antonio Malvado… who stood nearby.

Payaso reviewed the obvious. "After the shipment was delivered to Stepptoe…you followed the teamster?"

"He begged for mercy. They always do." Malvado sneered. "He said there was only one key. Even after I cut off his ear he claimed that was true. That story went with him to feed the vultures."

"Why would he lie?" Payaso struggled with the idea. "What happened next?"

Malvado picked at his yellow teeth with the point of a knife. "That night we pretended to break into the consulate to scare Stepptoe."

"That worked." Payaso agreed with Malvado's stratagem. "The next day Stepptoe moved the strongboxes to the Custom House."

"We both saw the coins when he opened the boxes with his key. The gold was there."

Payaso crossed his arms. "When Stepptoe came the next day we showed him the passage from the Custom House into the cathedral crypt — where we moved the strongboxes. He tried to tempt us with promises of more loan payments. Ha! But there was only one key that opened all these locks." Payaso held up the key Stepptoe exchanged for the documents. To prove he was right Payaso opened one padlock after another. With a peeved expression he flipped open the lids on all four boxes. All empty.

Malvado moved into the circle of light. "The Yankee gold may be gone for now…but we have the loan documents — and the *alcabala* — to get more." He smiled as he tapped the stamped and sealed certificates inside the vault that were stolen from Stepptoe's safe.

"And this transparent paper…whatever it is." Payaso pulled the revised overlay map out of the armada vault. "These markings are important…but they do not make any sense."

"Maybe Stepptoe returned later and took the gold for himself?"

"You never found a second key in Stepptoe's consulate?"

Malvado scowled and shook his head emphatically.

Payaso stared back toward the passage to the Custom House.

"There's only one way out. My Custom House guards would have seen him."

Payaso locked the stolen loan documents and strange diaphanous paper into the great chest. When he sensed Malvado's doubts Payaso cut him short. "Trust me. Whoever took the gold has no reason to come back. The documents and that paper will be safe here now. Anyway...we can't take the Consul's strongboxes into the Custom House. That could connect us to the Americano's murder...instead of framing Stepptoe for the missing gold."

Malvado shrugged. "Dead men reveal no secrets."

Payaso gave the killer a smirk. "The thief must have come from inside the Custom House. How else could this have happened? Now we have the only keys. Whoever had a key to the strongboxes will never be able to open this impenetrable chest."

Payaso snapped his final orders and tried to hide his insecurity with overconfidence. "Post two of your best men in the Custom House outside the passage. If the thieves return...grab them."

A half smile rose on Malvado's upper lip as he contemplated the pleasure of another torture.

CHAPTER 73

DAY AFTER DAY AFTER DAY the results of unceasing bombardment filled the Mexicans with confidence. Arista and Payaso swaggered with the greatest delight. Even greater than the glorious victory of Thornton's ambush. Or the cowardly retreat of Taylor's precipitous run for the shelter of Point Isabel on 1 May. Church bells clamored as enthusiastic bell ringers frantically spread the news of the latest Mexican triumph. Dispatches to the Mexican press heralded daily accounts of decisive victory. Great rejoicings in Matamoros celebrated the brilliant achievement.

Mexican collaborators hastened S. Thomas Swift's daily dispatches to *The Picayune*'s express pouch and steamships waiting at Point Isabel. All designed to guarantee the continued Mexican victories reached the American newspapers quickly. Again Swift was the first recipient of the official Mexican releases.

Arista barely contained his enjoyment as Payaso read the latest litany to Swift.

> *As Aurora dawned yesterday we began to fire from our*
> *ramparts on the fortifications of the enemy. At last the hour*

arrived when we were to give a terrible lesson to the American camp…whose odious presence could no longer be tolerated. Our ramparts remained immovable. The same did not happen to the American fortifications. Whose bastions were so completely demolished that towards eleven o'clock in the first morning their artillery ceased to play…and their fire was hushed. They had not courage to load their guns. The intelligence and practice of the Mexicans sufficed to conquer those who had superior arms.

As many of our cannonballs passed through the enemy's embrasure the loss to the Americans has been very great. And although we do not know exactly the number of their dead the most accurate information makes it amount to 56. It is probable that such is the case…Bombs so well aimed…Indeed the enemy has suffered a terrible loss. Why did they not dare to repair their fortifications in the night? Cowardice alone could force them not to put themselves in harm's way…and not to return the fire that poured upon them at daylight.

To conclude Payaso announced he would now read a brilliant paragraph by the most excellent *Señor* General-in-Chief as to the part his superior took in the events of recent days.

General Mariano Arista — His Excellency — says thus: "From the news we publish today we anticipate before the end of the present week to witness the total discomfiture of the enemy. From our account of the war the world will judge of the great superiority of our troops — in courage as well as skill — over the Americans. The nation with which we are at war is most savage in its proceedings. The enemy has fired red shot against this innocent city…and we publish they are unworthy of being counted among enlightened nations. Let us oppose the unbridled ambition of the Anglo-American with patriotic enthusiasm so peculiar to us. Indeed we need only follow the glorious example of Matamoros — that noble city — which will be known in future by the name of Heroic."

Confident beyond reach Arista paced rapidly back and forth. "Taylor has retreated." Arista made the exclamation for the benefit of Swift's notebook. "His force is split. One-fifth in the works…no more than five hundred…our spies tell us. He cowers in Point Isabel with little more than two thousand. Paralyzed by fear. We have surrounded their fortifications with Ampudia's infantry to the north and Payaso's artillery to the south. Malvado guards the chapparal. Now our main force — under my own direction — will sit in wait on the road to Point Isabel. Our constant presence will strangle the fort. Starve it into submission. Then to surrender. If Taylor dares to attempt a rescue — which his honor must require — we will be waiting in a trap astride his only avenue south!"

General Arista stopped and planted both feet. His figure framed by a large gilded portrait. "This will be one of the greatest victories for our nation. Yes! We have the Americans trapped between the horns of a hopeless situation. Victory will be ours!"

☒   ☒   ☒

When Swift returned to the hotel black storm clouds filled the northwest sky. As she led Peony into her stall under the arched entry Swift heard the rejoicing Mexican officers loudly singing in the saloon beyond the courtyard.

When she turned to put her saddle and pad on its rack two men confronted her. Swift instantly recognized the scar-faced deserter and his skinny sidekick.

The two men backed Swift into the empty stall next to Peony. The stink of chewing tobacco and cane liquor filled their breath. The skinny soldier quickly moved behind Swift. Grabbed both her arms. The revolting reek of his filthy clothes stung her nostrils.

"We've got a message for you…Missy." Scarface hissed. "My boss says you been sticking your nose where it don't belong."

Swift gaped at the ugly brute with the jagged scar.

"Cat got your tongue? Do not play innocent with me. We know you've been asking around about Stepptoe and the gold."

"What are you talking about?" Swift bluffed. Her mind raced. *Let them play their hand first.*

Scarface gave her a vicious look. "Don't give me that crap. You found Stepptoe's body. Now you and your friends are asking too many questions."

"What do you mean?"

"I mean Anoche and Big Tim and that priest. Any more nosin' around and you and your friends won't have a nose for smellin'." Scarface laughed at his own joke. He kissed the flat of his Bowie knife and leered at Swift.

Swift twisted in the grip of Kelly the Weasel but couldn't budge.

"Who is your boss?" Swift asked.

"For me to know and you to find out." Scarface smirked.

Swift repeated her earlier assertion. "I don't know what you're talking about."

"You heard what I said. Now…I'm going to leave you a little present of my own. Hold her — Weasel — while I leave a little calling card." Scarface hissed.

Swift lifted her right knee. Drove her bootheel down as hard as she could on the skinny attacker's instep. Instantly he released Swift and yelped in pain. "Dang strumpet stomped me!"

Scarface deftly moved toward Swift. Swung a heavy fist toward her face. Swift ducked. The blow glanced off the crown of her head. Swift whipped her stunned attacker with her riding crop. Momentarily surprised…Scarface touched his bleeding cheek. "You little bitch!"

Swift braced herself. Took one step forward. And gave a mighty kick with her right leg — toward Scarface's crotch.

The kick stopped short of any damage as Swift's riding skirt restrained her foot a fraction short of her target. The words "Take that…you bastard" died on her lips.

Scarface grabbed Swift's leg in midair. The powerful grip wrenched Swift off her feet. And dropped her backward onto the straw. The skinny attacker again locked her arms in a viselike hold. Swift was helpless.

The point of the razor-sharp Bowie knife was inches from Swift's face. "All high-and-mighty—are ya? Now we'll see who is king of the beasts. Once you lose that pretty nose you'll know better than to stick it in other people's business. Hold her!"

In her stall Peony kicked the walls and released a shrill cry of agitation.

"Nice to have an audience." Scarface snarled as he extended the blade toward Swift's nostril.

Out of nowhere something blocked the light behind Scarface.

A powerful force spun the attacker around. Then a stout pitchfork handle cracked across his skull. Momentarily senseless Scarface dropped to his knees. The skinny accomplice released Swift. Jumped to his feet—and grimaced.

Michelena Anoche threatened Scarface with the business end of the pitchfork. Big Tim grabbed the smaller man by the collar and lifted him off the ground. His feet pedaled the air.

"What's going on here?" Anoche demanded.

"Nothin's going on." Scarface confidently peddled his claim. "Just having some fun. No harm done. Tell 'em…Kelly."

"Just funnin' we was." Kelly the Weasel stammered his explanation. "Din' mean nothin' by it."

"Doesn't look like funnin' to me." Anoche shot a glance at Swift as she knelt in the straw. "You boys were lucky we came along when we did. Any harm come to Swift—and you'd have to answer to me. Got that?"

"Like I say…we was just deliverin' a message. No harm done." Scarface inched toward the stable door.

"If I catch you doing this again…Scarface…I'll personally see your balls strung up on these rafters. Goes for you too." Anoche menaced both deserters. "Take your worthless hides outta here. And never show your faces around here again. Git!"

Scarface sprinted out through the stable entrance. The skinny man hobbled after him as fast as he could with his bruised instep.

Anoche turned to Swift. "You alright…dear?"

"Thanks to you." Swift brushed straw off her suede vest. "They were waiting for me in the stable.…If you hadn't come along…" Abruptly just how close a call she had came over Swift. Her knees felt weak. Big Tim steadied his friend.

Anoche pulled a hiltless sticking knife and sheath from her belt. Presented the weapon to Swift.

"Take this. Keep it in inside your right boot. Like my Daddy always said. 'Nothin' like a stickin' knife to help with close work.' No telling when you may need it."

Recovered somewhat from the attack Swift accepted the razor-sharp dagger.

"Come on. I'll buy you a sarsaparilla. And show you how to fasten

that great equalizer securely inside your boot." Anoche gave Swift her
arm as the first raindrops spattered in the dusty courtyard.

Beyond the secure walls of Hotel Casamata the incessant bass of
Harp's riverbank cannons roared miserable death toward Fort Texas.

CHAPTER 74

FOR TWO DAYS the Mexicans had raised the ante. Arista placed a heavy mortar battery less than a half mile from Fort Texas. Masked by a thick mesquite grove to the northwest the pointblank guns beleaguered the Americans from the great river bend that overlooked the Paso Real ferry. On the north side of the fort Ampudia emplaced more guns and a mortar. Constant fire now poured into Fort Texas from three sides. Ampudia soon brought more guns and twelve hundred men to complete the investment. From the edge of the wooded lagoon flashes of musketry rattled continuously from the Mexican *cazadores* sharpshooters. Balls buzzed through the air like mad hornets toward anything that moved in the fort. Or over the drawbridge.

Before dawn brightened that fourth day of the siege a lone Texas Ranger galloped through the Mexican ring. Draped low on his horse's shoulder like a Comanche warrior Walker reached safety across the drawbridge. His report from Point Isabel was curt. The Louisiana volunteers were delayed. No reinforcements had arrived. Taylor could not relieve Fort Texas. The Cottonbalers were on their own.

Late on that fourth day rain clouds formed in the afternoon sky.

From out of the northern wood a bugle sounded. The hidden Mexican muskets went silent. A Mexican officer accompanied by two horsemen advanced halfway across the open ground. Captain Edgar Hawkins — to whom the command of Fort Texas had devolved upon Major Brown's horrific wounding — remarked with an attempt at gaiety: "Maybe they want to plead for a truce." Although never authorized Hawkins often referred to the works as "Fort Taylor" — some thought in an attempt to curry favor with his commander.

Dancer accompanied Walker to meet the Mexican officer. The duo brought a message from the Mexicans back into the fort. Arista demanded the fort's capitulation. Walker repeated the points detailed by the officer. "General Arista informs the Americans they are surrounded by an overwhelming force." Walker spoke formally. "Any assistance from General Taylor's army is utterly hopeless. If Taylor advanced he would be forced to retire. We must be aware in the case of an assault the rights of individuals cannot be observed to the extent desirable by an orderly surrender." Walker added his opinion. "They are suggestin' no quarter will be spared."

The Mexican ultimatum ended with a demand for unconditional surrender.

"We are given one hour to decide."

Taylor had assumed he left two weeks of supplies for the fort. Help was unlikely to return within less time. Now only five days since Taylor's departure Dancer and Walker — and every man within earshot — knew those assumptions were meaningless. From the damage and intensity of firing the fort's supplies had been consumed at a far faster pace than the undisturbed camp life known before the siege.

Rendered frantic by the imminent assault — and fearful for the loss of life — Captain Hawkins called a council of war. His officers discussed the ultimatum. A vote must be put on the one question that mattered: Surrender unconditionally…or not?

Hawkins prattled through a list of despair. Supplies of powder and shot ran low.…With no wagons or enough horses an attempt to leave the fort would be folly.…We're surrounded.…We're outnumbered.… The worst is yet to come. Hawkins fiddled with a brass cuff button. He longed for the uneventful routine at the two Southern posts he had served in recent years. Pass Christian Mississippi. Baton Rouge Louisiana. These were in fact construction projects more than commands. His captain's rank some said was a purchased commission by his father-in-law. Now that rank hung on his shoulders like a hundredweight. Hawkins had never seen true action in all his years in the army. The mind of the accidental commander darted from consternation to accusation. *What would a reasonable person do? Why sacrifice the men on a principle…now made ridiculous by circumstances? Anyway…it's Taylor's fault he abandoned the fort. Taylor didn't leave adequate supplies. How could anyone expect to defend a position with so little?*

Successively the other officers put in that it was not hopeless. Bragg and Lowd. Lieutenants Ebsey and Lansing. One officer pluralized John Paul Jones's famous Revolutionary War retort. "We have not yet begun to fight!" Hawkins heard little of it as he paced back and forth. His pocket watch ticked in his palm. The ultimatum from Arista grew heavier. In his mind the demand was like a final judgment.

Into this void stepped Sarah Borginnis. "I didn't march with you boys from the Nueces to be whipped without a fight." Attention turned toward her presence as she began. "Sure we've taken a few rounds…and we've given as good as we got. Them Mexicans can't hit a target if it was three hundred yards long and only one hundred fifty away. Why haven't they attacked already? Ask yourself that. I'll tell you why. They know they'll get whipped if they do. These walls are nine feet high. Then add in that eight-foot ditch. We can take anything they throw at us. From the advantage of these walls our boys will pluck them like ducks sittin' in a row. Arista knows it. That's why they sent us a message…instead of a charge."

The Great Western drew herself up to her full height. She looked every man in the eye. Her voice grew forceful. "If you gentlemen think these Mexicans can fight…you've got another thing comin'. If I have to…I'll go out there right now and straighten out the entire Mexican Army by myself." Her words drove home with the invincibility of a battleship.

Just then two men carried a stretcher into the midst of the cluster of officers. Major Brown was pained and pale. A crimson patch spread a fresh red stain in the sheet below his thigh. Only one solitary boot rise could be seen beneath the cotton cover.

Brown winced. "Dancer…prop me up." Then he began as he gathered himself: "I am no longer in command here. But I have something that must be said. Our orders are not to leave the fort… and to hold out." He coughed as sweat from a fever beaded on his drawn face. "Those are our orders. But we have a higher calling. That calling is to defend this new state…this new Texas…and to prove by our courage that Texas is the rightful ground of the United States. To surrender is meaningless. This is our nation…our land." His white-knuckled grip clutched the stretcher's edge. Dancer stood to one side. Borginnis on the other. Ready to catch the wounded Major at any moment.

"We will be remembered not for what we do here." The Major's voice was a barely audible rasp. "We will be remembered for the honor we bring to how it is done."

With that admonition Dancer eased the ashen-faced Major gently back onto the stretcher. All of Brown's strength spent in those two poignant statements.

Secret ballots were counted in the stifling hospital tent. Unanimous but for one dissent the results rejected the notion of surrender. The Americans chose to defend Fort Texas to the end. Quickly the council drafted a simple reply. The signature stated "E. S. Hawkins — Commanding" to give the impression of a general's rank. Yet honor bound not to elevate Hawkins's status beyond captain.

Dancer and Walker delivered the reply in English to the Mexican officer. Who in turn rode the dispatch to the awaiting Arista. Hawkins's words were diffident but clear. "My interpreter is not skilled in your language — but if I understand you correctly…I must respectfully decline to surrender."

☒ ☒ ☒

Upon the ultimatum's expiration the Mexicans recommenced firing. Inexhaustible shot and shell descended into the fort. Any misstep brought a reminder that death was everywhere. A corporal scratched out a melancholy last letter to his family. "We are like so many cattle placed in a pen for the Mexicans to try their skill upon. And they seem strongly disposed to do so." The soldier closed with a newsworthy final account. "The enemy has thrown about thirty-five hundred shots—solid and shell—amongst us."

The letter somehow found its way into *The Daily Picayune* in New Orleans weeks before the corporal's mother opened it.

Later that night upcountry storm clouds obscured the moon. Under that cover Walker and Dancer watched for an opening in the irregular musket fire that flashed from the edge of the traverse northeast of the works. Through a gap in the darkness the pair rode hard toward the old *hacienda* at Rancho Ramireno. Then broke off onto a dry sidetrack that ran between the scrub and wetlands known to locals as El Camino de los Indios. The old Indian trail cut six miles off the distance to Fort Polk in Point Isabel.

After a hard gallop and alternating cantor some three hours later Dancer and Walker reported to General Taylor. "The Cottonbalers resolved to hold the fort to the last man if necessary."

Musketry spattered against the log ramparts through that fourth night. The fort's dense earthen walls and timber works absorbed the big guns' battering balls. Unlike a stone and brick fortification its walls refused to be worn down…to the frustration of the Mexican gunners. As Harp and the Mexican officers scanned their progress even the point-blank range of incessant cannon fire did not smash openings. No breech appeared that infantry could swarm. No sign was visible of measurable reduction. The fort's construction withstood the onslaught. So far.

⊠   ⊠   ⊠

Borginnis watched as shells and shot descended into the fort from three angles. At one point during that fifth day an unexpected ball came over from an opposite direction. Took clean off the right arm of young Private Moody—H Company just as he stepped out of his company's bombproof. Borginnis's gaze followed another ball as it came low over the parapet. Skipped on the killing field. And careened toward two men. Henry Russell—just that day a discharged army volunteer…and now a private citizen—let the ball pass as if he was a casual pedestrian. The ball came to rest near a pile of collected cannonballs. Russell picked it up. Added the warm Mexican sphere to a stack of 273 cannonballs and seventy-three unexploded shells. And duly noted the addition on a notched post near the guardhouse that faced the drawbridge.

Moments later Private Stewart—also in H Company—heard an incoming shell. The soldier threw himself on the ground. The only casualty was a broken crystal face on his pocket watch. Stewart ambled into his tent to put the damaged timepiece away. Without warning another cannonball ripped through the tent. Blew through the Private's barracks box with all his worldly belongings. Then a third ball fired from Harp's same battery struck the earth not three feet outside Stewart's tent. Minutes later Stewart hurriedly relocated his remaining gear to another place of comparative safety. Unscathed.

☒ ☒ ☒

Borginnis stepped out of her bombproof near Dancer's empty boudoir. To her left her gaze traced back and forth along the hospital tents beneath the western bastion. The canvases looked like a ghostly gale had torn them into flapping tatters.

When The Great Western took a first step on her rounds a ball flew right over her right shoulder. Bounced toward the commissary stores in the center ground near the well. Blasted through a molasses barrel from Dancer's stores. Shattered a box of tea. And rolled along the parade… coming to rest not twenty feet from the third hospital tent. Where it exploded. Red-hot splinters of murderous metal rent the air. Astonishingly no injuries were taken.

Harp had sent a man to station himself in a large mesquite tree on the right bank opposite the fort. Not far from the Paso Real landing. From his high perch he could see the trajectory of every shot fired at the Americans. His observations were conveyed to a horseman below. Then promptly delivered to Harp's officers at the Mexican works. The officers in turn graduated their powder charges to rectify—or repeat—the results. Steadily the precision of the fire neared perfection. Only when the Mexican guns grew so heated by continual firing was the deadly storm given an interval of peace.

Borginnis knew the unending bombardment weighed a considerable uneasiness on the minds of the men in the fort. Some grew morbidly indifferent to the exploding shells. Others listlessly let bombs burst in dangerous proximity. Hard labor and constant vigilance wore down every soul in Fort Texas. Sleepless exhaustion was the rule.

Hunkered deeper into their ratholes Dancer's clerks joined civilians… and teamsters…and quartermaster men in unspoken speculation on what they would do if Taylor's army were beaten.

Gradually a strange sense of complacency fell upon the troops. Fear expended itself into a numbness of uncaring disregard. All knew inevitable death drew near.

CHAPTER 75

TIME RAN OUT. General Zachary Taylor issued a general order. *No telling how long those brave Cottonbalers can hold out.* The army would march from Point Isabel at three o'clock that afternoon to relieve Fort Texas. Taylor spoke to his trusted scouts Dancer and Walker. "If the enemy is on the route…we will give battle."

Dancer distributed the written orders. Every officer studied the closing watchword. And took its meaning to their troops for the campaign ahead.

> *General Taylor wishes to enjoin the battalions of infantry that their main dependence must be in the bayonet.*

That afternoon the army marched seven miles west…toward the north-south Corpus Christi-Matamoros road.

CHAPTER 76

THE NEXT MORNING the Americans struck out again across the flat plain. Dancer gauged eleven miles were covered in the slow sand track before the army reached the pond called Palo Alto eight miles north of Matamoros. Shortly before noon Walker's scouts uncovered Arista's army. The Americans halted on the main road near the Palo Alto pond. Their advance guard drank their fill. Topped off canteens. While the rear units in the long column straggled onto the field.

From her vantage in the Mexican command post known as "Arista Hill" S. Thomas Swift knew the Mexicans blocked the road to Matamoros. As her gaze swept to her left Swift crudely sketched the Mexican regiments drawn up in line of battle a mile in length. Double the length of the American line. Now accumulated beyond a wet marsh that separated the two armies.

Swift realized Taylor was surprised. Not Arista. Arista had chosen his ground and waited. He now held the advantage.

Swift mingled self-consciously among the Mexican officers. Yet she joined the group as they gathered under their commander's tent. Swift moved closer. On the opposite side of Arista's large map stood Patrick

Harp. His eyes narrowed when he recognized Swift in the huddle under the tent's marquee.

Arista swept his finger over the detailed map. "To reach Matamoros the only way is to pass through the prairie of Palo Alto." Arista spoke in a confident tone. Swift followed Harp's gaze as he scanned the road — which formed a low levee in the cordgrass. The track ran north from their position past the pond to the west. A rain-created bog spread on the east of the sandy levee as far as the eye could see to Swift's right. Like a shoreline this wetland marked the farthest limit of the western plain before the ground deteriorated into salt marshes toward the Gulf. Arista continued. "We outnumber the Americans by nearly three to one. The only chance the Americans have is to break through our superior force. As our spies inform us — and knowing Taylor still lives in the old school of the bayonet charge — we can expect a frontal infantry assault. Given the old man has no imagination — and that he is confined by the recent rains — the invaders have no other choice."

Overhead carrion vultures soared lazily as they observed the imminent battlefield far below. Their skin-red heads and cold black eyes followed as the human folly moved into a large open expanse of grassy plain.

The Mexican officers returned to their units confident in victory.

Arista motioned Swift to stay. "In my years as the commander of the Tamaulipas Department I had this map — and several others — created in painstaking detail just for this day. With this knowledge I anticipate every move Taylor will make…before even he knows what he will do. He is caught like a mouse in my maze. I am the cat who knows his every move. You shall see today how Your Excellency is always right. It won't be long now before my great victory allows me to take my rightful place as president of all Mexico. Let me show you."

Bending over the precious map Arista showed Swift how a great spread of scrub covered the terrain before them. Low rises and dry *resaca* levees belted the battlefield to the north. East. South. Tall mesquite woods closed off the plain on the western side beyond the road. Arista pointed smugly. "Those mesquite obscure a marsh and low levee that runs parallel to the road on the Americans' right flank."

Swift's gaze followed Arista's gesture as she saw dense stands of mesquite at the Mexicans' backs spreading for miles to Matamoros.

From her prominence on the *motita* dune Swift saw only occasional patches of open ground that broke the dense woody landscape as it occupied the land southward toward the Rio Grande.

Arista exhaled deeply as Swift sketched in her notebook. The Mexican General waved his palm over the map. "Think of the field of battle like the face of a timepiece…now without hands. In the center — around which the entire contest will pivot — stands a wetland made boggy by the recent heavy rains. Here at the top is the Palo Alto pond." Arista tapped the map where the numeral twelve would be. "Palo Alto will give its name to this battlefield…and our great victory."

Arista returned to the map confidently. "Across the face — on a diagonal cut from twelve to seven — is the road from Point Isabel to Matamoros. The initial battle line of the Americans faces south…here." The General drew a horizontal line that traced from east to west… with the American left positioned toward the two and Taylor's right nearest the ten. Next Arista drew his battle line. Swift saw Arista's troops faced north. The Mexican left anchored itself at the eight and its right anchored itself at the four on Arista's detailed battle map. Arista's battle line was twice the length of Taylor's.

"Today will be a great day for Mexico." Arista unleashed his boast as he folded the invaluable map inside its leather cover and placed it in the drawer of his writing desk. Swift's quick glance told her there was more than one map in the drawer.

To the circling buzzards the movements of the armies appeared to twist counterclockwise on the plain as the dark lines rotated around the central bog.

Within minutes the Americans moved forward onto the field. Taylor's army formed in a predetermined battle order to the left and right of the road. Dancer and all the American officers knew Taylor's battle plan. The General planned to mass troops on his right — along the road. Then use those troops to hit the Mexican left with a bayonet charge across the open prairie. A simple strategy. Direct assault. Accept casualties. Drive the enemy back from its position.

Taylor reviewed his battle plan with his key officers. Dancer watched as the commander used a charcoaled stick to scratch a rough map on the lid of a powder keg. "On our right wing astride the road is Twigg's command. Within the right wing is the Fifth Infantry on the extreme right. To their left is our field battery. Holding the road are two eighteen-pounders supported by the Third Infantry…here. Last comes the Fourth Infantry as the easternmost unit. Behind the right wing a dragoon squadron is in reserve. Walker's mounted Texas Rangers are on picket duty west of the road—in the mesquite thicket behind the right flank…here."

Dancer and the other officers huddled closer to see the sketch Taylor made. Taylor continued scratching the crate with his stick. "Our left wing between the road and the central marsh is under Belknap. Within the left wing…from west to east…is first the artillery battalion nearest the road. Then another field battery. Then the Eighth Infantry. That—gentlemen—completes our left corner. Another dragoon squadron has the double duty of guarding the train parked on the road in the rear of Palo Alto Pond…and supporting the American left wing. Take your positions…and God be with you."

Dancer watched as Taylor's officers galloped to join their men.

CHAPTER 77

NOW POSITIONED with less than three-quarters of a mile separating the lines the two armies stared at each other.

Swift's pencil noted how the sunlight glinted from the Mexican bayonets and lance heads. Their battle pendants and flags rippled in the midday Gulf breeze.

From out of nowhere Harp appeared on horseback. His presence surprised Swift. "Got yourself a front row seat I see…Swift." Harp smirked.

"I see you have found your true colors at last…Lieutenant Harp." Swift blurted her biting quip without thinking. *Don't forget he's the enemy. In more ways than one.*

Harp glowered at Swift. "To each his own. Battlefields are a dangerous place…especially for those that have no place being there."

Swift remained silent a moment longer as she let Harp's intention evaporate. "Hard to tell who will be in the wrong place at the wrong time."

"Watch your back…Swift. You're not among friends here." Harp spit a stream of dark tobacco into the sand.

"We'll see…won't we." Swift added her comment gamely.

As he wheeled his horse hard Harp snapped: "Yes. Yes…we will."

⊠　⊠　⊠

Swift turned her attention to watch Arista ride his horse along his battle line. As the General reviewed his soldiers in their brightly uniformed green tunics he exhorted them to repel the invaders. The rallying cry of "*Viva la República!*" rolled along the Mexican line. The men's voices mingled with strains of martial music from the regimental bands. Satisfied. Arista took up his position with a cabal of officers on the *motita* dune that anchored his right flank.

Near at hand Swift could see where the Tanques de Ramireno track from Longoreño passed behind the dune. The trail bore in a general direction from the prairie road between Palo Alto and Point Isabel. Southeast. Past the Rancho Ramireno. To the river. Recent heavy rain had turned the Ramireno Track's black clay into sticky mud that made the shortcut almost impassable. Beyond the path in either direction the deluges had turned many once-dry *resacas* and meander scars into boggy marshes or standing ponds.

In response to the Mexican battle cries Dancer watched as the Americans stripped the coverings from their battle colors. Unfurled the streamers to the breeze. And raised a deafening cheer in defiance.

⊠　⊠　⊠

Arista chose his position well. As he explained to the correspondent from the *Brooklyn Eagle.* To Swift Arista pointed out how the Mexican Army had set a perfect trap for the Americans. He expected an attack head-on down the road or across the plain. Exactly as Harp's spies had reported Taylor's plan. "As the Americans move forward the Mexican cavalry on each wing will envelop the attackers from both flanks. Our superior numbers will hold the middle. While our cavalry crushes them like a vise. Victory is certain." Arista spoke confidently. "We will destroy the Americans."

"What forces have you kept in reserve…General?" Swift asked — as if the question was simply a matter of record. *Be careful what you ask. You don't want to hurt the Americans' chances. But they don't seem to have much chance anyway.*

Arista gave a condescending smile. "Reserves are not needed to contain a breakthrough or counterattack. Our numbers will paralyze their first strike…and our cavalry will crush them from both sides."

As Arista's "Army of the North" waited the General lectured Swift. "Torrejón's mounted lancers hold the road on the Mexican left. Ampudia's brigade has been pulled away from the siege of Fort Texas to reinforce Torrejón's immediate right." Arista pointed proudly. "Secreted separately in the mesquite woods west of the road—over there on our extreme left flank—is Antonio Malvado and his four hundred mounted *rancheros.* We are content to defend. The pressure is on Taylor."

⊠   ⊠   ⊠

Lieutenant Jacob Blake of the Topographical Corps galloped past the other Americans and volunteered in his clumsy way. As he jostled past he shouted over his shoulder: "I'm going down to observe the enemy lines!" Blake's horse bounded forward. Reached full speed before its rider had his right boot securely in the stirrup. He held onto his reins with his left hand. And before the wind blew away his cap he resettled it with his right. Blake rode forward within Mexican musket range. Then turned his mount to the right. Dancer watched as Blake bounced parallel to the enemy's lines. Dancer's eyes met a look of surprise from Blake's fellow topog Lieutenant George Meade. To their mutual astonishment at a random point Blake stopped. Dismounted in the thigh-high cordgrass. And—being slightly nearsighted—drew out his telescoping glass to scan the enemy lines.

Also somewhat astonished by this solo rider Swift heard mutterings among the Mexican command. Arista confided with his aide. "He must carry an offer of conciliation. Or a suit of peace…no doubt." Under the assumption the solitary officer had some important communication for His Excellency Arista dispatched two lancers forward to communicate with the lone emissary.

Unaware of the two advancing Mexican officers outside the circle of his spyglass Blake made general note of the troops in his line of vision. Then he remounted. Blake continued his ride along the entire enemy line. The flummoxed Mexican officers like jilted suitors were left alone in the tall spiky grass. Swift held her breath as the Mexicans followed the rider in their gunsights. Trained to fire in volley and not "at will" the riflemen held off their triggers for an order to fire. Blake continued his oblivious and careful assessment of the enemy. Swift exhaled as she realized the screen of protective sharpshooting *cazadores* skirmishers thinly spaced in front of the Mexican line were equally surprised to see Blake blundering past.

Blake returned toward the American lines. Trotted along the levee road. Dismounted and attempted to salute the General. Instead he fumbled his riding crop…and this toppled his spyglass case. Once he brought these under control his gloves fell to the ground. Blake struck attention and reported to Taylor. "The artillery is masked by the infantry and grass…sir. But they are there. Two batteries of artillery. One battery of five four-pounders in the center and another two-piece battery of eight-pounders facing our right. Judging by the green 'Maid of Erin' banners…sir…the two-piece battery is commanded by that Irishman Harp and his Saint Patrick's Battalion. Another four-pounder stands alone on our left—the enemy's right. On both far wings they have cavalry lancers…sir. Guessing by the colors again…our right faces Torrejón. He's the one who ambushed Thornton…sir."

"Good work…Blake." Taylor commended his officer. "Stay close to me…Lieutenant. With your knowledge of the field I will need you to carry my orders to the lines."

"Yes…sir!" Blake beamed as he mused: *Jiminy…the boys back home will never think I'm a dawdling simpleton or call me "Dipsy Doodle" again!*

CHAPTER 78

THE FIRST SHOT
PALO ALTO
8 MAY 1846/2:28 P.M.

JAMES COLLINGSWORTH TURNER watched from the rear as a single round shot from the Mexican artillery arced toward the American lines. Turner and the rest of the reporter pack noted the time. 2:28 p.m. The ball smashed into an artillery caisson nearby. The unfortunate Corporal Jonathan Bleak who sat on the caisson exploded in gore. His was the first casualty of the first battle of the war. Turner retched on their shoes.

The contest of the Mexican war opened in earnest.

Dancer heard Taylor shout. "Infantry…advance in column. Then move into line formation!" Two batteries of field artillery quickly bounced one hundred yards in front of the American lines. Then set up within eight hundred yards of the Mexican left flank. At the same time the ponderous 18-pounders pulled by four yokes of oxen creaked past Dancer into position on the road. Taylor personally supervised the big guns from the height of Old Whitey. His white battle stallion.

Dancer watched as the American fire was concentrated on Torrejón's cavalry on the Mexican left flank. Beside them Ampudia's 4th Infantry moved into position near the road. Where Dancer sat next to Taylor this movement suggested the massing of troops for an attack. "Pour more fire onto these regiments!" Taylor shouted to his artillery command. Alive with nervous excitement Dancer stared as a dozen Mexican rifleman were thrown down. The dry grass spattered red. Sergeants dragged the dead and wounded aside. The enemy's ranks behind quickly closed the gaps as they shouted "*Viva Mexico!*" The closed gaps were then reopened by another round of decimating American fire.

Swift flinched at the sudden roar when the Mexicans opened their heaviest guns onto the battlefield. Fired at flat-zero elevation. At three hundred yards Swift saw the cannonballs make their first graze. Then rise up and fly farther until they made a second graze at about six hundred yards. Anything in their path was crushed. By design the entire trajectory was below human height. For herself Swift now experienced what Arista had told her. As a killing machine an 18-pounder was three times more effective than a 6-pounder. "That is because…the heavier the shot…the greater its speed…and disastrous effect upon reaching its target."

The Americans watched these fearsome projectiles emerge from the flash and smoke. Sergeant O'Callahan spotted several balls coming directly for this rank. "Steady…boys." He hoped his stoic command would calm his men. "Hold your order now." With devastating result the shot sliced men and horses in half. Bodies literally exploded from the impact. Fragments of equipment and body parts hurtled about the ranks to kill and maim even more soldiers. Even when a shell slowed to the pace of a bowling ball a round shot easily lopped off any limb in its path. Destroyed any weapon or supplies it found.

Many troops stood at order arms as if spectators. They watched the effect of the American shots on the enemy. And watched the Mexican balls come their way. So as to throw themselves out of their way. Dancer saw others kneeled on the ground or flattened to avoid the bouncing balls. As Taylor had explained Dancer saw the most destructive fire came from the American batteries. Thus the Mexicans focused their fire there in return.

Lieutenant Blake directed Dancer's attention to see Ringgold's "flying artillery" dart about the field. Loaded. Fired. Displaced. Before counterbattery fire could catch up with them. The lighter bronze guns and rapid fire picked specific targets. Instead of simply taking blank aim at masses of men. Harp was not surprised when an American gunner carefully aimed at the Mexican regimental band. Just as it began to play the martial tune *Los Zapadores de Jalisco*—or "The Engineers of Jalisco." With one explosive shell the American fieldpiece destroyed the entire band. Scattered bodies. Silenced instruments. And sent soldiers screaming as they clutched their bloody wounds.

To Dancer the American gunners looked more like butchers than military men. Coats stripped off. Sleeves rolled up. Suspenders dropped below their waists. As Dancer's gaze traced back and forth only their red flannel undershirts kept them in matching colors. Ringgold's men limbered and unlimbered their guns. Fired a few shots. Then dashed through the gun smoke. And fired again. With practiced rapidity. All the time hidden from Harp's sharpshooters by the dense clouds of powder smoke. Like deathly apparitions the American gunners threw shot after shot into the Mexican front rank. Men screamed. Went down. Gasped in pain.

"Something must be done!" Swift heard Arista exclaim. Arista ordered action from Torrejón. "Take some one thousand lancers and two four-pounders from the left and turn the American right flank." Swift scribbled the words rapidly. Then shifted her gaze as the Mexican cavalry raced west. Across the road. And charged into the chapparal. What Swift could not see was the lancers' horses soon bogged down as they plunged into the low brush. Ground softened by recent downpours that drained into a depressed *resaca*.

The Mexican advance was observed. And reported to the commander. Dancer overheard Taylor respond to the report. From the General's position behind the 18-pounders on the road he nodded. "Keep a bright lookout for them." Then calmly went back to business.

Quickly the flanked American infantry responded. Dancer saw their lines move right and back. The officers knew the command would be vulnerable to an aggressive cavalry charge. *Their long lances will reach us before our bayonets are useful.* Dancer picked out that Torrejón intended to roll up and trample the American flank beneath his charge. As they were trained Dancer knew the American infantry would "form square."

His memory flashed to the endless drills. The square formation positioned men in four-deep rows on each side. That created a hollow center. For officers. Baggage. Battle flags. And wounded. The ranked volley of fire from the faces of the square would be daunting. Each row reloaded while the ranks behind fired to the roll and beat of the drummer. Fire. Reload. Until the front-most rank fired again. The deafening volleys came ceaselessly. Behind the smoke Dancer knew the square presented a bristling hedge of bayonets. A fearsome wall against the Mexican cavalry lancers.

Yet the Mexicans planned an answer. On Harp's advice Mexican field artillery would direct fire point-blank into the massed square. Though he embellished history before it happened Arista explained to Swift that Torrejón brought the 4-pounders and canister shot just for that purpose.

From the road Taylor and Dancer watched the 5th go into square. Would the Mexican 4-pounders be still slowed by the wetland? Dancer grit his teeth. The Mexican lancers bore down rapidly. The west face of the square held its fire. Closer the lancers raced. Now within fifty yards. Like a thunderclap the square let loose its volley. The Mexicans reeled. Regrouped. Charged again. But without the devastating fire from his 4-pounders Torrejón's lancers fell. Then retreated approximately three hundred yards. Inside the square the Americans bandaged their wounded. Troopers moved up to fill the gaps.

Not that far away Swift overheard the word arrive from Torrejón. The terrain and dense mesquite wood made a charge impractical.

"Try again!" Arista screamed at the messenger.

Minutes later Torrejón's cavalry maneuvered farther north. Then rode wide to avoid the murderous fire from the assembled square. As he saw this attack unfold Dancer realized the lightly defended supply train offered a tempting target. The Mexican lancers did not give a wide enough berth. As the lancers rode near they received a devastating volley from the right face of the square. Ahead of Torrejón's lancers the Americans' 3rd Infantry moved forward to protect the wagon park. Dancer saw Torrejón hesitate. Dissuaded from pressing the attack further. Having suffered considerable losses — the Mexicans retreated.

A moment late and a charge short Torrejón's two 4-pounders arrived…only to be surrounded by the retreating lancers. Quickly the Mexican cannons unlimbered. Prepared to fire on the stationary square.

Not four hundred yards away. Just in time Dancer saw two flying batteries arrive at full speed to cut off the Mexican threat. Torrejón's horse artillery pounded forward. Dancer watched as Walker's Rangers moved forward beside their batteries. The marksmen leveled their rifles at the approaching enemy 4-pounders. With their usual coolness the frontiersmen took deadly aim. At the same time the riflemen and the American cannon opened fire. Musket ball. Canister. And spherical shot ripped their targets. The effect was devastating. Without firing a gun the enemy's artillery was completely routed. And immediately retreated. Dancer knew Torrejón left dozens of dead in the bush. The rest were driven back into their lines.

At that moment Dancer's ears picked up a change. A lull fell over the field.

CHAPTER 79

SHADE OF A MESQUITE
NEAR PALO ALTO POND
8 MAY 1846/MINUTES LATER

LIEUTENANT JACOB BLAKE took advantage of the lull. And reflected on his good fortune. *To make detailed notes and study the terrain is one thing. To race helter-skelter with urgent orders to this commander or that—from one end of the battlefield to the other…that honor is quite a different matter.*

Blake looked exhausted. During the lull he dismounted to obtain a few moments' rest in the shade of a mesquite tree near Palo Alto pond. The wagon train formed a circle of safety nearby. Blake unbuckled his holster. Dropped the heavy belt on the ground at his feet. Instantaneously the percussion-cap pistol exploded. The single ball smashed upward into Blake's jaw—just above his buttoned collar. Blake's body jerked. Then toppled over backward as straight as a surveyor's stake. Soundlessly his body came to rest on a bed of trampled cordgrass. His lifeless eyes turned up at the sky. What remained of his face held an odd expression…as if another of life's mysteries had confounded him.

"Damn fool." So Taylor said when he received the news. Almost as an afterthought the old soldier unconsciously spoke Blake's epitaph.

"I must say…he gave one helluva report. One of the best topogs we had." The General paused. Settled his straw hat back into place. "Now what?"

Taylor spun around and almost bumped into Dancer behind him. Beside Dancer was the large black stallion from Rancho Valdez. The horse was a reverse image of Taylor's Old Whitey. When the two men's eyes met the bottom of Dancer's stomach fell away. Something told him this was the wrong place at the wrong time.

"Dancer"—Taylor commanded—"I've got a job for you. Take this order to our forward right. Tell the light Colonel to move those eighteen-pounders down the road and take the Fourth and Fifth with him."

"Wait a minute…General." Dancer said. "I appreciate the honor… but I'm an observer. My job is to see that supplies come in…and keep my eyes open." *Not to mention figure out that indecipherable map…and find Wildfire's treasure and the missing loan documents.*

"True. That's what I asked." Taylor conceded Dancer's point as he recalled their agreement on the wheelhouse of the *New York* exactly nine weeks before.

As Dancer sensed the worst he tried reason. "You'd be much better served by one of your own… sir."

"Be that as it may…son." Taylor leveled his gaze on Dancer. "You are a man of action. And that is what I need now."

Dancer blinked. Then tried a different gambit. "Don Carlo's cattle and mules and sheep have fed this army for a month. Surely that must count for…" Nonetheless the sinking feeling grew stronger in Dancer's belly.

Taylor's raised hand put an end to that thought. "Ah yes…that deal you struck with Juan Baptiste…the land reimbursement…confiscating Payaso's lands…the payment in specie coin. That went beyond your call. I agreed because I needed the supplies at a time when peace was possible. Now this is war. You can leave if you want. But…Dancer… in the next few hours you'll be much safer close to me."

Dancer felt cornered. His mood sank as his failure hit home full force. The shooting had started. His mission was blown away. In fact everything he had set out to do since Mustang's cryptic orders. And Jones's death. And Jace's execution. His mind boiled with defeat.

Taylor continued. "After we win this…you'll get your payment… wherever it was stashed. But we have to win this contest first."

Dancer considered playing his but-I-saved-your-life card…then thought better of it. *Damn. So close.* Dancer tossed all risk to the wind. Looked Taylor in the eye. "General…if that's an order. I'll do what I can to help." *Maybe Jones was right. I attract trouble. Pressed into service and promoted in one stroke. Must be my fate. But as Maybelle and Tony told us: "Play with a winner every chance you get. You can change horses later."*

"Good…I knew I could count on you…son. Now take these orders to the light Colonel."

Dancer leapt into his saddle. Taylor shouted up toward the back of his newly brevetted topog scout. "Once they take their positions! Report back immediately!"

Dancer galloped away. *What the hell.* Soon the commanding general's number one courier rode orders to all commanders in every corner of the battlefield.

CHAPTER 80

EIGHT MILES AWAY in Matamoros Payaso's batteries rained shells on Fort Texas. From noon onward the attack was the heaviest bombardment yet. Inexplicably — around two o'clock — the Mexicans ceased fire. In the silence a new sound came to the trapped denizens of Fort Texas. The sound of distant cannon came from the north. From the road to Point Isabel. The rapid firing sounded like one continuous volley of field pieces. Every man strained to listen. The dull boom of distant artillery rolled across the mesquite prairie.

At that moment something unexpected took place. From the men in Fort Texas a thunderous shout rose.

"The army's advancing!"

Those who sprinted out of their bombproofs and ratholes were disappointed. Taylor's army was not already at the drawbridge.

Within minutes the heavy bombardment resumed from Matamoros. Yet Borginnis and those trapped in Fort Texas gave their attention to the sounds of battle to the north. Soon clouds of smoke could be seen over the northern treetops. The sound and fury told plainly of a terrible contest being waged.

The continuous cannonading spread over the low country like thunder. No one knew if they were American or Mexican guns.

Sentries returned from their lookouts. They reported the Mexican infantry that had surrounded the fort on the north side just the day before had disappeared. Musket fire no longer harassed their redans from the woods.

After perhaps two hours the furious sounds of cannon ceased from the northern road. Sarah Borginnis asked Captain Hawkins the time. "Sixteen hundred hours." The lull carried foreboding. Had the Americans been forced to retreat…as Arista predicted? Was Taylor collecting his dead and wounded? Had we been defeated? What terrible fate was next in store for those who refused to surrender Fort Texas?

A cluster of men near the drawbridge considered the inevitable surrender. Once and for all they decided to break their swords in two. Rather than give them up to the enemy.

CHAPTER 81

DANCER CHECKED his watch. Four o'clock. On his face he felt a warm wind increase from the Gulf. Grass smoke smarted Dancer's eyes. A smoldering cannon wad discharged by a battery had ignited the tall cordgrass between the two armies. Smoke and flames of the prairie fire quickly spread across the field. With their targets obscured cannon blasts from both sides slackened. The Mexican lines had fallen back. Occasionally now Dancer heard the strangled screams of Mexican wounded. Unable to pull themselves beyond the burning grass line. Mercifully their cries were overcome by the sound of the searing blaze that quickly consumed them.

As he chatted with officers Taylor rode along the American line during the lull. He looked casual while all waited for the contest to begin anew. Dancer trailed Taylor to one side—and a length behind. The intense heat of the day was only worsened by the flames of the prairie. Officers let their men fall out to get water.

Taylor ordered his entire battle line into a realignment. Dancer rode off again to send the 18-pounders on the right still farther forward. Down the road. To a spot close to the original position of the

Mexican left flank. The 4th and 5th Infantries moved along the road. To anchor the American extreme right. And prevent a repetition of Torrejón's earlier flanking attempt.

High above in the heavy updrafts hungry black eyes watched the two lines of men pivot. Yet kept the wetlands between them. The entire American line moved counterclockwise. Now aligned beside the road. The opposing Mexican lines realigned to remain parallel with the American battle line. The Mexican right flank advanced counterclockwise about four hundred yards while the left flank remained in place. Swift stood in Arista's camp slightly east of the road. The Mexican advance now left Arista Hill exposed. In the eery quiet the deadly danger of her position dawned on Swift for the first time.

The Mexican front shifted to be nearly perpendicular to their first line. The wagon road was now open for an American advance. Two pools of water as before lay between the two forces. These barriers discouraged a frontal assault by either side. The flanks offered the only ground for effective infantry or cavalry attacks. The effect of these maneuvers Swift recorded on a fresh notebook page with rising unease.

Dancer again checked the time as he saw the breeze had thinned the smoke. Five o'clock. In a thunderous roar both sides resumed their deadly artillery duel. Arista's batteries now directed fire toward the 18-pounders and the men of the 4th positioned next to them. From the vantage of the elevated road Dancer watched as the 4th received a galling fire from the Mexican batteries. Men were thrown down. Gaps opened in the lines…only to be quickly filled by those behind. The big American guns continued to blast bloody breaks in the Mexican ranks. Holes that got even bigger as they remained unfilled.

Taylor signaled Dancer amidst the din. "We must do what Torrejón could not!" Taylor shouted. Dancer spurred his stallion to order the dragoon squadron of light cavalry in reserve on the right to turn the Mexican left. Supported by the 4th Infantry and Ringgold's artillery.

Swift watched with concern as the dragoons advanced in the direction of the camp where she stood. Intense cannonading and small-arms fire from the Mexicans poured into the squadron. Within a short distance they faced Torrejón's massed cavalry. Quickly the sixty-eight dragoons realized they could not press an attack. And fell back after two men were wounded and four horses butchered.

At that instant Dancer stood next to Second Lieutenant Ulysses "Sam" Grant. They both gaped in horror when a few feet in front of them a solid shot blew off an enlisted man's head. Bounced. Then tore away the lower jaw of a captain who stood to Dancer's immediate left. A shell exploded overhead. Dancer picked up the enlisted man's campaign cap and handed it to Grant. "Don't suspect he'll be needing this anymore." With that Dancer turned his back on the gore. To his right both the dragoons and the supporting 4th were forced to pull back. Shortly they rejoined the right wing.

Dancer remounted his black horse — now lathered white. Pounded off with orders for the artillery battalion to move up the road and take the place of the 4th. They must fill the gap between the 18-pounders and the 5th Infantry. Dancer raced past sergeants as they bellowed at the infantrymen to sit down in the grass. Anything to find some protection from the deadly Mexican round shot and canister. Thankfully Arista's cannon fire consistently flew well over their heads.

Partially shielded by the tall grass Dancer spotted Torrejón as his cavalry organized a massive charge against the Americans' far right. Dancer careened hard to alert the heavy artillery commander. Just in time the 18-pounders loosed their fury. Leveled canister and grape slammed into the charging cavalry. Dancer saw a shell burst in their midst and heard the canister balls strike flesh. A decapitated horse reared. Pitched its dismembered rider into the tall cordgrass with a heavy thump. The cannon fire repulsed the charge. Instantly the Mexican horsemen wheeled on the supporting infantry battalion now in square formation. The front rank fired a single devastating volley as Torrejón's riders came into close range. Lances lowered. Again Torrejón's horsemen were driven back to the main Mexican battle line. Harp's San Patricios artillery covered Torrejón's escape.

As Major Samuel Ringgold rode forward near his guns he was hit by a Mexican 4-pounder shot. The ball tore the flesh from the front of one thigh. Passed through his horse. Then ripped through Ringgold's other thigh as it exited. Mortally wounded the officer and horse collapsed together. Dancer and Grant raced to their comrade's side. Blood poured from his shattered legs. White splinters of bone protruded through his light blue regimental trousers. Little could be done.

The Mexican artillery continued its thunderous fire. As Patrick Harp held the spyglass to his eye he enjoyed a small measure of sweet revenge.

CHAPTER 82

ON THE BATTLEFIELD
PALO ALTO
8 MAY 1846/ MOMENTS LATER

TAYLOR AGAIN redirected the action. The old warrior moved like a boxer who sideslipped the trap of a corner. Taylor sent Dancer to the opposite end of the battle. The orders called for the light artillery to pour continuous fire into the inactive Mexican troops opposite Taylor's far left. The battery's guns belched lethal fire. A butcher's bill lengthened rapidly.

In formation the Mexicans soon tired of being slaughtered for no use. With a shout the troops demanded to be led on to the enemy with the bayonet. "Let us fight hand to hand! Let us die brave men!" Swift noted the exchange. Arista hesitated. Then granted their wish. The General ordered his light cavalry at the end of the battle line to turn the Americans' left flank. The cavalry was to be supported by the 2nd Light Infantry or *zapadores* engineers. Followed by the Tampico Coastal Guards. "Do whatever it takes to turn the Americans' left flank!"

Dancer rode hard. As he approached the American light artillery position he realized the artillery's view was partially obscured by the grassfire smoke. The American Captain stood on his caisson and strained to view the enemy. He expected to roll to the assistance of

Ringgold on the American right. At that moment Dancer arrived at full tilt and shouted. "Mexican cavalry! There! Leaving the chapparal!"

Dancer pulled abreast of the caisson and shouted at the Captain. "If unchecked that cavalry could reach the American wagon train!" The Captain responded. With understatement he shouted at Dancer. "Tell Taylor I'm occupied!" First the Captain positioned one battery directly in front of the two charging Mexican cavalry columns. Then Dancer watched as the 2nd flying artillery unit raced forward. After a brief moment the mounted artillery took up a point where they could fire canister point-blank into the Mexican right flank.

The first battery opened on the two squadrons of cavalry with round shot. Shells. And spherical case. As fast as the ramrods could reload. Surprised to be met by fire the entire cavalry advance scattered into the bushes. Then fell back in disorder.

The Mexicans tried to return the fire on their flank that came from the west. But were frustrated by the blinding sun directly in their eyes. In short order the *zapadores* light infantry and Coastal Guards fell back. The American artillery again moved to the attack. Without hesitation they pushed their flying batteries to within three hundred yards of the Mexican right flank. From the height of his battle stallion Dancer saw the batteries open an *enfilade* fire. In minutes this withering attack rolled back the Mexican right flank. At the sound of cannon fire coming in her direction Swift turned to look up the battle line to her right. Men broke ranks. Ran desperately toward her position. Swift watched in horror as the regular cavalry increased the panic among the Mexican infantrymen. The horsemen raced away from the American guns. Thundered through their own lines. Scattered foot soldiers left and right.

Arista and some of the San Patricios men halted this flight. Incensed the Mexican General ordered a counterattack by the broken infantry units—supported by what remained of the light cavalry regiment. Swift stared in disbelief. The Mexican troops—now too disheartened to push home the attack—were easily turned aside by a sweep of flying cannon fire along the lengths of their columns.

The rout now became general. Each infantry regiment joined the ones that flooded past. Like a growing torrent the wave moved toward Swift. The 1st fled. That exodus demoralized the 6th. Which swept the panic along to the center of the Mexican line. As quickly the general contagion broke over the 10th. And then the 4th Infantry in turn. The entire Mexican line collapsed and ran toward Swift's position.

⊠   ⊠   ⊠

The western sun now burned low behind the Americans' backs. The fiery ball glinted blindingly in the Mexicans' faces. Every Mexican red plastron breastplate reflected. Every polished bayonet glistened. Every white-leather cross belt centered by a brass plate stood boldly outlined in the Americans' sights. From the brilliant sunlight only the powder smoke and smoldering grass fires gave the Mexican troops a fleeting screen. Darkness could not come soon enough.

Dancer galloped back to report the flying artillery's sweep. The Mexican line rolled back like a carpet. Taylor considered a bayonet charge to turn the retreat of the enemy's right into a rout. Dancer counseled caution. The wetlands. The prairie fires. Darkness. Not to mention exposure of the American supply wagons to a possible cavalry raid or capture. He had traversed the entire battlefield. Several times. A charge at this time was unwise. Taylor decided against an attack. Not that far away the routed Mexican troops poured past Arista Hill like an island in the stream.

⊠   ⊠   ⊠

Arista ordered his army to withdraw to a sheltered bivouac for the night. Not far from his original right wing. The troops moved to the mesquite-covered ground — perhaps a cannon's distance from their earlier position near Palo Alto pond. From Arista's relocated command tent Swift penned with pride the day's events into another fast-paced dispatch for her exclusive readers.

Next came a macabre business. By torchlight patrols searched the field for their dead and wounded in the high fresh grass and the charred stalks. Many of the Mexican dead could not be buried. Swift learned the Mexican quartermaster anticipated victory. That was his excuse for no need to provision the army with pickaxes and shovels.

When wounded were brought into the field hospital Swift uncovered another truth. The surgeon in charge of the medicine chests had disappeared. And during the battle he absconded with all the supplies. Swift's neutral detachment almost broke its bounds as she watched the ghastliness unfold around her. Wounded after wounded were piled into wagons. Then trundled back over the jolting road toward Matamoros. Every movement a tortured agony that reopened their wounds. Cries of pain shot into the night.

⊠   ⊠   ⊠

American search parties brought in their wounded from the darkness. Through the night Dancer heard the cries of men as the surgeon's saw cut away mangled limbs.

Ulysses Grant wrote home that evening.

> *We then encamped on our own ground and the enemy on theirs. We supposed that the loss of enemy had not been much greater than our own and expected of course the fight would be renewed in the morning.*

Neither side had accomplished its objective. Taylor had not reopened the road to Fort Texas. And Arista had not destroyed the American force. The Battle of Palo Alto was a draw.

⊠   ⊠   ⊠

Without cover in the bright moonlit night no messenger risked the run to Fort Texas. Worries swirled through the American bastion. Had their little American Army been beaten at Palo Alto? Midnight came and went. The darkest hours passed in agonized doubt. The night had not yet left the chapparal as the dwindling darkness thinned toward morning.

Still with no word.

CHAPTER 83

HORROR OF WAR
RESACA DE LA PALMA
9 MAY 1846

BEFORE SUNRISE Arista withdrew his army from the mesquite bivouac. The Mexican camp moved in darkness down the road. Toward Matamoros. Swift watched as supplies were followed by artillery. Then infantry from the Mexican left. Next came the right wing of elite *zapadores* engineers and Tampico Coastal Guard. The entire army moved in battle order. Several field pieces and Torrejón's cavalry formed the rear guard for the orderly line of march. Malvado's *rancheros* took their own path south. Like ghosts they moved silently among the mesquite thickets.

At sunrise the Americans discovered Arista had decamped the field. Taylor again gathered his war council. Dancer knew Taylor's own inclination was to press on to pursue Arista...and relieve Fort Texas. Yet strong arguments existed for breaking off contact.

"The Mexican Army has not been destroyed." So one officer argued. "And they still outnumber us. My guess is four to one."

Another officer favored caution. "The Louisiana volunteers are expected to arrive any time. The requisition was sent how long ago... must be twelve days now. Considering the odds...waiting for reinforcements is the prudent course."

"We showed what we could do yesterday with cavalry and our flying artillery. Look how we rolled them up like a rug. Given a clear field we can do it again." The artillery subaltern barely contained his enthusiasm.

With a wave of his hand a senior topog put the junior officer in his place. "Palo Alto was prairie. From here to Matamoros is woods. Thorn thicket. Ravines. Not the best terrain for flying artillery."

"Gentlemen…gentlemen…what did we learn yesterday? How can we turn it to our advantage?" Taylor probed.

In that moment of contemplation Dancer spoke up.

"Sir…if I may…I'd like to throw into the hopper some observations from my experience."

An unwelcome stir went through the tent. As if a nonmember had stepped into the club.

"You all know Jack Dancer." Taylor gestured to his trusted recruit. "He is acting as my courier with Blake gone. He may have something to add…because he has seen the Mexicans' guns up close."

Dancer began: "Your men know their business better than anyone…General. Yesterday's results show that. My purpose is to share what I know. It may aid your decision." Dancer paused then stepped forward. "The Mexican guns are serviceable…but twice as heavy as ours. Most are old. Obsolete. The dates I've seen on their guns go back to 1776. I know because Payaso showed me personally. The old Spanish cannons are iron. Heavy. Not easily repositioned or re-aimed. The quoin that elevates the barrel is cumbersome. You have to drive it in with a sledgehammer like a wedge. And it loosens with every shot. Thus the Mexican balls tend to go high…over our heads. As we saw. Simply put…their guns are made for siege work not fieldwork. That's why they've played more havoc at Fort Texas than they did against us yesterday…or will do today."

Officers of the 4th and 5th agreed. Simply having their men sit in the grass yesterday gave them some protection.

Dancer chose his words carefully. "What we didn't see yesterday from the Mexican infantry was their muskets. I've seen them. They are old British Brown Bessies from India. They're relics of the past. That's why the Brits unloaded them by the shipload for years. Most of the

Bessies were condemned as unserviceable."

"So what?" One officer was quick to counter Dancer's observations. "They can still put a ball through you before you get to their lines."

"True." Dancer agreed. "But only under one hundred yards. And then only if they are pointed directly at you. I've watched the Mexicans practice. To a man they overload their powder. That makes the Brown Bess kick like a mule. The Mexicans compensate by firing from the hip. When they do that even within twenty yards their volleys go high."

General Taylor added under his breath…just loud enough for all to hear: "As Sam Walker would say…'They couldn't hit a bull's ass with a handful of banjos.'"

A murmur of agreement fluttered through the club.

"Most important…the Mexicans were promised victory yesterday. Arista has pumped them up with illusions of easy victories. The Thornton ambush. Taylor's retreat to Point Isabel. Fort Texas not returning their fire. Victory is theirs for the taking…that's what their officers told them. Contempt for the invaders was a common phrase they used."

Dancer directed his last comment to Taylor. "After yesterday my guess is their infantry and the conscripts in the line feel betrayed by Arista. They don't much want to be here…but the ruling class and the stupidity of their politicians got them in this mess. My sense is the time to attack is now."

The young officer blurted out his enthusiasm. "General…we whipped them yesterday—and we can whip them again!"

Taylor counted the secret ballots of his war council. Out of his ten commanders seven favored remaining at Palo Alto and awaiting reinforcements. Only three voted to attack.

Taylor had heard his officers out. Now the veteran General sided with the minority of three…and Jack Dancer.

"Gentlemen…prepare your commands to move forward within the hour."

CHAPTER **84**

ON THE ROAD TO MATAMOROS
RESACA DE LA PALMA
9 MAY 1846/SOMETIME LATER

SWIFT RODE her nervous Peony amidst the Mexican Army as it retreated four miles. In an orderly fashion the battalions took up an even stronger position at the old riverbed meander of Resaca de la Palma. At that place Swift again sketched the battlefield. The road crossed at right angles a ravine about sixty feet wide and four or five feet deep. Recent rains left standing water knee-deep in places. Or up to the waist in the lowest part where the *resaca* met the narrow Matamoros Road. Over this road the Americans had to pass.

The American war correspondent accompanied Arista to his camp on the south side of the muddy ravine. From the elevated position Swift added details to her sketch. She watched as entrenchments and earthworks were thrown up on the cutbank above the southern side of the *resaca.* Three batteries of guns were positioned to command the road to Fort Texas. One battery on the north bank of the *resaca.* Two others flanked the road on the south side. The Mexican troops deployed in double rank. Arista told Swift his force was six thousand strong. Reinforced during the night by Payaso's fresh troops withdrawn from their siege of Fort Texas.

North of the ravine a wall of men now waited on both sides of the road. Their backs to the *resaca*. Another Mexican battle line on the ravine's south side behind them had a clean line of fire across the open *resaca*. This second line made the most of the cover provided by a dense thicket of chapparal that ran along the southern edge of the draw.

An American company of the 4th Infantry led an advance scouting party south on the Matamoros Road. The chapparal was quiet until they neared the Resaca de la Palma. As the party moved into the sunlight two Mexican guns roared from their masked position on the near side of the *resaca*. Instantly one American in the front rank was thrown down. Gasped in pain as his blue waistcoat turned dark red. A shell exploded overhead. Three others were driven down— grievously wounded. Fellow troopers pulled them up behind their own saddles and galloped back to Taylor.

The contest exploded.

✠　✠　✠

Taylor drew in the dirt…and briefed Dancer on the battle lines. Every detail critical for Dancer's assignments…and survival. Two hundred and fifty men must protect the train of three hundred wagons in the rear. Two heavy 18-pounders—which had proved less effective than the flying artillery the day before—bolstered the supplies. In front of the train on the road to Matamoras sat the 8th Infantry with the mounted infantry dragoons before them. Looking south to the left of the road in column was half of the 4th Infantry positioned behind the 5th Infantry directly in front of it. On the right of the road the remainder regiments of the 4th watched the backs of the 3rd Infantry in column before it. In the foremost vanguard the flying artillery formed the point of attack on the road itself.

Mounted on his black stallion Dancer stayed close behind the left shoulder of Taylor as the General rode forward on Old Whitey to scan Arista's position through his telescope. The topogs were right. The thick chapparal precluded reliance on long-range fire. The Mexicans occupied two solid lines along the *resaca*. Taylor knew only a small portion at the center point counted.

The key to victory was the road to Matamoros.

Taylor ordered the attack. Dancer raced orders first to the flying guns to engage the enemy. Then to the infantry commanders and the dragoon horsemen. Finally Dancer's horse raced back to Taylor's second-in-command to inform the 8th Infantry in the rear reserve.

Dancer watched as the horse artillery charged forward. Unlimbered their guns on the road within range of the enemy. And fired. At that moment from their left — hidden from view by the chapparal — a column of Mexican cavalry bore down on their position. Unseen until almost on top of them came the sparkling Mexican lances lowered toward the chests of the gunners. In the blink of an eye the Americans fired one point-blank cannon blast into the oncoming cavalry. No time to reload. The men dropped their ramrods. Raised their carbines and sabers. The Americans prepared to defend hand to hand. But the blast of canister and grape had its intended effect. The lancers wheeled aside. In their place both infantries contested the chapparal. Battle cries and screams of pain broke out as close fighting continued on all sides.

Into the maelstrom the Americans advanced. On the left the American 5th Infantry. On the right the 3rd led the charge forward toward the ravine. The Mexican guns roared but their work had little impression. The shots rent the air above the heads of the American infantry. Dancer's assessment was right.

As Dancer moved forward on the road his gaze saw a brigade of the 8th Infantry receiving galling musket fire. The volley came from a body of Mexicans lodged in a thicket of chapparal to their left. The commanding officer shouted to his men to turn and charge the thicket. A lieutenant on the far side appeared personally to charge the enemy. In the next moment the lieutenant was hit. And lay wounded upon the ground. A Mexican soldier towered over him — about to run a bayonet though his body. An American officer sprang forward. His Colt revolver blasted toward the Mexican. Just as the enemy bayonet was to be driven home. The soldier looked up. Hesitated in alarm. Then thrust down hard. His razor steel missed the lieutenant's chest. But hit the arm of the wounded American. At that same moment the officer swung his Colt's barrel like a baton. Split the Mexican's skull with a thunderous blow. Beside the officer and his wounded lieutenant his men reloaded their hot carbines and fired. Three Mexicans fell. The Americans gave a great shout of rage. "Kill them!" And charged. Another lieutenant — also of the 8th...and at the head of his squad —

fell on their left…mortally wounded. Blood gushed red from the hole in his belly ripped by a Mexican musket ball.

Dancer strained to see ahead of this contest. High in his stallion's saddle he watched as the 5th charged a thicket. An officer madly beat down the bushes with his horse and hacked through the branches with his sword. The instant the officer emerged from the brush three Tampico Guards fired at once. With a scream his horse fell dead under him. A crowd of Mexican muskets and lances rushed at him. As best he could the officer desperately swiped his saber to defend himself. An instant later a bayonet slashed through his mouth. And came out below his ear. The officer seized the weapon with his bare hand. Raised his sword to cut his tormentor down. But he was surrounded. Another bayonet rammed into his lacerated arm. Still another steel jabbed through his hip. Borne down. Outnumbered. The 5th's officer fell. Literally pinned to the earth.

With that first charge the infantry masked the gunner's view. The flying battery suspended its fire. For fear of galling their own troops. The horse unit now raced the battery to the head of the charge. The gunners closed on the melee where the officer from the 5th engaged the enemy. Here an artillery colonel met the officer. Who stood awkwardly. Supported by his sword used as a cane. In his haste the New York artillery veteran did not see the officer was wounded. In crisp fashion the gunner barked. "Sir…request a party of your men to support my battery. We must cross the *resaca* on the road." At that moment the officer turned. And presented a most terrible sight. Blood clotted on his mangled face. The officer of the 5th answered with difficulty. "I will give you the support you need." The officer slurred his blood-soaked promise.

As the artillery man realized the situation he asked with some emotion: "You're wounded…sir! What can I do for you?"

The wounded lieutenant colonel replied laconically. "Give me some water…and show me my regiment."

* * *

Moments after Dancer delivered the orders a portion of the 4th Infantry moved forward to the left of the road. In minutes they reached the northern bank of the ravine. From their far left on the edge of the *resaca* came a squadron of Mexican lancers that charged like a whirlwind. The band of Americans steadily leveled their fire upon the charge. Two green tunics pitched to the ground. Most of the Americans melted back into the chapparal. At this point a lieutenant remained in the open space. His squad received the whole charge. The lieutenant defended himself with his sword briefly…but was beaten down. He twitched in death as seven lances skewered his body.

On the right of the road Taylor and Dancer watched as the 3rd moved in column rapidly forward. Directly into the teeth of deadly fire from a Mexican battery. The roaring guns were positioned on the north side — where the road crossed the ravine. The captain who had voted in secret ballot to advance threaded his command through the dense chapparal. Kept a distance from the open road. When they neared the ravine they met the enemy entrenchment to their left that supported the artillery piece. Twenty-five or thirty men wheeled to their left. Charged along the ravine. Their advance slowed momentarily as they slogged knee-deep through fetid water. Then their carbines roared. Revolvers thundered. Swords met flesh. A trooper screamed as a bayonet pierced his thigh. In that moment the forces clashed like two titans in an unmoving grapple of death. Close-quarter slaughter engulfed the blue and the green. The defenders wavered. Then… soon…the enemy was routed. A Texas lieutenant leapt forward. Seized the leading mules attached to the artillery piece that held the road. The fast action prevented the guns from being driven back across the *resaca* to the Mexican camp. Another lieutenant from the regiment of Texans thrust a handspike between the spokes of the caisson's wheel. Locked the gun carriage against a tree. Bayonets silenced the last Mexican gunner.

To save the field piece a large force of Mexican cavalry now charged the Americans. Taylor sent Dancer to order the 3rd to bring a column up on the right side of the road. Just in time. The column drove off the enemy cavalry with the point of their bayonets. A corporal's carbine banged. And the Mexican lieutenant colonel that led the Mexican charge dropped from his horse grievously wounded. As the officer rolled over the American corporal in remorse handed the enemy his canteen. A moment later the corporal lay dead on his back. Killed by a musket ball fired from across the *resaca*. His stiffening body clutched a cartridge in his hand. The bitten-off paper casing was still clamped between his rigid lips like a last cigar.

Dancer's respect grew as he saw the Mexicans fight with valor and bravery. They defended their land. Resolved upon victory or death. The contest in the *resaca* was bloody. Every inch of ground contested.

An American officer pitched down in the front rank. He gasped in pain as his comrade's blue jackets trotted double-time past him.

A sergeant shouted. And a shell exploded behind him. Dancer watched as a boot twisted up in the air. And fell in the *resaca*. With a heavy splash. Half the sergeant's leg was still inside.

The balls and cartridges Dancer had supplied the Americans now pressed the green-jacketed Mexican regulars back. A Mexican rifleman shot in the lungs fell draped over a mesquite bush. Drawing his bayonet an American volunteer stabbed the wounded man until the rifleman stopped twitching. Then ransacked his haversack for rings. Or a watch.

Even from her rear vantage point Swift sensed the Mexican advance front beyond the *resaca* beginning to waver. Men on the far side of the ravine floundered across the wet *resaca* to reach their comrades on the south bank. At last the line gave way.

One of the *zapadores* trapped on the north edge of the ravine swung his spent musket like a club. And put down two Americans before a third blue jacket lunged a bayonet into his chest.

Frequently the blue waves of Yanks tried to charge across the ravine. But a murderous fire of artillery turned their work to bloody frustration. The Mexican artillery and entrenched muskets leveled directly into the faces of the oncoming Americans. A shell burst barely over their heads. The blast drove down two more Americans and ripped the flesh of several horses.

Dancer saw a shell explode right at the edge of the chapparal. Canister shot rattled through the mesquite branches around him. From out of the chapparal another American seemed to step slowly. His blue coat turned scarlet before he jerked down into the grass. Another trooper ran toward the *resaca* just as he was hit in the shoulder. The man stumbled down the ravine's side. Shuddered to a stop. Fell facedown in the muddy water.

Only decisive action would turn the battle to either's favor.

CHAPTER 85

"CHARGE THE GUNS!"
RESACA DE LA PALMA
9 MAY 1846/WITHIN THE HOUR

TAYLOR TURNED TO DANCER. "The Mexican guns must be dislodged!" He shouted. "Tell Captain May's dragoons to charge the guns! We must break through like a fist through a pane of glass. Breach the Mexicans' line…and victory is ours. Fail…and we'll be trapped in Arista's chapparal."

Dancer needed no reminder to recall the fate of Thornton's debacle. He wheeled. And cantered away from the front of the action at Taylor's command position. Directly behind and to the left of the flying guns. Within several caisson lengths Dancer approached the dashing Captain May at the front of his dragoons. Dancer relayed Taylor's orders. The Captain — known to savor recklessness — snapped a brisk salute. "We will do it…sir!"

The cavalry man turned his battle steed to face his mounted light dragoons on the road. Raised his sword. Then bellowed so every man could hear him. "Remember your regiment…and follow me!" The Captain and Dancer rode forward at the head of the column — toward Taylor and an artillery officer.

The officer shouted to the Captain. "Wait — Charley — until I draw their fire!" The Captain and Dancer pulled up at the front of the mounted dragoons. The squadron behind them filled the road. Four abreast in column. The lips of some were pale. Their eyes wore a fixed expression. Dancer knew danger was at hand. Two soldiers with clenched teeth nervously laughed. All took a tighter grip on their reins or settled themselves with care into their saddles. Quiet words of confidence and bravado were passed from each to his neighbor like a canteen. Others prayed.

With a roar the horse guns fired through the thin smoke toward the Mexican battery. Harp's Mexican artillery immediately returned fire. Murderous round shot punched a hole in the air above the Americans' caps. Just then the swashbuckling Captain stood in his stirrups and bellowed. "Charge!"

At precisely that same instant a Mexican shell burst with a thunderous explosion immediately behind Dancer's spirited stallion. Dancer's terrified mount bolted uncontrollably forward. In tandem the dragoon Captain and Dancer raced ahead of the charge. With pounding hoofs and rattling sabers the dragoons swept like the wind up the road. Stirrup to stirrup. They raced forward on the narrow track. Their Captain and Dancer led the charge.

Now out of control Dancer galloped headlong into the teeth of the Mexican gun line. Onward the pair charged. Side by side. With flowing beard and long mane the captain screamed at the top of his lungs: "Men! Follow!" Dancer's horse thundered forward…scared out of its wits. Unresponsive to its rider's attempts to turn him. Or rein him in. The maddened stallion careened around trees felled into the dusty road. Leapt over obstacles scattered like cordwood to block the way. Eighty dragoons thundered forward like a train. Four abreast in a solid mass that filled the small roadway behind their leaders. Every dragoon hell-bent on blasting all before them to smithereens.

So fast was the charge that Harp's Mexican artillerists had not a moment to reload. They dropped their ramrods and plunges. Took up pistols and swords. Anything to defend themselves against the screaming blue banshees on horseback that brought dreadful slaughter into their midst.

The Captain and Dancer pounded across the ravine on the levee road. Came opposite the enemy breastworks. Dancer's mad stallion thundered forward. Straight up the road. Ears back. Eyes bulged white with terror. Uncontrolled. Dancer cracked a bayonet aside with Blake's sword. Then hacked downward into a man's neck. The stallion reared then bolted forward. Dancer gripped the crazed horse. Then heard a musket bang near at hand. Ducked. Swung his sword at another Mexican. And raced farther up the road.

As the Mexican earthworks and guns loomed ahead Captain May bellowed again. "Follow me!" Like a mad wolverine he careened to his left. Leapt over the works. Several of his horsemen followed.

From left and right Dancer heard the crack of muskets from the defenders of the enemy guns. Every Mexican turned his musket toward the dragoons. The horsemen whirled like madmen in their midst. Two new and not well-trained horses of a pair of fresh dragoons balked at jumping the works. Their desperate riders turned them hard left to ride along the lip of the ravine. In the vain hope to turn the breastworks at another opening. A private pointed toward a low rail fence. His shout transformed into a terrible scream as a volley of musket balls took his life.

As a dragoon lieutenant passed the first works a mounted Mexican lancer dashed at him. The lieutenant parried the Mexican's thrust with his saber. But received a flesh wound from the sharpened point. Just then a cannon shot slammed through the right side of the lieutenant's horse. Killed it instantly. Shattered the officer's left side. The lieutenant shouted an oath as his horse collapsed. The shout cut short as two Mexican bayonets drove him to the ground.

Another *zapador* was hit in the back...and the man tumbled down the ravine's side.

A ball hit Dancer's hat. Jerked it back on its cords so it hung from his neck as his horse careened through the Mexican lines.

The Mexicans momentarily were driven from their guns by the furious charge. But just as quickly they rallied. Again they got possession of the battery. The horse squadron became scattered amongst the enemy entrenchments on both sides of the road.

Though the battery had been silenced for a time the guns were not captured. Harp's Mexicans remanned their guns beside the road. Prepared to pour deadly fire again into the oncoming ranks of American infantry. Now behind enemy lines the dragoons found themselves the targets of fire that came from Mexican riflemen on both sides. The courageous Captain realized he was in no-man's-land. His command caught between a hammer and an anvil. As the enemy closed in the Captain knew they must retreat. Or be slaughtered by the point-blank fire of the Mexican infantry.

"Fall back! Fall back!" The Captain screamed to his dragoons.

He signaled a sergeant to lead the dragoons back toward their own lines. Collected several dragoons himself. Then turned them around from where they had just come. The last of the blue-jacketed horsemen retreated. Their work was done. The gap they created in the enemy's defenses resealed. The Mexican infantry fired aimlessly at the backs of the retreating dragoons.

CHAPTER 86

BEHIND ENEMY LINES
ARISTA'S CAMP/RESACA DE LA PALMA
9 MAY 1846/A FEW MINUTES OR SO LATER

THE EXPLOSION OF SHOTS receded behind him as Dancer steadily took more control over his horse. The beast had rushed headlong—breaking clear of the Mexican lines. Dancer now found himself a few hundred yards beyond the fray and in the midst of General Arista's camp. Everywhere stood the military wealth of his army. Stands of small arms. Ammunition boxes. Thousands of buck-and-ball paper cartridges. Scores of splendid packsaddles. The empty camp was arranged to form a small village. Walls of baggage. Stacks of trunks. Piles of private property. All neatly arranged. Without the slightest thought of a defeat.

An elaborate tent with tasseled marquee caught Dancer's eye. Under the canopy each object was intentionally placed on a large Alicante carpet of discerning Moorish design. As if transported from a Spanish gentleman's library. An ornate writing desk sat ready for grandiloquent dispatches to be written by a confident victor. A silver tea service still steamed on a side table. Within easy reach of the abandoned desk cartons of fine writing paper sat near at hand.

Dancer's still-skittish stallion carried him forward. The aromas of a great victory feast reached his nose. The deserted preparations were in suspended animation. About this scene camp kettles filled with savory meats simmered over fires. On the shoulder of the road were carcasses of half-skinned oxen. Over several red-hot charcoal spits great sides of beef broiled deliciously. The hangers-on who had moments before been busy in their feast-preparing work were gripped by a sudden panic. They fled in haste toward the river.

His horse finally reined in Dancer jumped down. Led the stallion between a wall of baggage and a covered supply wagon. No sooner had he turned the corner than he stopped short. Reached for his Colt.

Who came toward him in an elegant Spanish riding outfit? A look of surprise on her face? Flushed in the heat of the thick Texas air? None other than Samantha Swift.

"What the hell?" Dancer stuttered.

"I could ask you the same question." Swift quipped her retort as they took cover momentarily out of sight of the camp. *What's Dancer doing here? Has he deserted?*

For a long stunned moment the two Americans looked at each other. Swift looked different somehow…or so Dancer thought. *Less naïve and more experienced?* Their horses moved together. The stallion and the mare snuffled each other in dim recognition of days past in the Rancho Valdez pastures.

Swift broke the silence. "Arista invited me to observe the battle firsthand from his headquarters. I think it made a damned good story."

"More than a good story…Swift. It will make a great obituary."

"What do you mean? What's happening?"

"We charged right up their middle and broke through."

"That doesn't explain how you got here." Swift pressed her onetime friend.

"Well…let's just say…I came along for the ride." Dancer removed his forage hat. Stuck a finger though a hole the size of a musket ball.

Swift noticed a red gash on Dancer's right forearm.

"You're hurt." Swift touched Dancer gently. Dancer winced for the first time. Then shrugged off any attention.

"This is not a good place." Dancer said to Swift with alarm. "The Fifth Infantry is right behind me. The Mexicans have fallen back from the northern side of the ravine. It won't be long before the dogs of hell are loosed."

Swift peeked from behind the wall of baggage. The din of battle came from the Resaca de la Palma. Not a quarter mile away. Quickly she turned back. In a hoarse whisper Swift gave Dancer a dire warning. "General Arista was convinced this was only a skirmish…not a full battle. When he realized the Americans had taken his batteries on the north side he left his tent. Arista was right here minutes ago."

"Taylor's men are coming." Dancer spoke impatiently. "They've tasted blood. They won't ask questions before they shoot first at anything that moves. And the Mexicans won't be as friendly as your General when they see an American woman. Take this." Dancer pulled from his holster the Paterson Colt that had once belonged to Blake. "Thumb the hammer back to lock a cylinder in place. That will drop the trigger down. All five cylinders are loaded and capped." Dancer handed Swift the heavy revolver. "Watch out. It's got a hair trigger."

Swift took the weapon. Then slipped it into her sling bag that hung down to her hip.

"You've got to get out of here right now!" Dancer said as he recognized a grudging respect for the correspondent.

"And how about you?"

"I'll get back to our lines…somehow."

Swift shot back with a mix of concern and irritation. "You better…because you have to take this to Taylor." Swift handed Dancer two leather-covered cases.

"What's this?" Dancer asked.

"Maps. I stole two maps from Arista's writing desk when he left. One shows north of the Rio Grande River. The other is a detailed map of the entire Mexican terrain south of the river to Monterrey."

"Do you know how valuable these are?" Dancer hefted the two folding maps with fine leather covers.

Swift shot Dancer a look. "These maps could decide the war…Dancer. With them Taylor will know the territory ahead. Without them Taylor's army will stumble around in the Mexicans' backyard like blind men."

Dancer stuffed both book-like maps into the inner pockets of his jacket. "This is the break the topogs have been looking for!"

A split second later an unexpected shell exploded under a supply wagon. Debris rained on their heads.

"You've got to get out of here now…Swift! While you still can. Go! Go now! Ride to the river. Take the flat ferry to Matamoros. Just get out of here. Taylor is about to bring the entire army right up this road."

"Don't worry about me…Dancer." Swift began to gather the reins of her horse. "At least I'm on the side of the lines where I'm supposed to be. I'm here to report on the battle…not be a part of it." *Let's hope Arista doesn't find out I stole his maps. I'd be executed on the spot as a spy.* Swift swung up onto Peony with ease.

Swift grinned slyly. "Tell the boys…if they get here soon…they can eat the Mexicans' lunch." Then steadied her horse. "And…Dancer." Swift paused as she bent forward in her saddle and brought her face close to his. "Thanks…and take care. I owe you one." Swift craned in the saddle to see if the way was clear. As Peony moved forward Dancer gave the edgy quarter horse a sharp smack on its rump. Rider and horse bolted toward the river.

Dancer mounted his stallion — now calmed by the familiar smell of Swift's quarter horse. For a moment he watched until Swift disappeared into the chapparal. *Without a doubt…Swift — you are a most disconcerting woman. Godspeed.*

With authority Dancer spurred his stallion into the open camp. Then reined the steed north as they bolted up the road. In moments Dancer returned to the fury and thunder of full battle.

CHAPTER 87

BACK INTO THE FRYING PAN
RESACA DE LA PALMA BATTLEFIELD
9 MAY 1846/A LITTLE WHILE LATER

DANCER LEANED LOW over his horse's neck to reduce his profile. He rode hard. Came from behind the surprised clusters of Mexican troops. Infantry and cavalry ran in every direction. Turned toward any peril that presented itself. Dancer darted between them. Drove into the wind toward the road north. Like lightning from his right a Mexican horseman bore down on him. Lance leveled like a medieval knight. Dancer reined hard to his left. Flailed Blake's short sword wildly. Parried the thrust lance. For his troubles Dancer received only a slight flesh wound from the point. This time in his upper right arm. At that moment a bloodthirsty war cry rose from the far *resaca*. The lancer turned and fled.

The black stallion danced between equipment and barricades. Hit the flat draw at a gallop. At that moment a ball slammed into Dancer's horse. Passed through its right side and out the left. The shot killed the horse instantly. Horse and rider twirled in a pirouette of death. Dancer went down into the bed of the *resaca*. Together rider and horse came to rest in the damp ravine. The horse's body pinned Dancer's left leg into the soft churned sand with its dead weight.

Dancer lay there in the midst of the action. Carnage ran riot on all sides. Shots from the American and Mexican guns tore up the earth around him. He tried to raise his horse. But was unable to move. Dancer fell back helpless. He was still astride the horse…with his right leg over the stallion's neck. No pain came from his pinned left leg. But Dancer was trapped.

From nowhere a riderless horse came careening toward Dancer. The animal struggled and reared in pain. Blood pumped from three musket ball wounds as the maddened horse's hooves pulverized the ground. Two or three times the crazed animal came near to trampling Dancer. At length—with a scream of agony and a last death twist—the horse fell dead. Its body half rested on Dancer's fallen steed. Just then a musket ball glanced off Dancer's exposed right boot—which lay across his stallion's neck.

Exhausted from pain and exertion dullness came into Dancer's eyes. *So this is how it ends.* The tide of the action now rolled away from him. The green Mexican uniforms began to disappear from the top of the ravine bank. Squadrons of blue trousers passed in apparent pursuit.

Dancer's brain nursed disconnected thoughts of Charleston. Belle Ashley. MayBelle's honey cakes.

Not far from Dancer a villainous-looking *ranchero* came into view. Armed with an American sergeant's short sword the bandit dispatched a wounded American and robbed his body. The next form the *ranchero* came to was a Mexican. Whom he dispatched in the same way. He rifled the rags for any treasure. In this way the *ranchero* came on. Methodically. Murderously. He slew three more. Dancer peered over his horse's neck. Watched the *ranchero* work. Fate expected Dancer to be his next victim.

Slowly Dancer reached for his Colt on his right hip. His fingers found Blake's holster. But the hard leather was empty. Onward came the *ranchero* doing his butcher's work. As he awaited the vulturelike business to take his turn Dancer gritted his teeth. A shadow fell over Dancer's eyes. The *ranchero*'s menace cast a final pall over the trapped American. Dancer's last vision was of the *ranchero*'s red blade raised at a killing angle. In a blink the *ranchero* stiffened. Frozen in place as Dancer watched powerless. Then the murderous *ranchero* lurched forward. Fell across the neck of Dancer's dead horse. The killer's elbow smacked Dancer's wounded right upper arm. The assassin fell to the sand. Twitched. And lay still.

"Got yerself in a bit of jam…I'd say…Dancer." A familiar voice crowed over him.

Dancer squinted into the blinding light. Not quite comprehending if he lived. Or if his unaccomplished life was being called to account by Saint Peter. Dancer felt the weight of his horse lift from his leg. Several strong hands pulled him free from his desperate situation. Someone put a canteen into his hands. Tilted the elixir to his lips.

"We wondered where you'd gone off to." The voice was remorseless. Unapologetic. "Taylor's been askin' after you."

As reality returned to Dancer's senses he recognized the voice.

"Next time…get off your horse before it lays down for a nap." The unmistakable drawl came from Texas Ranger Sam Walker.

Dancer fumbled in his jacket. "The maps." He stammered. "I've lost the maps." Dancer patted every pocket. Inside and out. Every space. *Where are the maps!* His mind cried out as pain shot through his stiffened arms.

"Lose something…Dancer?" Walker drawled with a low chuckle.

Dancer looked up as Walker wiggled two fingers through holes in Dancer's hat. And wiped the sand from a pair of embossed-leather map cases.

CHAPTER 88

ALL ORDER OF BATTLE WAS LOST. Yet the Mexican soldiers—
driven from their entrenchments and without artillery—still
doggedly—but unsuccessfully—disputed the onward march of the
American troops. Both flying batteries opened on the retreating enemy.
Drove them from their last holds. Those who still lingered were soon
routed. Cavalry and infantry were seen in confused masses. Figures flew
in every direction. Many rushed toward the Rio Grande.

✠　✠　✠

Samantha Swift's high-spirited quarter horse raced along the road to
Matamoros for almost four miles. In no time they broke from the
chapparal near the river. A scene of bedlam greeted Swift. In terror the
defeated fled. Camp followers. Support troops. And contract teamsters
were joined by dozens more. Who all sought the river. At the crossing
there was but one flat ferry. Civilians swarmed the small platform. In
the midst of the panic Swift recognized the calm figure of Father
Thomas. The padre tried to help those who wanted to come onto the
flat. His serene presence restored order to a certain degree among

the fugitives.

Father Thomas spotted Swift as her horse came close to the ferry platform. "Come…come…my child." The Welsh priest beckoned her. "Join us to cross the river of sorrows. Come now…before it is too late."

Swift hesitated. "There's no time."

"What is time in God's presence?" Father Thomas smiled calmly.

Swift's throat tightened as her worst fear gripped her with a shudder. That deathly fear of drowning paralyzed Swift. In that instant from over the riverbank came a thunderous pounding of horses. Mexican cavalry poured onto the ferry. The horses crowded the frightened people to the back. Pushed them closer to the far edge. Still more horses and riders came. These pushed onto the already crowded flat. Rearing. Twisting. Heavy hoofs made the flat list and angle treacherously. People began to fall off into the water. Around the simple ferry the swirling waters of the Rio Grande fairly boiled. Swollen by up-country rains.

Floundering souls disappeared under the muddy water. Dozens upon dozens clutched each other in their agonies of death as they slipped below the surface. Others screamed for help as the merciless waters swept them away. Father Thomas's priestly robes were muddy at the ferry's far edge. He braced himself against the towline stanchion. The good Father extended his last weapon. His wooden crucifix was held up to the advancing cavalry. Like a shield to protect his flock. But the horses slipped on the wet planks. Wild-eyed in terror. The beasts knew no understanding of his appeal.

Out of the chaos two riders different from the rest bulled their way on board. From the shore Swift recognized the horse and the saddlebags of carved leather. Branded black with a crude harp of Erin. Patrick Harp. The second rider was General Francisco Payaso. With vicious determination the pair forced their horses onto the crowded flat undeterred. Father Thomas raised his crucifix higher above his head. Offered a talisman to ward off the stampeding horsemen. As the ferry tilted even more Father Thomas slipped. Tried to regain his footing. He held his crucifix high. Harp's horse twisted. Its massive flank swept the priest backward into the river. His billowed robes were the last to be seen going under.

For a terrible moment Swift watched the water for a sign of the priest. There was a thrashing. Father Thomas's bald head burst out of the water. Gasped for breath. His simple cross still held high overhead. His priestly cowls steadily became insurmountable. Soaked with water. The great weight of the robes became too much to bear. Slowly down went the kindly face of the priest under the torrent. His arm elevated above the current still held high.

"Rise again…Father!" Swift cried out. "Please…Father!" Nightmare flashbacks of her mother's drowning played in her head.

Like a cork Father Thomas burst to the surface. Struggled.

Quickly the river came for Father Thomas. As it did for so many that day. Swift watched through fearful tears. She clasped both hands before her mouth to stifle a cry. Stared as Father Thomas gripped the wooden crucifix and was carried away by the muddy waters. Slowly the cross sank below the surface. And was gone.

Swift shivered in despair. "There but for the grace of God go I…" Swift whispered as she clasped the cameo of her mother about her neck. The necklace her father had commissioned upon Swift's birth.

Swift again hesitated. The once gentle waters of the Rio Grande were swollen into a malicious torrent. Now the surging rush was a death trap. Hapless men and horses tried to swim across — too terrified to wait for the ferry's return. The tenders strained to keep the ferry in position against the swirling river. Barely able to control the boat they struggled to take the mass of horsemen to the far bank. The deck was wet and slippery as the lucky few thrashed about the flat.

As dark clouds massed in the afternoon sky Peony jostled nervously. And Swift came to a fateful realization.

I must find another way.

CHAPTER 89

EACH MAN LISTENED at Fort Texas with intense interest. Sounds from the raging battle at Resaca de la Palma boomed in the near distance. The echo of every gun created an agonizing need to know which side the gun belonged. And its effects. Bombardment from the Matamoros batteries continued only sporadically. Yet the defenders gave the incoming shells little notice. Occasionally the fort fired a volley from its 18-pounders to let General Taylor know all was still well in Fort Texas.

As the afternoon wore on the heavy thud of firing on the battlefield grew less and less powerful. The discharges became more irregular. "Have they charged the guns?" One of the officers was less than certain. Yet another and another gun was silenced. "Did they carry them?" Sarah Borginnis murmured her question in ecstatic hope. In time all distant cannonading ceased. Volleys of musketry were next heard. And then stillness. The silence spoke of a hand-to-hand contest. At Fort Texas every ear strained to understand what result was known at Resaca de la Palma. Did General Taylor and his men conquer...or die?

⌗ ⌗ ⌗

Samantha Swift stifled a cry as the unfeeling water swallowed Father Thomas. Mechanically she secured her correspondent's bag—with its precious notes—and Dancer's pistol across her body. Turned Peony's head. Then raced forward up the embankment to find a way through the rising bedlam at the riverside. Peony knew as well as her rider which way to go. Together they worked the edge of the chapparal. Avoided the mesquite woods to their left with its impenetrable understory of prickly pear and yucca. Skirted the riverside bogs and sand swamps. Rider and horse gingerly picked their way downstream toward the Paso Real ferry…and Fort Texas.

Along the extended oxbow of the Rio Grande about three miles separated the upper ferry and Fort Texas. Swift soon discovered the terrain before her was more broken by gullies and rivulets than the interior. Here the chapparal put up a barrier of strong dense growth. Into these intricate thickets a majority of the Mexican troops fled. Now that the rout at Resaca de la Palma battlefield was complete. Hundreds—even thousands—of troops buried themselves in the brush. Waited for the veil of night to aid them in their escape.

As Swift worked her way between the thickets two Mexican soldiers sprang from the bushes. One grabbed Peony's reins. The second grabbed Swift by the leg. Ripped her right foot from the stirrup. Swift kicked her leg free. Then lashed out with a sharp boot kick. The blow caught the soldier on the temple. Her star-wheel spurs slashed a bloody furrow in his scalp. Infuriated the soldier pulled Swift from the saddle. Flung her to the ground. Surprised momentarily to discover his adversary was a woman he hesitated. Swift leapt to her feet to confront him. When his hand came away red from his bloodied head his eyes blazed with anger. Awkwardly Swift reached for Blake's revolver. Deep inside her correspondent's sling bag.

When the pistol come into view the soldier cried out. Kicked Swift's forearm. The pistol turned end-over-end. Flipped high in the air. Swift dropped into a crouch. Fumbled for Michelena's dagger secreted in her boot. *"Comes in handy for close work."* Mitch's words echoed in her mind. The soldier lunged toward Swift. Grabbed her by the throat. The impact spun them around. At that moment the pistol landed on a flat stone. Handle butt first. The capped chamber discharged. Swift felt the bullet whip past her ear. And smash into the soldier's head. His brains blasted into the air with a red spray of fragments and blood. The man dropped to the ground like a bag of butcher's offal. Swift felt the sticky splatter on her cheek.

The second soldier struggled to mount the little mare. They danced in place for a moment several yards away. Then the soldier turned in the saddle. Looked back as he regained his balance. His comrade's blood spread in the sand at Swift's feet. When the mare twisted to the side the soldier panicked. Drove his heels into Peony's sides. As the mare bounded forward Swift put two fingers between her lips. Gave a shrill whistle. It was the newsboys' call her father had taught her. The street sellers used the whistle to announce new editions as the fresh papers arrived on the streets. Or bring the other lads at a run to give help.

Peony responded to Swift's call. Without warning the bounding horse lowered her head. Slammed to a stiff-legged halt. Spun left. Then thrust right. Peony unsettled the terrified rider. Confused him to no end. The angry mare reared high on her hind legs. Beat the air with sharp front hoofs. Then jerked forward. The Mexican flew into the air. There was a heartbeat's silence. Then the sound of a curdling scream as the man landed on a deadly Spanish Dagger stand. The thick yucca spines stabbed through every part of his body. As if he had landed on a bed of swords. He gasped in terrible agony. Then fell back. Silent.

Swift ran to her mare. Took the reins and quieted the agitated horse. She talked in deep calm tones. Peony looked into Swift's eyes. The intelligence of the mare almost had an expression of satisfaction at a job well done. "We make a good team." Swift whispered as she stroked the mare's jaw and neck. *To be safe…better take the firing caps out of the Colt before I put it into my bag.* And she did. Then she swung up into the saddle.

After a short distance through the thickets Swift could hear she approached the middle ferry road. The track led to the Paso Real crossing under the walls of Fort Texas. She inched forward. Through a break in the undergrowth Swift watched the scene of panic before her.

The roadside was littered with equipment. Fleeing Mexican soldiers stripped off every encumbrance to their flight. Scattered everywhere were muskets. Cartridge boxes. Green military cloaks. Shiny lacquered hats. Among this detritus flooded a tide of terrified and wounded men. Some fell exhausted. Amongst them were horses with bleeding wounds. The animals kept their feet until pressed to full speed. Then rolled to the earth and carried their riders with them. The heads of the forsaken horses rose and fell. As they feebly attempted to fight against their death throes.

Swift watched as horsemen pounded down the road packed with men stumbling forward in their frightened flight. Squadrons of cavalry thundered forward. They rode over those whom the fate of war had spared. The horses scattered bodies left and right. And trampled others.

Frequently the wounded and defeated men threw worried glances over their shoulders. Did the American devils pursue them? Gradually it dawned on the routed remnants that the Americans were not coming. Perhaps for want of sufficient dragoons? Perhaps from occupation with their own wounded and dead in the chapparal of Resaca de la Palma? Little did they know Taylor had made no plans to cross the river with force or speed to consummate a victory. With the approach of night all offensive measures ceased. Onward in the twilight the defeated trudged with one mind. Reach the river. And cross before death caught them from behind.

Swift waited for an opening. When it came she darted from her hiding place. Crossed the road. And disappeared into the thicket on the far side. Now free to put distance between herself and the road of retreat Swift skirted the watery low depression north of the fort. Where Ampudia's muskets had fired on the ramparts only the morning before they reinforced at Palo Alto. Quickly she broke into the open ground. Two agitated sentries spotted the charging figure. Without thinking they shouldered their carbines and fired. Both balls spit up sand behind the rider. Swift raced toward the drawbridge of Fort Texas. Muttered a prayer the pickets would hold their fire. With one arm the solo rider held her white handkerchief high. Her other held the reins and her sling bag against her chest. While she lowered her face into her mare's wind-whipped mane.

✹ ✹ ✹

No bells rang now across the Rio Grande in Matamoros. The gay noisy music that had filled the air had been silenced since the evening of 8 May. To the Americans in the fort this silence was rife with meaning.

Yet they waited for the truth to be told. At a little before six o'clock S. Thomas Swift—war correspondent for the *Brooklyn Eagle*—galloped into the refuge of Fort Texas. A gaggle of soldiers gathered around the rider.

"We whipped them!" Swift shouted the news. "Taylor has won! The Mexicans are routed! The enemy is scrambling to get across the river!"

At that moment an officer of the 7th Cottonbalers jumped onto the far western rampart that overlooked the ferry road. A confusion of cavalry and men and wagons and wounded struggled toward the Rio Grande on the road below. Boats of every shape and size came from Matamoros to carry back what remained of the Mexican force. Every available person worked the ferry feverishly. At the bedraggled sight from the parapet the American officer turned to the open parade ground inside the fort. Then gave three cheers.

The defenders of Fort Brown—as it was now known (in honor of their commander Major Brown…who had died of his wounds that afternoon)—all loudly responded with a resounding cheer that was heard as far as Taylor's bivouac near the *resaca*.

From that moment the guns of Matamoros across the river never fired again.

PART V

MADNESS

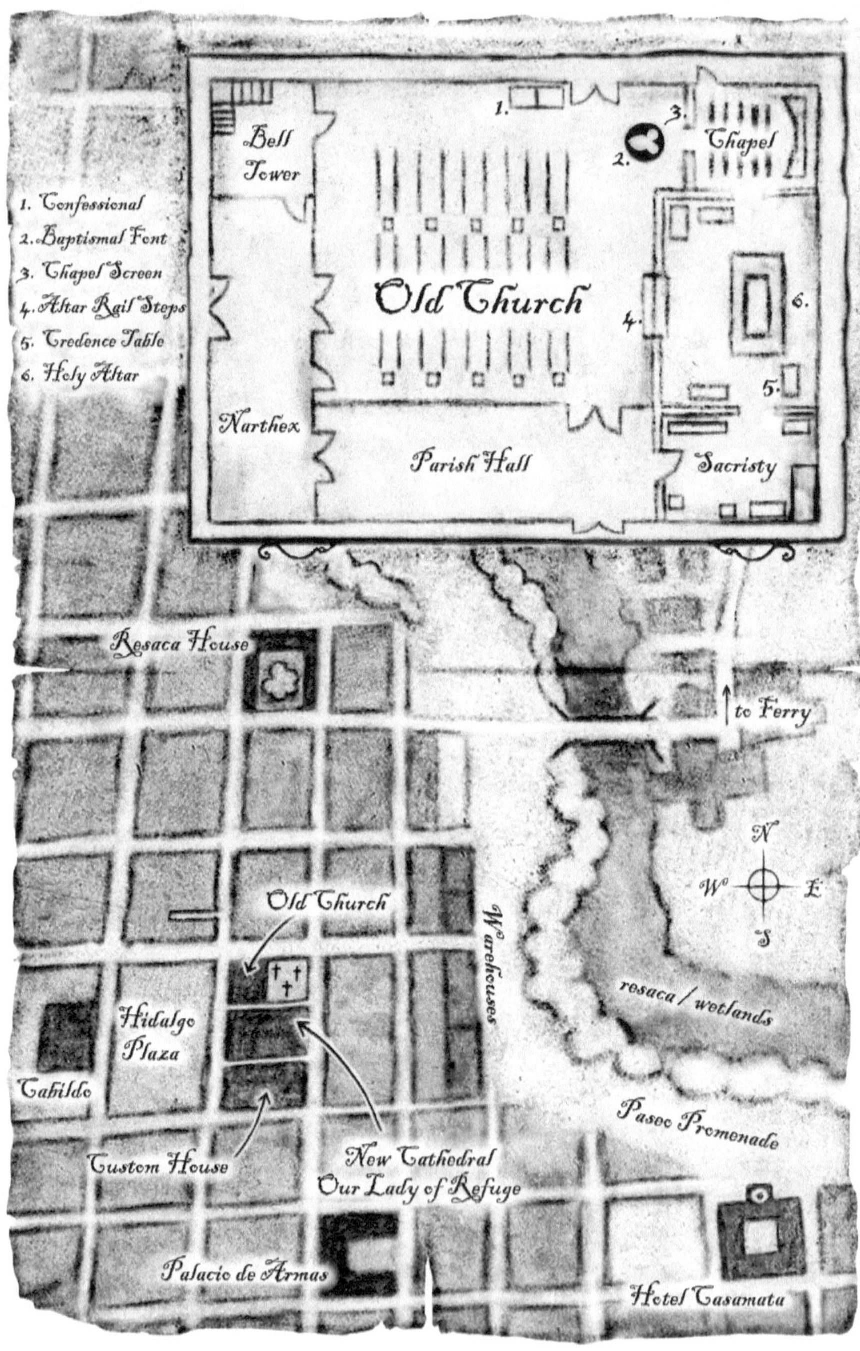
1. Confessional
2. Baptismal Font
3. Chapel Screen
4. Altar Rail Steps
5. Credence Table
6. Holy Altar

Bell Tower
Chapel
Old Church
Narthex
Parish Hall
Sacristy
Resaca House
to Ferry
N
W E
S
Old Church
Warehouses
resaca / wetlands
Hidalgo Plaza
Cabildo
Paseo Promenade
Custom House
New Cathedral
Our Lady of Refuge
Palacio de Armas
Hotel Casamata

CHAPTER **90**

AMERICAN CAMP
FORT BROWN/FORMERLY FORT TEXAS
9 MAY 1846/AT DUSK

TWO BATTERIES of flying artillery arrived at Fort Brown as dusk descended. Then a "foot" artillery battalion and dragoon squadron—together with an infantry brigade—tromped up to the fort. They made camp on the same ground they had left eight days before to the northeast between Fort Brown and the Rancho Ramireno. Swift and a clutch of war correspondents occupied a collection of tents inside the fort. Pitched hastily under the comforting bastion walls. Even though the earthen fortress was no longer required to protect against the defeated Mexican Army.

In the glow of several flickering candles Swift penned her final dispatches. She crafted a victory series: Siege of Fort Texas. First Blood at Palo Alto. Victory at Resaca de la Palma. The Aftermath of Battle at Fort Brown. No other correspondent's words that night carried as unique and coveted a perspective of the battles. None told the tale as an eyewitness behind the Mexican lines. Swift's words flowed from her pen.

For the occasion Swift used Arista's personal stationery. Captured from the General's camp that had been abandoned in such haste. As she signed the last dispatch the voices of correspondents beside the fire outside her tent related war stories.

"The Mexican victory feast was superb."

"Too bad the Mexicans never got a taste."

Among the baggage captured from Arista's camp they found a wooden leg. The appendage crafted for the General…who had lost that limb in Cuba as a younger man. "Makes it harder to run away!" The reporters laughed.

"Many an officer's triumphant letter home tonight will be written on that fine Castilian writing paper. Did you get some?"

Beyond the camp to the east the buildings of Rancho Ramireno smoldered. That *rancho* had been successively occupied by American pickets. During the days before Taylor's retreat to Point Isabel. Then by enemy pickets. During the bombardment of Fort Texas. After Ampudia broke off to reinforce at Palo Alto an American sergeant and ten men went out one evening and set fire to the *rancho*. As the special correspondent detailed in the fourth part of her series some officers regretted the arson. Though the official line claimed the *rancho* was burned to deny the enemy a protected observation post. Regardless of regrets the once-beautiful ancient *hacienda* of the family of the wife of Don Carlo Juan Baptiste smoked in ruins.

Swift pushed the flap of her walled tent aside. Inhaled the cool twilight air. Then buckled her dispatches into her leather case. *Now that the shooting has stopped…there's no need to make insurance copies.* She raised her eyes across the flats toward the dark silhouette of Matamoros. Frequent pistol and musket reports traveled back over the river. What was happening? An expression of concern clouded her brow. Swift worried for Michelena Anoche and Big Tim.

⊠　⊠　⊠

As Swift witnessed at the ferry General Payaso had fled from the battlefield. With Arista's debacle behind him General Francisco Payaso led the rout across the river. On the upper ferry Payaso narrowly escaped being drowned when he crossed the river. Yet he was one of the first men who appeared in the main plaza of Matamoros after the defeat. Exhausted he circled the plaza almost unconscious of his actions. "All is lost! Arista is defeated!" Payaso exclaimed to anyone who half listened. The little Creole General denounced Arista. Blamed others. Heaped ignominy on all but himself. "Had I...General Francisco Payaso...been in command...by my bravery alone...we would have swept the Americans from the face of the earth!"

With his mad rants Payaso also brought the news to Matamoros that for Mexico the day was lost.

CHAPTER 91

ILLUSTRATOR AND DAGUERREOTYPIST William Beacon trotted up beside Swift. "I'm so glad you're safe…we had no word except a few reports from Dancer." The friends exchanged an awkward hug. "I've got something you should see." Beacon looked almost apologetic. Swift held her tent flap back. Welcomed her friend inside. Without ceremony Beacon handed Swift a packet of *Brooklyn Eagle* newspapers. Each edition neatly folded and bundled in date order. The last edition dated eight days before on 1 May 1846. Beacon then handed Swift a similar packet of *The Daily Picayune* newspapers. Headline after headline screamed the war news from Mexico. Every *Picayune* story was capped by the name of James Collingsworth Turner.

Swift stared at the *Eagle* newspapers one after another. Then at *The Picayune* editions. Disbelief spread in her expression.

"Where's my name? These are my stories in *The Picayune*!" Swift blurted out. "Why is Turner's name on my stories? How could this happen…?"

In a flash the full impact of what Turner had done hit Swift like a kick in the stomach.

Her eyewitness report of the murder of U.S. Consul John Stepptoe.

Her interview with Captain Hardee captured during the Thornton ambush.

Her exclusive access to the Mexican commanders. Payaso. Ampudia. Arista.

"He stole all my stories…He used my words as his…How could this happen?" Swift implored Beacon for an answer.

Beacon tensed. "He did it with *The Picayune*'s express pouch. All the correspondents used the same pouch. Officers sent letters in Turner's pouch. Even the Mexican collaborators used the pouch. It was faster than the army courier…got to New Orleans three — sometimes four — days earlier. Turner must have gone through your dispatches and — "

Swift choked back violent anger. "He stole my dispatches…and passed them off as his own! Did anything I wrote get published over my name?" Her voice shook as she rifled through the New York newspapers in rapid succession.

"Some of your society observations and a profile sketch or two made it. But nothing that was exclusive" — Beacon said dejectedly — "or had anything to do with hard war news."

Swift collapsed on a canvas campstool. "Everything I've worked for…everything I've done…none of my war news reached the *Brooklyn Eagle*?" *How will I ever prove myself now…and win back Father's newspaper from his thieving brother? Swift seethed with anger. And despair.*

Like an avalanche the disaster of losing everything descended on Swift. She pressed her fist to her mouth to stifle a scream. While her whole body quaked in shock.

Just at that moment who sidled up to her open tent but James Collingsworth Turner.

"You've made a name for yourself…Swift."

Swift turned toward the condescending scribe. A look of rage rose in her eyes.

"Smart move to report from the Mexican side." Turner rambled on cheerfully. "Your human-interest features weren't bad. The one about the priest was very touching. What was his name? Father Lomas? But your best piece was the one about the *fandango* fashions. You've got a real nose for design…Swift. Good stuff for that women's monthly. What's it called? *Godey's Lady's Book?* Are you planning a piece on the victory dance? I heard the Hotel Casamata *señoritas* are especially fashionable. Too bad the *Eagle* didn't let you cover some real news."

Swift rose from the stool. Her eyes fell on her shoulder bag. Then she remembered she removed all the firing caps from the Colt. As she stepped toward Turner Swift stooped slightly. Reached toward her right boot that held Anoche's dagger. The fire of hatred burned in her eyes as she straightened. The blade hidden just arm's length behind her hip. Beacon saw the blood revenge in Swift's face. He jumped forward. Took a position between Swift and Turner.

"You better leave." Beacon spoke to Turner even as he was barely able to restrain Swift.

Turner scoffed. Then ducked out through the tent flap as he muttered just loud enough for Swift to hear him: "Maybe next time you'll stay home…where a woman belongs."

CHAPTER 92

AS LANTERNS GLOWED General Taylor—accompanied by several officers—walked into the correspondents' camp. A slightly lame Dancer limped behind him. The journalists rose as a group at his arrival. Desperation—and the commotion outside—prompted Beacon to push Swift through the tent opening.

"At ease…at ease." Taylor spoke in a fatherly tone. The General responded calmly as the correspondents fired questions pell-mell about the day's action. Taylor thanked the reporters for their valuable work. "As you know this is the first time the press has worked alongside us during a war. So far…so good. I'd particularly like to thank Mr. Turner and Miss Swift. Are they here? Ah yes. Thank you…Mr. Turner…for your enlightening dispatches." Swift felt the slight bulge of the dagger now returned to its boot sheath. *Just you wait…James Collingsworth Turner. Just you wait.* With one hand Swift clutched the tent pole as she gathered herself.

"And…Miss Swift…your work from the Mexican side took a special kind of courage. When we are finished here please join me privately for a stroll on the parapet…if you wish. I'd be happy to give you some exclusive insights from the victor's vantage point." Taylor smiled then gave a small laugh as if he almost forgot something. "Oh…by the way…Miss Swift…thank you for the maps. The one of northern Mexico will be invaluable for the next stage of this campaign."

Swift was shaken but collected herself. "You had made a point how important a good map would be…General. When I saw them in Arista's writing desk…I thought you might appreciate them more than he does."

Taylor laughed heartily. "I dare say you are absolutely remarkable. Tell me one thing. How did you get the maps to Dancer?"

"He was riding by…you might say…and I was going in the other direction. Just handed them off to him. Glad he made it."

"So am I. We'd be lost without the maps…and both of you." Taylor clasped Swift's hand in both of his and shook it with heartfelt warmth.

Taylor wished the correspondents a good night. Gave Swift a nod. Then turned to walk away. Swift fell in behind Taylor. Neither spoke for a few moments as they climbed to the wide rampart. In several paces past the flagpole the pair came to the four-sided *redan* bastion that overlooked the Rio Grande. There the commander paused as they looked into the night at the sight of multiple fires blazing. The sounds of distress that traveled from Matamoros were unsettling. Shots were heard irregularly from across the river. A pall of smoke hung over the city. Evidence of flaming cane roofs appeared as an orange red tumult against the night sky.

"It looks like the fires of hell." Swift spoke quietly as she stood side by side with the General. "What's happening over there?"

The veteran of the War of 1812 and the Blackhawk War and the Second Seminole War paused and then replied. "Madness."

The old soldier shook his head. "For regular order there is only one worse place to be than with a victorious army…and that is with a defeated one. It is insanity there now. Dead being counted. Wounded constantly coming in. The Mexicans put their wounded in gunnysacks. Many on the ferry road yelled like fiends from the rough handling. You can't imagine how that treatment reopens bleeding wounds afresh. Lookouts tell me many others were found dead in their sacks…drowned while crossing the river draped over the backs of swimming mules."

At that moment from the far bank came cries of wild despair. The sounds mingled with the screams of the grievously wounded.

Taylor recalled old memories. "Regular Matamoros citizens will flee into the countryside. Many will fall prey to cutthroats. Other outlaws will pillage and rape the defenseless. Terror reigns in the streets. All is disorder. Imagine four or five thousand lawless men…angry in defeat and utterly mad with grief." The General spoke in a grizzled low voice. "They are gripped by panic…striking out at everything. They loot. Drink. Terrorize anyone in their way. And they are armed. Carbines. Pistols. Knives. It is madness."

From across the river as they listened a breeze carried to them a woman's cry for mercy. Then a pistol shot. Next a scream of anguish. Then a second pistol shot. The silence was followed by raucous laughter. Then a glass bottle shattered on the far embankment.

"That is not a place any soldier wants to be right now." Taylor turned quiet as he confided his thoughts. "Nor would I wish it on any sane soul."

CHAPTER 93

**AMERICAN CAMP
FORT BROWN/TEXAS
9 MAY 1846/AN HOUR OR SO LATER**

SWIFT WALKED BRISKLY back toward her tent pitched against the bastion wall inside Fort Brown. Resolved to make critical insurance copies of her four-part series. *I'm done for if these dispatches do not get to the* Eagle. Just then who came toward her but Jack Dancer. He carried a folded note. "This is for you….One of the cantina boys just brought it over." Dancer handed Swift the letter. On the outside was scrawled "SAM" in a large childish hand.

"Looks like Big Tim's attempt at writing." Swift glanced at the front and back of the mysterious note.

She read the message out loud to Dancer. "D C Tra Bel War Hos Help." Swift's eyebrows knit in concentration and her head turned to the side. "What is this? I know it's from Big Tim." Swift again looked at the blank reverse side. Then reread the words silently. "But what does it mean?" Swift and Dancer moved closer to the lantern light beside her tent as they examined the note together.

"Tra Bel?" Swift said the words slowly…like Big Tim would. As he tried to find the letters to the words he sounded out loud. "Tra Bel. Trabel. Trable. Trouble. Somebody is in trouble." Swift glanced at

Dancer in realization.

"War Hos." Dancer pronounced the words slowly. "War Horse. Ware Hos. Warehouse. Somebody is in trouble at a warehouse?"

"And they need help. But who?"

"D C? Dicey? Do See?" Dancer looked mystified. "D C? What do you think Big Tim was trying to say?"

Swift snapped her fingers. "Got it. D C stands for Don Carlo. Big Tim knows Don Carlo but he doesn't know how to spell it. He could only sound out the first letters." Swift deciphered the message. "Don Carlo is in trouble at the warehouse. We've got to do something!"

"What can we do? Going over to Matamoros tonight would be a wish for death." Dancer reasoned for a moment. "Don't you have to finish your dispatches? If you don't get them out tonight with the army courier to Point Isabel…all the other correspondents will tell the story as they see it. If you wait…your work will be old news. Think about it…Swift. Every dream you had about coming out here would be lost. Your entire journey would mean nothing! You would be crazy to give that up…and even crazier to try to cross the river tonight!"

Swift turned her back on Dancer. Bit her lip. Faced the madness in Matamoros. *Dancer is right of course. If I don't send my dispatches tonight nobody will want to read them when the story is cold. Even General Taylor said it was madness in Matamoros. Do you want to throw away everything you've worked for? What about your exclusive interviews with Arista? Your series implanted side by side with the Mexicans on the battlefield? Your firsthand reports must be your only focus. You don't have to go. There's nothing you can do anyway.* Swift reviewed her dilemma logically. Ticked every reasonable option. Tick. Tick. Tick.

Then something happened that Samantha Swift had never experienced. Her heart challenged the reasons in her head. *Are you sure? Don Carlo is in trouble. He made all this possible for you. His kindness. The clothes. The horse. What's more important to you…Swift? What does your gut say? Your name in print…or your friends? If it was your father over there…what would Mother do? You're right. No question.* Samantha Swift listened to her heart.

"I've got to help Don Carlo. I'm going across the river." Swift's voice was determined.

The words of Dancer's reply formed on his lips. *"Don't be crazy!"*

But he caught himself.

Swift held Big Tim's note in both her hands as she looked over at the fires of Matamoros and said: "Yes. I *do* have to go. And…yes… I must try."

Dancer was stunned. But he understood. In a split second he made his decision too.

"Well…in that case…no use you having all the fun alone." Dancer kept his tone light. "I'm coming too."

Swift shot a surprised look at Dancer. "Do not be stupid. You've got nothing to gain. This is my problem…not yours."

Dancer let her words roll off without the sting. "A promise is a promise. There is no higher duty than a man's word. If a man forsakes his honor then he has nothing to live for." He spoke as he gestured toward Matamoros.

"What are you talking about?" Swift asked in a bewildered tone.

Dancer turned toward Swift. Looked her in the eye. "I promised Jones I'd find the bastard that bombed the *Decatur*…the same bastard that killed him."

"But that's crazy." Swift stood in front of Dancer. "Jones is dead. Your dying won't bring him back."

At that moment the sound of a gunpowder explosion rolled across the river from Matamoros.

Dancer spoke in a low determined voice. "It's more than Jones. Santa Anna killed my brother Jace. Murdered Jace at Goliad after the Alamo. That's why I must do this."

Swift's gaze took in the darkness over Matamoros. "This is my mission. I must do this. But you don't." *No need getting us both killed.*

Dancer clenched his teeth. "That's where you're wrong. I must do everything…anything…to defeat the evil of Santa Anna. Only then will the honor of Jace…and Jonesy…be revenged. I gave them my word. That's why I'm coming with you." *And see what the situation is with Wildfire's treasure and documents. After all…orders are orders.*

Swift was secretly relieved she was not going alone. *Maybe I misjudged Dancer. Perhaps there is more to this man than profiteering and greed.*

Swift held up one finger for Dancer. Signaling him to wait. "But first I need to do something." She bolted into her tent. Grabbed the leather bag with her four dispatches. Dancer held the flap open for her. Then followed as Swift rushed away from the tent. And ran over to William Beacon standing with the other pressmen. She took him aside.

"I know you work with Turner…and we are competitors."

"Friendly competitors." Beacon's tone was amiable. "I only illustrate for *The Picayune*."

"Be that as it may…I need you to do me a favor."

"After what Turner did to you…you deserve a break. How can I help?"

"Here are my dispatches. There are four. They're all ready and addressed to my editor at the *Brooklyn Eagle*. These are the only copies. No time to make more. Here is the favor I need. Can you see they are included with the army courier tonight to Fort Polk in Point Isabel? That's all. Just put them directly into the courier's pouch. By all means…make sure Turner doesn't get his hands on these too. Can you do that for me?"

"I'll do my best…but no promises. Turner checks everything." Beacon's tone had turned doubtful.

Even as S. Thomas Swift handed over her series of four victory dispatches to William Beacon she felt a twist in her stomach that all was lost already. So much of her work had been stolen. Her *Decatur* dispatch. Rancho Valdez. The riverbank parley. Payaso's interviews. Stepptoe's murder. The Thornton ambush. All lost. Would these reports while implanted in enemy territory be stolen too? Swift questioned if misfortune was her destiny. Was the end of her story already written? Was writing her own life page by page with free will even possible? As if from a deep well an answer floated up into her thoughts. *Like Charles Morgan said…"A story untold is only a dream." Now or never.* She touched Beacon on his chest. Mouthed a silent *Thank You.*

Within the hour Swift met Dancer in front of his bombproof. Together they slipped through the sally port near the burying ground in darkness. Raced along the riverbank toward the middle ferry.

CHAPTER **94**

**MIDDLE FERRY LANDING
OUTSIDE FORT BROWN
9 MAY 1846/WITHIN THE HOUR**

BEDLAM GREETED Swift and Dancer at the ferry. Frantic civilians jammed onto the approach road. About them lay the wounded. The dead. As if they lay where death's scythe had cut them down. Scores of desperate souls begged passersby for help. For water. Others brandished weapons to force assistance. Torches illuminated the calamitous scene. Braziers burned on the ramparts of the American fort at the top of the embankment—closer than a grenade toss away. Upon this scene seemingly from Dante's inferno the low glow of fires reached across the channel from Matamoros.

Dancer grabbed Swift by the elbow. Yanked her back. "Nothing for us that way. Follow me."

The pair scuttled back into the willow bushes. Worked their way downstream a distance. Up ahead two Georgia regulars stumbled through the brush away from the river. Drunk. With one hand each man held a bottle. And kept his balance. With the other arm around his companion.

"Good thing you nabbed that canoe this afternoon...Jacob... before the Mexies ran like rabbits."

"Made a quick visit to the cantina for supplies. Simple child's play." The second trooper's voice was thick.

The soldiers stumbled up a game trail toward the American camp.

Dancer pointed. "Those two left a canoe in the bushes. Let's grab it."

Dancer steadied the crude craft with both hands. Put a knee against the wooden side.

Swift stopped before she stepped into the narrow canoe. Her constricted breath came fast and shallow. "I hate water." She spoke her fear out loud. *This is how Mother died. And Father Thomas.* Swift inhaled deeply. Steeled herself. "You can do this." *You must do this. Face your fear.* She held onto both gunwales with white knuckles. Then stepped into the ribbed hull. She edged her way past the center yoke to the front bench of the canoe. Steadied herself with both hands on a paddle that rested across the gunwales. Behind them was the order and camaraderie of the victorious American camp. In the darkness before them was the chaos of Matamoros.

With a powerful push Dancer thrust the canoe into the strong current. Grabbed the second paddle. Dancer pointed the bow upstream at a severe angle. He knew the force of the swollen waters would land them downstream from the crossing. *Plus the sandbar at the river bend will shield us from any sentries still in the breastworks.* He set his sights on a spot on the levee more or less beyond where Payaso's lower batteries stood. *Let's hope the riflemen are gone.*

In no time the swirling waters drove a heavy object against the side of the canoe with a rocking thump. The boat tilted. Swift swallowed her cry. "What was that?" Swift whispered. "A body." Dancer continued to paddle. "The sentries reported scores of them floated down the river. Some were caught in trees by the high water." The canoe reached the middle of the powerful current.

Swift dropped the paddle into the canoe. Clutched both sides. Stared straight ahead as the skyline burned on their right. From out of nowhere they both heard a sodden thump against the upstream side. Both felt the drag from a large object. This time the current lodged the object under the bow. The canoe tilted low toward the waterline. Dangerously close to the surging current. Swift gripped both gunwales tighter. Water splashed her right hand. Next came a dull scraping along the side of the boat. Swift snatched back her fingers from the upstream gunwale. The object slowly traveled toward the middle of the canoe. Then twisted.

Without warning a hand shot up over the gunwale. Wet. Gray. In its cold dripping grip was a wooden crucifix. A leather thong hung down from the watery cross as the macabre hand slid slowly along the boat from its bent wrist. Swift flinched away. Almost capsized the canoe. Dancer's quick counterbalance with his paddle righted the small craft. Swift and Dancer stared transfixed at the deathly fist as it made slow progress along the side. Scraped. Pulled. The death hand hooked over the edge of the boat. Inexorably the weight pulled the craft dangerously closer to the waterline. It was Father Thomas's crucifix clutched in his death fist.

If the body pulled the boat lower — if it tilted the gunwale under the water — the powerful current would send black water rushing over the edge and swamp the canoe in the middle of the river. The image of her mother drowning flashed again in Swift's mind. *Slick stone walls. Nowhere to grasp. Clothes like a weight. A dark water puddle under the table. Cold. Unfeeling. Suffocating. Blackness.*

Dancer gave a powerful backwash stroke with his paddle on the right side as the deathly crucifix came toward him. The bow pivoted to the right. The drag from the body and its wet cowls partially released its weight from the canoe.

At that moment an object knotted at the end of the cord caught in a notch where the thwart met the gunwale. For a breathless blink of an eye neither Swift nor Dancer knew if they faced oblivion in the dark waters. Dancer again stroked a backwash. The canoe pointed directly upstream. The corpse slid toward the stern. And the crucifix was yanked from its death grip. The cross clattered softly into the bottom of the boat. From the wooden crucifix — tied by a leather thong — was a signet ring. Dancer reached forward between his boots. Handed the cross to Swift. Just as the wet dripping crucifix appeared out of nowhere. The now empty death hand slid away. Then disappeared into the river behind them.

Swift shuddered uncontrollably. Grasped the crucifix to her chest.

With mighty strokes Dancer drove the canoe forward until it reached the willow flats of the far bank.

CHAPTER 95

DANCER AND SWIFT jumped from the canoe. Ducked into the shadows on the grassy slope of the levee. Above them to the right—beside the splintered *gabions* of Fort Guerrero—two drunken soldiers fought over possession of a blanket. A thing not worth two copper *reales*. The second soldier shot the possessor with a pistol. Swift and Dancer bent low and ran to their left. Stayed in the shadows. Sprinted across the *resaca* bridge. Once they gained the *paseo* promenade they again zigzagged left. Darted from tree to tree. Took great care not to be seen. Or heard.

In this way they worked their way to the back alley that led to the Hotel Casamata stables. On the far side...away from Independence Plaza. Swift and Dancer looked both ways before they moved. With a nod the pair slipped around the corner. Then stopped short. The heavy iron door blocked the gateway passage. Locked into place to secure the courtyard.

A trio of drunken soldiers stumbled into the street up the way. They began to come toward the gateway.

"I know where the key to the livery door was kept." Swift slipped into the guard booth under the passage. In the darkness her hand patted the underside of a bench for a hidden nook. She withdrew a large iron key.

Dancer took the key. Ducked toward the livery door beside the heavy gate. Tried to find the keyhole. The iron key slipped from his fingers. Swift took it up from the sand. Felt for the lock. Her fingers found the keyhole. In slipped the key. Retracted the bolt. Pushed the door open slowly to not make a sound. Silently Swift stepped through the opening. Dancer followed. Closed the door. Swift locked the small door behind them. Just as the drunken soldiers passed the barred gateway.

When Swift and Dancer peeked into the courtyard the hotel was dark. As silent as the old barracks-arsenal it had been in recent times. Swift and Dancer felt their way around the corner. Slipped under the gallery *portale*. Then along the right-side colonnade. Only a faint light ahead showed a glimmer from a ventilation chink. Placed high in the wall. Hidden by the great viga beams. The dim light seemed to come from the area of the strong room at the far end of the courtyard.

Dancer tiptoed into the hallway that led to the saloon. Partway along the passage he stopped at the door of the strong room. He rapped quickly three times. Paused. Then rapped twice.

"It's Dancer." He spoke in a low whisper to the bolted door.

A peephole opened for an instant. Then shut.

Inside Swift and Dancer heard the heavy iron safety bar being withdrawn. Then the ancient-lock tongue slowly turned. The door opened partway.

Swift and Dancer slipped through the slight opening. And the door was rammed shut behind them. Bolted. And barred.

CHAPTER 96

THE HOTEL STRONG ROOM held everything valuable one would need on the frontier. The original Mexican engineers built this room to be an armory at the core of their *casamata* fort. Swift and Dancer's gaze swept the strong room. From cases of whiskey to crates of percussion caps every inch was stacked high along aisles off a middle space. Bags of coffee. Tea. Stacks of rifles. Saddles. Rice sacks next to dry goods. Horse blankets. Swords. Gunpowder kegs topped by Indian tonics and liniments. Tobacco. Dried beans and hardtack biscuits. Rope and lanterns. Even a dusty old piano. Two coffins hung from the rafters. One large — for an adult. One small — for a child. The smells of leather and spices mingled into a *mélange.* Somewhere between an arsenal. A stable. And a kitchen. All blended with the sour undercurrent of stale alcohol.

"Dancer! You're alright!" Anoche cried as she leapt forward and threw herself into Dancer's arms. She kissed his neck and ear passionately.

"Tried to save myself for you…darlin'." Dancer spoke dryly.

"And…Sam!" Anoche cried as she threw her free arm around Swift. Anoche hugged both the interlopers at once. "I was so worried.

We didn't hear a thing since you crossed the river with Arista. No telling what could have happened."

Swift gave Michelena a warm hug in return. "Had to get my war reports firsthand. But I got a little closer than I planned."

"Thank God you're alright." Then Anoche checked her enthusiasm. "My apologies…let me introduce someone."

Out from a darkened corner a confident man stepped into the sphere of lamplight. Swift's gaze took in the black polished riding boots to the knee. The black pants with a swirl of white pearl embroidery up the outside seam. From his belt hung a bladed rapier. Swift recognized the thrusting weapon favored by fencing masters like Pepe Llulla. Under the collar of a black shirt a black silk kerchief was stylishly knotted around his neck. Swift blinked as she took in the features of the handsome face. Black hair barbered carefully down to long sideburns. The angled razor cut pointed to a full strong mouth. A trimmed mustache was separated cleanly by the ridges of the cleft under his aristocratic nose. His eyes were dark. Almost black. And they seemed to penetrate Swift until she involuntarily gave a slight shiver.

"Let me present someone to you both." Anoche gestured warmly to her guest. "Diego Juan Baptiste…eldest son of Don Carlo."

"Good to see you again…Dancer."

The men enveloped each other in a masculine hug. The two comrades clapped each other on the back. Dancer said warmly: "It's been too long."

"Yes. New Orleans…wasn't it? As I recall you were on your way to the Irish Channel in search of stevedores." Diego's expression took on a serious look. "Sorry to hear about Jones. He was a good captain. A good friend. Word around Exchange Alley had some Irish deserter mixed up in it somehow."

"That would be Patrick Harp." Dancer paused. "He's been up to his old tricks around here too."

Swift composed herself. Her eyes did not leave Diego before she interjected. "I saw Harp yesterday at the upper ferry. Just across from Fort Paredes. It was his horse that knocked Father Thomas into the river." Swift's hand caressed the wooden crucifix inside her vest pocket.

Anoche glanced at Swift. Then Diego. Then Swift. And back again to Diego. *What is this I see?* Then Anoche filled the void. "Diego — this is Samantha Swift. Samantha — this is Diego Juan Baptiste. Samantha is a war correspondent for the *Brooklyn Eagle* newspaper in New York City. Diego has been away for several years reading law in Philadelphia. Then he schooled for a short time at West Point…in a foreign officer exchange with the elite Topog Engineers…if I have that right. He just reached the Rancho Valdez day before last."

"Yes…the American blockade made it a longer trip from New Orleans than usual." Diego's rich Spanish-accented English was spoken with assurance.

Diego Juan Baptiste stepped forward. His body moved easily. And his fine boots made no sound on the flagstone floor. He took Swift's extended hand. Then with a bow brought it to his lips. His left hand rested on the caged hilt of his rapier. Swift thought she heard a soft touch of leather. As Diego brought his heels together gently.

"My father wrote me about you." Diego began as he looked into Swift's face. He was slightly taller than Dancer. With the broad-shouldered physique of a *gaucho.* "I am so pleased you accepted Don Carlo's gift of my mother's clothes…and her horse. It renewed my father's spirit. Once again he knew those gifts were put to beautiful purpose."

Swift blinked as her suntan deepened. Then recovered her composure. "The honor was mine. Your father is a good man…which is why we are here. What do you know?"

Swift. Dancer. And Anoche looked at Diego. "As Mitch says… I arrived at the *rancho* little more than forty-eight hours ago."

"That was the day Taylor marched from Point Isabel toward Palo Alto?" Dancer noted.

Diego nodded thoughtfully. "I barely arrived when Josefina told me about your contract with Don Carlo. She told me my brother Luiz had forced her to show him the document. She said Luiz had given a copy of the contract to Payaso."

Dancer smacked a fist into his palm. "I knew Payaso was mixed up in this somehow."

"When I confronted Luiz he confessed." Diego kept his voice even. "He broke down totally…as second son he said he had no life. No prospects at Rancho Valdez. Hoped to ingratiate himself with Payaso. But instead of currying favor…Luiz implicated Don Carlo in treason."

An expression of confirmation came over Dancer's face. "Just like Stepptoe said…it was Payaso who stole the *alcabala* tax money from the Custom House."

"Yes. We have suspected for some time. Now we have proof it was Payaso and Malvado and their gang." Diego confirmed the conspiracy. "Shortly after…Luiz left for California. He thought he may have prospects in the north. Said something about contact with a Swiss man named Sutter who has a fort on the American River. There is nothing for Luiz here. He can never return to Matamoros ever again."

"What did you do next?" Swift asked.

"Josefina said Don Carlo had gone to the old church. I know now that Don Carlo meant to deliver Dancer's commission to Father Thomas to be secreted in his church."

As she touched the crucifix again Swift asked: "Did you see Father Thomas?"

"Yes. Father Thomas told me many things. Most of them made sense."

In the next minutes an extraordinary story was revealed.

"After he left the church Don Carlo went to the Presidio to confront Payaso with an ultimatum. Confess to his theft…or leave Matamoros forever. Instead…Payaso took Don Carlo prisoner."

Anoche asked the question. "Do you know where they're holding him?"

"No. The Cabildo town hall? Maybe a military depot? He could be anywhere."

Dancer nodded in agreement.

"Especially after Father Thomas gave me this." Diego placed an odd map on the table. Beside the lantern. The map was drawn on transparent vellum paper with the look of frosted glass.

Dancer stared. "This map was made by Stepptoe to show where he put the treasure in the Custom House." Dancer's eyes met Diego's. "Then Stepptoe revised this overlay map when the gold was moved into a passage leading to the cathedral crypt. He told me he put the overlay map and the loan documents in the consulate wall safe. Both were stolen when Stepptoe was murdered. The loan documents alone are worth a million dollars to Wildfire."

Swift picked up the fine-grained smooth paper. "It feels like velvet.

Where did Father Thomas get this?"

"You know those three fine watches the Father carried?" Diego smiled. "Each one was a different time? Father Thomas could never remember which was which."

Diego leaned into the lantern light. "Turned out our good Father was a master watchmaker…or at least that was his occupation in Wales before he felt the calling to become a priest."

"What do watches have to do with strongboxes…and the treasure…and this unfinished map?" Dancer wondered.

Diego chuckled. "Father Thomas shared one of his favorite sayings. 'If you can open a watch…you can open anything.' You know the twinkle Father Thomas got in his eyes?"

Dancer leaned back and clapped his hands. "It was Father Thomas that emptied Stepptoe's strongboxes…not Payaso!"

Swift's brow knit in uncertainty. "When I found Stepptoe's body… his safe was empty. If the killers stole Stepptoe's overlay map and the loan documents…how did the overlay map and loan documents get into the Custom House armada vault?"

Diego answered the question. "Payaso. But Father Thomas made a second visit."

"How did he get into the Custom House?" Swift wondered.

Diego replied: "He didn't. When the cathedral was built years ago by the labor of the *rancheros* Father Thomas arranged for the *rancheros* to dig a secret passage from the cathedral catacombs to his old church. 'Never know when you need another mousehole.' Or so he liked to say. Father Thomas used that secret passage to get to the strongboxes…and the armada chest."

And take the treasure to hide somewhere. Dancer knew he had looked everywhere — from the bell tower…to the chapel…to the sacristy office. Now he threw up his hands as if pleading for mercy. "But where did he stash the gold? I've looked everywhere."

Diego looked from face to face. "Father Thomas gave me this map because he thought it was his fault Don Carlo was taken hostage. He kept saying…'I know now. It was my fault.' He wouldn't listen to my objections. Kept muttering…'It's all my fault.' I tried to comfort him. But Father Thomas took that guilt with him."

"To his death." Swift whispered the words. She explained about the chaos at the upper ferry earlier and crossing the river in the canoe with Dancer only an hour before. And the crucifix. Swift took out the cross from her pocket. Cradled it in both hands on her lap as she idly stroked the signet ring.

Silence fell over the foursome.

Staring at Father Thomas's cross Swift put two and two together. "Payaso thinks Don Carlo has Stepptoe's revised overlay map and the loan documents. He's convinced the overlay map will lead him to the gold."

"And the loan documents would be his bonus insurance with Wildfire." Anoche — too — reasoned.

Diego gripped his rapier's hilt then chimed in. "That's why Payaso is holding Don Carlo ransom…for the map…which he thinks will lead him to the gold and the documents. But how?"

At that point Dancer reached into his jacket pocket. Pulled out the parchment base map that Kaufman gave him in New Orleans. The same street map he showed to Stepptoe before the Consul was murdered a month ago. Dancer spread the base map on the table. Diego placed Stepptoe's translucent tracings over the base. Swift carefully aligned the edges. Dancer studied Stepptoe's encrypted maps against the lantern light. On the transparent overlay map a distinct "X" near the lower middle appeared to correspond on the base map with an alcove at the end of a short passage that ran from the Custom House to the cathedral catacombs. The "X" marked where the treasure should be…in the alcove.

"It makes no sense." Dancer scratched his head. "The base map and the revised overlay map line up…but they point to a spot in the passage between the Custom House and the catacombs. That's where Payaso moved the strongboxes in the first place…but the treasure was stolen from there."

Anoche bent closer to the vellum overlay. "What is that second mark farther up? It looks like a cross. On the base map the cross looks like it marks the Resaca House."

Dancer pulled at his ear. "What are we missing?"

Swift inhaled a short breath as she realized she held the secret. "That's what these rings are for…I'm sure." Swift slipped her signet ring from her finger. Then removed the matched ring from the crucifix cord. When pressed together she discovered they formed a perfect nested pair.

Diego shook his head as if to clear the cobwebs. "Yes…but…what do they mean?"

Swift examined the hazy overlay map on both sides. Then gave the same careful inspection to each side of the base parchment. "See here?" She pointed. "These markings on the porous underside of the overlay map are made with a graphite pencil or charcoal stick. Father Thomas must have added these to Stepptoe's overlay map!"

"But they don't line up with anything." Anoche looked confused.

Then Swift remembered an old printer's technique her father had taught her. She had never forgotten those days when she toured the newspaper with him. Showed her how newspapers and typesetting and printing worked. "Let me show you how printmakers pull a woodblock proof before it's locked into the frame with all the type."

Swift continued in all seriousness. "When printmakers carve a woodblock two ridges are left in the block to register the paper into the correct position. Traditionally the registration marks are called *kento*. One is a backward 'L' in the lower right corner. The other a straight ridge at the bottom. The paper is carefully placed into the *kento* and dropped down on the woodblock. When printmakers pull a proof they sometimes use the clean side of a previous proof sheet to save paper." Swift demonstrated. "To get a clean proof the printmaker flips the paper end-over-end so the top edge of the fresh side fits into the *kento* at the bottom."

The other three leaned closer to the maps.

"Watch this." Swift unraveled the mystery as she turned over the vellum map. There on the transparent paper were two marks several inches from the bottom edge. One straight line. One backward 'L.' Swift carefully adjusted the overlay map to align the 'L' with the lower right corner of the base map. And then the straight *kento* with the bottom edge of the parchment map. "These must be the markings Father Thomas made with a different pencil."

Anoche gasped. "Look! The location of the Resaca House cross has completely changed!"

"They say 'X' never marks the spot." Dancer managed a bemused look.

Diego's finger traced the marks. "These two each look like a woodblock *kento*. But this one… we now see backwards through the paper. It doesn't look so much like a cross…but more like…the face of a mouse?"

Dancer cracked his knuckles in frustration. "That's crazy. What does it mean?"

Swift beamed. "It means Father Thomas is telling us where the mice took the treasure!"

As Dancer and Anoche and Diego watched closely Swift walked them through the secret of the treasure map of Matamoros step-by-step like a magician who revealed a trick.

First. Swift placed the overlay map right side up over the parchment base map. And aligned the corners of both maps. The "X" position on the overlay marked the cathedral alcove on the base map that showed through underneath. The "cross" marked the Resaca House. Everyone nodded.

Next. Swift flipped the transparent vellum map using her proof-sheet technique. Both the "X" mark and the "cross" showed through. And now Father Thomas's two faint *kento* registration marks were clearly visible on the upper side.

Then. Swift aligned the two printmaker *kento* marks with the base parchment paper. One at the lower right corner. One at the lower edge. Everyone saw the hazy vellum map now overlapped the parchment on two sides…off center by an inch or two. Instantly the meaning of the map was entirely different. The original "X" spot was now wildly out of position on the base map.

"I think we're still following you…sort of." Dancer frowned as he and Anoche held the two maps together.

Swift pointed out something the others had not seen. "These dotted lines on the underneath side lead to the "cross" mark on the front. The lines are the mousehole passage between the cathedral catacombs and Father Thomas's church. Diego was right. That's how Father Thomas got into the catacombs…where Payaso had moved the money from the Custom House. In short…Father Thomas relocated the money from Payaso…the same money Payaso stole from Stepptoe. Father Thomas carried the treasure back from the catacombs' alcove into his own church along this passage. See the dotted lines drawn on the reverse side? They are drawn in orientation with the 'cross' on the other side that marked the Resaca House."

Anoche and Dancer held the two maps between their fingertips so the maps didn't slip out of position.

Finally. With her finger Swift traced the dotted lines until they met the mouse-face symbol on the overlay vellum. Swift placed the in-cut intaglio engraving of her signet ring on the round mouse-face symbol. Then very carefully…from the underside of the parchment map… lined up Father Thomas's raised-image signet ring to align with her ring on top. With everyone spellbound Swift pressed the two rings together. Hard. Then again even harder as she used the crate table to maximize her downward pressure.

"Printers call this a blind emboss. It leaves a raised impression—but no ink is needed."

Dancer removed the top overlay and looked at the bottom parchment map. There on the base map was a raised emboss. As he touched the distinctive mouse-face he realized where the treasure of Matamoros was hidden. Clearly the signet ring impression indicated a location inside Father Thomas's old church near the north door.

"Is that where the treasure is hidden?" Dancer blurted out. *Could that be the baptismal font?* Then Dancer hesitated. "How is that possible? Surely the font is too small to conceal four boxes of gold.

Swift gave Dancer a look of frustration. "At least we know the treasure and documents are hidden in the church. Exactly where…is up to us to find out."

"And thanks to Sam…we have a place to start." Anoche cut any tension.

"That's amazing!" Diego exclaimed. "With only half the map to work with Father Thomas still showed us where he hid the treasure!"

Swift acknowledged Diego's perceptiveness with a smile. "That's how Father Thomas kept the hiding place in his church a secret. Father Thomas realized Stepptoe's 'X' marked the cathedral. By using the Hidalgo Plaza outline on the vellum he guessed where to place the cross so it looked like it marked the Resaca House. The cross was a red herring to confuse Payaso if the overlay map fell into his hands. Father Thomas's secret was safe until it was revealed by the blind emboss of the signet rings."

As Dancer touched the raised emboss on Kaufman's map he grasped the secret of the rings. "On the back of the overlay map the dotted lines have no meaning. Only when they are aligned with Stepptoe's parchment map do we know where they lead."

Anoche exhaled with relief. "With the printmaker's marks Father Thomas used the old 'X' on the overlay to show us his new location on a map he had never seen. Brilliant."

Swift added happily: "And nobody else knows but us!"

Anoche embraced Swift. And Dancer. And Diego.

After a moment Anoche asked: "Now what do we do?"

Diego looked at the others. "Payaso's men are holding Don Carlo hostage. Payaso claims Don Carlo traded with the enemy and is a traitor to Mexico. But in fact Payaso is just trying to save himself by discrediting Don Carlo."

"And cover up the fact that he's been stealing tax money for years." Swift frowned.

"Where is Don Carlo being held?" Dancer asked.

"We do not know." Diego frowned. "Maybe one of the levee warehouses…or the Cabildo?"

"What are we waiting for?" Dancer said. "Let's find Don Carlo and get him to the old church before the Mexican Army regroups and restores Payaso's authority." Dancer turned toward the door.

"That's not our only problem." Anoche's words made all eyes turn toward her. "Big Tim is missing too."

"What do you mean?" Swift said. "I got this note from him. That's why we came across the river. All he wrote was that Don Carlo was in trouble."

"That's Big Tim's writing all right." Anoche confirmed the penmanship. "At dusk tonight—about the time we heard the cheers from the American fort—Big Tim said he was going into town to ask about Don Carlo. We haven't seen him since. That was four or five hours ago. It's madness to go out there now. The soldiers are drunk. Outlaws are everywhere. And Payaso and Malvado will kill Don Carlo if they don't get the gold and the loan documents. Tell me how it could be worse?"

"You're right." Dancer nodded. "We're in a lot of trouble. But I've got an idea."

CHAPTER 97

MATAMOROS was a hell of drunken soldiers and violence. Earlier that day the northern border town was full of merchants and teamsters and camp followers that worked for the army. By night all those good citizens had abandoned the town. Now replaced by the quasi-military guerillas. Outlaws. Bandits. Opportunists that looked for plunder and personal advantage. No one knew when the Americans would charge across the river. No one knew when the end would come. But come it would. And with it the end of an opportunity.

The lawlessness transformed the principal streets into scenes of death and debauchery. Clusters of troops occupied the storefronts and warehouses. Fires fueled by broken furniture and dismantled wagons burned like specters in the open plazas and dark alleys.

Men wandered in search of their units — and in search of more cane liquor. Women and wives and families who came along with the soldiers scuttled in the shadows. Avoided encounters as best they could. Many searched for fathers. For husbands. For brothers. Among the wounded and dead. All asked for any word. Chased any hope. Women of easy virtue found the pickings to their liking among the drunken soldiers. Many of the drunken men lost their weapons—and then their lives—to the *rancheros*. One by one the *rancheros* lured them into the outlying areas…and killed them. As much for sport as for bounty.

Into the madness and terror the common sight of a coffin proceeded. The box gravely carried by four grim-faced bearers. Passersby stopped. Gave the sign of the cross. And gave the large coffin room to pass. At the front with the casket on their shoulders walked Anoche and Diego. Able to toss a phrase of greeting in the local dialect that cleared the path in front of them. At the rear Dancer and Swift shouldered their burden…now disguised in Mexican serape and sombrero. All four coffin bearers slowly moved forward in their solemn duty.

About them was riot and arson. Looters did their beastly work. Dancer saw two men come out of a fine brick house. Their arms filled with sacks of silver goods. Candlesticks. Serving pieces. Utensils. Fingers laced with necklaces of turquoise. Multiple gold chains dangled from their necks. One stopped a moment to toss a torch back through the window of the merchant's home. A Mexican officer nearby stood watch. But did nothing. The men snapped the officer an exaggerated drunken salute. Then went on their way.

The funeral cortege worked its way slowly through the streets from the warehouse area.

Drunkenness was universal. Made riot by the pillaging of a cane liquor distillery beside the levee. A trail of men staggered from the scene. Their senses twisted. Buckets of liquor in their hands. Souls unhinged in drunken furies. Soldiers lay passed out in the alleyways. Several men ran from a house overloaded with loot. Dropped expensive clothes in the street. The sounds of bottles smashed against stone came from alleys as the coffin passed on.

As the somber mourners turned into the plaza they were surrounded by a swirl of lunatics from the city insane asylum. Recently escaped when the madhouse was set ablaze. The insane were frightened. Bewildered. They stumbled and wandered. Lost. Their filthy clothes and uncombed wild hair formed a parade of madness that flowed randomly about the plaza. Moaning and screaming the mad argued with the voices in their heads. And each other. Dangling chain restraints gave the scene an undercurrent of ghoulish rattling. Their insanity seemed not out of place that night in Matamoros.

Through this eddy of human flotsam the casket bearers pressed on. At a side street Anoche and Diego turned off the main plaza. The cries of now homeless maniacs faded behind them.

In a dark alley between two buildings the small party hid the coffin. Anoche and Swift sat on the end. While Dancer and Diego hunkered down in the shadows.

"We must find where they are holding Don Carlo and find Big Tim." Dancer spoke quietly but with assurance. "We'll make better work if we split up. Diego and I will search the Cabildo town hall with its courtrooms and mayor's office across the plaza. It's the most likely place. Mitch…you and Swift check out the warehouses along the levee *paseo*. That's what Big Tim's note said. But be careful. Just scout the buildings. We'll meet you there in twenty minutes."

"What do we do if we run into trouble?" Swift asked.

"Don't go inside." Dancer paused. "If Diego and I miss the rendezvous…it means we ran into resistance. You go back to the hotel…wait and regroup. It will be our safe house."

"What do we do with the coffin?"

"We'll hide it here in the alley for now." A nearby pile of fodder hay quickly hid the empty casket.

Dancer and Diego peered around the corner of the alley. Then slipped into the street. Through a streaming thicket of babbling maniacs they made their way toward the Cabildo on the far side of the main plaza from the parish church.

Anoche and Swift raced to the rear door of the first warehouse. Typically a holding place for cattle hides. The warehouse was not large…and in minutes they satisfied themselves it was empty. They moved to the military warehouse down the promenade. Threw hasty glances through a window. Then impulsively cast Dancer's caution into the night. And entered from the middle of the building.

"I'll check the stores area." Swift moved to her left.

"I'll look in the office section this way." Anoche indicated the opposite end of the building.

CHAPTER **98**

ANOCHE SAW A LIGHT came from the crack under the office door. She put her ear to the entry first. The lever handle gave under pressure. Slowly she pushed the office door ajar. Peeked inside. There across the room was Big Tim. Or what looked like Big Tim. A form slumped in a chair at the far end near a flickering candelabra. He was asleep. Or motionless. The room appeared empty.

No sooner had Anoche stepped three paces into the darkened room than she sensed something wrong.

Out of the darkness behind her a powerful arm wrapped around her throat. Another rough hand clamped across her mouth.

"Looking for something…you slut?" The words came from a shadowy figure. Anoche recognized the voice of Kelly the Weasel. "Rat got your tongue?" The deserter giggled. Kelly planted his feet spread wide to avoid getting his other instep crushed. The Irish deserter dragged Anoche toward the light cast from the candles. The figure of Big Tim stirred in his binds.

"Bring her over here." The second captor's voice was menacing.

Anoche was half carried half dragged into the light by Kelly the Weasel.

"Ah…the mistress of the Ladies Hotel." The scar-faced deserter snarled. "Maybe our luck has turned…Weasel. Hold her. I'll get some rope."

Weasel's breath reeked of cane liquor. His scrawny paw closed tighter over his prisoner's nose and mouth. Anoche struggled to breathe. The Weasel's forearm locked her elbows behind her like an iron bar. In one vicious move the deserter slammed her to the floor.

Even though Anoche kicked violently with all her might she was trapped. Scarface fell on her legs. Began to tie her ankles. The man behind her breathed whiskey and tobacco into her face. As he held her down to the floor. Big Tim tried to shout. But the gag jammed in his mouth only allowed a low growl to be heard. His chair was firmly roped to the fireplace irons. Immovable.

"What have we here?" Anoche's tormentor hissed as the light revealed a hideous scar that bulged from his ear to what was left of his nose. Scarface bent to his work as he wrapped the coarse rope around Anoche's ankles.

"Now we got two birds in hand." Weasel grunted as he struggled to hold Anoche. "We can ransom them both." The deserter's black and missing teeth showed in a grin.

Scarface looped the rope between Anoche's feet. "We can ransom them to the Americans. Or we can kill them if they don't pay up."

"Or kill 'em first. Gives us more time to collect the ransom." Weasel cackled at his own joke.

Anoche struggled. But her arms were gripped by Kelly the Weasel behind. And Scarface held her knees with one arm.

"Now we're getting somewhere." Scarface spit as he tried to thread a knot. "Our little hotel mistress will bring a pretty penny from all her lovers."

Anoche closed her eyes. And strained. She bucked. Kicked. Twisted. Her jaw clenched as she fought the inevitable.

Out of the darkness Anoche felt the grip of the skinny deserter around her neck unexpectedly loosen. Then a warm stickiness spread on her neck. A muffled groan came from behind her as a hiltless sticking knife withdrew from the deserter's throat.

"Hold her…Weasel. I've got to set this half-hitch knot." Scarface snarled as he straddled Anoche's legs.

He didn't see the hickory axe handle coming before it crushed the side of his skull. Scarface fell sideways across Anoche's legs onto the floor.

Swift stood over Scarface's body. Still hunched slightly in a fighting stance. Ready to strike a second blow. A moment later she let the stout axe half drop to the wood floor.

Anoche sensed freedom. Gave a huge kick with both knees that rolled the deserter's limp body on its back. She sat up. Unwrapped the rope around her ankles. Bounded to her feet. In the same motion she pulled her Bowie knife from her belt. Anoche stood over the scar-faced deserter with retribution on her face. The razor-sharp knife glinted in her right hand.

"Guess this isn't your lucky night after all...Scarface." Anoche growled in a voice Swift did not recognize: "Now you'll get what you deserve."

Swift touched Anoche's arm. Without a word spoken Anoche realized they had to get Big Tim out of harm's way and meet up with Diego and Dancer any minute.

Anoche relented. Slipped the twelve-inch knife back into her belt sheath. Gave Scarface a sharp kick. "Today you don't die...so you can live to tell the tale." Anoche leaned over the unconscious figure. "Never again will you look upon a woman like you did tonight." She touched the hilt of her Bowie knife. Then Anoche spoke an epitaph. "We will give it to you for love. Or you can pay for it." She paused as she spit into the scar-faced deserter's face. "But you will never take it by force. Never."

Anoche straightened. Her gaze turned toward Swift in the candlelight. Unconsciously—with the back of her right hand—Swift wiped spittle from the corner of her mouth. The motion left behind a crimson smear of courage. Anoche saw in Swift's face the look of a lioness. Bloodied. Eyes blank. Astride her kill. The look of primordial survival. It was the look of a wild beast. Instinctual. Unthinking. And deadly.

Swift rose up to her full height. With a slight stagger she caught her balance and squared her shoulders. Again Swift raised the back of her right hand to brush away a fallen lock of hair from her forehead. Again it left a streak of color across her brow. Anointed like a warrior after the initiation of battle.

Swift blinked several times rapidly. Anoche looked again into the face of the young woman she knew. Now Swift's expression was as if to say "What happened? Where was I? What have we done?" Swift's startled eyes searched Anoche's face for an answer. Where before a tear might have formed...now there was the look of a survivor.

Anoche and Swift exchanged an embrace in triumph.

☓ ☓ ☓

Swift and Anoche jumped to the aid of Big Tim. Swift removed the gag. Cut and untangled the ropes that held him in the high-backed Spanish chair. Still seated his bewildered face looked up at them. Then he wrapped his great arms around the waists of both women. Hugged with some of his gentle might that almost lifted them off the floor.

"You save me." He spoke with joy in his eyes. "You save me."

"Are you all right?"

"Me all right."

"Where is Don Carlo...Big Tim? Was Don Carlo with you?" Swift coaxed.

"No. No Don Carlo." Tim stammered as he nodded toward the still figures on the floor: "They talk. Say Payaso take Don Carlo to Custom House."

Swift looked at Anoche. "That must be Malvado...and Harp as well."

Big Tim said: "Bad. Harp bad. Malvado bad."

Swift put a comforting hand on Big Tim's forearm. "I got your letter...Big Tim. You did good."

"They made me write. They said kill Don Carlo if I don't. I sorry."

"You did the right thing...Big Tim. Without your letter we wouldn't be here." Swift comforted the distraught giant. "I'm proud of you. You did good."

"Good. I did good." Big Tim happily repeated the words.

Just then Dancer and Diego came through the door. Their eyes traced back and forth at the two bodies on the floor. Then they stopped. Looked at Swift and Anoche. Then at Big Tim. "I guess we didn't have to worry about rescuing you girls after all." Dancer's words carried a warm admiration.

"Why do you think we need rescuing? And…don't call us 'girls.'" Swift's words carried an icy emphasis.

"We can take care of ourselves." Anoche tilted her head toward Swift as she touched her Bowie knife.

Together Swift and Anoche helped Big Tim to his feet.

"Big Tim said they've got Don Carlo at the Custom House." Swift gave Big Tim a canteen.

The five now moved to the door. Checked the dark side street. It was empty.

Dancer spoke in a low tone. "We've just come from the plaza. Except for enough raving lunatics to fill a madhouse…the side streets on the river side of the main plaza are quiet. The Custom House only has four guards. Let's go give them a surprise."

CHAPTER 99

CUSTOM HOUSE
HIDALGO PLAZA / MATAMOROS
10 MAY 1846 / WELL PAST MIDNIGHT

THE FIVE collected the coffin from the side alley. Then the small procession made its way to the Custom House. Two soldiers stood guard outside the building. Where the taxes and tariffs were collected and vaulted.

"Let me handle this."

Anoche took two large jugs of cane liquor she had stashed in the casket back in the strong room. Diego strapped on his rapier while Dancer buckled a Colt pistol onto his belt and Big Tim tucked away a jimmy bar that had been hidden in the coffin.

Michelena Anoche made herself known as she approached the guards.

"*Hola…amigos.* This is a fine night for guard duty. You must be the only *guardia civil* left with honor tonight. That is why I have brought you a reward." Anoche pretended to take a long draft from a doughnut-shaped ring jug.

"Michelena…it is me…Roberto. You remember me? You see me in your saloon always?" The first city guard nodded warmly to Anoche.

"Of course…my brave heart. Here is a small gift for you."

The first guard took a long draft. Passed the clay jug to the second. Who took an even bigger snort.

"Do you have some more friends inside?" Anoche asked. "It is not fair at this moment to not share. There is plenty for everyone."

One guard went inside and brought the other two onto the front portico. Every man took a long drink. Michelena appeared to join them. Then the mistress of the Hotel Casamata added a second loop-handled canteen to the circle.

"Hey *amigo*…wait for me. My turn to drink." The fat sergeant of the interior guards wanted more than his fair share.

"You tell me you are *hombre*…but you lie to me. You stink so much I cannot breathe."

All four guards tried to keep pace with Anoche's cane liquor. As they took more long slugs from the two jugs.

"This Michelena is all right. She's not as fat as your sister." The short one joked and the other two laughed at the expense of the sergeant.

"She looks good to me…and so does your sister." The first guard turned lewd as he became unsteady on his feet.

"You got caught in bed with his sister? But you said her ass meant nothing to you!" This sent them all into gales of laughter.

"Don't keep that jug all to yourself. You are free to pass it to me now?"

"We was going to wait for you…*amigo*. You be too slow!" The interior guards passed one ring jug between them even faster.

Almost on cue three guards stumbled against the wall. Both jugs dropped to the ground. Shattered in a splash of liquor and clay shards. Then the three slid down the adobe and hit the flagstone. The fourth aimed for a low side wall. Then simply collapsed on the portico where he was. All four passed out cold. Their party was over.

Anoche relieved the sergeant of the Custom House keys. Then signaled to the others to bring the coffin as she opened the Custom House door.

"What did you put in there…Mitch?" Dancer asked.

"Learned it on the Savannah docks from some Chinese sailors from Shanghai. Comes in handy in the saloon when you get a live one that doesn't know when to stop. Does the trick every time. We call it a 'Mitchy.'" Anoche smiled at her success.

╳ ╳ ╳

Don Carlo had been battered by Payaso's men. They had tried to force a confession of treason from him. But Don Carlo knew the men from the garrison. And their mothers and families. And their forefathers. He had talked them into a reasonable doubt. Into belief that he was not a traitor to Mexico. Then into the realization that the true traitor to Mexico was Payaso. Payaso's maniacal rants in the plaza—and his indictment against Arista's incompetence—helped Don Carlo's argument. The men abandoned their orders. And left Don Carlo to find their solace in the streets.

Swift and Dancer and the others searched the Custom House. Within minutes they found Don Carlo shackled in the prisoner's dock in the great *sala capitur* courtroom. Don Carlo was not in any condition to walk away by himself.

"That's where the coffin comes in." Dancer instructed in a muffled voice: "There are plenty of air holes and gaps. We will carry Don Carlo back to the hotel. It will be like before. Take it slow and look mournful. Don't worry. Nobody stops a funeral procession carrying the dead."

"It's not someone else's funeral I'm worried about." Anoche voice was deadpanned.

The procession descended the wide stairway gingerly as they supported Don Carlo. Moved toward the grand double front door. Diego and Dancer eased Don Carlo into the casket. Closed the lid gently. All four lifted the coffin. As Swift opened both doors. Then they stepped onto the flagstone portico outside. And stopped. A gaggle of madhouse denizens milled about in front of the Custom House. At the sight of the coffin the escapees backed away. As if their disordered minds told them to distance themselves from death and the devil's work. One by one the ragged wretches mumbled and shuffled away into the darkness. While the others waited beside the coffin Swift took Dancer aside. Near the front corner of the Custom House.

Swift gave Dancer a sharp look. Her anger boiled over. Reason finally released by her desperate bloody work in the warehouse. "I was a fool to trust anybody. Even you. Why didn't you stop Turner from stealing all my dispatches! You should have known!"

"How would I know? Anyway…Beacon will get your last four dispatches through. Won't he?" *Whoa. This is a side of Swift I've never seen. What happened in that warehouse?*

"He works for Turner's newspaper. Who knows? He better. Or I'm finished as a serious correspondent." A brown smear of dried blood was still visible above Swift's right eyebrow.

"What can I say? Think positive. That's all we can do."

Swift gave Dancer another withering look as her self-possession returned. Just then several shots came from the streets north of the parish church. A shriek rose from the mad escapees as they scuttled in fear back toward the main *zócalo* plaza and into the thinning night. "How are we going to get through town all the way to the hotel?"

"That's a good question." Dancer hesitated. "I guess we'll just have our own funeral."

"You make it sound so easy…Dancer."

"Yes. You're right. Makes me forget how scared I am." Dancer replied seriously for once as the desperation of their situation sank in.

Swift shook her head. "What am I going to call this plan of yours in my next dispatch?"

"A long shot." Dancer submitted his suggestion without humor.

Swift frowned and gathered herself. *If I live to write a next dispatch.*

"Okay…are you ready?" Dancer said to the group.

Swift caught him by the arm…and whispered into his ear: "If things don't work out. I'm sorry my nerves got the better of me back there."

"Nobody said we'd live forever."

Dancer swept his eyes over the plaza in front of the Custom House. Then looked right up the street…past the cathedral in the middle of the block. Like a scout in enemy territory he surveyed Father Thomas's parish church on the next corner…beyond the imposing cathedral. Knots of mostly immobile soldiers were dark shapes in the gloom. Darkness might prove to be their friend. If it lasted. Dancer signaled to the others. Together they hoisted the casket to their shoulders. Heavy now with Don Carlo secreted inside.

"Let's go!" Dancer muttered through clenched teeth.

The funeral procession eased off the Custom House flagstones. Angry voices from near the *cabildo* shot across the plaza space. The procession moved left. Turned the corner. Toward the river. Down the Calle de Morelos. Diego and Anoche in the front. Dancer and Big Tim in the back. Within steps the corner of the brick Custom House shielded them from any plaza revelers.

Swift walked behind. Her head bowed. Veiled with a mourner's *mantilla* lace. She looked the part of the forlorn widow.

CHAPTER **100**

WITH EVERY STEP the solemn procession put the Plaza de Hidalgo farther behind them. And the brick-walled Custom House. Slowly they moved toward the next corner. Dancer glanced to his left — into the Calle de Rio Bravo. Up the street on their left the deathly still bell tower of the parish church rose against the dawning sky. The group took a few steps forward into the intersection. Several blocks ahead — along the sandy track of the Calle de Morelos — was the *paseo* promenade. And beyond the *paseo* was the safety of the Hotel Casamata. At that moment in their path — a few yards ahead…on the opposite corner — appeared a stumble of four drunken soldiers. The skirmishers eyed mischief. And raised up to block the procession.

Diego made an instant calculation. "Let us pass…*amigo*. We are taking our father…a true son of Mexico…to the church for final absolution. He died not moments ago…before the last rites. If he receives a merciful pardon for his sins while his body is still warm…God may still open the gates of paradise to him. *Por favor.*" Diego made a gesture of appeal to their left.

A spindly corporal in a soiled green tunic rose unsteadily on his feet and filled the space before them. He planted his feet wide. Two other infantrymen shifted menacingly to surround the coffin. The fourth evil-looking rifleman with a bloody rag around his blackened hand moved toward the grieving widow.

"Stop! We are the tax collectors." The tallest soldier shouted his order in an officious voice. "No one dies in Matamoros without paying for the privilege."

The procession halted. Gently lowered the coffin to the ground.

"There has been enough blood lost today…brothers." Diego did his best to appease the soldier. "Now is a time for peace…and to lay the spirit of the dead to rest."

"Now is the time to look out for ourselves." The gangly leader spit his words. "The death tax must be paid…or you cannot leave the *zócalo*. You pay…or the coffin stays here. Those are the new rules."

At that moment Swift played her part of the grief-stricken widow. She stepped forward. And collapsed across the coffin as she wailed in bereavement. *"Mi amor! Mi amor!"* Swift cried as she hugged the coffin. For effect she pounded on the box with her fists. *"Mi amor! Mi marido!"*

Dancer's hand touched the handle of his pistol. While Big Tim's iron jimmy bar and Anoche's blade were checked. Diego tapped his coin purse as a distraction but checked his rapier was ready for action.

Swift's display drew all the drunken soldiers' attention toward the coffin. Abruptly — with drama — Swift staggered a step back. Screamed. *"Oh…Dios mío! Dios mío!"* Swift dropped to her knees. Clapped a hand over her heart. Pointed with the other at the coffin. A terrified look in her eyes. Slowly — with all eyes on the coffin — the lid moved on its hinges. Inch by inch the lid of the coffin opened. *"Marido! Mi marido!"* Swift screeched as the lid fell completely open. Unexpectedly two corpse-like hands grasped the sides of the wooden box. The Mexican troopers' eyes bulged from their sockets. Slowly a sepulchral body began to rise from inside the casket. As the cadaver rose it pointed an accusing finger at the spindly drunken tax collector.

The two wide-eyed drunkards beside the coffin crossed themselves repeatedly as they stumbled backward from the macabre scene. The third conscript fainted dead away. Helped by a soundless blow to the back of his head by Big Tim.

The angry corporal shouted at his two fleeing comrades. "Cowards! What is a dead man? He cannot hurt you!" The tall soldier turned on Diego. Then drew a short infantry sword.

In a flash Diego's rapier whipped through the half darkness. *Zip...Zip...Zip* went the razor-edged blade. Baffled the drunken corporal took one step backward. Just as his green pants fell around his ankles. He stumbled. Almost fell. Bent over to clutch his pants. And took a blow to the back of his head from the heel of Anoche's knife...which would have dropped an ox.

Don Carlo lay back in his private coffin. A slight smile on his lips. In his hands he held Father Thomas's crucifix. As a precaution the procession abandoned the safe house of the hotel. Instead they turned left up the Calle de Rio Bravo. Continued toward the parish church and its small graveyard. Now not even a block away as the rising sun promised a new day.

CHAPTER **101**

NO SOONER had the procession passed a narrow alley in the middle of the block than up ahead at the next corner several riders appeared. Weapons bristled in the early light. At their center Malvado on his black horse blocked their path. The cutthroat and his bandits advanced down the street slowly. Filled the space from wall to wall. The coffin procession came to an abrupt stop. Dancer turned his head to look behind them. Another phalanx of horsemen led by Payaso blocked any hope of escape. Next to his Mexican benefactor sat the venomous deserter Patrick Harp at Payaso's shoulder.

In a moment Malvado and his henchmen surrounded the small funeral procession.

"My guess is that coffin doesn't have a dead body in it…yet." Harp's supposition was accompanied by a malevolent sneer.

Trapped. The attending mourners lowered the coffin to the sandy street. Don Carlo pushed open the lid — and Diego helped him stand.

"I've seen what you did to my two men in the warehouse. Drop your guns and blades. Now!" Harp shouted.

An impressive array of weapons struck the dirt around the coffin.

"Don Carlo…I don't care if you are a traitor or not…but I do know you have been trading with the Americans." Payaso hissed. "Those 'ᏠB' brands on the mules and cattle were the work of Dancer. As you know your son Luiz told me. But it doesn't matter now. My spies let me in on your little secret." With a sneer Payaso pulled a paper from his inside pocket. Don Carlo and Dancer immediately recognized their contract. "Now only one thing matters that will save your lives. Tell me where Stepptoe's money is. *My* money!" Payaso demanded. "Tell me! Or I will have the pleasure of watching each of you die one by one."

Malvado motioned to his horsemen to round up the hostages.

"Take them into the church. All of them!" Payaso ordered.

The *rancheros* jumped to the ground. Surrounded Dancer and Anoche and Big Tim while Diego supported Don Carlo. The bandits herded them roughly forward. All five captives were pushed through the church's dusty graveyard toward the side-porch entrance.

Only then did Dancer realize Swift was nowhere to be seen.

CHAPTER **102**

THE OLD PARISH CHURCH was once a grand edifice but had seen better days. When there was only one church to vie for patrons' support it had flourished. The dim light of sunrise revealed the neglect that showed in the peeling plaster and faded gilt paint. Payaso. Harp. Malvado. And their band of killers marched the five hostages through the church graveyard. Through the south porch door. And into the open choir crossing…where the transept met the center nave before the altar. Then the captives were herded harshly across this crossing…to the space between the first pew and baptismal font.

"Let me make it simple for you." Payaso's tone did not suggest he would welcome any questions. "I know about the deal Don Carlo and Dancer made for the supplies…and my lands. Your son informs me the price was to be paid in specie coin. And the payment was to be collected now — after the battle — here in this church. Your job — if you want to live — is to tell me where Wildfire's treasure is hidden. There isn't much time. Soon this old church will fill up with more peasants who consider this a sanctuary. And I am not a patient man. So tell me… where is the money?"

No one moved. Payaso's icy glare fixed on each in turn.

"I see the lady correspondent is not with you?"

Dancer answered before Diego. "She is with the American Army in their camp…to report on the occupation of Matamoros any time now."

"Ah…no matter. My question is the same. I see…you will need some persuasion."

Payaso gave Malvado a nod. In a second Malvado grabbed Juanita Sanchez…who had come from her village to sell bread. Malvado had caught her in the church with a handful of other villagers. Now packed into a huddle in the front pew. Payaso bellowed. "Tell me where is the money… or this peasant dies!"

No one spoke a word. Only the peasant woman's muttered prayers were heard. At Payaso's signal Malvado pulled a hideous knife from his belt. Held the blade to the helpless woman's throat. Then dragged the terrified peasant toward the north aisle side door. As they struggled past the carved baptismal font its wooden cover crashed to the stone floor. In a moment a muffled scream came back through the open door. Then ended in a low strangled gurgling moan. When Malvado returned a sneer lifted his lip. All eyes watched as the bandit cleaned his blade in the holy water of the baptismal font. Then disdainfully wiped it dry on his sleeve. For Malvado the peasant woman was nothing more than sacrificial fodder.

"Where is the money!" Payaso shouted. Malvado grabbed an old man from the huddle of hostages. Dragged the poor soul to Payaso.

"No! Wait!" Don Carlo countered. "Take me as a hostage. But do not hurt these innocent people."

Payaso bounded forward. Smacked Don Carlo across the head with his horse pistol. Malvado leveled both revolvers at Dancer and Diego and Big Tim and Anoche.

"Tell me where the money is…or more will get hurt!" Payaso frothed.

Don Carlo pulled himself up by the support of a pew bench. Pressed a hand to his bloody temple.

"Where is it?" Payaso roared.

Not getting the answer he wanted Payaso raised his pistol. Spun around. Fired point-blank at Big Tim. The force of the shot knocked Big Tim backward. His huge bulk splintered a pew and knocked two more benches across the stone floor. Big Tim lay still on the cold limestone. Wooden shards around him.

"Stop!" Dancer shouted. "I'll tell you where the money is…on one condition. That you take the money and leave us. We have done you no harm. As you say there is little time. If you don't get out of here with your blood money…soon you won't be able to escape. Taylor is preparing to attack Matamoros this very morning." Dancer's lie was an act of desperation.

Harp turned on Dancer. The obsessed Irish deserter for weeks had gnawed on the bone of settling his score with Dancer.

"Show us the money…and everybody can go. Except you… Dancer. If you want to survive…you must give me the loan documents to buy your life. Looks like my little trick with the coal oil in the *Decatur*'s water tanks missed its target. That won't happen again."

Dancer's body tensed. *It was Harp.* "You killed Natchez Jones." Dancer's accusation was hurled with clenched fists. "I'll kill you… Harp. You bastard son of a bitch."

Harp laughed. "You're the one to die now…Dancer. Just like Wildfire sent me out here to do. And I'll brand your crucified corpse too…just like I did to Stepptoe. Now where are the documents!" Harp exploded.

Dancer stood his ground.

Harp hissed malevolently. "You should have died the day we blew up the *Decatur*. Now you will today."

Dancer bargained. "I'll give Payaso the money…Harp…and you can take me hostage. But only after you've let the others go will you get Wildfire's loan documents." Dancer stared Harp down. "The money now…and the documents when everyone else is safe. Take it or leave it."

Payaso stepped forward. "Where is the money! Tell me now!" Payaso shouted impatiently.

"You get nothing unless you swear to let them go. Swear in the house of God!" Dancer countered.

Payaso hesitated. Then gave Harp a slight nod of ascent.

"You're almost sitting on it." Dancer let his words hit their mark. "The strongbox is in the priest's confessional. Under his seat."

In a flash Don Carlo and Diego realized Dancer had given up his commission share of the contract.

Every reason for Dancer's privateer mission to Matamoros was lost. Yet Father Thomas's money was safe. A part of Dancer wanted to believe it couldn't be helped. But Dancer knew that was not true.

Malvado made sure all six of his men had their guns pointed at the group of four remaining hostages. Then he stepped to the confessional situated in the aisle near the northside entrance. With his short sword he pried up the seat. There was a strongbox too heavy for one man to lift. Two men struggled to raise the locked box out of the confessional. They dragged it with a hollow scraping sound across the stone floor… toward the baptismal font. Malvado angled his pistol at the lock. Then shot it open with a deafening blast that echoed throughout the church. Malvado twisted off the lock. Quickly Payaso opened the lid. Inside was a mass of white canvas bags. Each filled with gold half-eagle coins.

"There should be more!" Payaso demanded.

Dancer bluffed. "That is all there is. Don Carlo's payment was held back by the quartermaster until Matamoros was occupied. That moment may come within the hour. What you have is my commission payment. Every last cent."

Malvado gripped his pistols. Payaso fumed. "Don't tell me about Don Carlo's payment! Where is Wildfire's gold? There were four strongboxes! Someone stole them from the catacombs! Even when Malvado and Harp tortured Stepptoe…he still claimed the gold was stolen by someone else. But who? Where is Wildfire's gold hidden?"

"That's a good question." Dancer's voice was even. "Maybe you should ask the Americans…when they get here."

"Take it away!" Payaso ordered. Two of Malvado's men moved four bags of treasure out the nave's northside door — opposite the porch door they had entered minutes before. Payaso followed them out the door.

Harp turned on Dancer. "Where are the loan documents?" Harp demanded.

"Not until you let the others go."

"Just to be sure you aren't lying to me — Dancer — or want to follow us…I'll be taking this as insurance." Without warning Harp grabbed Don Carlo. Put his pistol to the aristocrat's temple.

Harp cocked his gun and gripped his hostage. Just then Samantha

Swift stepped from behind a great pillar…into the open crossing. Swift spoke in an even voice. As she leveled Blake's Colt at the deserter. "Leave him…Harp. If you take one more step you all die." Harp and Malvado stopped. Pointed their pistols at Dancer and Diego and Anoche and Swift.

"Says who?" Harp bluffed.

In that moment from behind the nave columns—and what seemed like every shadow in the church—stepped out Sam Walker and his Texas Rangers. Four rifles and Walker's long-barrel Colt cocked in unison. Aimed at the heart of Malvado and each of his four henchmen.

"We say so." Walker's calm assertion reverberated through the silent church. His men leaned into their aim. Locked onto their respective targets. Only Harp was not targeted—for the sake of Don Carlo.

Swift repeated: "Let him go."

Harp hesitated. Slowly he backed his way toward the door. The deserter held Don Carlo hostage as a shield. Four of Malvado's men used their own leader—and Harp with his hostage—as their cover. They stood frozen just inside the church door. Their guns moved back and forth. Unsure which Ranger to watch. Or Swift by the altar steps. Malvado aimed both his pistols at Walker. The scene crackled with tension. Walker raised his sword in his free hand. With that signal his men took the careful aim of a firing squad.

Harp lunged forward. Shoved Don Carlo toward the leveled guns. Then bounded for the side door. Two of Malvado's men beside the nave door were thrown down by the first volley. Crimson spattered on the plaster walls. Malvado's blasts exploded chunks of plaster off the wall where Walker's head had been. The boom of Walker's Colt caught Malvado squarely in the forehead. Spun around by the bullet Malvado fell headfirst into the baptismal pool. The holy water turned as red as the blood of Christ.

Harp bolted through the door behind two *rancheros*. Slammed the door shut behind them. Outside Payaso—with the remnants of Malvado's gang—leapt on their horses from the steps. Pounded away from the main plaza and up the street—toward Resaca House—as the bright early morning sunlight shone on their backs. Bags of coins danced in their saddlebags. Close behind Dancer chased the thieves out

into the Calle de Comercio. As Payaso and his men — and Harp —
escaped Dancer realized he had no weapon.

"Dancer!" Walker shouted.

Dancer turned toward Walker. In a blink of an eye Dancer caught
the Ranger's long rifle as it lofted into his hands. *One shot. Make it
count.* Dancer dashed to the corner. Settled his elbows atop the old
cemetery's low adobe wall.

At full tilt Payaso led several riders around the next corner. Harp
galloped behind. Dancer calmed himself. Took a breath. Held it. And
squeezed the trigger. Walker's buffalo gun roared. The last rider took a
bullet square between his shoulder blades. Flopped forward. Then
tumbled backward off his horse. He was dead before he hit the sand.
Thirty coins fell to earth without a sound beside Harp's body.

CHAPTER 103

INSIDE THE OLD CHURCH
MATAMOROS
10 MAY 1846

BACK IN THE CHURCH Anoche propped up Big Tim. As he came back to life he opened his jacket. Then slowly removed a thick leather-bound book from his shirt pocket. The ball from Payaso's gun was lodged in the pages of *Brownwell's Primer for First Readers.* The force of the ball had only knocked Big Tim unconscious.

Diego helped Don Carlo to a pew. While the Rangers dragged Malvado and the other bodies into the street. Dancer then gently guided several villagers to use the coffin left outside to carry Juanita Sanchez's body to the cemetery yard. Anoche and Swift dabbed Don Carlo's wound with handkerchiefs wet with holy water brought from the carved-stone stoup at the west front entrance.

"What was this about your commission and the loan documents?" Don Carlo asked Dancer.

"Just a bluff." Dancer smiled mildly. "Bullies like Payaso and Harp are greedier than they are brave. Stand up to them and they back down."

Don Carlo turned toward the American. "Dancer...I don't have good news for you." Don Carlo explained slowly: "Father Thomas hid your share in the confessional…as you knew. As to the rest of the gold…he was the only one who knew the hiding place….Now Father Thomas is dead. I'm sorry."

Dancer shrugged as if to make the best of it. "Quickly come… quickly go."

Anoche crossed her arms and turned thoughtful. "But didn't Stepptoe's map and Swift's signet rings point to the church's baptismal?"

"A fifteenth station of the cross would be too easy a clue. I checked." Dancer shook his head as he kicked the carved font. "Maybe Swift has some ideas."

Swift worked her mother's signet ring with her thumb. Then took out Father Thomas's ring from her coin pouch. As everyone looked at Swift a thoughtful expression came over her face as she thought of her mother's words. *Find the mate to this ring and you will find the truth.*

"Father Thomas said these rings were inspired by wood carvings of church mice back in Wales. That may be a clue. Maybe he left a mouse trail for us to follow?"

Anoche lifted the baptismal font cover from near the side door where it had landed. To her surprise there was a mouse subtly carved onto the wooden lip. When she placed the cover on the three-basin font a notch fell into place. "Look. The mouse is headed in that direction. Almost as if the mouse pointed toward the wooden screen in front of the Lady Chapel?"

Swift walked to the carved screen. Looked left and right. Then by her feet. Nothing. When she looked up high on the screen she spotted another mouse. This one looked like it ran toward the altar rail. "Diego…look around the wooden altar gate. Near the three steps."

Diego saw the mouse right away. "Here! On the baluster just under the railing. The mouse is carved to point into the sanctuary. But where?" Anoche examined the inner altar rail. No running mark. Swift checked the ambo lectern just inside the altar railing. Nothing.

Then Big Tim spotted it. "Bishop's chair. There!" He pointed to another wooden mouse. This carving clung to the front apron just underneath the clergy's seat.

Swift traced where the mouse's nose pointed. Followed the line as it led her gaze toward the back of the altar ledge. All eyes were on Swift as she walked toward the credence cabinet against the back wall. Just to the right of the altar on the raised ledge. In an almost inaudible voice Swift spoke. "The tabernacle?" Swift stepped to the credence cabinet used in celebration of the Eucharist. Swift opened the latched ambry-cabinet door. Inside were vestments. Communion items. And a sacred vessel. With both hands Swift lifted the ornate object from the cabinet and placed it on top of the credence table.

"What's that?" Dancer asked.

"Maybe what you've been searching for?" Swift answered with some mystery.

Swift opened the hinged lid of a large pewter pitcher. Inside the empty wine flagon was a scrolled set of papers. She pulled them out and handed the scroll to Dancer.

A smile came over Dancer's face as he unrolled the packet. "I owe you one…Swift." After a quick glance Dancer explained. "These are the loan documents that Wildfire wanted…and now the boys in Washington will be glad to get them instead. In fact…very glad. See here. The documents claim a loan of one million dollars. Not a bad insurance claim…if you are Wildfire. A mite more than the hundred thousand they actually delivered. Nice work…Swift."

Again Anoche gave Dancer a soft stroke on his back.

"But what about the treasure payment?" Diego glanced at Dancer and Swift and Anoche. "Father Thomas's markings on Stepptoe's map…and Swift's mouse faces indicated the treasure was some place in the church."

"But where?" Anoche asked. "Clearly not in the confessional."

Dancer snapped his fingers with another realization. "Father Thomas isn't the only one who understands the secrets of the Lord's house. Not everything can be learned in the confessional alone." Dancer turned. And walked slowly behind the altar. "My guess is Father Thomas reserved a very special place for Wildfire's blood payment." Dancer pulled up the sacred antependium cloth that draped the holy table. There under the altar cloth was another wooden compartment.

Everyone gathered behind the altar. Except Big Tim…who stood a wary guard at the altar-rail gate. Diego and Dancer held back the textile drapery. Swift and Anoche bent down on their knees. Their fingertips traced what looked like a strange lock on the double doors. In fact there were two locks. Or—more accurately—two rectangular metal plates.

One on each door. Newly installed. The brass plates were still shiny. On each plate was a circular keyhole. Though not a hole. More of an indentation. The two indentions were near the center edge. But one was positioned a hole-width higher than the other. Swift took off both signet rings. Placed one on each hand on the middle phalanx of her forefinger. Secured by her thumb. Her ring with in-cut intaglio engraving on her left. Father Thomas's ring on her right…with its raised image. With great care Swift pressed one ring — then the other — into the two corresponding circular impressions. They fit like precision keys. Swift slowly rotated her left ring clockwise. The right ring counterclockwise. The locks clicked as she moved each ring a half turn. Behind the locked plates a master mechanism turned like a finely crafted Welsh watch. The twin lock tongues of the ingenious device withdrew soundlessly. Each into its rectangular plate. A moment later the altar doors opened.

Inside — under the sacred altar — were four church-donation tithe boxes. As sturdy as any strongbox. Each one the size of Dancer's lost commission.

"This is Wildfire's payment…the money that Payaso stole from Stepptoe…and Father Thomas — how should I say — reclaimed for his church." Dancer blinked several times. Then considered for a long moment. With a sudden upwelling of realization Dancer made a fateful decision. "The boys in Washington will get these loan documents. That's all they really want. Who knows what happened to Wildfire's money? As best I can tell…the money was stolen. In fact…stolen several times. In the end the money disappeared without a trace. End of report."

Don Carlo stood amazed. "Thank you — my son — for your sacrifice. The only sorrow is you have lost your entire fortune." Don Carlo looked at Dancer quietly. "But now I too realize there is much more in life than money. Having Diego return home — and the Americans push that scheming Payaso out of Matamoros — is payment enough for me. On this day…with God as my witness…I pledge this money shall remain with this church. The money came from the town…and should be returned to the town. Maybe someday we will see a school for orphans — and all children — here. It would be fitting if it were named after Father Thomas. That is my wish."

By this time Walker's men had carried Harp's body and Malvado and his dead bandits into the church graveyard. Dumped the bodies in a shallow pit hastily dug days before in anticipation of war casualties. They next carried the strong tithe boxes out the northside door. Placed the heavy boxes in a wagon on Calle de Comercio. Then mounted a well-armed horse guard.

Walker pointed out even the parish church was not a safe place to stay much longer. No one needed to be convinced. Together with Walker and his Rangers Swift and Dancer—with Diego and Anoche and Big Tim…and a battered Don Carlo—made their way safely back to the fortress called Hotel Casamata.

CANTINA
HOTEL CASAMATA
10 MAY 1846/THAT EVENING

IT WAS WELL PAST DARK. The streets were still active. But the cane liquor for many had reduced the bedlam into a morose slumber.

The troop of Texas Rangers safeguarded their horses and wagon in the courtyard of the hotel. The heavy tithe boxes were secured in the arsenal strong room. Already the aroma from the cantina's kitchen reached the barrack's sleeping rooms. The smells promised the best-cooked meal they had had in weeks. And maybe best of all it would be served by Anoche's girls. A case of the finest Kentucky whiskey was involved. The kind that came in glass bottles with actual labels.

In the cantina glasses soon passed among the tired band.

As night settled over Matamoros it was clear the ladies of Anoche's hotel were relieved to be protected. And the Rangers were happy to oblige. "We are men who know our duty and do it." Or so one Ranger rhapsodized as he gave Gabriella a pull around her wasp-like waist. His buddy warmed to the large smile coming from the latte-skinned Sharice.

Sam Walker pushed his dinner plate away after he cleaned it to metal with a last tortilla. "No man in the wrong can stand up against a fellow that's in the right…and keeps on a-comin'." Several Rangers raised their glasses to their leader in agreement.

Walker rose. And offered a toast to his Texas Rangers. "Free as the breeze. Fast as a mustang. Tough as a cactus." Each and all drained their glasses.

Walker now faced Swift. "And to Samantha Swift. If she had not sprinted back to the hotel. And led us through the Custom House…and then the catacombs of the cathedral…and found the secret passage to the church with her map…me and my boys would never have been able to get the drop on Payaso and Malvado. Swift saved the day. To you…Miss Swift."

Swift raised her mostly full glass toward Walker. Gamely she accepted the cheers that went up from all at the table. On the outside Swift did not let her failure as a correspondent show. Yet on the inside her gut twisted with the knowledge that all her dispatches had been stolen. *Fortitude…Swift. Restraint. Hold your emotions in check. This is a day for celebration. Make the most of it.*

Don Carlo reached across the table to Walker. And shook his hand heartily. "Thanks to you…that scoundrel Payaso has been sent packing. Now the whole town will know Payaso stole the *alcabala* tax money for himself and the other Creole generals in Mexico City. Payaso's lands will be sold to recover that lost revenue. I'll guarantee the Rancho Valdez next door—with its 'right of contiguity' as the Creoles call it— will be the high bidder for his lands. With special thanks to the tax-free receipts from the cattle and horses sold by *Señor* Dancer to the American Army. A rightful end to that little Payaso's schemes." Don Carlo raised his glass.

Diego reached out. And gave his father's forearm a proud squeeze.

"What about you…Dancer?" Don Carlo spoke frankly. "You lost out on your commission in the church. My friend…I'm sorry."

Dancer looked at Don Carlo with an expression of feigned sadness. "The President's Secret Service isn't everything it's cracked up to be." Dancer counted his fingers as he talked. "Since this all began… my partner was killed…and I've been keelhauled…ambushed… wasted good champagne on a bad bomb…nearly got skewered by a *ranchero*…held hostage…and lost all my commission. But to be honest…I think I'm going to miss the excitement." A light chuckle went up among those gathered.

Dancer wrestled with his conscience for a moment. "Don't worry…Don Carlo." Dancer continued: "From the sale of Kaufman's supplies to the army — and the deposits in my account in New York — I dare say that will cover my expenses. And with some luck I may still turn this into a profitable adventure. At most your commission — Don Carlo — would only have been a most generous gift."

Dancer paused then spoke in a serious voice. "Most important was to obtain these loan documents. That was my true mission in Matamoros…at least that is what Mustang and the Inner Circle sent me here to do. Keep these documents out of the hands of Wildfire… and we keep a million dollars out of the hands of the slavocracy. Those were my orders. Plus I'll let you in on a little secret." Dancer paused for effect. "After Jones and I bought the goods with Kaufman's Citizen's Bank of Louisiana account…we increased the prices on the supplies to the army to cover that commission…just in case the war got in the way of true commerce."

Anoche moved close behind a seated Dancer. Placed her hands on his shoulders.

With a thoughtful look Dancer turned his glass with the fingertips of both hands. "Now I know it was Harp that bombed the *Decatur.* And it was Malvado that killed Stepptoe…."

"And it was Harp who crucified him" — Don Carlo added — "and branded his body with the calling card of Wildfire…to make it look like Wildfire stole the treasure."

"My work is done here." Dancer had concluded his speech.

"Why the long face…Sam?" Anoche asked with concern.

Swift's attention snapped back to the cantina. "Last night I learned all the dispatches I sent throughout the war were stolen. Now all my work here — all my reputation — rides on my victory series of just four dispatches." *More than anything I want to be respected for my work. And — of course — to earn back Father's newspaper from his monstrous brother.* "The series was given to the army courier from Fort Brown last night…at least I hope it was. Before Dancer and I crossed the river to Matamoros. I won't know if my dispatches even made it through…or how the stories are received…for weeks. Until then I must cast about to find something to do. I need to find a new interest."

Her eyes met Diego…and he smiled in return.

Dancer broke the silence. "By the way…where is Dolly O'Hara?"

Anoche helped Sharice and Gabriella clear the dishes. "Hadn't you heard? She dropped Harp and ran off with Luiz Juan Baptiste. Something about California…and a fresh start."

Dancer nodded. "Good choice."

Anoche shook her head. "I reckon we won't be seeing the red-haired Irish goddess around these parts again. Isn't love a crazy thing?"

⊠　⊠　⊠

At night's end Jack Dancer and Michelena climbed the stairs to the balcony rooms. Followed by Diego and Samantha Swift.

Samantha's gaze followed the pair as they disappeared arm-in-arm into Michelena's room.

At Samantha's door the war correspondent turned to Diego. "You are a most unexpected man…Diego. You keep me off-balance somehow."

The courteous Diego replied: "My apologies."

"No…I think I like it." Samantha spoke softly as she placed her hands lightly on his chest.

"Would you care to come inside?" Samantha said looking up into Diego's eyes.

"That's quite an offer."

"Is that a yes…or a no?" Samantha said playfully.

Diego leaned forward. And kissed Samantha on the cheek.

"Tonight…I think it is safer for both of us if I camp with Don Carlo downstairs. I must return to the Rancho Valdez tomorrow to care for Don Carlo and take stock of our lands." Diego smiled.

"My work in Matamoros is finished too." Samantha realized the bleak future before her was a confrontation with Jacob Swift in New York—with little to show for herself. Somehow she summoned a happier thought. "When will I see you again?"

Diego wondered if Samantha knew how strongly the same thought had come to him that evening. "I see now what my father saw in you. Strong-willed. Brave heart. Much like our mother." The heir to Rancho Valdez paused. "I'll be at the *rancho* for at least a month. But now that the war has mostly moved west—and with Don Carlo and Roberto at home—I wonder how much there will be for me to do?"

Samantha looked into Diego's dark eyes. "Is that an invitation?"

Diego's smile raised the corners of his thin mustache. "Of course… long rides will be needed…and the small *casita* with its garden near the river will need attention after all this time."

"I can't imagine anything I would like more than to see the *rancho* again. But on one condition." Samantha turned a mock-serious expression toward Diego. "No branding and no prairie oysters this time."

Diego leaned forward. And kissed her again. This time warmly on the mouth. He felt Samantha's cool fingers touch the back of his neck as she pulled their bodies together. Gently. And then completely. When Samantha relaxed and settled back off her toes she looked into Diego's eyes. Her entire expression was full of hope.

"Until tomorrow then…"—Diego said with promise—"…and the Rancho Valdez."

❁ ❁ ❁

Some minutes later Samantha Swift fell asleep as soon as her head hit her pillow. She was not disturbed by the joyful commotion in the next room that came from Dancer and Michelena for most of the night in the defeated city of Matamoros.

QUO VADIS?

WORD OF THE THORNTON AFFAIR that occurred on 25 April reached Washington D.C. on 9 May 1846 via military courier and telegraph. The news arrived fourteen days after the event. Expansionists immediately labeled the skirmish a "dastardly ambush." Polk readied an appeal to Congress for war. He trumpeted the *cause célèbre* as the shedding of "American blood on American soil." Despite the fact that the soil was disputed territory claimed by both nations between the Nueces River near Corpus Christi and the Rio Grande near Matamoros. On 13 May the United States Congress agreed and officially declared war on Mexico.

War fever was at a peak in Washington. Yet nothing was known to America of the Battle of Palo Alto on 8 May and the Battle of Resaca de la Palma on 9 May…or the Mexican defeats and retreats that opened the way for Taylor to occupy Matamoros on 18 May without resistance.

Into this information void William Beacon made sure Swift's four dispatches were delivered *posthaste*. In person Beacon raced Swift's victory dispatches to Point Isabel. Then accompanied the pouch by steamer to New Orleans. Rather than turn the precious series over to

Turner's express network Beacon made a fateful decision. *I can do better than that. I'll take them to New York City myself. Personally. While there I can print my daguerreotype plates with Mathew Brady…and get them exhibited. Your precious dispatches are safe with me…Swift. Consider it done and dusted…as they say.* Beacon nabbed the last ticket on the last steam packet north. Swift's victory series was received at the *Brooklyn Eagle* in New York City 16 May 1846. Within seven days of the action. An unheard-of record time. Only three days after war was declared in Washington. And seven days before plodding military channels to the War Department in Washington delivered Taylor's official battlefield reports on 23 May.

S. Thomas Swift's four-part series of victories in Mexico caused a sensation. Bold front pages featured the courageous correspondent's name. Capped by an exclusive interview with old "Rough and Ready" himself. General Zachary Taylor. Soon exchange newspapers across the nation reprinted Swift's four eyewitness reports. American patriotism fueled by bravado and bluster rose as the clarion call of the day. Volunteer regiments formed overnight. Politicians demanded the floor to fume self-righteously about how much territory Mexico should cede in reparations for its resistance. Editor Walt Whitman made sure the "Special War Correspondent of the *Brooklyn Eagle*" was hailed in *absentia* as the guest of honor at numerous banquets and benefits for the war effort.

Sensational daily headlines from 17 May to 21 May 1846 drove sales of the *Brooklyn Eagle* newspaper to new heights. On the streets the newsboys hawked their papers loud. "'Ere's your *Eagle!*" "Buy an *Eagle!*" "Tremendous victory!" "Read all about it!"

VICTORY IN MEXICO!
Review of the Actions
As Seen from the Mexican Side
!!! EAGLE EXCLUSIVE !!!

Loss of the Mexican Army
Flight of the Defeated

Death of Major Brown
Fort Texas Renamed

A Cowardly Mexican General
Pursuit of the Fleeing Mexicans

Direct from the Battlefield
Part 1 of a 4-Part Series

MATAMOROS MEXICO—9 MAY 1846. Today on the Texas plains near a dry ravine called the Resaca de la Palma the first great act in the history of the operations of our Army of Occupation ended in victory in Mexico. And with the imminent capture of Matamoros on the Rio Grande all immediate prospect of fighting was terminated.

"Our victory has been decisive." General Zachary Taylor told your correspondent these words personally.

Although no accurate data from which to determine the enemy's force on this day are available Taylor told the Brooklyn Eagle *a rough estimate is possible. "General Arista's army is known to have been reinforced after the action of the 8th at Palo Alto by both cavalry and infantry—and no doubt to an extent at least equal to his loss on that day. It is probable that six thousand men were opposed to us." Taylor exclusively revealed these details to the* Brooklyn Eagle.

The enemy was "in a position chosen by themselves and strongly defended with artillery. The enemy's loss was very great. Nearly two hundred of his dead were buried by us on this day."

Taylor's final battlefield assessment indicated that the Mexican "loss in killed—wounded—and missing in the two affairs of the Eighth and Ninth is—I think—moderately estimated at one thousand men."

American losses in the two days' battles Taylor reported: 34 Americans killed. 113 wounded.

Your faithful correspondent has learned the Americans captured eight pieces of Mexican artillery. Much ammunition. Three standards including the revered colors of the Tampico Coastal Guards. Some 100 prisoners with 14 officers included General de la Vega...who commanded the guns taken by

Captain May's cavalry charge. According to Lieutenant George Meade of the Topographical Engineers — your correspondent learned — the Mexican losses may have been even greater. Meade placed the Mexican loses at 1,200 killed and wounded. 300 drowned while swimming the Rio Grande. And between 1,000 and 2,000 deserters.

The Mexican Army was almost literally annihilated. The broken fragments fled for safety from our victorious troops as this dispatch was written. That proud and confident army of the best troops Mexico had — but a few days before — marched into Matamoros without a doubt the Americans would fall an easy prey to their arms. So certain were the Mexican officers that magnificent preparations for celebration had been made well in advance of the Resaca de la Palma action. This army — so certain of victory and its superiority to General Taylor's force — was today cut to pieces. Driven in confusion from the Rio Grande.

Such was the battle of Resaca de la Palma — and such too was the outcome of Palo Alto on the day preceding — in the opening salvo of the Northern Campaign.

The disputed territory was completely subdued in little more than six weeks from the day our army reached the riverbank opposite Matamoros now occupied by Fort Brown.
Your humble servant on the battlefield:
S. Thomas Swift
***Special War Correspondent of the* Brooklyn Eagle**

# # # # #

ON 30 MAY 1846 the following notice appeared in the *Brooklyn Eagle* exchange classifieds deep on an interior page. The note was inserted between a ticket announcement for the return show of the infamous "Feejee Mermaid" at P.T. Barnum's American Museum and a City Corporation Notice for the regrading and repaving of Water Street from Jay to Main streets.

> ### *IN MEMORIAM*
> *It is with great sadness and grief that the editors of* The Daily Picayune *in New Orleans — an exchange newspaper associated with your* Brooklyn Eagle *— report the melancholy death of their Mexican War correspondent: James Collingsworth Turner. After Mr. Turner served with distinction to bring readers the latest news from the battlefront at Matamoros on the Rio Grande — upon his return to New Orleans — Mr. Turner died by yellow fever on 18 May 1846. The date General Taylor occupied Matamoros. He was 29.*

# # # # #

TIMELINE OF HISTORICAL EVENTS

1845

4 March 1845	James Knox Polk sworn in as eleventh president of the United States.
25 July 1845	General Zachary Taylor's "Army of Observation" took position at Corpus Christi in Texas.
November 1845	Louisiana Congressman John Slidell sent by President Polk to Mexico City to secure boundary adjustment between United States and Mexico; Polk authorized $50 million offer to Mexico for northern territory.
December 1845	Mexico formally refused Slidell mission/ U.S. purchase offer.
29 December 1845	Texas admitted as twenty-eighth state; entered as a slave state.

1846

2 February 1846	Beloit College founded in Beloit in the Wisconsin Territory.
8 March 1846	Taylor's "Army of Occupation" crossed Nueces River for Rio Grande River through land claimed by both United States and Mexico.
28 March 1846	Taylor arrived at Matamoros on Rio Grande.
25 April 1846	American troops attacked by Mexican troops on north side of the Rio Grande in "Thornton Affair."
3 May 1846	5 a.m. Mexican artillery opened fire on Fort Texas from positions directly across Rio Grande.
8 May 1846	Battle of Palo Alto — first official battle of the Mexican-American War; although no clear winner — Taylor declared victory after Mexican troops retreat.
9 May 1846	At Battle of Resaca de la Palma Taylor's troops are victorious and end six-day siege of Fort Texas; Major Jacob Brown's men rename the post "Fort Brown" in his honor.
11 May 1846	President Polk — unaware of Palo Alto or Resaca de la Palma battles — referred to Thornton Affair before Congress: "Mexico…invaded our territory and shed the blood of our fellow-citizens on our own soil."
13 May 1846	U.S. Congress officially declared war on Mexico; Taylor unaware of this development.
18 May 1846	Taylor and troops occupy Matamoros after Mexican troops retreated to Monterrey.
15 June 1846	Treaty of Oregon signed between United States and Britain; ended twenty-eight years of joint occupation and established border between the two countries at the 49th parallel.
16 August 1846	General Santa Anna returned to Mexico…landing at Vera Cruz.
20 – 24 September 1846	Taylor negotiated with General Ampudia to surrender Monterrey…including an eight-week armistice.
19 November 1846	Polk appointed Major General Winfield Scott — not Taylor — to command expedition to Vera Cruz.
28 December 1846	Iowa admitted as twenty-ninth state; entered as a free state.

1847

22–23 February 1847 — Taylor — outnumbered by Mexican troops — countered Santa Anna…who eventually withdrew at the Battle of Buena Vista.

9 March 1847 — Scott and more than 8,000 U.S. soldiers arrived via sea just south of Vera Cruz — the largest amphibious landing in U.S. history.

29 March 1847 — Scott captured Vera Cruz and San Juan de Ulua fortress.

18 April 1847 — Scott defeated Santa Anna at Cerro Gordo.

Summer 1847 — Polk sent Nicholas Trist — clerk to Secretary of State James Buchanan — to negotiate with the Mexicans; Trist — ultimately defying delayed orders sent by Polk — secured purchase of California and half of Mexico's territory for $15 million.

19 August 1847 — Scott victorious over Mexican General Valencia.

20 August 1847 — In Battle of Churubusco…Scott and forces defeated San Patricio Battalion (composed mainly of American Army deserters) and Santa Anna's troops to seize Churubusco five miles from Mexico City.

24 August 1847 — Santa Anna negotiated truce with Scott.

6 September 1847 — Truce between Santa Anna and Scott terminated.

8–15 September 1847 — The Battle for Mexico City — with major actions at Molino del Rey and Chapultepec Castle — culminated with Scott occupying Mexico City. Battles. Skirmishes. And sieges continued until March 1848.

9 October 1847 — Samuel Hamilton Walker — Texas Ranger and co-inventor of the Walker Colt revolver — killed at Huamantla.

1848

2 February 1848 The Treaty of Guadalupe Hidalgo signed by Nicholas Trist and representatives of a collapsed Mexican government without Polk's knowledge; the treaty formally ended Mexican War…created U.S. southern border along the Rio Grande… and—for a $15 million settlement—added territory including all or parts of: Present-day Arizona. California. Colorado. Nevada. New Mexico. Utah. Wyoming.

10 March 1848 Treaty of Guadalupe Hidalgo ratified by the U.S. Congress in 38 to 14 vote; abolitionists objected—fearing expansion of slavery into the former Mexico territories.

29 May 1848 Wisconsin admitted as thirtieth state; entered as a free state.

4 July 1848 Treaty of Guadalupe Hidalgo proclaimed.

7 November 1848 Zachary Taylor elected twelfth president of the United States.

1849

18 March 1849 Taylor sworn in as president.

15 June 1849 Former President James K. Polk died in Nashville/Tennessee.

1850

9 July 1850 President Taylor died in office.

9 September 1850 California admitted as thirty-first state; entered as a free state.

As a work of historical adventure fiction all the fictional characters are imagined. Yet the historical events and some historical figures such as those listed in the forward's Historical Characters pages are real. For example: the battles of Palo Alto and Resaca de la Palma in 1846 did occur in the context and order described. The details of those battles and the events leading up to the first fighting of the Mexican War come from well-documented reports. Another example is that many of the commanders in the American Civil War began their careers in the Mexican War. Union commanders included (in alphabetical order): Ulysses S Grant. Joseph Hooker. George C. McClellan. Gordon Meade. George Thomas. Confederate commanders included (in alphabetical order): Braxton Bragg. Thomas J. "Stonewall" Jackson. Joseph E. Johnston. Robert E. Lee. James Longstreet. (Source: *U. S. Grant in the War with Mexico* by Jeffrey Mauck.)

For the fictional characters of Colonel John Ashley and his sister-in-law Lady Belle Ashley the story named the family after the Ashley River where its tidal backwaters form the southern shore of Charleston Point. Inspiration was drawn from the historical figure of James

Gadsden from Charleston South Carolina. The fictional "Wildfire" conspiracy and loan payment scam was entirely imagined. After the Mexican War then Secretary of War Jefferson Davis strongly influenced U.S. President Franklin Pierce to acquire land from Mexico for a transcontinental railroad along a southern route to avoid the Rocky Mountains. Pierce had defeated Winfield Scott for the presidency in November 1852 with a pro-slavery view that appealed to white southerners. In 1853 James Gadsden served as the American ambassador to Mexico. In that role Gadsden negotiated the purchase of territory from Mexico that took effect 8 June 1854. The Gadsden Purchase today comprises much of southern Arizona — including several towns: Yuma. Tucson. Sierra Vista. And the southwest corner of New Mexico as far east as Las Cruces. Despite the land acquisition from Mexico sectional differences over slavery ended progress on a transcontinental railroad until after the Civil War.

The plot to make claims of loss accredited to the "Wildfire" plotters was inspired by the fraudulent Mexican War claims made by George A. Gardiner for $428,750 from the loss of a silver mine in Mexico that never existed. After a congressional investigation ("The Gardiner Investigation" Serial Set Vol. No. 687; Session Vol. No. 1; 32nd Congress; 2nd Session; H. Rpt.1) and subsequent perjury trial (*The United States vs. George A. Gardiner* 1853) upon conviction in March 1854 Gardiner swallowed strychnine and died in his jail cell a few hours later (*New York Times* 6 March 1854). Gardiner's Mexican War claim was only surpassed by a legitimate $602,682 claim by Louis S. Hargous a former U.S. consul in Mexico City before the war that claimed the loss of two steamships on the Isthmus of Tehuantepec. The isthmus is a narrow span in Mexico from Veracruz state on the Gulf to Oaxaca state on the Pacific. In early 1851 real-life Judah Benjamin and Louis S. Hargous formed a company in New Orleans to create a railroad across the isthmus. In 1853 Hargous's son Peter A. Hargous launched a bark named *Wildfire* from New York. Many years later after the documents were released by Congress in 1890 Peter A. Hargous pursued further Mexican claims for repayment of twenty-seven lost bonds extended to Mexico in 1845. That claim was rejected. For this avenue of research I am indebted to the 1989 PhD thesis of Peter Mark Jonas "United States Citizens vs. Mexico

1821–1848" at Marquette University.

The historical influence for the character of Patrick Harp was drawn from the Irishman John Riley and the events of his life. We are indebted to the insights into the nativist-versus-foreign-born conflicts that motivated Irishman John Riley and the Saint Patrick's Battalion in Peter F. Stevens' *The Rogue's March*. A fictional look at the proud and doomed *Saint Patrick's Battalion* by James Alexander Thom also provided great insight. Riley did desert the American Army and served heroically on the Mexican side—where he is revered as a hero today. In his court-martial—because he deserted before the official declaration of war—Riley was not hung along with about fifty of the eighty-five *San Patricios* troops captured and tried as traitors. Actor Tom Berenger played the titular role of John Riley in the 1999 movie *One Man's Hero*.

The inspiration behind the character of Israel David came from the biography of Judah Benjamin. For information about the real-life Judah Benjamin the work of Robert Douthat Meade's outstanding biography *Judah P. Benjamin: Confederate Statesman* was inspirational. Although Benjamin was not involved in the fictional "Wildfire" conspiracy he did go on to have a distinguished career with the Confederacy. Benjamin has been described as "the brains of the Confederacy" and a favorite of Jefferson Davis. Benjamin is a fascinating figure who held three successive Confederate cabinet posts: Attorney General. Secretary of War. And Secretary of State. After the Civil War Benjamin built another career in England.

For scenes in New Orleans to establish Jack Dancer's credentials as a profiteer I thank Elliott Ashkenazi's insightful work *The Business of Jews in Louisiana 1840–1875* which describes in remarkable detail the way the cotton trade operated and was financed in New Orleans. And the roles that commission merchants and cotton factors played in that trade. Like Israel David (Judah Benjamin) the fictional characters of the Kaufman Brothers were loosely based on the historical figures of the Lehman Brothers—who in fact had no involvement in the imaginary conspiracy and loan arrangements described in the novel.

George Wilkins Kendall inspired the author to create the character of James Collingsworth Turner. Kendall was born in Vermont and gained experience on Horace Greeley's *New York Tribune* until he relocated to New Orleans and co-founded the first cheap daily newspaper in the city: *The Picayune* in 1837. Lusting to see battle firsthand Kendall attached himself to General Zachary Taylor's command. Kendall served the army in several roles. Staff Officer. Aide-de-Camp. And organized his own Pony Express (and later steamers from Vera Cruz to New Orleans) which doubled as a courier service for official dispatches known as "Mr. Kendall's Express." More than one of his messengers was murdered en route with a grotesque note pinned to his jacket: *"Correo de los Yanquis"* or "Return to sender." Kendall was credited with inventing Taylor's famous order at the Battle of Buena Vista: "A little more grape…Captain Bragg" popularized in an 1847 Currier and Ives print. One of Kendall's main rivals was James L. Freaner of the *New Orleans Delta*…who published under the pseudonym "Mustang."

The political biography by Henry Montgomery titled *The Life of Major-General Zachary Taylor: Twelfth President of the United States* (Auburn: Derby Miller & Company 1850) — with preface dated 1847 and Taylor's letter of 5 July 1850 that ends the volume — was especially useful for Taylor's own words from Mexico. Of great assistance was the firsthand account of Major John Henshaw written not years later while in Mexico between March 1846 (Corpus Christi) and December 1847 (Mexico City). The New Englander's record is part memoir and journal entries and reflections while serving under both Generals Zachary Taylor and Winfield Scott. Henshaw's day-by-day account of being inside the siege of Fort Texas in May 1846 is richly detailed. The collection was edited by Gary F. Kurutz in *Major John Corey Henshaw's Recollections of the War with Mexico.*

The lack of good maps on the American side is a historical fact. The high-quality maps the Mexicans used — particularly those captured in General Mariano Arista's camp after Resaca de la Palma — were drawn by Jean Luis Berlandier. Berlandier is an interesting and colorful character who lived in Matamoros. When war broke out he was a captain in the Mexican Army of the North. Berlandier's "fly on the wall" service at the side of Arista and Payaso as an aide-de-camp and cartographer was the primary inspiration for Samantha Swift's fictional experiences from the same eyewitness seat within the Mexican lines. Born in southeastern France Berlandier studied botany in Geneva

Switzerland — where he also apprenticed to be a pharmacist and taught himself Latin and Greek. In 1826 Berlandier joined a scientific expedition to Mexico to collect botanical specimens in Mexico and Texas. By 1827 he had been hired to prepare detailed maps of Matamoros and the nearby region as part of the Mexican Boundary Commission that published its works in 1850. At the dissolution of the commission in 1829 Berlandier settled in Matamoros. He married and became a physician where he ran a pharmacy and doctor's clinic. And also kept detailed meteorological and astronomical journals. During the war Berlandier served as interpreter and was in charge of Matamoros hospitals in 1846. When war broke out in spring 1846 Berlandier served as a captain and cartographer and aide-de-camp in Mexico's Army of the North under the command of Generals Mejia and Arista. Berlandier's extensive knowledge of southeastern Texas and northeastern Mexico from his botanical field collections was invaluable to the generals. In the Battle of Palo Alto Berlandier served as adjutant and cartographer to Generals Arista and Mejia. Captain Berlandier drew the first sketch maps of the battle of Palo Alto (8 May 1846) which now reside in the Library of Congress. The battlefield sketches are considered today by researchers and archeologists Haecker and Mauck as the most accurate renderings of that battlefield. After the war Berlandier lived in Matamoros but drowned when he tried to cross the San Fernando River south of the city in 1851. Some of the best specimens of Berlandier's papers and maps of Texas and Mexico are now archived in the Library of Congress and Yale University's Beinecke Rare Books and Manuscript Library and the University of Texas at Austin's Briscoe Center.

For students of history here are some of the fictional departures from strict historical accuracy. The fictional character of General Francisco Payaso arose from the historic records of General Francisco Mejia — who was commandant of the Matamoros Garrison at the time the Americans arrived on the Rio Grande River. Although history records that General Francisco Mejia made his offer to foreigners to desert on 20 April 1846 with an offer of 320 acres of land and free passage anywhere in Mexico….for dramatic reasons the author moved this episode to 24 April. The evening before the Thornton ambush.

The character of John Stepptoe is loosely based on the events and situation of John Marks—who served as U.S. Consul in Matamoros in 1846. Stepptoe's involvement with the Wildfire conspiracy—and his murder—are entirely fictional.

One historical liberty taken by the author was in placing Father Thomas's mouse carvings in 1846 Matamoros and describing the mouse marks as fictionally created by an "anonymous woodcarver they nicknamed the 'Mouseman.'" In fact the inspiration for the story idea came from Robert "Mouseman" Thompson (1876–1955). Thompson was a British Arts and Crafts furniture maker who left his trademark "church mice" in the real Bangor Cathedral in Wales in the 1950s. Robert Thompson's Craftsmen Ltd workshop in North Yorkshire is now run by his descendants—whose oak furniture brand still honors "The Mouseman of Kilburn." To this day children delight in searching for the five mouse carvings around the Bangor Cathedral in Wales…and some say they have found an extra special sixth mouse. Although that discovery may be inspirational as well.

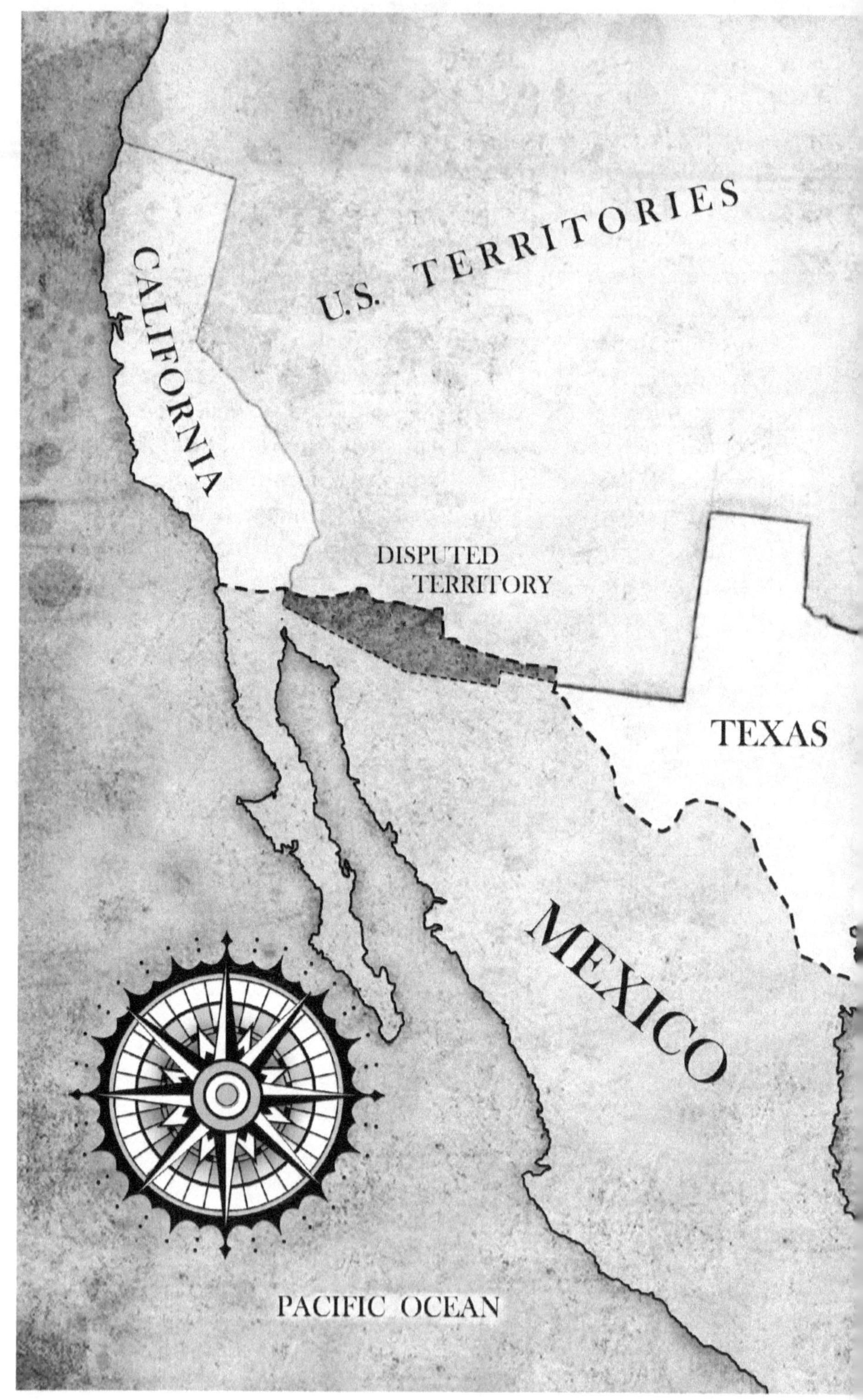

CALIFORNIA
U.S. TERRITORIES
DISPUTED
TERRITORY
TEXAS
MEXICO
PACIFIC OCEAN

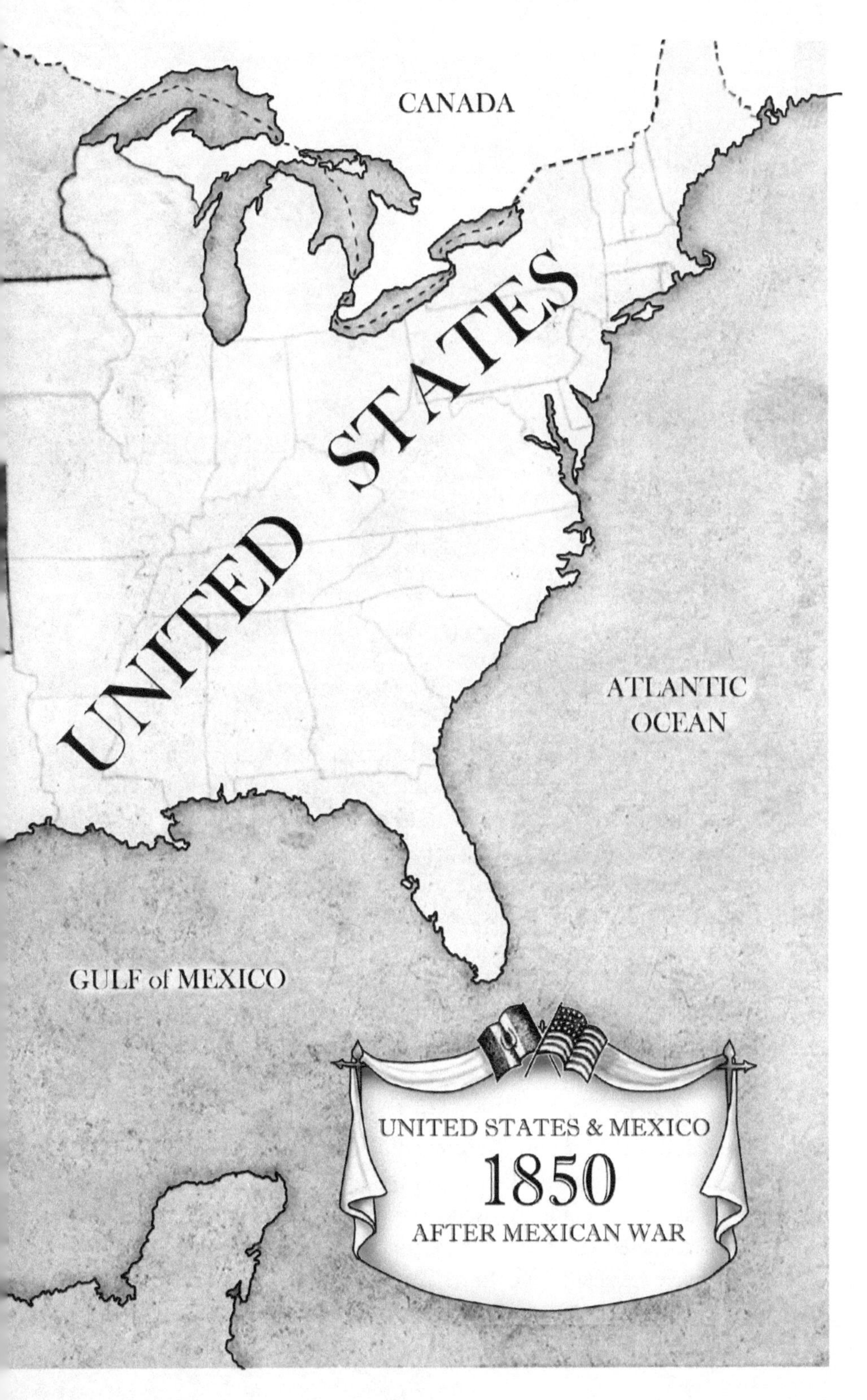

CANADA
UNITED STATES
ATLANTIC
OCEAN
GULF of MEXICO
UNITED STATES & MEXICO
1850
AFTER MEXICAN WAR

ACKNOWLEDGMENTS

The purpose of this book is historical fiction not fictional history. The aim is to entertain…and at the same time share with readers the exciting outline of history the *Swift and Dancer Adventures* bear witness to. A work intended to be a mix of fictional adventure and fact based on true events. With that intention every effort was made to not fight the facts. And instead to be inspired by them.

For this narrative actual events and the lives of historical figures inspired several fictional characters. Any motives and actions of these fictional characters are entirely the author's imagination. Any resemblance to current events or locales…or to persons living or dead…is entirely coincidental.

In that effort to reflect real history I must first acknowledge my gratefulness for the Merriam-Webster.com Time-Traveler dictionary. With this invaluable resource I tried to time-check every word. Phrase. And idiom as best I could to weed out every anachronism. When modern words failed the test by entering the English language after 1846 they were rejected. We hope this historical authenticity is a pleasure to readers. Please let us know what was missed.

For research and historical details of New Orleans in 1846 I am indebted to the unfailingly helpful staff of The Historic New Orleans Collection Williams Research Center in the French Quarter. The personal help of Pamela D. Arceneaux (then Curator — Rare Books); Daniel Hammer (then Head of Reader Services); and Eric A. Seiferth (then Reference Assistant) was invaluable. In particular their assistance helped uncover the character sketches written by Walt Whitman during his three-month employ as an editor/reporter at the *New Orleans Daily Crescent* March to May 1848…where his brother also worked as an office boy. Whitman's time in New Orleans immediately followed his work as editor of the *Brooklyn Eagle* in New York City from March 1846 to early 1848 during the Mexican War years. Also of great interest was the Williams Center's extensive card collection of duels and dueling accounts in New Orleans.

The author gives particular acknowledgment to the outstanding historical scholarship of John S. D. Eisenhower's *So Far From God: The U.S. War With Mexico 1846–1848*; K. Jack Bauer's *The Mexican War 1846–1848*; Martin Dugard's *The Training Ground: Grant, Lee, Sherman, and Davis in the Mexican War, 1846–1848*; the richly illustrated work from both the Mexican and American perspectives in Krystyna M. Libura's and Luis Gerado Morales Moreno's and Jesus Velasco Marquez's *Echoes of the Mexican-American War* (translated by Mark Fried). For detailed historical archeology of a U.S.-Mexican War battlefield the careful scholarship of Charles M. Haecker's and Jeffrey G. Mauck's *On the Prairie of Palo Alto* was essential. For details on Samuel Walker and the Texas Rangers I used Paul Foos's outstanding *A Short Offhand Killing Affair: Soldiers and Social Conflict during the Mexican-American War*. And for a fresh perspective on the United States invasion of Mexico I recommend Amy S. Greenberg's *A Wicked War*.

A work of this scope takes a village. Without the unfailing and professional help of an incredible group *THE GOOD OR EVIL SIDE* would not have made it to print. First acknowledgment goes to my wife — Synnöve Granholm, whose love and support made completing this project possible. Accolades to my editor — Amy Hausman — who put down the kibosh on every anachronism and historical hiccup she found. I couldn't have done it without you. To the best book mapmaker in the business — Rhys Davies — I owe the adventure of accurate and inspirational maps that illustrated every section. My invaluable proofreader and copy editor—William Oppenheimer—added as much perfection into the final manuscript as humanly possible. Not only did Barbara Uebelacker's proofreading immeasurably improve the final page proofs but her home base in Beloit Wisconsin added a special historical connection. David Wu—who designed the book text and always makes me look good—I have unending respect for. And to Richard Ljoenes Design LLC whose "Quill-and-Pistol" series logo and book cover made this Swift & Dancer Adventure jump off the shelf.

And finally to all the other "late bloomers" out there getting that book inside them out on paper…I salute you. Keep your butt in the chair.

ABOUT THE AUTHOR

Dan Gooder Richard's love of adventure stories began as a boy. The first two novels his mother gave him at age ten are still on his shelf: Margaret Armstrong's *Trelawny* and Herman Melville's *Typee*. That boyhood love of a good tale was reinforced as Dan listened to his father weave cowboy yarns during family trips from Iowa to his father's childhood home in Montana. After earning a bachelor's in history Dan blasted water wells in India with the Peace Corps. Ski bummed in Taos Ski Valley. Motorcycled across the Sahara. Then earned his master's in journalism at Missouri.

Dan's middle name comes from his maternal grandfather: Leslie MacDonald Gooder who was a publisher in Chicago from the early 1910s through the 1950s. Dan carried on the family name in publishing. After he and his wife sold their marketing/publishing business in 2016 Dan turned his full-time attention to writing historical adventures. Dan lives in Virginia with his Swedish-speaking Finnish-born wife who also loves adventurous travels. Their 40+ year life/work partnership—without the loggerheads—inspired the Swift & Dancer Adventures.

In Dan Gooder Richard's previous life as a publisher and one of the real estate industry's leading authorities in marketing and lead management he wrote two top-selling books on real estate marketing: *REAL ESTATE RAINMAKER®: Successful Strategies for Real Estate Marketing*, and *REAL ESTATE RAINMAKER®: Guide to Online Marketing*; both published by John Wiley & Sons. Dan also authored two non-fiction books in the popular *SMART ESSENTIALS* series: *SMART ESSENTIALS FOR COLLEGE RENTALS: Parent and Investor Guide To Buying College-Town Real Estate*, and *SMART ESSENTIALS FOR REAL ESTATE INVESTING: How To Build Wealth In Real Estate Today*. You can follow Dan's recent work at www.DanGooderRichard.com.